praise for
Meant for Me

"WOW! 🤩 What a conclusion to this really great trilogy of stories by Betsy St Amant. I loved this sweet story of redemption, love and friendship that turns so much more.."

—DANA, GOODREADS

"Great conclusion to the series! Loved the humor sprinkled throughout the novel. Magnolia Bay is a fun setting with its quirky and heartwarming characters and small-town issues such as a lightning-fast gossip line and small budget for town repairs. I enjoyed every minute spent in the pages of *Meant for Me* starting with the first page."

—STACI, GOODREADS

"I've always enjoyed being in Magnolia Bay and my favorite part of it is the core group of friends that is there. Mama D is also pretty fabulous as she comes alongside the younger people. The book takes some interesting turns and you will cheer and sigh as the story unfolds."

—LAURA, GOODREADS

"This was such a fun, sweet read involving friends to more, close proximity, grumpy/sunshine, marriage of convenience, and insta-family. St. Amant weaves spiritual truths into this story such as being chosen by God and that God works things out for good."

—ALLYSON. GOODREADS

Meant for Me

· MAGNOLIA BAY ·
BOOK 3

Meant for Me

BETSY ST. AMANT

SUNRISE PUBLISHING

Meant for Me
Magnolia Bay, Book 3
Published by Sunrise Media Group LLC
Copyright © 2025 Betsy St. Amant Haddox
Print ISBN: 978-1-963372-52-6

This book is a work of fiction. Names, characters, places, and incidents are either products of the author's imagination or used fictitiously. Any similarity to actual people, organizations, and/or events is purely coincidental.

Scriptures taken from the Holy Bible, New International Version®, NIV®. Copyright © 1973, 1978, 1984, 2011 by Biblica, Inc.™ Used by permission of Zondervan. All rights reserved worldwide. www.zondervan.com The "NIV" and "New International Version" are trademarks registered in the United States Patent and Trademark Office by Biblica, Inc.™

For more information about Betsy St. Amant please access the author's website at the following address: www.betsystamant.com.

Published in the United States of America.
Cover Illustration and Design: Raya Decker

· MAGNOLIA BAY ·

Where I Found You
No Place Like Home
Meant for Me

Topher –
I'm so glad you were
meant for me.

"You did not choose me, but I chose you."
JOHN 15:16A NIV

Amazing Grace, how sweet the sound
That saved a wretch like me,
I once was lost but now I'm found
Was blind but now I see.

One

THERE WERE TOO MANY PEOPLE IN HIS boat. No, there were too many *kids* in his boat.

The evening sun began its lazy late summer descent, casting a golden glow atop the waves of Magnolia Bay. Linc Fontenot held back a scowl as yet another sticky-fingered, freckled-faced child grabbed for the steering column of Linc's twenty-foot pontoon. Of all the nights for Anthony, his college-aged tour guide, to call in sick. Should have told him to pop an ibuprofen and get to work.

"We'll be off shortly." Linc attempted a less-fake smile at his pontoon full of eight Croc-wearing, camera-clutching tourists. He probably sounded as annoyed as he felt, which wasn't great for the five-star reviews he was in desperate need of, but some things, like the weather and this wind stirring up waves, just couldn't be helped. The boat rocked again, and he braced his legs as he stood starboard, arms crossed.

The dock—unlike the boat—sat annoyingly empty as they bobbed. Where was Zoey? She'd sworn she was on her way ten minutes ago. And not that she'd lie, exactly, but it'd be just like her to leave him hanging, stretch him to his max before swooping in to help at the last minute.

"What's this do?" The same freckled, sunburnt kid reached for one of the levers on the steering column.

Linc swatted his hand away, let his scowl free. "Blows up the boat."

"Really?" The kid lowered his hands to his side, blue eyes wide against red cheeks.

Linc narrowed his eyes. "Wanna find out?"

Freckles adamantly shook his head and cowered into his mother, who wore a buckled life jacket despite the fact they hadn't even set sail yet and vests were optional for participants over twelve. The mom frowned at Linc, wrapping her arm around her son.

Five stars, five stars. "Uh, help yourself to the sodas in the cooler there." Linc stepped away, turned his back. See? This was why Anthony did Boiling Bayou tours in the off-season. Linc was better with crawfish than people.

He shaded his eyes and gazed up the dock, toward the boat house and the slightly leaning, boarded bathroom facility and the minuscule concession counter that made them able to pitch this bay-side tour business more legitimately. In the bow seat, a middle-aged couple wearing straw hats started arguing, one of them sounding like they'd already hit up happy hour at the pub before boarding. Great.

He could probably only stall about five more minutes, and then he'd be forced to drive the boat *and* talk, God help him. Maybe they'd get lucky and see a dolphin, despite the last sighting having been weeks ago. No way would Linc be able to create the same energy Anthony did—giving facts about bay life and stats about the gulf beyond, making the tourists laugh and want to come back. Honestly, it was just a bay.

But he'd come back years ago, hadn't he? So maybe it was more.

Two kids started a loud game of rock, paper, scissors, and Linc wondered for the tenth time if he could raise his age limit for tours. But then he'd be turning away families, and exhausted dads with fat wallets looking to sit down for an hour were the only reason he was able to keep things running in the off-season. The hurricane last year made this past crawfish and shrimp haul the smallest Linc had ever had. He just had to make up the difference this fall and winter with these side hustles, then hope for a solid season next spring. Problem was, he wasn't generating enough traction on the tours yet, and Elisa, who'd helped market his buddy Noah's inn recently, suggested he focus on getting people to leave reviews.

Positive reviews. He winced. This was all doable, right? No need to worry.

Except for the fact Zoey might not show up and he might have to play the role of fun-loving guide. *That* was reason to worry.

But there she was, finally, jogging over the sun-warped planks, dark hair bouncing over her small, fairy-like frame. Her slouchy, oversized bag slammed her jean-clad hip with each step, her smile wide and knowing as she barreled straight down into the boat.

"Took you long enough." Linc kept his voice low, his stance solid as she braced one hand on his shoulder to soften her abrupt landing. Wasn't that what he always did for her? Had done while she'd stood and watched her own business burn to the ground several weeks ago?

He wasn't the only one needing to make up profits. At least his status wasn't emergency. Yet, anyway.

She blinked up at him, blue eyes large beneath thick bangs, her smile far from innocent. "Now, did you think I left you here alone with all these"—she dropped to a horrified whisper—"*people* on purpose?"

"Yes. I did." His shoulder tingled under her touch. Been doing that lately. Somewhat bothersome.

"And yet you called me anyway." She winked, moving her hands to plant on her narrow hips. "I sort of like being your only hope."

He scowled again as he made his way to the wheel, shaking off the lingering burn on his arm. "Desperate times."

"Am I getting paid for this?" She unzipped that ridiculous bag and pulled out a black band.

He plopped down on the captain's chair. "No."

She affixed the band over one eye and struck a pose. Good grief, she'd brought an eye patch. "What about now?"

He snorted. "I asked you to lead the tour, not channel your inner Captain Hook."

"Same thing, right?" She pulled a fake goatee from her purse, peeled off an adhesive strip, and affixed it to her cheeks and chin. Then draped a gold chain over her neck, rolled up her shirt sleeve to reveal the fake—*please* be fake—bicep tattoo of a heart reading MOM, and turned to the tourists with a grand gesture. "Ahoy, mateys! Welcome aboard."

Oh, brother. Linc shifted into reverse, and the boat puttered away from the dock as Zoey launched into an even thicker accent, sounding more British than pirate. But the kids had quieted down, and even Mrs. Uptight looked relaxed now, leaning back against the seat and smiling as her son stared, mesmerized, at Zoey.

Same, kid, same. Linc threw the throttle into drive. Hard not to stare at Zoey lately. Which obviously was just proof Linc needed a vacation. He'd been working too hard the past month, was getting tired. Or something.

Something dangerously close to vulnerable.

He squinted into the sunlight as he navigated them out of the inlet into deeper water, keeping an eye on the wind still sending rogue gusts. Zoey might be goofy, but she'd rake in those five stars for him. He'd pay her for helping today, even though she wouldn't be expecting it. She'd been couch-surfing over Magnolia Bay since her apartment lease ended and the insurance from the fire at Bayou Beignets had yet to pay out. She needed all the money she could get, despite insisting she was fine. He knew better, knew that was why she'd been scrambling to create her own side catering business in the meantime.

She also insisted she couldn't stay with him, even though he had two extra bedrooms. Said she'd cramp his style. And she would. He rather liked his high ceilings and cedar beams and wide windows with a view of a pond, his own private corner of Magnolia Bay. It was peaceful. Quiet.

But maybe some temporary company didn't sound *too* awful.

Zoey leaned in toward her audience, casting one leg straight out to the side like it was a peg. "Who can tell me why one pirate pushed another one overboard?"

The parents exchanged knowing grins while the kids shook their heads.

"Because they got into an *arrgh*-gument, of course!"

Linc rolled his eyes as the adults chuckled. "I thought Miley was the resident comedian around here." The moody young barista had shocked everyone with her comedy skills at the Cajun Circus fundraiser his friend Cade hosted earlier in the summer. "You should probably keep your day job, Zo—"

Oops. She had no day job anymore. He winced.

Zoey narrowed her eyes, the wind brushing back her hair and giving her an even more genuine pirate-like appearance. "If you're going to insult me, commit already. Don't stop mid-sentence like a coward."

"Sorry." He briefly released the wheel and held up both hands in surrender. "I didn't think it through."

"Since when do you care about that?" She turned back to the tourists, thankfully before she saw the grin Linc fought to hide. Maybe that was why he tolerated Zoey. Okay, more than tolerated. She had moxie. Always told him what he needed to hear.

Never seemed to be scared of him, unlike most of the rest of the town.

"I've got one more question for ye, then we'll turn our attention to the murky, treasure-laden waters of Magnolia Bay." Zoey wiggled her fingers toward the freckled kid.

The boy jumped up from his seat and grinned. "I have a question too!"

"Please remain seated at all times," Linc droned.

The kid reluctantly perched on the edge of the bench seat. The engine hummed beneath them. "What's your pirate name?"

"Oh! Um." Zoey cleared her throat, cast a quick look at Linc.

He shook his head, stoic. Nope, not helping. She'd gotten herself into this . . .

"It's, ah—" She adjusted the eye patch that had slipped. "Captain Z, of course."

Freckles sank back, skinny brows furrowed. "That's *bor-ing.*"

"I mean, that *was* my name. Before . . . the fire." Zoey squared her shoulders.

Freckles blinked and the rest of the crowd grew still. "The fire?"

What was she doing? Linc steered them toward the open water, where two jet skis raced. He scowled. In this wind? Those arrogant idiots better follow the traffic rules . . .

"Argh, that's right. I'm homeless." Zoey lifted her chin, patted her goatee as if she were making up a simple story and not merging fiction with reality. "Did you not see the burnt building on Village Lane?"

"I did." A younger girl, life jacket securely buckled, raised her hand, eyes wide. "That was yours?"

Anyone else, he'd worry about the story sending them into a PTSD episode. Even his stomach twisted when he remembered the flames, the sweat pooling on his back as Zoey buried his face into his shoulder, hiding as her award-winning business burned to a crisp.

But to Zoey, it was apparently just one more obstacle to pole-jump over onto a sunbeam. One more silver lining to an already gloriously metallic cloud. Did anything *ever* bother the woman?

Though she did refuse to walk past the shop in its current

shape—the shape on hold while she waited for the claims department to sort the whole mess out.

"Arrgh, it's true. Cannon fire." She wiggled her fingers again and this time, Freckles's grin returned.

"What's your new name?"

"Did you get a promotion to captain because you won the pirate war?"

"Did anything else burn down?"

"Where will you live next?"

The kids ignored Linc's stay-seated command and jumped up and down, shooting rapid-fire questions, while the moms exchanged mildly concerned looks—as if they weren't entirely sure how to reconcile the very real, burned building with Zoey's story about very unreal pirates.

Anthony never gave him these kinds of problems.

Linc shook his head, gearing down to keep his distance from the jet skis still racing in a zig-zag. His fingers stuck to the lever, residue from Freckles, no doubt. *Why* were kids so sticky?

"Hang on, guys. You have to answer a question for me, first." Zoey raised her arms for attention, wobbling as Linc turned the boat portside to avoid the worst of the jet skis' wake. She planted her feet. "Why were the kids so restless in pirating class?"

Freckles blinked at her. Life Jacket Girl shrugged. Linc couldn't look away, either, Zoey holding the entire boat captive as she rose on tiptoe, face light, eyes sparking with drama and life and sun.

Man, she was pretty.

"Because they were . . . over-*bored*!" Zoey lunged forward, arms splayed, as the kids jumped and shrieked. Then the wind slammed a wave into the wake of the second jet ski. Linc jerked his attention back to the wheel, two seconds too late. The boat launched. And Freckles went flying.

His mom screamed at the splash. Zoey caught herself, tripping over the younger girl who had fallen to the slippery boat floor. She popped up like a wide-eyed gopher. Two dads jumped up, raced to the edge of the boat, slipping in their Crocs. Every other gaping-mouthed, wide-eyed head on board turned accusingly to Linc.

He cut the boat to idle and sighed. So much for five stars.

Zoey Lakewood had never fancied herself a betting woman, but if Magnolia Bay ever lowered itself enough to host a wet T-shirt contest, she'd put her life savings on Linc.

Not that there'd be any left, the way she was currently plowing through her savings account after the fire.

Linc's flip-flops squished as he unceremoniously deposited the freckled boy back into his mother's arms. His shirt stretched taut against his broad back and biceps. One of the men—the boy's father?—reached to shake Linc's hand, but Linc brushed it off, returning to his captain's chair as his mane of wet man bun coursed rivers of water down his thick neck.

He was mad.

Zoey winced as the chaos meter in the boat escalated a notch, everyone swarming the kid with exclamations of concern. Did anyone blame her? Maybe she shouldn't have been so dramatic with her pirate vibes. But how was she supposed to know the boat would lurch at the *exact* wrong moment? Wasn't that Linc's job as captain to know?

She tried to catch Linc's eye, but he only jammed the boat into gear and scowled as he flipped his dripping hair out of his face. "Tour's over."

Oh, dunkin' donuts, he wouldn't look at her. So he was mad. Which wasn't fair, but he'd get over it. Not much had been fair lately, and *she* wasn't complaining. "Well, that over-bored joke sure was timely." Zoey plastered on a bright smile for her damp audience, who didn't smile back as the boat began puttering—slowly, to Linc's credit—back toward the dock. She quickly pulled off her eye patch, blinking against the sunset glinting off the bay. "I guess I should have mentioned swimming was optional at the *end* of the tour only . . ."

Crickets. Make that soggy crickets. She gulped.

The boy's parents continued fussing over him, while the young girl in a life jacket wrinkled her nose and tried to scoot as far from his spreading water puddle as possible. Linc muttered stuff about "*told* them to remain seated" as they neared the dock. Which was valid. So maybe it was a little of everyone's fault.

Still. She tried to think what else she had in her purse that could help save the tour, the bag her best friend Elisa often referred to as Mary Poppins's. Personally, she'd rather think of it as Hermione Granger's, but same concept—endless supplies.

She began digging. Eye patch, ChapStick, the keys to her tired but trusty Jeep, her Alice in Wonderland coin purse, tissues, a mini screw driver, phone charger, a folded jump rope, pepper spray, emergency stash of candy—*aha*. This sure qualified.

"Who wants Starburst?" She tugged the colored bag free and held it up. The kids cheered and more hair ties sprinkled to the floor like confetti. "Plenty for everyone. Parents too." She handed the candy to the mom of the overboard boy. "Here, enjoy." Maybe this would buy some time to fix this.

She scurried to Linc's side as the others gathered around the Starbursts. Time to test the waters. *Waters*, ha. That was a good one. "Ahoy, Captain."

"They're going to want refunds." A muscle ticked in his jaw, his eyes hidden behind dark sunglasses. Probably calculating how much gas he'd already spent and wouldn't get reimbursed for by the time he gave everyone their money back.

She shuffled her feet, frowned. She hated when he was upset. Ironic, maybe, as she seemed to upset him the most.

"Maybe offer refunds?" Zoey reached up to adjust the strap of her bag around her shoulder. "It's only one tour, and hey, it got cut short, so now you can go home. Alone. To be, you know—*alone*."

As he liked. Which was part of why she kept refusing his offer to stay in one of his guest rooms while she waited on her insurance payout. Linc didn't really want her there—he just felt obligated since he had unused space.

"True." Linc's lower lip tugged to one side, as if fighting a smile. Ahh, a moment of humanity. "There's not *always* a bright side, you know."

"Oh sure there is. Just gotta *look* for it." She pulled his sunglasses off his face and immediately regretted it.

His laser gaze slammed into hers without blinking. Linc. Always steady. Strong.

Annoyed, maybe. But there.

For her.

She'd never really figured out why. He'd certainly never made a move on her, so it wasn't romantic intention. He'd been there when she was younger too. Like that one day back when she was in middle school and took baking lessons from his aunt, and he—

"*Or* maybe some people see things that aren't there." Linc snatched his glasses from her, returned them to his face.

Okay, then. Mr. Grumpy was back. Zoey stepped back as he secured the boat to the dock. The tourists stood, grumbling and shucking off life vests, one of them mumbling about one-star reviews.

Oh no. Linc needed *good* reviews. And everyone leaving the tour squishy and annoyed wasn't going to get those. She had to salvage this for him, even if it wasn't technically her fault. At least, not all her fault. *Lord, a little help? Something happy?*

And then, like the parting of the Red Sea—okay, slightly less dramatic—the sun glinted off a distant wave and revealed . . .

"Dolphin!" Zoey pointed. Her heart soared.

The kids squealed and the adults whipped around to look. "Where?" Everyone rushed portside, and the boat rocked precariously.

"There it is!"

"I see it!"

The grumbles turned to delighted murmurs. Everyone stood still, watching, as a second dolphin crested the water. The pair bobbed in the setting sun, cruising back out toward the gulf, slick backs shining like—well, like a silver lining. Zoey breathed a sigh of relief. *Thank you.*

Linc joined her, crossing his arms as several people began snapping pictures of the dolphins. His sunglasses were tucked into the collar of his wet shirt. But for once, his brow wasn't furrowed, his jaw wasn't tight. "Good save."

"I prayed."

"Figured."

She shrugged. "Least I could do."

"Was it?" Turning, Linc's eyes lingered on hers, then dropped to her lips.

Um. Huh? Her mouth went dry. Her stomach dropped. "I—"

"You forgot to shave." He ripped the goatee off her chin like a Band-Aid.

"Ow!" She rubbed her jaw, more surprised than hurt. "I forgot it was there."

Linc smirked. "Then I'll amend my earlier statement to include that some people don't see what *is* right there."

"You're right." She ignored the flutter in her stomach, the slight shake in her hands, and forced her brightest smile. "They sure don't."

She rolled in her lower lip, trying not to watch as he meandered back to the captain's chair.

And maybe they never would.

Two

Y OU KNOCKED A KID OVERBOARD?"
Elisa plopped on the bench seat opposite Zoey in her booth
at Magnolia Blossom, interrupting the sounds of dwindling
evening chatter and pie forks scraping against plates. Her best friend's
ever-popular diner stayed open late on weekend nights, now that
tourism was finally booming again.

"That literally was less than an hour ago." Zoey steadied her
water glass on the table as Elisa settled on the bench. "I forget
how small this town is."

"No, you don't, that's why you love it." Elisa tucked her short
blonde hair behind her ears. She still wore an apron, as she enjoyed
cooking again as much as she did owning the place. "But don't
change the subject."

"I sort of accidentally scared a kid who *fell* overboard. Big difference." Zoey fiddled with a leaf on the magnolia centerpiece
between them, the one that propped up the newly printed menus
featuring the diner's magnolia logo. Hadn't even been a month
since the Bayou Beignets fire and she already missed brainstorming
marketing schemes, creating graphics, playing with new logos . . .
"Besides, Linc was the one who missed seeing that wave."

Elisa winced. "I'm sure he loved hearing you point that out."

"God sent us dolphins, so it all worked out." Of course, there was that still weird moment with Linc where she thought he'd—where she'd almost—oh, forget it. Stupid.

"You prayed for dolphins?" Elisa asked.

"I pray for everything." As her parents always said, *faith and prayer—that's what moves mountains. You do your part and God does His.* So she did. She prayed for her missionary parents' safety and ministry overseas, her friends, Pastor Todd.

She just apparently hadn't known she needed to pray for her beignet shop not to burn down.

"Are you praying for this wedding?" Elisa laughed. "We need it. Noah is driving me crazy. He's stressing over numbers and the catering budget and whether we should risk having a bar and offending people, or *not* having a bar and offending other people . . ."

"It's your big day." Zoey reached across the table and grabbed her friend's hand. "What do *you* want?"

"I just want to get married." She held up her left hand, diamond catching the overhead lights. "And Noah wants everything to be perfect for me, but I really don't care about the details like he assumes I do."

"That's sweet." Which was totally Noah. "Who would have thought, your former mortal enemy is now the man who wants to spoil you and can't even look at you without turning into a puddle of mush."

Elisa's cheeks flushed pink. "God works in mysterious ways. But good gravy, I'm being selfish." She waved her hand in the air. "The wedding will be fine—even if it is in roughly a month and there's still a ton to figure out. How are *you*?"

"Not any different since the last time you asked." Zoey made a show of checking her watch. "Roughly ten hours ago at the inn." Noah had insisted she take a spare room the past week, while she continued waiting on insurance to pay out. Elisa was doing the same until their big day. "Why does everyone keep asking me that?"

"Um, because you're homeless and lost your business?" Elisa winced. "Not to be blunt."

"I'm fine." Zoey leaned back in the booth, infusing her voice with brightness. As always, no reason to let anyone else know she was worried and ruin their day with her issues. "Chief Sanders said the fire started from that new commercial fryer I had just installed, so the claims department should get back to me any day now."

Talk about bad timing, since she'd spent most of her savings on said fryer—and since she and Elisa had chosen not to renew their lease on their shared apartment because of the pending wedding. Now Zoey couldn't afford it herself, even if she had kept it. She smiled anyway. "It'll all work out."

"Right, of course." Elisa's furrowed brow belied her confidence in Zoey's statement, but that was okay. Zoey had enough sunshine for them both. For everyone.

"I've been working on getting my catering business going, and looking up new recipes to dive into when I'm fully back in business and have a professional kitchen again." Speaking of, she had a batch of cookies out in her Jeep she'd experimented with that morning, stashed in a Tupperware she'd nabbed from the inn's kitchen. Had meant to bring them to Linc but forgotten in her rush to get to the tour.

"That's good." Elisa's frown eased a bit.

"And I've been dabbling more with my photography lately." Zoey smiled. "See, I told you. *Totally* fine." Not a lie. Not denial. Just being positive.

There was a difference.

"Okay. If you're sure." Elisa started to stand. "I better go check on Lucius in the kitchen, and get ready to start closing up."

"Yeah, I better go too. I'll see you back at the Blue Pirogue." Zoey scooted off the bench seat, knocking her bag she'd forgotten, nestled next to her, to the floor. The contents scattered across the tile. Oops. She scrambled to grab everything before Elisa could see, but her friend was faster.

"Dabbling, huh?" She picked up the photo Zoey had taken last week and gotten developed, a black-and-white shot of Linc on his boat, bun tousled in the wind, bicep flexed as he steered with one muscular arm. "Wow. Looks like a cologne ad."

"He's an interesting subject, that's all." Zoey snatched the photo back and stood, trying not to let her gaze linger on the image. Even though she'd stared at it quite a bit the past few days. Linc was attractive, sure—anyone who claimed not to see that would be an idiot.

But something about this particular candid, something about the gleam in his eye as he stared across the water . . . Linc looked so calm. Settled. Almost—happy? She didn't know what he was thinking about, what had removed his near-permanent scowl for this particular moment.

And that's why she kept studying it. It was a whole side to her best friend she didn't know.

"I think this is a very interesting subject indeed." Elisa grinned as she bent back down to pick up Zoey's ChapStick and screwdriver.

"You know it's not like that. *We're* not like that." Zoey dropped her belongings into the bag and hiked the strap up her shoulder. "We're besties."

Elisa's smile widened knowingly as she crossed her arms. "I thought I was your bestie."

"He's my *guy* bestie."

"I'm kidding. But I think you're kidding yourself a little too."

"Linc sees me as an annoying little sister type, at best." Zoey's heart raced beneath her hoodie. "He's *Linc*. He . . ."

"He what?" Elisa's voice lowered.

Zoey looked back at the photo still in her hands. "He makes me feel safe." Like maybe she didn't have to be in control after all.

Like maybe someone could take care of *her*, for once.

"I get it." Elisa's smirk shifted to a soft smile. "I'm just teasing you. You know, I probably just want you to have what I have with Noah, is all."

"I will." Zoey shoved the photo into her bag and zipped it. "Someday. With someone."

Just not with Linc. Because there was nothing safe about opening one's heart to a romantic relationship.

And—cologne-ad-model worthy or not—she wouldn't ever risk losing the security Linc brought to her life.

His life was chaos.

"You said it was an emergency." Linc crossed his arms over his chest and stared down at Zoey, who wore a hoodie and clutched a full Tupperware container to one hip. "You've got cookies."

The September night air washed over them, drying the still-damp-from-his-shower hair and warming his bare arms. He'd shoved himself into a T-shirt and track pants that might or might not have been washed since his last workout, and run out the door in a panic, wondering what could have made Zoey send him an "SOS, meet me at our spot" text. He'd just seen her a few hours ago at the dock, when they'd parted ways after he'd secured the boat for the night.

"You're very astute." Zoey opened the red lid. "Try one."

Crickets chirped from the bushes lining the walkway to the gazebo off Village Lane, mocking him. "*Aye.* You don't even care that you cried wolf?"

"Hold on." She pulled her phone from her back pocket and held up their text thread, feigning innocence. "Nope. As I expected—I never used the word *wolf*."

He closed his eyes, a headache forming in his temples. "Zoey, I've had enough emergencies for one day, and this sudden taste test of yours doesn't qualify as one." He could still hear the splash as Freckles went overboard. Still feel the judging stares boring into him afterward.

Could still feel the panic over the looming one-stars threatening him on the internet. He scowled. Too bad this wasn't the good ol' days of past generations, where one could run a business without needing FaceTok or InstaBooks or whatever the newest platform was called.

"Your perspective is wrong."

He opened his eyes.

Zoey grinned. "You should be grateful this wasn't an emergency, if you're tired of them."

"That's not the—oh, whatever." Her logic, while accurate, boggled his mind sometimes. And he hated feeling boggled. Especially at nine o'clock at night, after a near-disaster of a tour. They'd escaped without issuing refunds, thanks to Zoey and her dolphins. She was like Snow White, or whatever princess was good with animals.

He studied Zoey's dark hair, her thick bangs highlighting bright blue eyes, and his annoyance dissipated a notch. Yeah, Snow White was the dark-haired one. It fit.

"I worked on a new recipe at the inn this morning and need to know what you think. Just don't tell Noah I used his kitchen without permission." Zoey held a cookie up to Linc's mouth. "Try it. Then you can go home."

"I *was* at home. Quite content, for that matter." He ducked aside, which wasn't hard, given her short arm span. "Besides, I haven't been force-fed since I was a toddler." Before his mom died, his dad left. He'd gotten lucky, as far as foster parents went. He shoved away the memories.

"Those were probably vegetables." She wiggled the cookie and grinned. "This is sugar."

"That's even worse. You know I don't eat a lot of sugar."

"Just a taste."

He glared. "Why is this important right *now*?"

"Well, we're already here, aren't we?"

Why not? She practically had the cookie resting on his lips now, anyway. Besides, arguing with Zoey was an Olympic sport, and he hadn't adequately trained. He took a reluctant bite, rolled his eyes. "There. Tasted."

"And?"

"It's good."

She pouted, a breeze rustling her bangs. The moon peeked from behind a cloud. "You're just saying that."

Crawfish never argued back. Linc sighed. "It's *good*."

She adjusted the container on her hip. "I need description, Linc. My dessert catering business is on the line, here. Does it melt in your mouth? Does it make you want to order a dozen more? Is it too sweet? Just right?"

Kinda dry, actually. He frowned. "What am I, Goldilocks?"

She frowned back. "Imagine that you are."

"Then I would turn myself in to the police for breaking and entering."

"*Linc*."

"What? She committed a crime!"

A tree frog croaked, as if Zoey was interrupting its bedtime too. She pursed her lips, waited.

"Fine, it tastes better than porridge." Maybe. Linc licked his lips. What had she put in there, sawdust? The aftertaste grew worse.

"How am I supposed to believe you like it if you can't specify *what* you like?" Her eyes danced. "Okay, that's it. You have to touch the post."

She had him, and she knew it. He scowled, following her gaze to the ornate black lamppost stationed outside the gazebo. Its light glowed, soft amber rings reflecting on the worn sidewalk beneath. "That tradition is silly."

"Some traditions are, but this one works. You can't lie if you touch the post, and you know it."

"Just because you declare something doesn't make it true." But somehow, it did, and she knew it. He never should have gone along with this ridiculous "pinky promise replacement," as she'd put it years ago when she'd first dragged him there as a kid.

But he'd come and touched the post that day, just like he'd come tonight. And would do it again.

Because it was really getting hard to tell Zoey no.

Didn't mean she'd like his answer, though. He closed the distance to the lamp and slapped his palm against the solid black post. "Go ahead."

Her eager expression glowed under the light. She cleared her throat, squared her shoulders. "Did you like the new recipe?"

"No."

Her smile fell. "Linc!"

"What? You're the one making me do this." He shifted his weight, still touching the post. "Anything else?"

"What didn't you like?"

"Wasn't a good cookie." He shrugged. "Dry. Kinda tasteless—until the sawdust took over."

She winced. "Sawdust?"

"Stick to beignets, kid. You're good at that." Really good, actually. "Donuts, kolaches. Fried stuff."

"You forget I don't have a fryer right now." Zoey sighed. "Never mind. I just need to be patient. It'll all work out."

She kept saying that. Hopefully it was true. He let his arm fall from the post. "Why did this matter so much tonight?"

"I wanted to give you something after your nearly ruined tour."

"It wasn't, though." He moved to stand closer to her. "Your

dolphins saved the day. So what gives? You could have brought me porridge cookies tomorrow."

"I guess I didn't feel like going back to the inn yet." Zoey dropped down to the grass, pulled her knees up to her chest.

Oy. Linc dipped into a squat, refusing to camp out longer than necessary. It was a good stretch this way, at least. "Why not?"

She pursed her lips. "Weird decor?"

He held her stare.

"Fine." She looked away. "Sometimes the Blue Pirogue just reminds me of how much limbo I'm in. It *feels* like a hotel, you know?"

"That's because it is."

She ignored him. "I know it's temporary, but it's hard not being able to work. I'm used to cooking all day, marketing, being creative." She wrinkled her nose at the discarded tub. "That's part of why I'm playing around with catering efforts. Well, that, and the potential paycheck."

He shifted his weight in his squat. "And photography?"

Her shoulders stiffened. "What do you mean?"

"I saw you taking pictures last week on the boat."

Her eyes widened. "You did?"

"Yeah. Of the sunset, or whatever." He'd noticed because he'd been cruising the pontoon, eyes locked on the water, thoughts ruminating on the next day's schedule, when *bam*. Next thing he knew, his mind had drifted to thoughts of her. Of them. Of how nice it felt to have Zoey riding in the boat, like she truly belonged there. Like it'd be weird for her *not* to be there.

The click of the shutter had thankfully snapped him out of the near-mushy moment.

Zoey cleared her throat. "Right, the sunset was top notch that night." Her gaze lowered to the cookie tub. "Maybe I should give up on the cookie baking, work with you on the boat instead."

Oh, man. There sure hadn't been a camera shutter to snap him out of it today, had there, when he'd been watching her instead of paying attention to the water. The piling weather. His stomach tightened. She couldn't fill in for Anthony. It was too risky.

But how could he turn her down when she clearly needed money?

He shook his head. "Maybe we need to find you a part-time job with steady hours until your catering can take off, or you get back into a beignet storefront. The tours aren't consistent enough for what you need, I'm sure."

Not a lie. But not the full truth, and that felt bad. But what was he supposed to say? *Sorry I can't keep staring at you while you're performing that close to me*? He wasn't a creep.

Things were just . . . weird right now.

"You'd help me find something?" She raised a brow.

"Of course." Especially if that meant he'd get to sleep at night, not have to traipse around the town at nine p.m. "Maybe Elisa needs help at the diner."

Zoey shook her head. "She doesn't. Besides, can you imagine me carrying trays of food and drinks all day?"

Good point. She was a little clumsy. "What about Second Story? Or Chug a Mug?"

"Sadie already has all the part-time help she needs at the bookstore." Zoey wrinkled her nose. "And on second thought, I really don't want to get plugged in somewhere just to quit days or maybe weeks later when my claims check finally arrives." She hugged her jean-clad knees. "I'll just ride it out. Eventually, I'll be able to get a new storefront and everything will be like it never happened."

It wouldn't be exactly like that, though. He knew all about denial. Some decisions, some circumstances, some things out of your control simply left scars. He rubbed the tattoo on his ribcage, grimaced.

Zoey rested her cheek on her knee. "The Blue Pirogue is great for my situation, honestly. I shouldn't complain."

Linc drew a breath, let it out. "I keep telling you I have an extra room." Two, actually. He'd gotten the three-bedroom, log-cabin style house tucked into two acres of woods for a steal when he'd moved back to the Bay and started Boiling Bayou Crawfish six years ago.

"But I have a room at the inn." She grinned a little. "Better situation than baby Jesus was in, right?"

"Suit yourself." Probably for the best. He was starting to hope she would come stay, which was a red flag. He didn't need company—didn't *like* company. He just felt sorry for her, that was all. She was a friend, and in a tough spot. Nothing mushy about it.

Even if she was distracting him lately.

He stood.

"Look, I promise if my next option is a stable, I'll take you up on the offer." She smiled up at him. "Want me to touch the post?"

"No." He held out his hand, pulled her to her feet. "I believe you." Besides, he didn't want her getting any crazy ideas, like making him touch the post again while asking him if he really wanted her at his house. "Don't forget your container of sawdust there."

She smirked. "Funny."

He started walking toward his truck, then cast a glance over his shoulder. Zoey stood where he left her, staring up at the moon, arms crossed over her middle. "Coming?" he called.

"I think I'll hang out a little longer. I like the fresh air." Zoey waved him on. "Go ahead. Go to bed."

He waved good night, then climbed into his truck. Started the ignition, drove down the street . . . then made the block and killed the lights, parking just down the road from the gazebo. He cut the engine and waited. Watching. Protecting.

Because—for better or worse—something about Zoey Lakewood always kept him coming back.

Three

ZOEY SHUT THE HEAVY FRONT DOOR of the Blue Pirogue quietly behind her, not wanting to wake Elisa in her room down the hall on the first floor. Noah slept upstairs in the master that would eventually be theirs after the wedding, while Zoey conveniently bummed the room closest to the kitchen.

She eyed the full container of ruined cookies in her hands and winced. Maybe not that conveniently. At least Linc had told her the truth before she gave them to anyone else. She'd need to tweak her recipe, maybe use less salt. More vanilla. Something.

She crossed the welcoming lobby, full of potted ferns and carpet runners and fresh paint from this past spring when Noah had finished renovating the place, and headed for the kitchen to dump the cookies in the trash.

Goldilocks. She snorted. She should make Linc real porridge after all that. Would serve him right. Still, his words brought a smile, a rush of warmth and familiarity as she moved stealthily through the lower level of the inn. Linc was consistent, at least, in this current season of her life where nothing else seemed to be. She knew where she stood, what to expect from her grumpy best friend.

Even if he was rude about her baking efforts.

A light shone from the kitchen, and she paused around the corner. Another guest enjoying a midnight snack?

Low voices rumbled. ". . . booked solid."

"That's great!"

"It would be. Except we're losing money."

Zoey frowned. Oops. Noah and Elisa. She probably shouldn't be eavesdropping. Back-stepping, she shifted the Tupperware to her other hand. She could dump the cookies somewhere else and—

". . . Zoey."

She stopped again. They were talking about her?

"What do you mean?" Elisa's voice sounded confused.

Noah's tone lowered, nearly imperceptible. "We really need her room."

"Noah, she's my best friend."

"She's my friend too. But this is hundreds of dollars a week we're not bringing in—plus the groceries."

Zoey braced one hand on the doorframe. Guilt nudged. She'd given Elisa some grocery money, and despite her friend's insistence it was plenty, she knew it hadn't been enough to actually cover her costs at the inn. But her bank account was running so low . . . she really needed to get some recipes figured out for this catering venture.

"She has nowhere else to go. She couch-surfed for weeks before coming here."

Noah sighed. "I know."

"And it's only temporary." Elisa's voice pleaded.

"You really think the claims department is going to just suddenly hand her a check? After all this time?" Noah's tone dipped. "It's been almost a month."

"She believes they will."

"Zoey's an optimist."

She winced. That was a good thing, wasn't it? No one wanted

a Negative Nancy. Not her friends, her old boss, her missionary parents . . . Even now, her mom's voice from childhood rang in her mind. Tired after a long night of revival services. Weary after prayer vigils and ministry. *You're always my happy sunshine, Zoey. Never change.*

What other choice did she have?

As if reading her mind, Noah continued. "Being optimistic is great, but I'm trying to be realistic. She needs a long-term plan if this drags out much longer. We can't keep this up indefinitely—we're paying for a wedding and a honeymoon."

"I know. But we can't just kick her out."

Zoey winced.

"Of course I'm not kicking her out." Noah's tone gentled. "I just wanted you to know—business is up, but we're turning away guests."

"You know what would also solve this problem?" Elisa didn't wait for an answer. "Throwing your name in the hat for mayor. You could still run the inn too. It'd be extra income doing something positive for the town you love."

Noah sighed. "The town I didn't even know I wanted to stay in until I found you."

"That was then. This is now." Elisa's voice gentled. "Even my father warmed up to you. You'd be great at being mayor, sugar, and you know it."

She'd stood there way too long. Zoey eased away from the door, face burning. Not only was she a financial drain, she was an eavesdropper.

She slowly backed up and turned, but her shoe caught the carpet runner and she tripped. *Oomph.* The container of cookies dropped from her hands and landed with a loud thump on the hardwood floor.

Oh no. She scrambled upright just as Elisa and Noah came

hurrying from the kitchen. They both wore sweatshirts, jeans, and matching wide-eyed expressions.

"Sorry for the noise. Tripped on my way to the kitchen." Zoey stood, sheepish, hoping they couldn't tell she'd overheard. She gestured with the container as if proof.

"Ooh, cookies." Noah's brown eyes lit, and Elisa elbowed him in the ribs.

"Oh, you don't want these. It was a bad batch." She clutched it to her chest, filling her voice with cheer. "I'm actually glad you're up. I wanted to tell you both I got a new place to stay for a while."

Hopefully.

"Oh really?" Noah beamed. "That's great."

Elisa elbowed him again. "Where?" She tilted her head, eyes narrowed with suspicion. "That was fast."

"With a friend." Zoey waved her hand, starting to back away again. No more questions. If they knew it was Linc, they'd insist she stay at the inn, and then she'd be in an even more awkward spot. She couldn't stand to be the problem any longer.

Not when she was the one who always fixed things.

She cleared her throat. "They have an extra room for me to camp out a bit. I mean, no one can live in a hotel forever, right?"

"Right." Elisa nodded, staring hard at Zoey as if attempting to read beneath the surface. Even still, relief filled the gentle lines of her face. Maybe Elisa didn't want to look too hard after all. This was for the best, for everyone.

Except maybe Zoey.

"Anyway, I'll be out tomorrow after I pack up." Zoey kept her voice bright, her expression neutral as she gestured once more with the tub of cookies. "And I really appreciate you guys letting me stay here so long."

Noah's lips twisted guiltily to the side, and he shot Elisa a look. "Of course. Anytime."

Elisa offered a sheepish smile. "Good night, Zoey."

"Good night, guys." She hustled to her room.

Hopefully Linc was up for one more surprise.

He was a horrible person.

Linc scrubbed his hand over his face, his bristled jaw like sandpaper under his palm as he fought a yawn. He finished tugging his T-shirt over his head as he stumbled across the living room, toward the kitchen, squinting at the early morning sun glaring off the deck through the front door window. Only six thirty on Saturday morning, and he couldn't sleep for tossing in guilt over Zoey.

He opened the fridge and stood staring at the contents, the chilled air wafting across his bare feet. A jug of milk and several packages of defrosted chicken stared back, next to a bowl of fresh salsa and a carton of eggs. His stomach growled, but he wasn't in the mood for an omelet. Right now, anything he consumed would just churn with his guilt.

Zoey was obviously struggling—in vain—to branch out from her tried-and-true beignets for this catering venture of hers, and he'd spent much of the night debating on his decision to keep her off his boat. After all, it'd be easy money for her, and Anthony *had* been calling in a lot lately. She'd be a help playing guide, and the tourists seemed to like her.

But Linc remembered the way he couldn't keep his focus on the water, his eyes off her smile and her tanned shoulders and well—obviously, he couldn't afford the distraction she posed.

Maybe that was *really* why he felt like a horrible person—for having all these not-so-friend-like thoughts about his best friend.

He shut the fridge door with a thump. Maybe there was another way he could help Zoey out. Not that he had the funds to spare, until his own side hustle started booming. Besides, Zoey would never let him pay her bills.

Knock, knock, knock.

He frowned as he started for the front door, temper rising. Who in the world would be on his property this time of morning? Couldn't they read the *no trespassing* signs? He growled, mood tanking even further, and wrenched the knob. "This better be—"

"An emergency?" Zoey smiled hopefully at him through the screened door, wearing jeans and a Care Bear graphic tee. A suitcase stood beside her on the wooden porch, a pillow resting on top.

Oh. Something jumped in his gut, something he didn't want to examine too closely. And his mood lifted.

He opened the door, hinges creaking, and fought to keep his voice level, his face straight. "Guess you got banned to the stables after all. No more room in the inn?"

"Something like that." She attempted to wrestle her purple suit-case, nearly as big as her, inside the door.

"For crying out loud. Let me, before you hurt yourself." Linc nudged her out of the way and easily hefted the giant bag to the living room.

The screen door shut behind Zoey with a smack. "Guess this makes me Goldilocks, now."

"Searching for the right bed?" *Aye.* That sounded way different when he said it out loud. He quickly moved to the kitchen. Coffee. They both needed coffee. He started punching buttons on the machine he'd used a hundred times before and suddenly couldn't remember how to operate.

"For crying out loud." Zoey mocked him, elbowing him out of the way and taking over. "Let me, before you hurt yourself."

"Cute." Still, he sank onto one of the kitchen bar stools, propped his feet on the rung, and let her. "So. What happened?"

"No biggie." She opened the red container of Folgers. "The inn got booked up."

What? "Noah kicked you out?" Linc scowled, started to stand. Noah was a good guy, one of the few people Linc would call a real friend, but this seemed—

"*No.*" Zoey dumped the filter full of yesterday's coffee grounds into the trash can under the sink. "But I can't stay knowing that. Everyone has worked so hard to get tourism going again around here, and Noah almost lost the inn once. I can't be the reason his business suffers."

He grunted. "That's noble of you." Which was Zoey—always putting others first. He watched as she bustled around, like she already lived there, pulling out two mugs and using bottled water for the coffee pot. The picture was homey, cozy . . . downright dangerous.

"Is your offer still good?" She paused, mugs in hand, shooting him a look full of restrained hope.

Something stirred, something inside him he hadn't felt since Kirsten. Hadn't *wanted* to feel. Because look what that had gotten him? Betrayal. Sleepless nights.

Tattoos that wouldn't completely come off.

Zoey wasn't a girlfriend or an ex though. She was a friend, a constant in his life. She was different.

He opened his mouth to say yes, to assure her, then stopped. Was he really ready for her to be under the same roof if he couldn't focus while riding on the same boat?

He rocked back on the bar stool, thinking, holding her curious gaze. Maybe this was his answer of how to help her out without feeling guilty over the whole tour thing. He could spend more time on that, focus in during the day, only see Zoey in the evenings, when he didn't need to concentrate.

Yeah. This would be fine—so long as he kept all those errant thoughts like this one at bay.

He relaxed. "Like I always said, you have a room here as long as you need." He'd never had long-term company before. But if it had to be someone, might as well be Zoey. She knew him the best of everyone in Magnolia Bay, and the fact she'd finally accepted his offer was nice.

Not that he was lonely, exactly.

"It won't be for long." Zoey dumped the fresh grounds into the filter, talking faster than usual—even for her. Maybe she didn't need the coffee. "I'm sorry to just show up like this, but I really don't know where else to go."

He squinted.

"I just feel like a burden everywhere, you know? Rosalyn's house is so fancy, I wore my shoes in the living room once, and now I'm pretty sure I'm on the blacklist with their housekeeper." She started the coffee pot, jiggled the carafe into place. "And Mama D talks all night like an endless slumber party. Trish snores so bad I can hear her through the walls from the futon . . . which is sort of like sleeping on a lead pipe."

The coffee pot gurgled, as if trying to keep up with her spill. Linc rubbed his eyes.

Lot of words for six a.m.

"Sadie let me crash a night but then had to take care of her sister after that, which was fine because I think I'm allergic to her cat." Zoey talked faster, staring into the dark liquid brewing. "And Miley offered to let me stay with her, but I couldn't tell if she was serious, and honestly, she's kind of scary, even if she is a comedian now."

So Linc had been a last resort. Which he figured, but it still stung a little. Did she even *want* to do this? He hesitated. "Zoey, maybe—"

"It really is okay to stay here, right?" She turned a pleading gaze on him, and his heart twisted. "I won't bother you."

He fought to hide a smile. "Yes, you will."

She shoved her fingers into her hair and winced. "No more than usual, anyway."

He snorted. "I told you it's fine, and it's fine. As long as you're comfortable with it."

"It'll just be for a few days, week tops. That check is coming, any minute now." She snapped her fingers. "Then we're back in business, baby."

"Right." Somehow he doubted it was going to happen that quickly. He leaned forward, rested his arms on the island. "There're a few ground rules we should probably go over, then."

Her eyes widened. "Oh. Sure, yeah. I mean, it's your house."

Starting to feel more like a home by the minute, with her there. He cleared his throat. "First one being, don't you dare make me eat more porridge cookies."

Her lips twitched. "That's fair, I guess."

"Use the kitchen, if you want, but I'm only your guinea pig for the good stuff."

"Done. What else?"

"No noise after midnight or before six a.m."

She held up both hands. "For the record, today I knocked at six-thirty-two."

"Cutting it close."

"Rules are rules." She grinned. "What else?"

"Clean up after yourself. I hate dirty dishes."

"Also fair."

He pointed at her. "No touching my protein powder."

"Which one?" She gestured to the arrangement of black canisters lining the counter by the backsplash.

"I said the protein powder. The others are pre-workout and creatine, obviously."

"Obviously." She wrinkled her nose at them. "I have all the muscle I need for baking already, don't worry."

"Wouldn't hurt you to do a pushup every now and then."

She narrowed her eyes. "Maybe I'll have some rules too. Like no insulting your guests."

Linc scoffed. "Guest? This is more like a hostile takeover. I saw the size of your suitcase."

Her eyes lit in challenge. He loved arguing with her. Pretty sure the feeling was mutual. "Oh yeah? Don't change the subject. I'm not the one who implied you were scrawny."

They both simultaneously looked at his crossed arms, his thick biceps filling the sleeves of his T-shirt. He lifted a brow at her.

A tinge of color coated her cheeks. "Well, okay. Obviously that wouldn't be realistic."

He held up one hand. "I wasn't insulting your appearance when I suggested working out. You're obviously pretty . . ." Oops. Too far. He coughed.

Her turn for a brow raise. "Oh? You think I'm pretty?"

He cleared his throat. *Danger, danger.* "I was saying, pretty much in shape. You know, for your lifestyle." He swallowed, tried to look nonchalant.

"Why, Linc Fontenot, I do declare." Zoey dramatically fluttered her eyelashes, took on a thick southern accent that didn't sound too far from Elisa's real voice. "You sure know the way to a woman's heart."

"Come on, you know what I mean." He didn't know whether to laugh, insult her further to distract her, or simply take his coffee and vanish to the front deck. "Working out is good for you. Endorphins and all that chemical stuff. You could probably use some of that lately."

"Ahh, I see. I didn't realize you'd gotten a life coach certificate." Thankfully, this time she grinned, letting him off the hook.

Though catch and release was the last game he should be playing with her right now. It was all their usual banter and fun to her. To him . . . well, it was getting way too real, and she could never know that fact. He gulped his coffee just as Zoey's phone chimed.

She pulled it from her pocket, looked down. "Voicemail."

Huh. People actually set those up?

"That's weird. It didn't even ring." She frowned and began tapping the screen.

"I don't get great service out here." Exactly the way he liked it—minimal distractions. Except for this pixie-sized one taking over his kitchen. At least the coffee she'd made smelled good.

She held the phone to her ear, listening to the message. "It's automated." Then her eyes widened, cheeks flushed. "Oh no."

"What?" On second thought . . . "Wait." He couldn't handle anything else pre-coffee. He got up, pushed past her to the gurgling pot, and switched the carafe with a mug, expertly catching the stream of hot liquid before swapping them back.

Linc leaned one hip against the counter and took a long sip. The brew burned his mouth, but it would keep him alert for whatever was next. He inhaled a long sniff of steam. "Okay, go."

Zoey's face, for once, wasn't full of hope. "That was the insurance company."

He took another long sip, frowned. "Go."

"They said the claim was still pending." She paused.

Another sip. Swallow. "Go."

"Something about failure to disclose relevant information." Zoey rolled in her lower lip, eyes wide beneath her bangs. "I didn't report the new fryer or add it to the policy after it was installed."

"That shouldn't be reason enough to deny a claim." Linc tilted his head. "I'm sure that kind of oversight happens all the time."

She stared at her cell phone. "Apparently it's important."

"You'd only had that dumb fryer for a few weeks. Isn't there a grace period?"

"Maybe, but since they're chalking the fryer up to the source of the fire, then it gets complicated." Zoey closed her eyes, bracing herself. "Is this my fault?"

"Did you start the fire?"

Her eyes flew open. "Of course not."

"Then of course not." He took another sip. Ah, caffeine. Usually got to drink it in silence, but oh well.

"They said it could be another few weeks, maybe longer." She pulled on a strand of her dark hair. "This is getting more serious than I realized. I have no job. No income. All my stuff is in storage..." Then she abruptly stopped, drew a tight breath. Her smile returned. "But it's not that deep, right? I'll figure it out."

Oh brother. He set his mug by the sink and crossed the floor toward her, taking her by both arms.

She looked up, startled. He rarely touched her. Sure, he'd held her as her business burned. And numerous times she'd slapped him in the arm after a joke, or hopped on his back or tried to drown him in the bay by jumping on his head, but he very rarely initiated physical contact.

The feel of her slim, toned arms under his hands reminded him why. He ignored that, for now, held tighter. "You're already figuring it out. Like you keep saying—everything is going to be fine."

Weird, him assuring *her*. He didn't like this role-swapping, but she'd saved him enough times over the years from the pit—wouldn't hurt him to return the favor for five minutes. Not that he really knew how.

Should he hug her? When was the last time he'd hugged anyone? Besides Delia Boudreaux, maybe, when he ventured into church last.

Before he could decide, Zoey launched toward him, wrapping her arms around his torso and holding tight. Her warm body pressed against his, and she looked up at him, relief and gratitude swimming in her blue eyes. Her pink lips eased into a smile. "Thank you."

He stilled, gazed down at her, taking in the way she stared back at him like he was some kind of hero, absorbing the smell of her fresh shampoo, noting the heat of her arms and—nope. Definitely shouldn't hug her.

Linc pried free, stepped back toward the coffee. "Here. Drink this." He poured a mug, handed it to her so fast a few drops sloshed over the side onto the floor.

He grabbed a towel from the counter and swiped the spill with his foot, ignoring the bewildered look on Zoey's face as she took a slow sip of the brew. She'd be really shocked if she knew what had danced through his mind while she'd held him like that.

Had he made a mistake? He leaned against the counter, folded his arms over his stomach. Good grief, his heart thudded like he'd already done his morning workout. Blame it on the coffee, maybe. Then his gaze registered the Folgers container.

Decaf.

Well shoot. He scowled. He needed somewhere to put this adrenaline, or he'd do something *really* foolish. Like give in to another hug. "Forgot one more house rule."

"What's that?" Zoey sipped her coffee, eyes closed, relishing the brew, as if everything was, once again, all sunshine and roses.

"Ten pushups every morning before breakfast."

She blinked at him. "You're kidding, right?"

"I never joke about fitness." He dropped to the kitchen floor. Better crank out a quick twenty. Sure, he'd found a way to keep her off his boat and away from Boiling Bayou.

But he was pretty sure that with inviting Zoey to stay there, he'd just jumped straight from a sinking ship into a churning sea.

Four

I T'S LIKE I'VE NEVER BAKED A DAY IN my life." Zoey drummed her finger on the table she shared with Rosalyn Dupree, the aroma of fresh ground coffee beans wafting from the front of Chug a Mug. The coffee shop was hopping for a Tuesday afternoon, and judging by the scowl fixed firmly on Miley's face as she worked the milk frother behind the counter, the brew would be extra good today. "I'm not sure what I'm doing wrong with all these failed recipes."

"Have you asked Elisa to help?" Rosalyn leaned back in her chair, crossing her arms over her torso. She wore designer workout gear, her long blond hair tied up in a top-knot—per usual after she taught the noon aerial class at Madame Paulette's ballet studio.

"No, she's got enough going on with the wedding planning right now." Zoey shook her head. "I don't want to bother anyone."

She hadn't told Elisa specifically where she was staying yet, either—also on purpose. Her friend would have way too many questions, or worse yet, try to convince Zoey to come back to the Blue Pirogue. Which obviously wasn't good for her and Noah, and Zoey was tired of feeling selfish for being so needy.

"Friends aren't bothered by friends." Rosalyn offered her a smile. "But, I know what you mean. Elisa's plate is pretty full these days."

"I think my focus is off. I tried an actual recipe last night instead of winging it, and I think that batch of cookies would have been good, but . . ." Zoey wrinkled her nose and fought back a shudder. "I accidentally grabbed cumin instead of cinnamon." She could still taste the remnants of the mistake if she thought about it long enough.

Rosalyn grimaced. "Yikes. To be fair, though, you have a lot on your plate too."

"That's true." Zoey lifted her mug of half-drunk joe. "I just really need to get some income rolling, and I'm not sure how to go about it besides some form of baking."

"I'm not surprised it's hard for you to concentrate." Rosalyn winked as she picked up her teacup. "Especially if there's a handsome pirate lurking around the kitchen."

Zoey sprayed her coffee. "A *what*?" She swiped her mouth with the back of her hand, half laughing and half gurgling.

"What else would you call a massive, dark, brooding man on a boat?" Rosalyn leaned across the table with a conspiring grin. "Don't tell me you don't think Linc is attractive."

"Well, sure he is. I'm not blind." Zoey smirked as she wiped another dribble of coffee from the table. "And apparently neither are you."

"Of course not." Rosalyn lifted both hands. "But Cade is much more my type."

"Which type is that? Stylish pretty boy?"

"Exactly." They shared a grin.

"I'm happy for you two. But it's not like that with Linc, trust me." Zoey searched for a way to change the subject without technically changing the subject, before Rosalyn noticed her runaway heartbeat. "I mean, for one, the man must do his laundry like an elf makes shoes."

"What do you mean?"

"You know, in the middle of the night. Like an elf." Zoey gestured with her napkin. "I've been there three days, and I haven't seen so much as a single sock on the floor."

Hadn't seen much of Linc either, for that matter. He'd been working long hours, and most of his evenings were spent at the gym. Besides hearing the shower crank on after she was already in bed for the night, well, she might as well be living alone.

Which was fine, right? She didn't need companionship, she needed a roof over her head, which Linc was generously providing.

So why did it feel like he was avoiding her?

Rosalyn lifted her tea, pink lipstick staining the rim. "I'm not following."

"He's either a secret neat freak, or he's scared to let me see he's human." Zoey frowned. "Wait, scratch that. Linc's not afraid of anything."

Maybe he simply regretted her being there. She knew she'd be in the way to some extent, even though she'd made sure to clean the already-clean kitchen every morning after he left. Ran the vacuum cleaner too, after finding it stashed in the laundry room closet. And she'd been sure to keep to his quiet hours, as requested, though she'd skipped the pushups.

Linc was doing her a huge favor, and she had nothing to give back. Worse yet, nothing to do during the day to combat the fear and anxiety circulating her brain. The insurance company wouldn't return her multiple voicemails seeking more details on her case, instead sending a form email stating they'd received her inquiry and, due to "a high volume of inquiries," they could take up to forty-eight hours to return emails.

It was harder these days to be sunshine by herself, hence her desperate text to Rosalyn to meet her for coffee after the noon class today.

"Maybe he's just being courteous." Rosalyn set her cup down, her naturally arched brows furrowed. "You know, making sure you're comfortable being there."

Ha. "*Linc*? Courteous?" Zoey shook her head, hair swishing. "Sometimes I forget you don't know Linc very well. He has zero filter. He tells people exactly what he thinks, whether they want to hear it or not." She hesitated. Well, that was true with most people. With her lately, well—she had to make him touch the lamppost about her cookies. What was that about? Linc had never held back with her before.

Rosalyn nodded. "I've witnessed that no-filter dynamic between Linc and Cade. Though to his credit, Linc usually seems right." She chuckled. "Much to Cade's dismay."

"Yeah. I hate that part." More like missed it. The little gleam in Linc's eye, the hard-to-tell-if-he-was-joking-or-actually-mad expression, the arrogance—make that raw confidence—that accompanied his matter-of-fact, slightly sarcastic delivery of the truth.

She ran her finger around the rim of her cup. She'd always been jealous of that in Linc. What was it like, being able to say exactly what you thought, without having to worry about being too negative? Without having to worry about what would happen if you stopped being sunshine all the time?

And why had he stopped being that way with her the past several days? Zoey narrowed her eyes. "It's almost like he's being *too* nice."

"Yeah, I hate when men are considerate . . . and clean." Rosalyn grinned. "Such a hardship."

Zoey laughed. "I just mean because it's Linc. Like he's holding back now." She frowned. "I want him to be himself. I want *us* to be *ourselves*."

She'd actually set a trap to test her theory before she left for the coffee shop that morning. If Linc was holding back with her, then he'd ignore the bait. Though, to be fair, he probably wouldn't even go home midday to find it, so she might not know for a while.

Rosalyn leaned forward, caught Zoey's eye. Her gaze softened. "Look, you and Linc must be pretty good friends, or neither of you would have been comfortable with this arrangement."

"Best friends." The words flew from Zoey's lips on autopilot. And she still believed them, even though they felt slightly less true than they would have several weeks ago. Before the fire, when Linc held her in the raining ash and smoke. Before Noah and Elisa got engaged, and Zoey became homeless and unemployed and—

"Then I'm sure you'll find your groove." Rosalyn touched Zoey's arm. "And hey, if it gets too weird, you're welcome to come to my parents' house again." She winced. "I know Marta can be a *little* intense about her carpet staying clean, but—"

"I can't do that. But I appreciate it." Zoey squeezed her hand back. "You've only been back in Magnolia Bay for several weeks. I'm sure you're still adjusting to living with your parents and not out of a suitcase, yourself. I don't want to be a burden."

To Rosalyn, Elisa, Noah. Linc. To anyone. That's why she had to stay upbeat. Her friends had all been through enough the past year with the hurricane restoration, the lack of tourism, family drama, relationship issues . . . Rosalyn had been running from the Mafia a month ago, for goodness' sake. Zoey didn't need her friends worrying about her now that their lives had finally ironed out.

"It's been interesting moving back home, for sure." Rosalyn twisted her lips to the side. "But I'll find my own place soon."

"Unless Cade makes other plans . . ." Zoey grinned and wiggled her ring finger.

Rosalyn blushed. "*Way* too early for that."

"But?" Zoey raised her eyebrows. "I hear a *but*."

Rosalyn's blush deepened and her smile widened. "But . . . maybe one day. In the meantime, I look forward to being Cade's date at Elisa and Noah's wedding. Dressing up, dancing—"

"Catching the bouquet?" Zoey winked.

"I think Madame Paulette might body slam me for it." Rosalyn grinned, pausing to take a sip of tea. "Are you going to the wedding with Linc?"

Zoey's stomach flipped. "I hadn't thought about it." Oh, but now she was. Linc in a suit, long hair slicked back and styled, broad shoulders encased in a gray jacket . . .

"You're both in the wedding, right? I know Cade is best man, and Linc is a groomsman."

"I'm maid of honor." Zoey nodded. That excused her from needing a date, didn't it? She released a sigh of relief. Not that Linc would have asked her, or she him.

But good to have that out of the way.

Sudden footsteps sounded. "Girls!" Delia Boudreaux rushed toward their table as fast as her slight, post-hip-surgery limp allowed, her graying hair askew. "I'm so glad you're here."

Zoey pulled out the vacant chair between her and Rosalyn, frowning. "What's wrong, Mama D?" Surely not the diner again . . .

Rosalyn leaned forward in concern as Delia plopped into the seat, breathing hard. "Can we get you anything?" She craned her head toward the front counter, gesturing for Miley's attention.

"No, no." Mama D caught Rosalyn's hand, pressed it back down. "Don't bother Miley. I've heard the weather report is extra cloudy today."

"Cheers to that." Zoey saluted Mama D with her cup. "So what's wrong?"

She blew out a breath, chest heaving under her blouse. "I just had to ask—what are you both wearing to the wedding?"

Zoey and Rosalyn exchanged an amused look.

"Elisa's wedding that's in a *month*?" Rosalyn tilted her head to the side, lips tilting in a gentle smile. "Mama D, I don't know what I'm wearing *tomorrow*."

Delia waved her hand. "Maybe not. I bet your man does though. Cade seems the type to iron the night before." She turned her gaze to Zoey as Rosalyn snorted. "What about you, dear?"

"I'll be in a maid of honor dress." Speaking of which, she needed to go get fitted for her gown, which she'd refused to let Elisa pay for, despite being unsure how she was going to herself. Maybe the insurance money would hit before the fitting—

"Oh, that's right. Well, I've finally gotten away from that cane, and I've got to be snazzy. Can't let Madame Paulette show me up." Delia lifted her chin, her deep burgundy lipstick only slightly smeared today. No one could possibly show her up, though Lettie would try. "Nothing that requires Spanx. I'm eating that wedding cake comfortably, mind you."

"As you should." Zoey rubbed the woman's hard-working, blue-veined hand. "You'll look beautiful in whatever you wear. This whole town loves you."

"You're always so encouraging, dear." Delia patted her hand back. "Thank you, but also, don't flatter me. I need help." She narrowed her eyes as she swung her gaze between them. "Now, which of you will do my makeup for the big day?"

Zoey pointed at Rosalyn, just as Rosalyn timidly raised her hand. "I believe I have some experience in that department."

"Perfect." Mama D slapped her hand on the table. "I'm thinking a dramatic smoky eye."

She and Rosalyn began talking lip colors as the coffee shop door swung open, heavy boots clunking inside.

Linc.

Zoey's heart jolted, her vision narrowing until the chalkboard wall and bronze light fixtures faded from focus. He strolled toward her, gaze locked on hers, brow drawn. Her stomach somersaulted. Had her trap worked?

"What is this?" Linc dropped a bowl—one of the solid black ones from his house—onto the table. It clattered in a circle, spinning on its rim until it finally rested still in front of Zoey.

Rosalyn's eyes widened. Mama D leaned over to peer at the beige, lumpy contents.

Zoey blinked up at Linc, rolling in her lips and pressing them together. Joy bubbled. "Just some porridge."

"Very funny." Linc jabbed his finger toward the congealed mess, his mane of dark hair shifting on top of his head. "That stuff is like glue. You better get my bowl clean."

"Of course, Papa Bear." Zoey kept blinking innocently. "Nothing a little elbow grease can't cure."

Linc crossed his arms over his fishing shirt, glared. "I also heard you singing at six a.m."

"Six-oh-two." She tapped her watch with one window. "I set an alarm."

His lips twitched. "I went home for lunch. Now I'm late for my next tour."

"Better skedaddle, then." She wiggled her fingers. "See you later, roomie."

He narrowed his eyes, opened his mouth, then shut it. "If I come home and there's some little blonde creature in a pink dress sleeping in my bed, I swear—"

"Goldilocks wore blue."

Linc's gaze swung to Rosalyn, who winced and nodded.

He furrowed his brow back at Zoey. "You know what I mean."

She shrugged. "All I can say is, too bad you didn't like my cookies."

"So *this* is what I get for telling the truth?" He thumped the bowl, which clanked against the table again as if full of concrete. "I'd rather the cookies."

"That can be arranged too."

Linc's jaw twitched. He clearly wanted to laugh, she'd bet her next coffee on it. On second thought, she was only about seventy-five percent sure he wasn't mad, which made her grateful she wasn't a gambling woman.

Zoey cleared her throat. "No pink dresses, no porridge. Check, and check."

Linc started for the door without another word, leaving the bowl behind. Without turning around, he called over his shoulder. "You owe me thirty pushups. Ten per day."

"What in the world?" Mama D asked, face bewildered.

Zoey grinned at his retreating form. Linc was grumpy. Short. Annoyed.

Linc was back.

Which meant, for the moment at least, that Zoey didn't have to pretend to be happy.

Maybe one day he could relax again.

Salt water sprayed Linc's face as his boat raced across the water several hours later. Rays of afternoon sun bounced off the bay, and he turned his head into the mist, his shoulders tense under the warmth of early September air.

His fishing buddy Owen had referred to Linc once as that half-man, half-fish guy from the superhero movies . . . to which Linc had snatched him up by the shirt collar. But maybe it wasn't that far from the truth—he loved the water. Loved the smell of salt air, the crunch of sand and clay beneath his feet as he baited crawfish traps. The tug of the water against his waders as he braced against the waves, the pull of the tide. Being baked in the sun after a hard day's work kept him too tired to remember.

Too tired to want more.

Like now. For a minute, the stress of his off-season business ventures didn't exist. Worries about next season's crawfish haul didn't exist. Zoey's cornflower-blue gaze relentlessly haunting his dreams ever since she'd moved in didn't exist.

In fact, if he shut his eyes, took a deep breath, he could almost forget the fact that he wasn't alone on the boat.

"You probably shouldn't operate heavy machinery with your eyes closed."

Almost.

Linc cut the engine and leveled his stare at Delia, who sat across from the captain's chair, sleeves pushed up to enjoy the sun. "What's the urgency of this private tour, again? It's the middle of the day. In the middle of the week."

"I'm retired." Delia sniffed.

"And?"

"And I needed my vitamin D."

"And?"

"And you need life advice."

Oh, brother. He shouldn't have pushed. Linc sighed, moved a wet strand of hair out of his face. "Do I?"

"I'll say. Zoey is living with you."

Red alerts sounded. That was a way more intimate description than the situation called for. "She's *staying* with me until her check comes in and she can find her own place again. I have plenty of room." He shifted on the captain's chair. "And apparently, Trish snores and you talk too much."

"Ha." Delia hooked one sandaled foot over the other, folded her hands across her linen pants. Dark sunglasses covered her eyes, hiding the wisdom he knew brewed there on the regular. "Too much is relative."

He narrowed his gaze. "Right now I'd have to agree with her."

Delia laughed. "Lincoln Fontenot, honey, you don't scare me. Or even bother me."

Good. He didn't want to do either of those things. But he also didn't want the town mama freely offering her opinion on his life, uninvited.

He'd had enough sudden female input for one week.

As if reading his mind, Delia pointed at him. "If you didn't want my advice, you shouldn't have let it slip in front of me."

How had he let—oh, yeah. The porridge bowl.

Linc started the engine again, puttering against the inland curve toward the gulf. Things had felt odd with Zoey the past three days, their usual banter stilted. It was like they were so busy tiptoeing around each other, both trying to be overly considerate, that they'd lost their friendship dynamic. Which was the only reason why Linc had even offered to let her stay in the first place—he knew it'd be easy.

But it hadn't been.

So while he ran the tour that morning and tried to tune out Anthony yapping about Louisiana wildlife facts and hurricane stats, he realized the only difference was that he and Zoey had stopped arguing. He'd run home at lunch in search of something to pretend to be mad about, and bingo—porridge bowl. He'd had to fight back a smile in Chug a Mug at Zoey's pleased-with-herself smirk, at the light restored in her eyes.

Fighting a little smile now too, for that matter. Maybe he *could* allow himself to relax. Maybe things were slowly working out for everyone.

Maybe he wasn't destined to be alone.

"... parents are missionaries, you know."

Oh, yeah—Delia. Most people took his bouts of silence as a welcome cue to stop talking. Mama D did not.

He tried to keep up. "Whose parents?"

"Zoey's." Delia tilted her head, frowned. "You've never met them, have you? They would have already been overseas by the time you moved back to the Bay. They only come back to the States and see Zoey once or twice a year."

Linc frowned. He'd known that, but Delia made it sound . . . different. Like maybe it bothered Zoey that her parents weren't around. Every time she'd talked about them to him, she'd been proud of them. Happy they were living their calling, making a difference.

The sun dipped behind a cloud, casting a shadow over the water. "Anyway, just a heads-up that they might not understand this situation for what it is." Delia lowered her shades, stared at him over the rim. "A friend helping out another friend."

Aye. That stare could kill a shark in the water. What was she implying? Linc shifted in his seat, angled the boat back toward the dock. "Not sure what to tell you, since that's all it is."

Delia released a noncommittal hmm, lips pursed.

Man. He should have left that porridge bowl on the island at home. The last thing he needed was people getting into his business—or worse, questioning Zoey's reputation. His own was probably shot long ago.

The motor hummed. Surely they weren't doing damage with this temporary arrangement, were they? He and Zoey were friends, and everyone in town understood that. Besides, it wasn't like they were hormonal college kids in need of a chaperone—they were grown adults, making the best of a hard situation that wasn't anyone's fault.

He snorted. Besides, this was *Zoey.* He'd seen her trick-or-treating in embarrassing Halloween costumes, seen her when she was feverish and puking her guts out. Seen her stuff her mouth with a dozen jumbo marshmallows to win a contest, seen her burp-sing the national anthem at a baseball game on a dare. Hardly temptation-city.

Though lately, all of those memories were just making her more appealing. But Mama D didn't know that, nor did anyone else.

What wasn't Mama D saying?

Somewhere behind them, a fish jumped, splashed. The sun edged back into view. Linc guided the boat toward the dock, thoughts churning like the waves under the motor. For once, he felt slightly bad for all the times he'd left people in the wake of his silence. *Say something, Mama D . . .*

He finally caved. "Do you believe that's all it is with us? A friend helping a friend?"

Delia smiled. "It doesn't really matter what I believe, Lincoln." She replaced her sunglasses, draped one wrinkled arm over the back of the seat, and tilted her face toward the sky. "The question is . . . what do *you* believe?"

He cut the engine as the dock edged closer, the sudden silence making his thoughts all the more deafening. What *did* he believe? Was he only fooling himself?

He swallowed as they floated, one hand tight on the wheel as he guided the boat toward the wooden structure. "Me and Zoey have always been friends."

"Things can change, you know."

He shook his head. "Not with us."

Delia kept her face casually toward the sun, as if she wasn't probing his deepest thoughts. "Why not?"

Because he needed Zoey—needed *them*—to be exactly the way they were. Change was risky, and he'd lost enough over the years. The words burned the back of Linc's throat, and he coughed to clear it.

"Everything changes eventually, dear."

"No. We're different." They *had* to be an exception. Even though the small ache in his gut hinted to the contrary. He risked a glance at Mama D to see if she, at least, was buying it.

Oh no. She'd taken off the sunglasses, pierced him with a look.

Linc shifted his gaze back to the dock, grateful for the excuse as the boat gently bumped the wooden side. He stood to grab the ropes, heart thumping. Surely she'd see he was busy now.

"Lincoln, all I'm saying is you might be playing with fire here."

Like a sea bass with a baitfish, the older woman refused to let go. He wrenched the rope around the dock loop, pulling tight. Maybe he had to listen, respectfully, but he didn't have to agree.

"And I think poor Zoey's had enough fire in her life lately, hmm?"

Ouch. Okay, so that one hit the mark. Was this arrangement really that damaging for Zoey? He let go of the rope, blew out his breath as he turned to face Mama D. "What do you suggest?"

As if *he* was now the bass taking bait, she smiled smugly, tucking those dark sunglasses back on her face. "I'm sure you'll think of something, dear."

Oh, great. So there was that.

He finished tying off the rope, back muscles protesting as he wound maybe a little harder than necessary. If Mama D was right—and man, wasn't she usually?—he might not get to relax again for a very long time.

Five

 Zoey sang into the white spatula—officially the most boring spatula she'd ever encountered—and shook her hips before she resumed stirring the lumpy dough. The other day, she'd had to unearth the probably-never-been-used mixing bowl from the depths of Linc's pantry, behind an enormous open bag of sunflower seeds and a bulk-club box of white rice. No wonder the man looked like he did—the kitchen was full of nothing but natural peanut butter, avocados, and chicken.

She'd fix that.

"*…underneath the treeee.*" She sang along as she spooned clumps of dough onto the cookie sheet, pausing to wipe her cheek with her shoulder. Flour coated her hands, the apron she'd swiped from Linc's grilling closet—yes, an entire pantry dedicated to meat-cooking supplies—and the countertops. Oops, and the floor. Oh well, she'd get to that. Linc wouldn't be home for several hours and—

"It's September."

Zoey shrieked and spun, arm flailing. Cookie dough shot off

the end of her spatula and slapped against the wall, where it began a slow descent toward the floor.

Plop.

Linc stared at her from the doorway, his hair piled on top of his head, a slight sunburn streaking his nose.

Her heart restarted with a thud. "You scared me." She pointed at him with the spatula, and another piece of dough dropped to her feet.

"What are you doing?" Linc strode across the kitchen, scowl in place. He slapped the portable speaker, and Mariah abruptly shut up. "This place is a mess."

"Your bowl is clean, though." She gestured to the sink, where the black porridge dish nestled among the remains of burnt cookie crumbs, a rolling pin, and several measuring cups. She wouldn't tell him how long it had taken to soak the porridge free.

He ran a hand down the side of his jaw and, once again, she couldn't tell if he wanted to laugh or maybe sue her. "What are you wearing?"

Then his eyes widened a little, and she thought about teasing him for the phrase choice, but it seemed like he'd been through enough already. She looked down at the black apron. "You trying to say I'm not believable as *The Grillfather*?"

"Hardly." He sniffed the air. "Did you burn a batch?"

"Two, actually."

He leaned one hip against the island, then noticed the flour and backed away. "Remind me how you had an award-winning beignet business, again?"

"Apparently I'm really good at deep-frying stuff." Zoey winced and tossed the spatula on the counter. "Don't worry, I'll get the rest of this figured out."

Linc pried open the oven door. Smoke drifted out.

"Oops. Must not have heard the timer over Mariah." She hurried to the oven, donned a mitt, and wrenched out the tray. "Okay, so make that three burned batches. We still have one left." She gestured with the mitt toward the remaining lumps of dough ready for their turn. Or more like their fate.

He narrowed his eyes. "You really think that's a good idea?"

"Good point. I'll set two timers." She crossed her arms over the apron. Dough squished beneath her shoe. "The real question is, why are you so home so early?" Home. That sounded weird.

And nice.

"Oh, sure. You put an apron on and the nagging starts." He moved across the kitchen toward her, paused to brush flour off the leg of his jeans.

She held her ground, fighting a smile. "Evading my question, I see."

He was moving closer, now. Stopped directly in front of her. "Did you do your pushups?"

"I did five, and decided that was a ridiculous house rule." She lifted her chin.

He leaned in, and the smell of saltwater and sunscreen washed over her. She swallowed. Was he going to—

He reached around her, snagged an apple from the fruit bowl, and took a big chomp. Juice sprayed. "You're behind, then. You owe me thirty."

Why had she thought he was doing anything other than reaching for a snack? And why was the little voice in the back of her head whispering she wanted him to?

The stress of her situation was getting to her. She backed away, wiped apple juice off her face. "No sane person can do thirty pushups in a day, Linc."

"I do fifty."

"Like I said."

Gravel crunched outside. Linc frowned, stopped mid-chew. "Expecting someone?"

"I wasn't even expecting you." She tucked her hair behind her ear, then remembered the flour. Too late. She swatted at the white streaking her hair like premature gray. Ha. Another few days staying in close proximity with Linc and she'd be full-on silver.

Linc brushed past her, toward the front door. "Delivery truck might have taken a wrong turn."

She followed him, brushing at the front of her apron and leaving a trail of white powder in their wake. "How big a hermit are you that you're assuming a postal worker is lost instead of bringing you a package?"

"I rarely shop online. My protein powder lasts a month."

"People could send you gifts."

He grunted. "That doesn't even happen at Christmas."

It didn't? She frowned.

Linc peered out the screened door at an older model sedan parked halfway down the long, tree-lined drive. A middle-aged woman climbed out and began a careful trek in low heels over the gravel toward the porch.

Linc glared. "I have a no soliciting sign at the end of the driveway."

"Maybe she's lost, like you said." Zoey nudged Linc toward the kitchen. "I'll make you a deal. You go put the next batch of cookies in and set the timer—that way it'll be your fault if they burn—and I'll handle this."

"Fine." He obliged and headed back for the unsuspecting cookie dough. "I guess you living here is good for something besides making a mess."

"I'm going to assume you're joking," she called over her shoulder. But she smiled as she faced back to the driveway. See? They had their groove back. She was annoying, he was easily bothered, they bickered and bantered.

Best friends. They could make this work for a few weeks, if it took that long.

Everything was going to be okay.

The lady outside, dressed in a faded pantsuit with a floral-print blouse and carrying a manila folder, finally reached the door. Zoey opened it before she could knock, put on a welcoming smile. "Hi! Need some help?"

"I'm looking for Linc Fontenot." The brunette flipped open the folder in her hand and glanced at the document inside, as if to verify, before looking back at Zoey. Her foundation was a tad too dark for her skin tone, but her eyes were kind, if not tired.

A lawyer, maybe? Zoey frowned, shifting her weight to block the door as if that might keep Linc from hearing. "He's not available right now. I could probably help." If this was about the kid that fell off the boat, well, she definitely wanted to know first. Find a way to break the news gently to Linc.

Or better yet, have a chance to pack her suitcase and get a head start.

The woman shook her head. "I'm afraid I have to speak with Mr. Fontenot directly."

Yikes. Definitely a lawyer. Zoey drew a breath, smoothed the front of her apron, then realized how ridiculous she must look with flour everywhere. She tried to find her most professional voice. "Listen, Ms . . ."

"Bridges." She hefted her purse on her shoulder.

"Ms. Bridges." Zoey leaned in closer, lowered her voice as she propped open the screen door with her foot. "I think there's been a misunderstanding with this"—she gestured toward the folder—"suit."

Ms. Bridges frowned, looking down. "What about it?"

"It's not right."

"Not right?" She tugged at the hem of her jacket. "Really?"

Zoey shook her head. "Honestly, it's all wrong. Trust me."

Ms. Bridges tilted her head, lips pursed. "Do you really think that's your place to say?"

"Of course it is." Zoey reeled back. "I was there."

Ms. Bridges tilted her head the other direction. "You were at Macy's?"

This woman wasn't a very good lawyer. "No, I was on the *boat*. I saw everything."

"I certainly didn't buy this suit on a boat."

"I can guarantee you Linc has never even been to Macy's."

They spoke at the same time, then stared at each other. Zoey squinted. "What are you talking about?"

"What are *you* talking about?"

A car door slammed. Zoey looked down the driveway as a girl, maybe twelve or thirteen, emerged from the back seat, arms crossed over a cropped T-shirt. Her thick dark hair hung in waves over her skinny shoulders. "I told you he wouldn't be interested," she called.

"And I told you to wait in the car." Ms. Bridges released a sigh hard enough that her wispy bangs fluttered.

So maybe not a lawyer. Zoey frowned. "You're not here about the boat incident?"

The girl, ignoring the woman's instructions, began walking toward the porch. Zoey wondered if she should point out that fact to Ms. Bridges, who obviously couldn't see behind her.

But Ms. Bridges continued before Zoey could decide. "I'm here on official business for Mr. Fontenot. And honestly, it's been a long week. I could have done without the fashion advice."

Zoey jerked her gaze back to the woman. "Fashion advice?"

"My suit." She patted her jacket.

Zoey sucked in her breath. Oh, dear. She thought—"No! I was talking about a *law*suit."

"She's serving me papers?" Linc appeared in the doorway behind Zoey. She twisted around to look up at him just as his face darkened into a storm. He pointed to the road. "Listen, lady, I've got a no soliciting sign out there that you clearly barreled past."

"I saw it. And I'm not soliciting." Ms. Bridges pinched the

bridge of her nose. The wind ruffled her hair, sending a warm breeze across the porch. "Mr. Fontenot, I've been trying to reach you for over a week. It's urgent."

"Phone's not broken." He rested one muscular arm on the door frame, a clear signal he wouldn't be inviting anyone inside. Even if they had edible cookies, which they definitely didn't.

Ms. Bridges looked as if she'd aged a decade in the past sixty seconds. "Well, you don't answer it, nor do you have voicemail."

Linc tilted his head. "If you think back to the No Trespassing, No Soliciting, and Beware of Dog signs you drove by, you might realize you aren't that surprised."

They continued arguing. Zoey's attention drifted past Ms. Bridges, to the girl who had stopped at the foot of the porch stairs and tugged at the hair tie looped around her wrist. She scuffed one shoe in the dirt, leaning casually against the porch railing as if this trip was the ultimate in boring.

But her gaze kept drifting up to Linc, contradicting her alleged disinterest. She studied him like one might study a superhero. Or maybe a villain. Zoey snorted. With Linc, that was fair enough, depending on the day.

". . . I'm not serving you papers," Ms. Bridges was saying.

Zoey tuned back in.

"Glad to hear it. Now look, if you need money or directions, I'm sorry, but this isn't the place." Linc started to shut the door. Zoey jumped back just in time to avoid it slamming against her foot.

Ms. Bridges's eyes widened through the screen. "Mr. Fontenot, please, if you'll just stop one moment and listen—"

"Told you." The girl cocked one jean-clad hip, a smug smile creasing her face. Something about that look almost seemed . . . familiar. "You owe me ten bucks."

Ms. Bridges spun around to face her. "I most certainly do not. Amelia, you were supposed to wait in the car until I sorted this out."

Zoey took the opportunity to tug at Linc's arm. He looked down at her, the visible frustration in his gaze measurably softening. She whispered. "Maybe hear them out."

He rolled his eyes, but obligingly propped the screen back open, just in time for them to hear Amelia's response.

"It's hot in the car. And besides, it doesn't sound like it's getting *sorted*." Amelia air-quoted the word. "All this red tape is so annoying."

"I'll say." Linc scowled. "And for the record, you shouldn't be rude to your elders like that."

"Ha." The teen singsonged at Ms. Bridges. "He just called you old."

Ms. Bridges closed her eyes. Zoey was pretty sure if she'd been wearing red slippers, she'd have heel-clicked herself somewhere far away. "Mr. Fontenot, as I've been trying to explain to you, we have a situation on our hands."

"It's me." Amelia clambered onto the porch, a challenging gleam in her eyes that did nothing to conceal the dark smudges underneath. She looked . . . tired. Like an adult and a child, all at once. "I'm the situation."

"Who are you?" Linc frowned.

Zoey's gaze darted between Amelia and Linc, at their matching glares. Dark hair and eyes . . . no. Impossible. Linc wasn't—he'd never . . .

Amelia lifted her chin. "I'm your daughter."

Six

LINC HAD HAD PEOPLE MAKE UP ALL kinds of crazy reasons to come to his porch before—usually with an end game of selling him a vacuum cleaner or a set of professional-grade knives.

Claiming DNA was a new one.

"Nice try." He glared, crossed his arms over his chest at this unlikely duo. "I don't have any kids."

"And yet here I am." The girl—what was her name, Amelia?—matched his stance. She looked like she was past the sticky-hand stage, but the kid still needed some manners. Her mom, or whoever this Ms. Bridges was on the porch, had clearly dropped the ball.

"Here you are . . . and off you go. We were in the middle of something, so if you don't mind." *He* minded—a lot. He tugged at Zoey's elbow, wanting her to step inside so he could shut the door, but her face had washed pale. She stared at Amelia like she was from an Edgar Allan Poe poem instead of a sassy kid in need of some discipline.

Linc's hand slowly slipped off Zoey's arm, and his heart thudded as he studied her gaping mouth. *Aye.* She wasn't falling for this, was she?

His chest tightened. "Look, lady, you've either got me confused with someone else, or you're mistaken that I'm rich. Either way, this scam ends here." He started to shut the door. Zoey would just have to move on her own.

"Mr. Fontenot." Ms. Bridges stepped forward, lowering her voice. "Are you familiar with a Kirsten West?"

He caught the door before it slammed. Opened it again as the world dipped. The porch tilted. Now his mouth was the one hanging open. "How did you . . ."

In his peripheral vision, Zoey looked up at him, but he couldn't look at her. Could only look at Amelia . . . at her dark eyes and dark hair. No. How old was she? He was bad with kids. Really bad with ages. She looked, what? Eleven? That wouldn't be right.

He pressed his lips together, mind racing. Images of one fateful night, roughly fourteen years ago, flashed. He and Kirsten on a Valentine's date. Medium rare steak. Fake IDs, red wine. The fight, like always.

That particular makeup, which was definitely *not* like always.

He fought the urge to count on his fingers to be sure. "When is your birthday?"

"November. Why, you gonna get me a cake?" Amelia rolled her eyes.

He shoved his fingers into his hair. "The year, kid. The year."

Ms. Bridges opened her file. "2012."

Amelia was thirteen.

His ears roared. His vision blurred. He must have gasped, because Zoey's hand was on his arm, cool and steadying. Grounding him, keeping the sky in its rightful place. This wasn't possible.

And yet the impossible was glaring at him in low-rise jeans.

"Why don't you both come in?" Zoey's smile was bright, her grip firm on his bicep. "We have freshly baked cookies."

Next thing he knew, the oven timer was beeping, Zoey was clattering around the kitchen, and Ms. Bridges was perched on the edge of his leather sofa, while Amelia sprawled in his matching recliner, legs hooked over one of the thick armrests. A worn black backpack rested on the floor beside her, covered in marker doodles.

Linc paced by the door, his boots thudding on the hardwood floors. He tried not to stare, but Amelia was a dead ringer for Kirsten. How had he not seen it before? The waves in her hair, the narrow chin, the wide eyes with thick lashes—even the way she nibbled the cuticle of her thumbnail as she kicked one dirty shoe against the side of his chair.

"I don't understand," Linc muttered, paced, bumped the wall and spun to walk the other direction. "How could I be a father?"

Amelia huffed. "I took a health class in school last year that explains it, if you want my homework."

"Amelia!" Ms. Bridges gasped.

"I understand *that* part." Linc scowled. He ran a hand over his jaw. Why hadn't Kirsten told him? Why had she never—

"Here we go." Zoey hurried back into the living room, carrying a tray laden with cookies that were miraculously not burned, a pitcher of water he'd never seen before in his life, and several plastic souvenir cups from Magnolia Blossom Café. "Let's just all take a deep breath, hmm?" She shot Linc a pointed glare, as if the instructions were meant for him alone despite her general address.

Zoey deposited the tray on the coffee table, then sat next to Ms. Bridges on the couch. Linc preferred to stand. No, he *preferred* to bench press a couple hundred pounds real quick, but he'd have to make do with hydrating and breathing. He filled a cup with water, tossed it back, and then poured a second one while Zoey served their guests.

Guests? Make that *family*.

He had flesh-and-blood family.

The floor tilted again. He leaned against the wall by the television stand, found Zoey's eyes. She gave him a quick dip of her head, and he held on to her gaze like a life preserver. He clutched the cup in his hand and finally dared to look at Amelia—who was staring at him. He gulped, coughed.

"Thank you, Mrs. Fontenot." Ms. Bridges gestured toward the cookies with a smile. "You're very gracious. I know we showed up rather—"

"Oh, no. I'm not—we're not . . ." Zoey pointed to her chest, then at Linc, eyes wide. "I'm Zoey *Lakewood*."

Ms. Bridges winced. "Oh, you're not married? My mistake."

Any other time, Linc would have snorted at the panic in Zoey's gaze, the flush in her cheeks. He crossed his arms, his heartbeat thundering in his ears. "Can someone please tell me what's going on?"

"Mr. Fontenot, I take it you are familiar with Ms. West." Ms. Bridges set her cup back on the tray and opened her folder.

He fought back a snort. Familiar. That was one word for it.

"She's been gone for over a week. Neighbors reported their suspicions when her car never returned, but they saw Amelia still taking the bus every day."

Kirsten just left her? Linc frowned. "Where—what bus?"

Amelia stared at him like he was an idiot. "The *school* bus. I'm in eighth grade."

"No, I mean *where*? Where did you come from?"

"Lafayette." Ms. Bridges shuffled the papers. "That's where Amelia and her mother have been living the past three months."

"Lafayette—*Louisiana*? When did she move there?"

More shuffling. "I'm not sure. Where did you and Ms. West meet?"

"North Carolina." When his foster parents left Magnolia Bay and moved up north after he graduated high school. "We obviously lost touch." After—well, after *everything*. Cleanest breakup he'd ever had. Then he got that scholarship via weightlifting to finish his business degree at LSU and never looked back. Returned to the Bay after graduating to start his crawfishing business, to stop being a third wheel with foster parents who had raised him and were clearly done with the job.

Apparently, somewhere along the way, he'd missed a lot.

"Before Lafayette, we lived in Metairie. Then Ruston. Natchitoches." Amelia ticked the towns off on her fingers. "We get around."

In more ways than one in Kirsten's case, if she left her teen daughter home alone for a week or longer. His chest heated. Sounded like nothing had changed—betrayal, abandonment, zero loyalty. All these years, and she'd been in Louisiana, just a bridge or boat ride away. Sure, he'd blocked her number after the breakup, but she could have easily found him if she'd tried via his foster parents.

Why follow him to Louisiana but never reach out?

"She never told me." Linc looked between Ms. Bridges, Zoey, and Amelia, repeating the words he feared none of them believed. "I didn't know."

"I gathered as much. When we came to pick up Amelia, it took some"—Ms. Bridges shot the teen a side-eyed look—"*convincing* to get her to tell us who her father was."

Amelia scoffed as she reached for a cookie. "More like a threat."

"It was a choice, Amelia. Let us investigate your father, or go to a group home."

Amelia sort of looked like she wished she'd chosen the home. Why *had* she chosen him? Linc frowned. "How did you know who I was?"

"Mom talked about you off and on." Amelia lifted her chin, eyes back to challenge mode. "I didn't know much. But I knew you didn't ever want to be a dad."

He jerked, heat rushing to his head. His temples throbbed. "That's not—"

Zoey cleared her throat, caught his eye. Shook her head as she nibbled the edge of a cookie.

He released the hot sigh building in his chest, counted to three as he leaned back against the wall. So Amelia knew about him—knew lies about him, at least—but he never knew about her. A few choice words fluttered through his mind about Kirsten. What was this, her last-ditch revenge? Make him the bad guy and then bail after thirteen years of lies?

Ms. Bridges reached for a cookie, then seemed to think better of it. "I know there's a lot to process here, but the immediate point is you're Amelia's next—and only—kin that we're aware of."

"So tag? I'm it, just like that?" What was this, some kind of sick relay race? He couldn't take care of a teenager.

But he also couldn't abandon his kid like his father had abandoned him.

"Reuniting with family is usually the best course of action." Ms. Bridges glanced at Amelia, who seemed like she only half-agreed. "Especially when compared to the state options."

His kid, in a state home? This was all hitting much too close. He released another breath. "What are we talking about here? Watching her for a few weeks?" Linc's throat tightened. He didn't mean to sound harsh. But stringing words together had become a challenge.

"Watching me?" Amelia swung her legs around the chair, sat upright with a frown. "I'm not a television."

He frowned back. "You prefer iPod?"

She blinked. "What the heck is an iPod?"

Aye. He shook his head. "You know what I mean. I'm just trying to wrap my mind around this."

Ms. Bridges set her cup on the tray. "We're not certain of Ms. West's plan at this point. Like I said, she's been unreachable, and there—" Her gaze darted to Amelia, then back to Linc. "—there are some unknowns right now." She licked her lips, as if she wanted to say more but couldn't. "But as far as you're concerned, there'd be paperwork to complete. And we'll need a court hearing if this goes on indefinitely. But your background check obviously cleared, and she—"

Linc didn't even hear the rest of the woman's rambling sentence. He was stuck on that one word she casually dropped in her monologue.

Indefinitely.

Amelia's backpack seemed to double in size from its perch on the floor. Indefinitely was an option? Would Kirsten do that? He didn't know. Didn't know her anymore.

Apparently never really had.

Zoey suddenly stood, grabbed the half-empty pitcher of water, and gestured to Amelia. "Want to help me in the kitchen? We can refill this—and maybe find some edible snacks." She wrinkled her nose. "My bad on the cookies. They're a work in progress."

Amelia stood, brushed crumbs off her lap. "I know you're just trying to get me out of the room, but I'm game if you have Doritos."

"Probably won't find any artificial dyes in this house." Zoey widened her eyes knowingly at Linc, and he momentarily debated between expressing gratitude for her well-timed intervention or annoyance at her lack of health awareness. "But let's check."

"Good luck," he called as they disappeared around the corner to the kitchen. He quickly moved to the recliner Amelia had vacated and leaned forward, bracing his arms on his knees. "What's the part you're not saying?"

Ms. Bridges brushed her hair out of her eyes and sighed. "Ms. West has been in some trouble lately, including jail time."

Linc gripped his knees. "Jail?"

"She was released before anyone knew Amelia was home alone. There's also been a history of drug and alcohol abuse. Amelia has been passed around to stay at various friends' houses over the years, but since their recent move to Lafayette, she apparently hasn't found anyone to pass Amelia off on for her . . ." Ms. Bridges cleared her throat. "Adventures."

And he'd thought Kirsten was bad off when they broke up. "And Amelia knows all that?"

Ms. Bridges nodded. "She reluctantly admitted her mother has had different boyfriends over the years, but none that stuck around."

"And that's where she is now? Ran off with some guy?"

"We believe so."

He narrowed his eyes. "This isn't foul play? Should there be a missing person's report?"

From the kitchen, a cabinet door slammed, followed by female voices. Ms. Bridges stretched her leg, hooked one ankle over the other. "We have eyewitnesses who saw Ms. West leave the bar, where she rather abruptly quit her job bartending, and get in a car with a man she'd been cozying up with at work more than once over the past several weeks."

"So?" Linc shifted his weight in the chair. "Still could have been a kidnapping."

"She had a suitcase with her."

Oh. He let that sink in. "And you obviously don't want Amelia to know that part?"

"Amelia knows." Ms. Bridges sighed. "Apparently this isn't the first time something like this has happened. Though it's the first we've known about it. Obviously we'd have intervened sooner, but everyone kept their secrets. Hoped for the best."

Wow. Linc's stomach churned. "But if Amelia knows all that, then what was the cryptic *unknowns* thing about?"

Ms. Bridges glanced toward the kitchen, then back at Linc. Resignation clouded her face, and she lowered her voice. "This is the first time we have reason to think she won't be returning."

Linc had a kid.

Zoey stood out of the way by the living room fireplace as Ms. Bridges conducted a thorough search of Linc's house, confirming there were no firearms accessible, no alcohol or pill bottles in reach. A *kid*.

A teenager, for that matter.

She let her gaze flick to Amelia, who sat motionless on the couch with her backpack, expression neutral, as Linc led Ms. Bridges around his home. Sort of wished she could pull out her camera, document this moment, but that was obviously a bad idea.

"Did you draw those?" Zoey gestured to the white marker drawings covering the dark pack.

Amelia cut her eyes to it. "Yeah."

"Wow. They're really good." There was a cartoon turtle, a cupcake, a toaster with bread and steam escaping the top. An octopus with a lollipop in two of its eight tentacles.

Amelia just shrugged and looked away. Her mood had tanked since her earlier, faster tour of the house—since her part didn't involve investigating medicine cabinets. It hadn't taken more than ten minutes in the kitchen for Zoey to realize the apple hadn't rolled very far from a particular branch of the family tree. The teen had the same eyes, same snarky wit. Same sarcastic impulses. Especially fascinating, since Amelia obviously hadn't been influenced by Linc.

Had he really had no idea she existed?

Zoey's head reeled at all the implications—both known and unknown. Linc had obviously been in a serious relationship at some point with Amelia's mom—a fact that had no right to make her stomach twinge but did, anyway. And whether this girl stayed a few days, a few months, or a few years, his life had forever changed. Just like that.

Which meant what for Zoey? She would technically be homeless if this situation—however understandably so—meant she needed to move back out.

But this wasn't about her.

"Sorry again about the lack of Doritos. I'll try to grab some from the store tomorrow." Zoey smiled, but Amelia didn't smile back.

"It's just chips, no big deal." Amelia lifted her chin. "I can handle disappointment, trust me."

Oh. "I'm sure you can." Poor kid. But she didn't look all that torn up about this whole situation. If anything, she looked annoyed. Zoey took a chance, eased forward to sit on the floor in front of the recliner. "You really don't want to be here, do you?"

"Doesn't matter." Amelia tugged at a loose thread on her backpack strap. "Linc doesn't want me here."

He was going to hate having a kid call him by his first name. But it wasn't like anyone could expect her to throw the word *dad* around, either. "This is just a lot at once, you know? Everyone needs a minute to adapt. You, him." *Me.* But again—this wasn't about her. She needed to help everyone else find the sun.

Amelia squinted. "You really believe he didn't know about me?"

"There's no way he knew." Zoey shook her bangs out of her eyes, smiled. "We're close—he'd have mentioned it."

Amelia snorted. "Sometimes you don't know people as well as you think you do."

Maybe. But not Linc . . .

She frowned. Right?

Linc and Ms. Bridges came back into the living room, the tour concluded.

"Well, I'll be off." Ms. Bridges rattled off more comments about being in touch with next steps, then leaned over to hug Amelia, who stiffly allowed the brief embrace. "You know how to reach me, Amelia, if you need anything." She handed Linc her card, her earlier weightiness seemingly gone now that a plan was in place. "Have a good night, everyone."

And then there were three.

Zoey held her breath. Linc stood with his back to the room, staring at the front door, as if a part of him beseeched Ms. Bridges to come back. Amelia stared at him, eyes narrowed, fiddling with the zipper on her bag.

Someone had to do something. Zoey hopped up. "I think we should go shopping."

"I told you, I don't need chips that bad." Amelia flipped her hair over her shoulder.

"Not for chips—for bedding." She grinned. "We could get your room fixed up."

The teen frowned. "I'm not moving in forever. Seems like a waste of money."

Linc finally turned around. "We actually don't know how long this will be." He met Amelia's gaze head-on, to his credit.

She met the challenge. "I don't have to be here at all. I can take care of myself—I did every other time Mom bounced."

Other times? Zoey's heart twisted. She stepped between Linc and Amelia. "And I'm sure you did a great job—you're in one piece. But this time, you don't have to do it alone. We're here to help."

"Who even are you?" Amelia scowled. "You're just, like, here."

Zoey widened her eyes, risked a glance at Linc. Great, *now* he was starting to smile. She looked back at Amelia. "I told you—I'm Linc's friend."

"Ah. *Friend.*" Amelia air-quoted. "My mom had a bunch of those."

Dunkin' donuts. Zoey let out a quick breath. "It's not like that. I'm just staying in the other guest room until I can get my own apartment again."

"Uh-huh." Amelia folded her arms over her chest, pinned Linc with her stare. "Guess you're just a shelter for all kinds of strays, then."

Linc's smile vanished. He grabbed his keys from the end table by the door. "Let's go find you some unicorn sheets or something."

Amelia reluctantly stood. "I obviously made the wrong decision coming here if you think I want unicorn sheets."

Linc's brow furrowed. "Why not? You're a girl."

"Who is almost fourteen, not six."

His scowl deepened. "Then keep the blue ones already on the bed in there. Those mature enough for you?"

"Unicorns are out, Linc." Zoey stood by Amelia, hoping she'd see they could be a team. "What's in, Amelia? What's the vibe?"

"Adults trying to talk Gen Z slang definitely isn't," she muttered.

Right. Zoey let that one bounce off her back, found her smile. "You know what? I'll make a list before we go. You'll need toiletries, bedding. Maybe a lamp?" She started typing entries into the Notes app on her phone. "Oh, and a mirror!"

The sun might be setting outside, but Zoey could be—would be—sunshine for everyone.

Maybe there was a reason all of this—the fire, her homelessness—had happened after all. Maybe she didn't really need anyone to take care of her.

Maybe she was meant to take care of them.

Seven

THE PORCH ROCKER CREAKED AS LINC leaned back, turning his face up to the inky black starlit sky. Crickets chirped from the trees, and September wind wafted over the deck, stirring his hair, drying the sheen of sweat he hadn't been able to shake the entire time he and Zoey had wandered around the general store with Amelia.

His daughter.

He rocked harder, shut his eyes. But that only provided a backdrop for images, memories, to play like a projector. Kirsten's wild black hair, impish grin always suggesting trouble. The fancy picnic dinner he couldn't afford but had managed to throw together anyway. Charcuterie, wine, heart-shaped glasses.

Figured the *one* time he'd drunk underage he'd made an epic mistake. He'd just wanted to do something nice for Kirsten. Had felt her slipping away, thought a Valentine's date would interest her again. She'd been hanging with new friends, and he'd suspected the drug use even then.

He'd underestimated her.

The screen door opened, and Zoey joined him on the porch, wearing a giant sweatshirt and leggings, her face clean of makeup.

She took the chair next to him without asking if he wanted company and sank onto it, pulling her knees up to her chin. How she always sat like a fairy perched on a mushroom was beyond him.

"You okay?" She turned her head to face him, cornflower eyes shining against pale skin, lit by the nearly full moon above.

He rocked again, his chest heavy. "Define *okay*."

"My definition or Webster's?"

"Yours is probably more interesting."

"Hmm." She tilted her head. "*Okay*—an adverb meaning you could be worse but could be better."

"Sounds about right." He'd definitely be a lot worse if Zoey hadn't been there. He should tell her that, but his tongue felt thick. Vulnerability wasn't his thing, and Zoey knew that.

Surely she knew he appreciated her too.

His rocker creaked. "All these years, I had a daughter out there. This person just running around with my DNA."

"And your attitude." Zoey grinned.

"That too."

"She's finally asleep, though that new radio you got her is still blaring early 2000s pop hits."

Yuck. At least it wasn't country. "Maybe we can get her into rock." Sort of seemed like music was going to be the least of his worries in the days and weeks to come. Would it really be that long?

Too many questions. Zero answers.

Zoey tugged her sweatshirt over her bent knees. "So . . . you have a daughter."

He sucked in a deep breath. "I have a daughter."

"You really didn't know?"

"I wish everyone would quit asking me that."

She shrugged one shoulder. "Seems like a fair question."

He shot his gaze sideways to her. The urge to be vulnerable, to share, to seek relief, welled to the surface. But last time he'd poured out his heart, it had been to Kirsten, and they'd—yeah. It'd ended badly. So no.

Still . . . He raised an eyebrow. "If I had known, you would know."

A little smile tugged at Zoey's lips, and she hugged her legs closer. "I figured."

He shook his head. She liked knowing things, and especially liked knowing things about *him* that no one else did. Not really sure why that made her feel special. He wasn't exactly a jackpot of interesting information.

Well, before tonight, anyway. Guess that had changed too.

Zoey held his gaze. "What happened, Linc?"

Ugh. He hooked one leg over the other. At least that darn lamp-post wasn't in reach. "What are the odds of you letting me avoid this question?"

She squinted. "About as good as Pastor Todd replacing the baptismal font with a hot tub."

"Fine." He stopped rocking, shifted to face her. "I was nineteen, Kirsten was eighteen. Two kids made a dumb decision and made another kid."

Zoey blinked. "That's one way to tell the story."

He probably owed her a little more—after all, she'd saved him from being the bad guy when Amelia tried to buy a TV for her room. He tried again. "We were young, thought we were in love. But were always fighting."

Zoey listened, nibbling her cuticle. "Go on."

"There were rumors about her and another guy . . . she and I had been together several months, but I guess we weren't on the same page." Not even the same book, as he later learned. "Tried to do something nice for Valentine's, but she was acting weird, so I asked her if she was cheating on me, and she didn't like that. We had a big fight."

"Was she?" Zoey nibbled faster. "Cheating?"

He glanced toward the house where Amelia slept. Even now, years later—fourteen years later, to be exact—the word dropped a rock in his stomach. "Yes."

Zoey winced. "I'm sorry."

"After she stopped being so offended that I asked, she went the route of denial and then . . . distraction." That part of the story he could remember in detail, unfortunately. "I'm assuming I don't need to continue from here."

"Skip a page." Zoey swiped her pointed finger through the air. "What happened nine months later?"

"Well, we weren't together that long, obviously." He stared across the porch into the dark forest. "The truth came out about her cheating about a week after Valentine's, and we broke up a few days after that." He lifted one shoulder. "The end."

Or so he'd thought. Apparently it was just the beginning.

"That's a lot." Zoey gazed across the deck, her face drawn.

Did she think less of him?

The fact that it would bother him if she did sat heavy, an un-familiar weight. He'd never cared before. People's opinions were their own, and they could think whatever they wanted with no reflection on him.

But with Zoey—it mattered.

A frog croaked from a nearby tree, while a firefly danced through the woods. The hint of smoke from someone's burn pile lingered in the air. Linc swallowed hard, a ball catching in his throat. All these years, and he'd done the same thing to his kid that his father had done to him. Not the exact same. He hadn't *chosen* to leave Amelia.

The ball doubled. How was she going to know that differ-ence? How would Amelia ever trust him? Even Zoey had to dou-ble-check that he wasn't lying. Like she thought it was possible he would abandon ship that way.

Though to be fair, the word *father* sure jump-started his heart into overdrive.

"How are you feeling about this? Besides the shock, of course." Zoey tossed the question out there, like it was that simple to answer.

He thought a moment, wanting to shove everything down and back. But it kept bursting to the surface, threatening to erupt from his throat. "I feel like that one time when I was a kid, fell into the bay and caught a current."

Zoey tilted her head. "I don't know that story."

Still vivid, twenty-four years later. "Couldn't get up, despite being a strong swimmer even back then."

"Aquaman." She smiled.

He narrowed his eyes. "Don't you start too."

"Do you prefer water-baby?"

"I definitely don't."

"Fine. Continue."

"The pier was *right there.*" The sensation threatened him even now, the pull of the waves, the water soaking into his nose and ears. The roar rushing in his head. "I floundered until this old man in a fishing hat threw me a rope off the dock."

Zoey's eyes widened. "Who was it?"

"Don't know." Linc shrugged. "I'd never seen him before. Haven't ever seen him since."

She nodded slowly. "Wow."

"So, yeah. It feels like that." Like he needed rescue. He rocked in double time, fighting to fill his lungs even though he was no longer under the bay. "I never had a real dad. How the heck am I going to be one?"

"I know your parents died." Her eyes softened. "But your uncle was there for you, right? He seemed like a good man, the one time I met him."

"He's not my uncle. Uncle Lyle and Aunt Carrie were my foster parents."

Zoey gaped. "*Linc.*"

Okay, so maybe he didn't tell her everything. "It is what it is." Her mouth had yet to shut. "I had no idea you were a foster kid."

"Mission accomplished."

She frowned. "Why? It's not something to be ashamed of."

"I'm not ashamed. It just leads to questions I didn't—*don't*—want to answer." Like what had happened in the courtroom that day when he was eight. A week before, he'd nearly drowned in the bay.

Some days he sort of wondered if that old man should have let him.

Zoey still looked confused. "I thought your parents died when you were young."

"Mom did." Eyes stinging, Linc looked down at the boards in the deck floor. He should sand them again, paint a fresh coat of varnish. Keep them looking nice despite the wear and tear of age.

She hesitated. "And your dad?"

His throat tightened. "Let's just say I'm dead to him."

Zoey's hand was on his wrist, then, and he stared down at her white skin resting on his tanned forearm. "It's his loss, Linc."

The words slid like a balm over his heart, and for a moment, he relaxed into the warmth of them. The warmth of *her*. He stopped rocking, looked up to meet her steady blue gaze. Good ol' Zoey. Someone who saw, who cared.

Who chose to stick around despite his rough edges and sharp corners.

But no one stuck around forever, did they? He'd taken a chance with Kirsten, put down his guard long enough to realize it had protected him for a reason. It was much better for people to think of him as tough guy. As muscular Linc with the man bun and tattoos. Made them keep their distance, which he preferred.

Except with Zoey. She'd somehow decided years ago to vault over all his boundaries and nestle in like a burr on his sock. As a friend, that was fine. Nice, even, sometimes. But getting too open with her, letting down his guard . . . he couldn't risk losing what they had in their friendship. Couldn't risk something leading to more and blowing up in his face.

She was more valuable than that.

He stiffened, withdrew his arm, ignoring the tingles racing down his skin. "I've got to figure out what to do about Amelia. I mean, she'll have to start school and stuff soon, right?"

Zoey's hand fell to her lap, and she blinked rapidly, as if trying to catch up. "Right."

"I don't know how to enroll a kid in school." That task seemed downright impossible. "What grade is she even in?"

"She'll know. The school will know too."

"I've never bought school supplies. Do kids still use pencils?" Panic started a slow gnaw. "What is she going to eat?"

Zoey rolled in her lower lip, but not before he caught the smile forming. "She's a teenager, Linc, not a goldfish. She'll eat most anything." She wrinkled her nose. "Case in point, she ate one of those cookies."

This was a lot. "Does she need a bedtime?" He rubbed his chin. "Toys?"

"You realize she's not in diapers, right?"

He scowled. "That part I figured."

"Pretty sure she's outgrown Legos and Lite Brites too."

He stopped rocking. "*What* brights?"

"Forget it." Zoey shook her head. "Calm down—I'm sure she'll listen to music and just watch as much TV as you let her."

"I'm supposed to be picky about which shows, though, right? Oh, man, I probably need internet filters. What if she's a gamer?" He frowned. "And isn't there a whole thing about stranger danger?"

Zoey didn't even try to hide her smile that time.

"Go ahead, laugh it up." He rocked again, faster. He felt a headache coming on. "I don't know kids. They're all so . . . sticky, and opinionated."

"You'll get to know this one."

"Assuming she lets me."

"Ah." Zoey pointed at him. "There's the real issue. You're afraid she won't let you in."

Of course he was. He looked back across the yard, into the shadows. At the pile of gravel still piled up from the tires that, mere hours earlier, had brought a surreal situation into his life. "You saw how Amelia talks to me. I abandoned her."

"You can't abandon someone without intention."

"She doesn't see it that way."

"She will." Zoey matched her rocker to his pace. "Give it time."

"That's the problem." Linc glanced back at the house, where his daughter—his *daughter*—slept in a twin-size guest bed, probably listening to Avril Lavigne. He shuddered. "We don't know how much time we have."

"I guess not." Zoey nibbled her lip. "What did Ms. Bridges say when I took Amelia to the kitchen?"

"That this has happened before, but Kirsten always came back before the police got involved."

"That's a good sign, right?" Zoey raised her brows. "Except that's hardly a stable environment for Amelia to grow up in."

No kidding. But hard to convince a kid of that fact—ask him how he knew. "Ms. Bridges said they had reason to believe this time was different."

Zoey frowned. "How come? I mean, Kirsten is obviously flighty and impulsive, but I can't imagine anyone just leaving their kid home alone for—"

"Because." He pressed his fingers against his pounding temples. "She didn't renew her apartment lease."

"*Oh.*" Zoey reeled back. Nodded a little. "Oh."

"Yeah." Linc released a sigh as he sat upright. "Like I said—we don't know how much time we have."

And maybe that fact was both the problem and the relief.

Eight

MAGNOLIA BLOSSOM BUZZED, AND not with the typical pleasant banter of small-town folk waiting for their mid-week breakfast.

Zoey held the diner menu in front of her face, despite having the entire thing memorized—and despite the fact she didn't need to spend a penny on any of the items listed—and twisted side to side on the bar stool at the counter.

Linc and Amelia had still been asleep when she snuck out of the house a half hour ago, hoping to nab one of yesterday's discounted muffins from Elisa. She hadn't caught Elisa up yet on— well, anything, really, except a brief highlight of yesterday's events. Her friend's response last night had only read "eight a.m." with a string of exclamation points and shocked face emojis—which was only fair. Zoey winced as she ran her gaze over the laminated breakfast options listed in Times New Roman. It was time to face the music in the form of a short blonde in an apron. The plus side was it would give Zoey the chance to see how fast the Magnolia Bay gossip waters had started churning. The last thing Amelia—or Linc—needed was to blindly walk into a rumor mill.

Unfortunately, it seemed like word had traveled faster than Zoey's mini-SUV.

"I heard the girl is as blonde as a Barbie." Two middle-aged women sitting on the far end of the counter bent their heads together, but forgot to lower their voices.

Ha. False.

"Well, I heard she's goth." The brunette with curtain bangs shook the ice in her cup. "With tattoos!"

Definitely false. Zoey scrunched her nose, considering Amelia. On second thought . . . maybe give her a few years.

"Maybe she's a vampire." The second woman with tight curls projected spooky into her voice.

"Don't be ridiculous." The ice rattled again. "We're much too far south for vampires."

Oh, brother.

"Regardless, poor girl." The brunette slurped from her cup. "Imagine having to come stay with your father for the first time—and that father is *Linc*."

Zoey narrowed her eyes. What was that supposed to mean?

"Yeah, he's hardly Mr. Rogers." The curly-haired woman laughed. "He'll probably have her doing pushups for punishment."

From the booth nearest the counter, Mrs. Peters, the local librarian, sniffed loudly where she sat with her assistant, Harper, and the Second Story bookshop owner, Sadie. "Well, I've never. All this gossip is very unladylike."

Zoey mentally agreed.

The older woman cleared her throat. "So what have you two heard?"

"Mrs. Peters!" Harper scolded with a chuckle. "I haven't heard anything, personally—probably because of all your no-talking signs posted around the library."

Sadie piped up, her voice holding genuine surprise. "It's just shocking. *Linc*, with a kid. No one has ever even seen him date."

"Seriously. Much less parent." Trish, her long red hair tied in a low ponytail, stopped by their table, topped off their coffees. "I've only seen him make kids cry."

"He's just intimidating." Sadie shrugged. "It's not really his fault."

Trish giggled. "Well, intimidating or not—I'd co-parent with him in a heartbeat, if you know what I mean."

Grr. Zoey narrowed her eyes. She was this close to standing up and—

A plate clattered in front of Zoey. She lowered her menu to find a steaming waffle, complete with a pat of butter and a side cup of syrup.

Elisa.

Zoey grinned. "And I was just hoping for a muffin. Let me guess. Bribe?" Normally she'd turn down pity food she couldn't afford, but she had to admit, this smelled amazing.

"You'll tell me all the details anyway." Elisa leaned forward and rested her folded arms against the high counter, her shoulders hunched in her apron. "Your text last night was cryptic, to say the least."

Zoey reached for a fork. "It was late. I was tired."

"Obviously." Elisa pulled her phone from her pocket and read out loud.

Zoey
____

Magnolia General has a sale on desk lamps.

I've been craving Doritos for six hours.

By the way Linc just found out he has a daughter.

Zoey mumbled around her waffle melting in her mouth. "All facts."

"At least you gave me some heads-up. You've been pretty quiet since leaving the Blue Pirogue."

"Just been busy trying to get this catering stuff going. And fighting with my insurance company." Zoey forked another bite of breakfast. All true. Just not the full story. Should she tell her she was living with Linc?

Elisa put her phone in her pocket. "So, how is Linc? What's his daughter like?"

"Both impossible questions to answer." Zoey squinted at her friend. "Hey, do you have any milk you aren't going to sell? Like, old milk?"

"I'm not giving you expired milk just because you're on a budget." Elisa reached into the mini-fridge under the counter and poured a cup. "I take it there's been no further word on the claims check?"

"Nope." And she was refusing to panic about it. Thankfully, there were brand new things to worry about instead—like her best friend becoming an insta-dad. "I'm sure I'll hear something this week."

"You can't keep going like this, you know." Elisa cocked one hip, her knowing gaze accessing Zoey.

She ignored it, shoveled another bite of waffle into her mouth. "I'm fine, really."

"You should call your parents."

"They're evangelizing in a jungle." Zoey rolled her eyes. "They don't exactly have cell service or a way to send me money." Not that they had much of that, themselves, living off church sponsors. Zoey wouldn't take money from them even if they offered—it would feel too much like stealing from a ministry. Other people needed help more.

Elisa frowned. "I'm worried about you."

"I promise I'm taken care of until the check comes. It'll all be okay." Though there was still the risk that Linc could ask her to leave now that Amelia was there. Maybe she didn't have to worry about telling Elisa where she was staying, because she might not be staying there long after all. Somehow, last night's porch convo hadn't seemed the right time to bring that up.

Zoey poured the rest of the syrup on the plate, drowning her remaining waffle pieces and forcing brightness into her tone. Too bad she couldn't drown her problems in sugar too. Made everything go down easier. "Just wait. In a few days, my biggest issue will be needing help moving into my own apartment."

"If you say so." Elisa wet a rag, began wiping the counter. "So, back to Linc—how's he taking the news?"

"Like Linc."

Elisa nodded. "Stoic? Unbothered?"

Actually not so much, but explaining otherwise felt like betraying his trust. Zoey lifted one shoulder. "We're all still processing."

Elisa's brows lifted. "We?"

Oops. That sounded cozy. "Um . . ."

A small smile began to form around Elisa's lips. "Uh-huh?"

Heart pounding, Zoey shoveled in her last bite of waffle, then pointed to her mouth while chewing. How was she going to get out of this one? "You know . . . he tells me stuff. We're like a team that way."

"I see."

Zoey swallowed just as the bell on the café door clattered. She twisted around on her stool in time to see Linc and Amelia walk in, wearing dark T-shirts, jeans, and matching scowls. Oh no. Not yet. They weren't ready for this morning crowd.

Especially Amelia . . .

The diner fell silent, save for a handful of gasps and the clanking of silverware dropping against a plate. Everyone stared. Whispers hushed. Sadie elbowed Harper. Trish froze with a coffee carafe in hand. The two gossiping women at the counter gaped.

Amelia's eyes widened as she took in the people taking her in. Linc stopped short, his gaze darting around the room, expression darkening like a storm.

Not good, not good.

The last thing he needed to do was explode and prove all the gossipers right. Just because Linc had a reputation as being Mr. Tough Guy didn't mean he wouldn't be a good father. He deserved the chance.

So Zoey did the only thing she could think of. She hopped off her stool, climbed on the counter despite Elisa's shocked protest, and cupped her hands around her mouth. "Hey! Has everyone heard the big news?"

Dozens of eyes blinked up at her, a mixture of confusion and surprise. Except for Linc's. His gaze held . . . concern? She shot him a reassuring wink. No reason to worry. She had this.

She cleared her throat. "Noah Hebert is running for mayor!"

Linc owed Zoey about a dozen bags of Doritos.

"Thanks for that." He scooted over in the booth for her to take the seat next to him. Amelia had immediately headed for the restroom. She hadn't wanted to come in the first place, had argued the whole drive there. But they had errands to do, food to buy, school to enroll in—all the things Linc wasn't sure how to accomplish. Better figure it out soon, as school started next week. At least she wouldn't have to jump in midsemester.

If he knew anything about Magnolia Bay, though, he and Amelia had to face the inevitable gossip chain. Figured they might as well get it over with over a sizzling plate of bacon. Thankfully, after Zoey's announcement about Noah, the diner erupted into whistles and cheers, and everyone forgot about them. Apparently, his friend was a shoo-in.

Which begged the question—why hadn't Noah mentioned he was running for mayor?

Linc's phone buzzed in his pocket. The Gone Fishing text group had been blowing up for half an hour.

Cade
Um, Linc, anything you care to tell us tonight at the pier? 🎣

Owen
What do you mean?

Noah
He has a kid

Owen
A KID? 😳

Cade
I was going to let Linc tell it, but yeah

Owen
Man. I never hear the tea 🫖

Cade
Probably because you use phrases like that

Noah
Oops, I meant teenager, not kid. My bad

Linc
Looks like you guys already have it figured out. Catch a few for me

Noah
No way. You better show up!

Cade
Yeah, we need the real story, not the Magnolia Bay telephone game version

<u>Noah</u> ______________

See you ALL at 7 p.m.

Yeah, maybe. If he could get away. He paused. Would Amelia want to go with him? Not that they were exactly to the point of father-daughter fishing dates yet. He had to admit, the idea didn't sound awful. He had a lot of time to make up for.

Assuming she'd let him.

"Elisa is going to kill me." Zoey dropped onto the bench seat beside Linc, her wrist brushing his arm.

He grabbed for a napkin from the holder by the window. "Why are you sticky?" His first full day as a parent, and he couldn't avoid the stickiness—and it wasn't even from his kid.

His kid. So weird.

Zoey leaned past him for more napkins. Her long hair grazed his arm, and that balmy, fresh soap scent wafted up. "Syrup."

He took a deep breath of her, then caught himself. Frowned instead. "You already ate?"

"Just a pity waffle." Zoey craned her neck to look around the diner. "Oh no. Here she comes."

He tried to follow her gaze. "Who?"

Elisa appeared at the booth, wearing an apron, her fingers pressed against her lips. "I can't believe you did that."

"Are you mad?" Zoey winced. "I panicked. I was just trying to get the attention off"—she glanced at Linc, then back to Elisa—"you know. Everyone else."

Amelia started walking back from the bathroom, her head down, arms crossed. Linc held his breath, waiting. Would people start to—nope, they were all still locked in discussions, the words *mayor* and *campaign* floating around the room. He breathed a little easier.

"Mad?" Elisa snorted. "I'm ecstatic. I've been trying to convince

Noah to run for weeks—now he has to." She grinned. "Granted, *he* might be mad."

Zoey waved one hand in the air. "I can handle that. Not afraid of his flannel."

Amelia slid into the booth opposite them, braced her chin in her hands.

"What can I get you, sugar?" Elisa slipped into waitress mode and pulled a pad of paper from her apron pocket.

"Fries." Amelia scowled, dark brows furrowing. Linc blinked. Was like looking in a mirror.

"What about hash browns instead?" Elisa tilted her head. "We don't serve fries until eleven."

Amelia sighed long and loud, as if she'd been asked to clean the diner's floor on her hands and knees. With a toothbrush. "Whatever."

Linc opened his mouth to intervene with the attitude, but Elisa interrupted as she swung her gaze to him. "Let me guess—you want bacon?"

"You've seen *Parks and Rec*, right?" Zoey piped up before he could answer. Apparently he didn't even need to speak at this breakfast. All the women were doing it for him. "Bring enough for Ron Swanson."

Well, that was helpful, at least.

"Got it." Elisa flashed them a smile. "Be right back with coffees."

Now it was his turn. "Hey." Linc tapped the table in front of Amelia, who had started doodling on a napkin as Elisa bustled away. "You don't have to be rude."

Beside him, Zoey shot him a double-take, and okay, yeah. He could take his own advice sometimes. But this was parenting.

This was different.

"I wasn't rude." Amelia glared.

"You're being rude right now."

"I'm making the same face you are!"

Linc opened his mouth, then shut it again. Couldn't argue there. He tried to relax his features. "Fine. But . . . no fighting before coffee."

Amelia perked up, pushing away her napkin drawing. "Can I have some?"

"You're too young for caffeine." He hesitated, glanced at Zoey. "Right?" Man, there was so much he didn't know.

"How about a compromise? A little coffee mixed with milk." Zoey smiled, which immediately leveled out the tension hovering over the table. How did she always do that? "Miley over at Chug a Mug makes a mean decaf latte, if you ever want one." She paused. "Well, depending on the weather, of course."

"Whatever. This town is weird." Amelia grabbed a straw wrapper, began folding it.

She wasn't wrong, but still. This was *his* town. Linc took the wrapper from her. "Enough with the *whatever*s. This isn't going to work if you have an attitude."

"Great." She slapped her hands flat on the table. "Then send me back home."

He leaned forward. "There's no home to go back to."

Amelia's take-no-prisoners expression faltered. Zoey's hand landed back on his arm, still mildly sticky. "*Linc.*"

"What?" He looked between them. No time to gloss over anything. They'd already been tossed into the deep end—might as well start kicking. "She deserves the truth."

"What are you talking about?" Amelia frowned. "What happened to my apartment?"

Zoey shot a warning nudge into his ribcage.

But they didn't need to baby her. Like Amelia kept reminding them—she was almost fourteen. The social worker should have told her everything from the beginning. Now that, too, was being pawned off.

Would Kirsten's choices ever stop haunting him?

"Your mom didn't renew the lease." Linc held Amelia's gaze. "Looks like you're stuck with me for a while, kid."

Amelia's throat bobbed. She looked at Linc, then Zoey. Pressed her lips together.

Then bolted from the bench.

Aye. Guess hanging out with him was a sentence worse than death.

The bell clanged on her way out. Linc shoved his hands into his hair, forgetting it was tied up. The loose knot on top of his head slipped, and his fingers tangled. He growled, wrenching them free and scooting sideways against Zoey. "Let me out."

"No. Give her a minute." Zoey grabbed the edge of the table, holding on with both hands as Linc tried to bump her out of the booth.

He pressed against her again. "She doesn't know her way around town yet."

Zoey dug her heels in, held on tighter. Pretty strong for someone who refused to exercise. "She's not going far." She pointed out the window, where Amelia hesitated on the sidewalk by the stop sign on Village Lane. "See?"

The knot in his chest loosened, but only a bit. Was that how parents felt, all the time? Mildly panicky? He briefly closed his eyes. "I'm really bad at this."

"I'm glad you see that."

He opened his eyes, narrowed them at her. "Where is that annoying, perpetual optimism when I need it?"

"It's not very optimistic to lie."

His shoulders tightened again. She was one to talk. "Aren't you doing the same thing?"

Zoey reeled back to look at him directly, blue eyes wide. "How?"

"Lying to yourself. About your claim." He waved his hand. "Living like money is about to magically appear in the mailbox any day now when you know that it's tied up. You know you're stuck."

"Well." Zoey blinked. "Aren't you on a truth roll."

"I'm just trying to be honest." Someone had to be.

She frowned. "Truth can be *gently* delivered, you know."

"That takes too long." He looked back out the window, where Amelia had finally crossed the street. Great. Now where was she going to go? "Delaying the inevitable doesn't do anyone any favors. It's better to get the truth out, then *deal* with it instead of living in denial."

He'd had to learn that the hard way in a courtroom when he was eight, no reason everyone else couldn't catch up. He frowned. "Why are you women always so—"

Oops. Too far. Zoey's brow had disappeared into her bangs.

He swallowed the end of that sentence. "You know what I mean."

"Here's an idea. I'm going after your daughter, and you're going to look up the price of a muzzle on Amazon." Zoey abruptly stood. "Better get an extra large."

Okay, he probably deserved that. "Zoey—"

Elisa appeared with a tray laden with coffee, bacon, and hash browns. "Everything okay?"

"I'll be right back." Zoey patted Linc's arm. He grimaced—still sticky. He did *not* deserve that. "Enjoy your bacon."

Oh. Not sure how she'd turned a simple statement into a threat, but she'd managed. Zoey brushed out the door as Elisa put Linc's plate in front of him.

He stared at it. Not as hungry now.

The aroma of the still-sizzling meat met his nose, and he hesitated. Getting a bit of protein before facing either woman again probably wouldn't hurt. He never did operate well on an empty stomach.

He bent over his plate, shoved a piece into his mouth. Guilt nudged, but he couldn't quite determine why. He hadn't done anything wrong—had he? Didn't Amelia deserve honesty? Besides, he'd never been the compassionate type. Better for her to realize the truth right away, if she hadn't. Life hurt.

People left.

A throat cleared, and Linc looked up. Elisa still stood next to the booth, the empty tray tucked under her arm. She raised her eyebrows. "May I offer some advice?"

Linc picked up his second piece of bacon, stomach recoiling. He forcefully took a bite. "I assume you will anyway." He waited for the berating, the confirmation that he sucked, the *I used to be a teenage girl, so I know how they operate* stuff.

But Elisa only gave him a gentle smile. "Maybe give yourself a chance."

Oh.

He stared at the window as Zoey hurried to catch up to Amelia on the sidewalk. Hadn't expected . . . well, compassion. Definitely hadn't anticipated the way the sentiment washed over him, wiped away a bit of the guilt lingering.

Then his eye caught the napkin Amelia had been drawing on. A typical round, cartoon face, but with a frown instead of a smile. Two wobbly teardrops drifted from its comically large eyes.

He swallowed. Give himself a chance? Tempting. But . . . he looked out the window as Amelia stalked down the street. Wouldn't matter if he did.

Because it certainly didn't seem like his daughter would anytime soon.

Out of breath, Zoey caught up to Amelia a few blocks down from the café. The morning sun was in high gear now, a glaring contrast to the mood back at the diner—and the one reflected on Amelia's face.

She fell into step beside the sullen teen, dodging orange cones set around a newly repaired pothole. "Hey, all the good shopping is the other way."

Amelia didn't even look at her, just kept stiffly hustling down Village Lane toward the park and the gazebo. Across the street, a kid did a skateboard trick while a woman walking her Schnauzer chatted on her phone. Farmer Branson rolled by in his pickup truck, the bed full of crates of red and yellow vegetables.

Zoey took a deep breath and released it, along with her annoyance at Linc. He was doing the best he could—they all were. "Maybe you could just give your dad a break?"

Amelia snapped her head to look at Zoey. "He's not my dad. He's just a guy I don't know who gets to boss me around now."

"I can see how it feels that way, but . . ." Zoey tucked her hair behind her ears. "He would have been there for you sooner, had he known."

"Easy for you to say." Amelia huffed.

"Amelia, trust me on this one." Zoey touched her arm, stopped walking. "Maybe you don't know him yet, but I do." Better than anyone—the good, the bad, and the ugly. Unfortunately, Linc was showing the bad right now.

They were all overwhelmed.

"Why should I trust you?" Amelia crossed her arms, lifted her narrow chin.

Zoey resumed walking, slower this time. Was any of this even her place? And yet, how could she not try to help? "Because I haven't ever lied to you or betrayed you. Because I want to be here for you."

"For now." She rolled her eyes.

"What do you mean?"

"I've seen how this goes." Amelia hurried to keep up. "You're temporary. Just another live-in until the next shinier woman catches his atten—"

"Look." Zoey abruptly stopped again, turned to face her. "I don't know what you experienced with your mom and her relationships, but this is different. It has nothing to do with being *shiny*."

Had Kirsten been shiny?

The errant thought ricocheted in Zoey's chest, lodged a little. She tried to shake it off. Jealousy was a wasted emotion, and besides—Linc wasn't hers.

Not like that.

"I'm not an idiot." Amelia jabbed her finger into her chest. "I know how the world works, and I know how men and women work. So I know at some point"—she fluttered her fingers in a sarcastic *bye*—"you're out."

Zoey opened her mouth, then slowly closed it. How could she argue with such a fair assumption? She and Linc knew the truth between them, knew the innocence of their friendship and the circumstances surrounding their decision for Zoey to stay at his house. But Amelia . . . all she saw were facts filtered through a very jaded lens.

A lens she shouldn't have ever been forced to wear.

Amelia studied her from the corner of her eye, sniffed. "How old are you, anyway?"

"Almost twenty-nine."

She squinted, as if doing the math. "You're not even old enough to be my parent."

Ha. "Good thing I'm not, then, huh? Why don't I just be your friend?" Hope waved a flag. Maybe this could be a breakthrough moment. A tiny step toward bond—

Amelia shook her head. "You're way too old for that."

Ouch. Okay. "Well, what about a cool aunt?" Zoey struck a pose, both hands by her face in an old-fashioned *Vogue* pose—realizing too late that was the exact opposite move that a cool aunt would make.

"You can't be." Amelia scowled. "You're not related to my mom or dad."

So now she was getting technical. Zoey lowered her arms back to her sides. "What do you want me to be, then?"

"Probably won't be around long enough to matter."

Ouch again.

"Look, I know my mom isn't perfect, but I knew what to expect. And I knew how to take care of myself. I made myself breakfast, got to school on time, even made some B's." A warm breeze ruffled the teen's dark hair, the exact shade of Linc's, and her brown eyes watered. "Now I'm just starting all over doing the same stupid thing, but with different people in a different town."

Man. That was a lot. Just the thought of this young girl having to parent herself every morning—and having apparently done a decent job at it—made Zoey's heart ache. Attitude or not, Amelia needed help. Needed her.

Needed her dad.

Zoey shoved her hands in her pockets. "I get that, but—"

"No. You *don't* get it." Amelia's cheeks flushed pink. "You haven't been in my shoes."

"You're right. I didn't mean it like that." Zoey held up both hands, fighting to hold her optimism. Maybe she was just screwing this up as much as Linc. Then an idea struck. "I know it's different from your situation, but my parents moved across the entire world when I turned eighteen."

Amelia squinted with suspicion. "How come? Were you that bad of a kid?"

"*No.* They're missionaries."

"So they just left you at the first possible second to go serve God?"

Zoey blinked. "It wasn't like that."

But it'd felt like that a little, hadn't it?

She shook her head, pushing aside the past. She was proud of her parents—and they loved her. They were just . . . busy. "I'm only saying I know how unsettling all that felt, suddenly taking care of myself and being so responsible for everything. And I was legally an adult."

Amelia jutted her chin. "So?"

"So . . ." Zoey held Amelia's gaze. "I'm trying to say you don't have to do it alone this time."

"Well, maybe I want to." Amelia broke eye contact, jaw clenched, hands fisted. Across the street, joggers ran through the park, while a yoga group stretched under a shade tree. A sprinkler whistled across a nearby yard.

How was life continuing like normal when all three of their worlds had been completely upended? It didn't seem fair. Then again, neither was the fact that Zoey's shop had burned down.

She drew a breath. Thankfully, Linc wasn't catching the brunt of this conversation. Zoey felt better equipped to handle it than Linc right now—he clearly still needed time to process this massive change. Helping Amelia helped her best friend, so it was the least Zoey could do.

Besides, taking care of someone else helped her forget her own dumpster fire of a situation. "I'm sorry. I know you didn't ask for any of this."

Amelia rolled in her lower lip, remained silent.

"And I can only imagine how hard it is to trust someone. This happened really fast, didn't it?"

Silence. Then a small nod.

Zoey hesitated. How much could she say without speaking for Linc? Without committing to too much?

Then she had it.

"Follow me." Zoey headed toward the park and the gazebo across the street without looking back. Thankfully, Amelia fell into step behind her.

Zoey led her down the path, straight to the lamppost, hers and

Linc's, and turned to face Amelia with a somber expression. She gestured to the post with both arms, like a game show hostess revealing a prize. "Ta-da."

Amelia huffed. "What? It's just a light." She wrinkled her nose. "With a spider web."

Zoey brushed at the web. "Yes, it is, but it's more than that. Turns out, you can't lie if you're touching this pole."

"What?" Amelia rolled her eyes. "That's dumb."

"You sound like your dad." Zoey snorted. "But hey, even he believes it."

The teen's expression faltered a bit. "He does?"

"Yep." Zoey nodded. "It's like the ultimate pinky promise. Lying in this instance would be worse than even, say, lying in court."

Amelia studied the post, her expression morphing from skeptical to curious. "So why did you bring me here?"

"Because." Zoey slapped her hand against the black iron and held on tight. "I'm going to tell you some things that I deeply believe are true."

Amelia shifted her weight, crossing her arms once again. But her eyes darted between Zoey and the post with interest. "Whatever."

Zoey drew a deep breath. "Truth number one—I know your dad is doing, and will keep doing, the best he can."

Amelia frowned.

Zoey pressed on. "And number two—I know it'll get better." There. Now, if only Linc would prove her right.

Amelia studied the glow from the lamp. "Yeah?"

"Yeah." Zoey hesitated, then added one more. "And I'm here for you too. However you need me to be."

Amelia looked down at the ground, sniffed. Then lifted her chin, clearly trying to appear unaffected. "Can we get ice cream?"

Conversation over, apparently.

Zoey squinted up at the post as she let her arm hang back to her side. All the parenting books would probably suggest she say no to the obvious manipulation attempt but—as they'd just clearly determined—Zoey wasn't the parent, was she?

"Sure. Let's go." Seemed like the lamppost promise had worked a little magic, maybe bought a bit of time, but it wouldn't hold up for long. Only action would. If Amelia didn't believe Zoey was going to stick around long enough to fully trust her, then there was only one thing to do.

Zoey was going to have to move out.

nine

EVEN THE WATER DIDN'T BRING PEACE this evening.

From the pier, Linc cast his line into the depths of the bay, watching the lure sink under the gray-blue surface. The salty gulf air, the waves lapping against the wooden beams of the dock, didn't soothe his nerves like usual. In the distance, a seagull squawked.

He sort of wanted to squawk back.

"Watch out, guys. Linc looks pensive." Owen straightened from where he dug in the cooler. Ice rattled. "That's never good."

The local banker had a point. Linc cracked his neck to the side, but the tension didn't leave his upper body. "Something's gotta give."

"Parenting got you down?" Noah clapped his shoulder with one hand, rod in the other. "It's only been, what, two days?"

"I think that's an eternity in teen years." Linc stared at the red and white bobber off his line, blew out his breath. "Amelia hates me."

She and Zoey had finally come back to the café after their impromptu walk—escape?—earlier that morning. He'd paid for their breakfast, packing Amelia's hash browns in a to-go box she never touched as far as he noticed. And though Zoey kept up a running, cheery monologue while they enrolled Amelia in school, ran errands for said school supplies, and made another grocery trip that included Doritos, Amelia barely spoke another word to him the rest of the day.

How had he gone from living alone as a content bachelor to living with two women? Two polar opposite women, at that?

"I doubt she hates you." Noah joined him by the railing, adjusting the dangling bait on his hook. "She's just going through a lot, obviously."

One way to put it. At home that afternoon, Amelia had vanished to her room and slammed the door before blaring her music. Zoey had immediately headed to his kitchen, gathering bowls and spatulas like a woman on a mission to make the worst cookies ever. He'd stood in the middle of the living room and asked if anyone cared if he went fishing.

Apparently no one did.

So he went. Granted, he hadn't said the words very loud, but he *had* spoken them, so if anyone had a problem with it, well. He'd tried.

"You know the saying 'if looks could kill?'" Linc raised his eyebrow. "If I were a cat, I'd have used up all nine lives today."

"Of every animal in the kingdom, a cat is the last thing you'd be." Owen cracked open a can of sparkling water. "Except a lion, maybe."

He snorted. At least there was that.

"Wait. What animal am I?" Cade frowned.

Owen tilted his head, studied him. "A peacock?"

Noah guffawed.

"Very funny." Cade opened a new lure from a package. "Just because I dress nice and know brand names doesn't mean I'm flashy."

Noah grinned. "I think that's exactly what it means."

"Hey, remember that time my daughter I didn't know about showed up on my literal doorstep?" Linc raised his free hand in the air. "Can we insult each other later?"

"I think we might be insulting the animal kingdom at this point." Noah cast his line into the water.

Cade ignored him, looking back at Linc. "I think you two just have to grow into this. It's only been a few days—I doubt anyone adjusts to something this big that fast."

"How long is she staying?" Owen asked.

"That's part of the problem. We don't know." Linc felt a tug on his line, tugged back. Whatever it was slipped away. He began reeling in his empty line. "But I don't think they'll let her go back to Kirsten at this point after so many abandonments. Not without court interference."

"Maybe they'd make her do a program first or something." Noah twisted to look at Linc. "That'd be a good thing, right?"

Linc paused. "From what it sounds like, I don't know that Kirsten would commit to something like that. And the last thing Amelia needs is all this back and forth." He filled the guys in on what Ms. Bridges said about Kirsten's past absences. "There's been substance abuse too, but it's not just that. I mean, it's not like there are programs to convince mothers not to leave their kids for their new crushes."

Owen stared soberly into the water. "That's awful."

"Yeah." Linc knew how to pick 'em. Good thing he hadn't tried again much over the years—who knows what he would have caught? He pulled his line free of the water, frowned at the empty hook.

Was it even worth re-rigging bait?

"And Zoey is staying with you too?" Cade shot Linc a look over his shoulder as he fiddled with his lure.

"Wait. I didn't hear that part." Owen's brow furrowed. "Is that true?"

Linc groaned. "Relax, PK. Nothing shady about it."

"Hey, I had the same thought, and I'm not a pastor's kid." Noah reeled in his line. "I didn't realize that's where Zoey went when she moved out of the Blue Pirogue."

Wouldn't have had to move out if Noah and Elisa had kept their conversation private, from what Zoey had eventually admitted to him. She'd kill Linc if he let that slip, though, and he didn't need that. Zoey angry at him seemed to tilt the entire universe, and his was lopsided enough right now as it was.

He motioned for Owen to hand him a drink from the cooler. "It's not a big deal, guys." But maybe it was, if Mama D and his friends were all saying the same thing. His stomach clenched.

Cade recast his line. "I guess technically you guys have a chaperone, now that Amelia is living there too."

"We don't need a chaperone. It's *Zoey*." The same protest he'd given for years slipped free automatically, and the words tasted, well . . . not as true. Not a lie, really. But not true either.

The guys shot each other a look.

Owen passed him a sparkling water instead of a beer. Linc scowled at it, then popped the top.

"Besides, having another woman around probably makes Amelia feel more comfortable." That had to be true. Another thought dawned. "It's not like I can be home all the time getting this tour business going. And Amelia can't be alone." He lifted his can in a toast. "See? All's well that ends well."

The guys stared, unconvinced. Fair enough, since he wasn't really either.

Noah broke the silence first. "But you're playing house, dude." He rested his rod against the pier and crossed his arms over his flannel shirt. "That never goes well."

Linc took a long drag from the can, the bubbles burning his throat. "Isn't Elisa living with you?"

Noah frowned. "It's an *inn*. We're not the only ones there, and she's on a different floor."

"And Zoey is down the hall, along with Amelia." Linc shrugged. "What's the difference?"

Noah opened his mouth, closed it. "Elisa and I are getting married in a month. So—a lot of difference."

Time for a subject change. "You know what *I* didn't realize?" Linc finished the contents of his can in one big sip. "You're running for mayor."

"What? *More* tea I didn't get?" Owen shut the cooler with a thump and a frown. "Guys, come on."

"For the record, I didn't know this one either, Owen." Cade shifted to face them. "Does my dad know yet?"

"It's not official, hence my lack of telling." Noah shot Linc a pointed look. "Apparently Zoey took that liberty for herself."

For good reason, but it was fun watching Noah squirm. And at this point, anything to get the spotlight off his kid. Linc smirked. "Need any campaign posters?"

"Are you good with this?" Noah asked Cade, brow furrowed. "I mean, the town did essentially vote for you *not* to run a month ago."

"Yeah, on the same night I went to tell them I resigned from running." Cade laughed. "Of course it's fine. The town needs someone to step up, and right now I'm focused on passing the bar so I can get my freelance business started."

"And busy spending time with Rosalyn." Owen grinned. "*That* tea I have."

Cade groaned. "Can we get back to Linc and his problems? Before Owen starts trying to pour cream and sugar on me?"

The guys' banter continued, but Linc tuned it out as he absently dug around his tackle box. Noah's words cycled through his mind—similar to the warning Mama D had given him. *Playing house.*

A hook snagged a callus on his finger, and he winced as he tugged it free. He'd dismissed the idea when it was just him and Zoey. They were adults, they could handle whatever. But what about Amelia? *Were* they giving her a bad impression? He couldn't ask Zoey to leave. She had nowhere else to go—and he'd be lost without her. He didn't know how to do this dad thing, would screw it up worse than he was already doing alone.

Linc rubbed the sore spot on his hand. But what if Mama D and Noah were right? What if he was already messing things up with this living arrangement? He plucked a lure from the box and began wrestling it back on his line, imagining Amelia's scowl. Her glare, the rigidness in her back as she stalked away from him earlier that day.

Maybe at this point, things were just meant to be worse. Maybe there was nothing he could do.

"You know, there is one solution to this whole household thing."

Linc jerked his head up at Noah's quiet voice echoing over the water, seemingly reading his mind. "What's that?"

"Ask Zoey to marry you."

Owen choked on his drink as Cade burst into laughter. "What?"

Linc's throat went dry. He swallowed, narrowed his eyes. "Careful with those crazy ideas, or I won't have any confidence in you as mayor."

"I'm serious." Noah lifted one shoulder in a shrug as he recast his line. "Sort of checks the boxes you need, you know?"

"*Linc*, married? That'd be the day. Mr. Permanent Bachelor here." Owen clapped Linc on the shoulder, then dropped his arm at Linc's responding growl. "I mean, whatever you want, man."

Whatever he wanted? Linc dug through the ice chest and swapped his water for a beer. What he *wanted* was for things to stop changing.

And marrying Zoey would be the biggest change of all.

He guzzled half the can in a gulp. There was one other thing to consider . . . He stared across the water, stomach churning and not from the drink.

If his friends were already guessing at his shifting feelings for Zoey . . . how long was it before Amelia would notice too?

One of Zoey's favorite movies growing up had always been Disney's *Beauty and the Beast*.

Unfortunately, she seemed to be living it out in real time.

"What do you mean, you need to move out?" Linc growled as he dragged oars through murky pond water, his hair free of its usual tied-up knot, making him look extra beast-like. When he got home from fishing at sunset, Zoey had requested to speak to him privately. With Amelia in the house watching TV before bed, out in the middle of the pond in a canoe seemed to be the safest place. "That's ridiculous."

"This doesn't work." Zoey gestured between them, adding a swoop of her finger to include Amelia inside the house thirty yards away on the shore. She really wanted it to, but . . . "It was one thing for me to crash for a week while I got my ducks in a row, but those ducks are now, like, rabid squirrels." She shuddered. "And there *is* no row. There's just a frat party."

"That's ridiculous too." His scowl deepened.

Of all the elements of her favorite movie to come to life, she had to end up with the beast instead of a cute little talking teacup.

"You keep using that word." Zoey slapped at a mosquito. "And I know you think so, but this is my *life*." And Amelia's. And Linc's. But how much could she tell him of what Amelia had said without betraying the fledgling amount of trust she'd gained?

Linc pulled the oars again, water churning under the tired john boat that was not much bigger than a bathtub. "Seems to me if your life is full of rabid squirrels, then all the more reason for you to have somewhere safe to stay."

He had a point. Still . . . she crossed her arms. "And you have your own . . . well, you might not have squirrels, but you certainly don't have ducks either."

"I have a teenager. Sort of like both."

Zoey snorted.

"So . . . stay. Let's manage all these rabid creatures together."

Oh. That was almost . . . sweet. She studied him. "You don't want me to leave?" And here she'd thought she'd been more in the way of his suddenly chaotic life than anything else.

"Of course not." Linc pulled the oars into the boat, hooked them on the sides. A hush fell over the pond, save for the crickets overhead in the trees. Twilight shot streaks of navy and crimson across the sky. "Not to mention, you don't have a lot of options."

Also a good point. But it didn't change the facts. "We can't give the wrong impression to a teenager who is already in a state of trauma." She squared her shoulders, shifted her tone to unconcerned. Because she couldn't be concerned, not about herself. This was about what was best for Amelia.

And despite barely knowing the girl, Zoey cared—a lot.

"I know. I was thinking the same. And . . . I can't fix that." Linc leaned forward, elbows on his knees. "I can't undo any of this."

Man. He looked so defeated. So unlike Linc. She had to help him.

And this seemed like the only option.

Zoey lowered her tone to match his, despite the fact that only the frogs were eavesdropping. "So, for Amelia's sake, we're back to the fact that I need to find somewhere else to go. She thinks we're shacking up."

He scoffed. "Obviously we're not."

"Well, it's not obvious to her. She's used to seeing that kind of lifestyle."

Linc's Adam's apple bobbed, and he shifted on the seat, looking out over the water. Zoey rolled in her lip. Was he jealous at the thought of Kirsten being with other men?

Worse yet, was *she* jealous over the thought of him being jealous over Kirsten?

"I don't want to leave." Zoey shoved that away, pushed forward. He had to understand the whole picture. "But Amelia won't trust me because she thinks I'm just the girl of the hour. That I'll rotate out the door any day now and can't be trusted."

His profile sobered. "That's not how I am."

"*I* know that. She doesn't yet."

Linc cut his eyes to her. "So your solution to show Amelia that you're sticking around is to leave?"

"Exactly."

He sighed. "Makes as much sense as anything else does lately."

"Think about it. If I don't live here, and it's clear we're not . . . you know . . ." Zoey brushed her bangs out of her eyes. "And then if I *still* choose to hang out with her, maybe she'll realize I'm legit."

"Maybe. Or she'll think you just left anyway." The furrow in Linc's brow creased deeper. "Shoot. He was right."

Zoey matched his frown. "Who was right?"

"There's only one real solution."

Zoey doubted that—she'd just presented the only one. "What are you talking about?"

"We should get married."

A shock of cold flooded Zoey's body, like diving into the bay in January. Going under, under, under . . . Sounds hollowed, time froze.

Marry Linc? Her stomach flipped.

Marry Linc.

Just as suddenly, a rush of warmth. Like emerging back to the surface, stretching out on a sunbaked towel on the shore.

Okay, so maybe she hadn't presented the only solution. Her

chest tightened. "I can't—you don't—" She choked on her own half sentence. They'd never even discussed *dating*. Linc didn't date. Well, he had at one time, apparently, as evidenced by the low-rise-jean-clad evidence in his house.

But her? Him?

Them?

It was as if Zoey's secret wish and wildest dream collided in one simple statement. *We should get married.* Like it wasn't completely life-changing. Like he was casually suggesting they grab a latte from Chug a Mug or take a bike ride down Bayou Boulevard, playing dodge ball with the potholes.

Like he wasn't going zero to sixty with four words. How many times had they even hugged over the course of their friendship? And now he was going straight to—

Linc cleared his throat, leaned forward a little. "Zoey?"

She blinked. Realized for the first time she hadn't responded. "Um . . ."

"It makes sense." Linc shoved his hair back. "I can't do this alone. You don't have anywhere else to go. And Amelia needs a role model . . . a solid family unit."

Ah. So he was talking *practicality*. Of course. Her heart thudded.

But did he still think of her like *that*? Someone he wanted to marry and be with . . .

"It'd be just in name, of course."

Oh. All business.

"It'd legally be a marriage, but nothing has to change. We'd still be friends, exactly like right now." His eyes softened, like he was suggesting something noble.

Nothing has to change . . . Her heart drifted toward her feet. He was after function, not romance. Silly girl. She should have known better. This time, the cold seeping through her limbs felt like someone had yanked her off her sun-warmed towel and tossed her right back into the water. She tried to find words. What should she say?

What did she want?

"There'd be emotional stability for Amelia. Financial stability for you. Parenting help for me." He kept ticking off the pros on his tanned fingers. "I need help with her now, with these tours and the concession stand. And then when crawfish season comes, I'll be gone weird hours—can't leave her alone all the time. And hey, we'd even get a tax break. It's the easiest solution."

"Marriage isn't a numbers game." The words cracked in her throat.

"This one kind of is."

Ah, so romantic. Then again, this was Linc.

There were so many questions that Zoey had trouble narrowing them down. One slowly maneuvered above the rest. "What about later?"

"What do you mean?" Linc shifted his weight slightly, rocking the boat.

Or maybe she was rocking the boat, asking questions. If she wanted this . . . shouldn't she just go for it? It wasn't like she had a bunch of other men knocking on her door. There might be plenty of fish in the sea, but there weren't a ton of fish in Magnolia Bay.

Or maybe that was because she held them all up to a particular six-foot-plus man-bunned standard.

"I mean, Amelia is fourteen. What are we going to do when she goes back to Kirsten one day, or moves out, or goes to college in five years?"

"We'll figure that out then." Linc reached for the oars, tucked them back into the water. His short sleeves strained against his biceps. "We can only decide what to do with what's happening now. And right now, this solution makes the most sense."

Did it? And the fact she couldn't tear her eyes away from his muscular arms didn't concern him in the least?

He continued. "We have to put out the fire that's currently burning."

Oy. Zoey winced. "Really?"

"Sorry. Poor analogy."

She rolled in her lip. "What about Amelia? What will we tell her?"

"That we wanted to get married."

The word still sounded foreign coming from him. Zoey tilted her head. "But we've been denying we've even been in a relationship."

"No, we've been denying anything inappropriate was going on," Linc corrected. "We tell her that we realized what was between us and want to make it official, ASAP."

"ASAP." Zoey repeated the word, like a parrot. A dazed, bay-soaked parrot.

"Why not? I think waiting would do more harm than good."

In this particular instance, maybe he was right. Marriage wasn't something to rush into, but . . . people had arranged marriages all the time in different eras of history, different countries. Surely some of those worked out. At least Zoey already knew what to expect with Linc.

Grumpy before coffee.

Grumpy before bedtime.

Grumpy in crowds.

She smirked. And he was tidy—she wouldn't be worrying about laundry on the floor or toothpaste caps left in the sink. Wasn't that typically what wives complained about?

So why wasn't she sure?

"I know it's a little left field." A muscle ticked in Linc's jaw. "But Zoey . . . I'm drowning again."

She gripped the sides of the boat. *Oh, Linc.* As much as his grumpy aggravated her at times, this vulnerability was much harder. Had she ever seen him like this?

He stared at a spot on the rusty boat floor. "I can't screw this up. And I don't know how to do it alone."

Zoey inhaled, watching the way his muscles bunched and released under his shirt as he rowed. How could she say no? Linc was strong, capable. Solid.

Secure.

And he needed *her*.

There were surely worse things in life than marrying her best friend. She'd be doing him a favor, helping a teen in trauma . . . all pros. Except maybe one con.

Her heart.

He stilled the oars. "So what's it going to be?"

"Dunkin' donuts, Linc. Give a girl a second." She studied his face, searching for *any* sign that there was something more to this proposal—if one could even call it that—than a smart business plan.

He held her gaze, rowing them quietly through the growing darkness. Tangled dark hair, brown eyes holding sober sincerity. Everything that made Linc, Linc. And maybe . . . was that a little bit of hope shining in there?

He really wanted her to say yes.

A tiny thrill shot through her, and she squelched it. He didn't want her to say yes for the same reason she wanted to say yes.

Could she deal with that?

She briefly closed her eyes, prayed, and waited—for what? An audible voice? A finger writing in the sky? She opened her eyes. She knew God didn't answer prayer like that—at least, not hers. Which was okay. Maybe that just meant God was letting her choose this one. A pick-your-own-adventure, like those childhood books she used to read. Maybe everything would work out regardless of what she chose.

And marrying Linc was bound to be an adventure.

She drew a breath, looked at him. And mentally turned the page in their story. "Okay."

The oars stilled again. "*Okay*?" A frog croaked from across the pond. She'd halfway expected something more dramatic, like light-ning, maybe. But nope. Just pond creatures, and Linc's slightly heavy breathing, like this conversation had cost him something too.

"Okay." If he wasn't going to be romantic about it, there was no reason for her to swoon or give an ecstatic *yes*. Even if a tiny, backdoor part of her heart wanted to. She couldn't let him know that. Maybe not ever. It would mess everything up, and they had to do this. For each other, but mostly, for Amelia.

So instead, she lifted her chin and held out her hand to shake his, throwing on her sunniest smile. "Looks like we have a deal . . . hubby."

Ten

THE COURTHOUSE STEPS LOOKED TALLER than usual today.

Linc scowled as he tugged a finger into the tight collar of his blue button-up. He'd worn this shirt for approximately two business meetings and one funeral.

Looks like he was adding a wedding to the list.

Morning sun poured over the downtown building, sending a trickle of sweat down his back. He should have tied his hair up, but the occasion seemed to call for something a little more formal. So he'd left it down, slicked it back.

She'd said yes.

Linc wasn't in the habit of asking questions he wasn't relatively sure of the answer to. Maybe he hadn't been a straight A student over the years, but he considered himself a pretty smart guy over-all. Got his business degree with a respectable GPA. Started a successful business from the ground up.

But that *yes* the other night had caught him off guard.

Amelia stood next to him, wearing jeans, a lightweight hoodie, and a suspicious frown. "I still don't understand this. You guys said you weren't even dating."

"Things change." Linc motioned for her to climb the stairs. "This is the new plan."

"Marriage is a plan to you?" Amelia squinted at him, the sun highlighting her dark hair.

"What is it to you?"

She shrugged. "How am I supposed to know? Mom never got married."

But Kirsten was the last person he wanted to think about today. "Come on. Zoey's inside waiting for us." She'd left earlier than he and Amelia, with a bag packed to get dressed at the courthouse, spouting something about it being bad luck to see the bride before the wedding.

As if they hadn't had coffee that morning on the porch already, discussing the fact they should probably try to keep this elopement a secret for as long as possible. Let the three of them adapt as a family before dealing with the town's inevitable reactions.

He figured they had two, three days tops before word leaked.

Amelia reluctantly began to climb the stairs, huffing. "You didn't tell me exercise was involved."

"It's good for you." He started after her, feeling a bit of exertion too, which was weird. Was he nervous? He didn't get nervous. Then again, he hadn't felt exactly stable since Amelia had appeared on his porch, either. "Endorphins regulate moods."

She looked at him over her shoulder, lips twisted. "Is that some kind of hint?"

"If you'll take it, then yes."

A welcome rush of AC escaped the building as Linc tugged open the front door. The older security guard in a gray uniform nodded, scanned him half-heartedly with a wand. "Need any direction?"

With this brilliant plan of his? Probably, but—too late for that.

Linc shook his head, motioned Amelia to go past him. "Third floor." Then he added to her. "I'm assuming you want the elevator."

"Hey, maybe you're finally starting to know me after all." Amelia punched the button on the wall.

Linc flinched. See, that was why he had to go to these kinds of extremes to reach his kid. To show her he cared—enough to change his entire life to be there for her.

To prove he hadn't abandoned her on purpose like he'd been abandoned.

They rode in silence, Linc's heart thudding so loud he wondered if Amelia could hear it. Though if she could, she'd probably make fun of him, so he should be safe. Maybe he wasn't nervous, and this darn collar was just too tight.

"I still think this is weird." Amelia leaned her upper back against the paneled wall, staring at the row of lit buttons. "Really sudden."

"So were you."

She rolled her eyes.

"Like we told you yesterday, Zoey and I have known each other a long time." Longer than most people realized, which Linc was okay with. Meant people didn't pry into his past, wondering how he and Zoey met. Better to have everyone think they'd become friends as adults.

"And you just suddenly fell in love?" Amelia looked at him then, eyes questioning. Doubting. "Like, overnight?"

He hesitated. Love didn't need to have anything to do with this particular arrangement, but he couldn't get into that with Amelia. It would defeat the purpose of their forming a unit for her—because this was all for her. Zoey was someone he enjoyed being with, who he could trust to help parent his daughter. Maybe that wasn't enough for a typical marriage, but it was enough for them.

It was safer that way. Less room for getting hurt.

Of being left.

Besides, Zoey didn't have any interest in him as more than a best friend. She was only invested in Amelia, and needed help herself. Her reasons for saying yes were altruistic and more than obvious.

Even if it wasn't the reason a rogue part of him half-hoped for.

"That about sums it up." He cracked his neck. "You really want to hear the mushy details?" Not that they existed. But he and Zoey agreed Amelia needed to believe this marriage was as "normal" as possible.

"Ew." She wrinkled her nose. "Definitely don't."

As he figured. "Okay then."

"Why so fast, though? Why not plan a real wedding?"

"We're not exactly the big frilly type, if you haven't noticed." Linc frowned. Actually, Zoey might have wanted that. Should he have offered? But there wasn't time. They had agreed ASAP, for Amelia's sake. Surely if it was a big deal to her, Zoey would have spoken up.

The doors opened then onto a carpeted hallway, the scent of lemon cleaner heavy in the air. Two potted ferns waited on either side of a set of wooden doors with a plaque reading "chapel."

This was it. Zoey was in there, waiting to marry him. Or at least, she was supposed to be. His chest tightened. Nah, she'd be there. A few more minutes, and they'd be a family.

For better or for worse.

He rubbed his palm down the leg of his jeans. He didn't own slacks. And on second thought, he probably should have made Amelia wear something nicer, but that wasn't a battle he'd wanted to fight. He never knew which ones to pick—something else Zoey was going to have to help him learn. "Ready?"

Amelia raised an eyebrow at him, three parts attitude and one part concern. "Are you?"

Good question. He wrenched the door open anyway.

And there she was, standing next to Judge Morrow in a black robe. At least, he assumed it was Judge Morrow. He couldn't take his eyes off Zoey, wearing a knee-length, casual white sundress—one that showed a few curves she typically hid—her long, dark hair pulled up on the sides with flower clips. Her bright blue eyes smiled at him before her lips did, and his throat went dry.

"Hey." It was all he could push out. Maybe it was time to admit he *was* a little nervous, and it wasn't just the shirt collar.

"Hi." Zoey pursed her lips, hiding a smile. "Fancy meeting you here."

He snorted. A weird urge to give her a hug flooded his limbs, and he hooked his fingers in his pockets. It was *Zoey*. And this was business.

No need to confuse the matter.

She reached over, picked up a bouquet of pink and yellow flowers from the first row of chairs lining the other vacant room. Then she did a double-take at Amelia's outfit, raised her eyebrows at Linc.

He shrugged. "Don't ask."

Judge Morrow dipped his head as he moved behind a small podium, gray mustache lifting in a welcome smile. "Lincoln. Ready to get started?"

He started to correct him, but since Lincoln was the name on the official marriage license they'd secured yesterday, not much point. He nodded, cleared his throat. "Yeah, let's go."

Amelia slumped into one of the chairs in the front row.

"Want to stand with us?" Zoey inclined her head toward the podium, which Linc just then realized had been draped in some kind of white lacy cloth.

Amelia's face said no, but to Linc's surprise, she grudgingly stood and moved to stand just offset of Zoey.

Zoey tugged a few pastel flowers free of her bouquet and handed them to Amelia with a wink. A small smile tilted his daughter's lips as she looked down at them, and for a moment, it was like the sun had come out. Full blast. She was in there, his kid—somewhere under the layers of baggy clothes and attitude. And Zoey was helping her emerge.

If that didn't confirm they were doing the right thing, well. Linc drew a looser breath than he had all morning, and turned to face Zoey as the judge instructed. They could do this.

This was going to work.

"Wait." Zoey pulled another flower from the bouquet, bent off the bottom of the stem to make it shorter, and reached to tuck it into the pocket of his shirt. The scent of roses, mixed with whatever citrusy perfume she wore today, wafted toward him, her hands warm on his chest as she patted to make sure the blossom would stay. "There. Perfect."

She looked perfect, but he couldn't say that. Could he? It *was* their wedding day. Should probably say something nice. Linc cleared his throat, eyes flicking to meet hers, then bouncing away. "You look . . . nice." He dared a glance back.

Amusement danced in Zoey's face. Amelia groaned.

"I mean." He shifted his weight, loafers pinching his big toe. "You look pretty. Really pretty." Ugh. Would this awkwardness be the new dynamic of their life together? That's not what he wanted. He wanted everything to stay the same, just as they'd discussed. He cut his eyes to Amelia. Regardless, he'd do whatever it took.

He had a lot of time to make up for.

Thankfully, his edited compliment seemed to land, because Zoey's eyes softened and she smirked at him. "You clean up halfway decent, yourself."

Whew. There she was. The teasing eased his nerves—he had to admit that's what it was at this point, collar be darned—and his shoulders loosened. He and Zoey had always made a good team. Now they were just going to level up the commitment a notch.

Nothing else had to change. Well, except one thing.

He adjusted the flower in his pocket. "Ready for a new last name?"

"Thought you'd never ask." Then she grinned at him, and for a moment, he forgot it was all a show for Amelia's sake. Forgot

Goldilocks was just a fable, a way for Zoey to torture him with porridge.

Forgot that this marriage scenario wasn't supposed to fit just right.

He turned to Judge Morrow. "Let's do it."

This was really happening.

Zoey was grateful for the excuse to stare at Linc as they grasped hands in front of Judge Morrow, repeating vows as the scent of roses and Linc's spicy aftershave permeated the small room. The man looked too handsome for his own good with his slicked-back hair. Linc rarely wore it that way, but a little piece of Zoey's heart always rejoiced when he did.

Linc's gaze held hers, the steady eye contact doing all kinds of things to her heart. "For better, and for worse . . ."

Zoey swallowed. *Please, God, let there be some better on its way.*

"For richer, or poorer."

Well, she had that part covered.

"In sickness and in health . . ."

Amazing Grace played softly in the background, Zoey's request when the courthouse admin asked if she'd like any music. A thoughtful touch, even though she'd panicked and blurted out the first song she could think of.

I once was lost, but now I'm found, was blind, but now I see.

She certainly felt found in this moment. Safe, for the first time in . . . well, years. Like maybe someone could take care of her, instead of only ever having to take care of herself.

Like maybe God had been a little more involved in this impromptu decision than she'd thought. There *had* been that email that came through late last night. The insurance company had pointed the blame to the fryer manufacturer, who agreed it was an error but not theirs—rather, that of the supplier who had issued a part recall.

In other words, the investigation was still going, and Zoey was still indefinitely homeless and broke.

Talk about a finger writing in the sky after all.

"... 'til death do us part." Linc finished his vows, his voice deep. His dark brown gaze still held hers, a life preserver in an ocean.

The vows were standard, but Zoey meant them with her whole heart as she took her turn reciting after the judge. "In good times and bad ..." It wasn't hard to promise to be there for Linc. Wasn't she always? Wasn't that why she was even standing there in the first place, wearing a strapless bra of all things?

And she had no doubt Linc meant his vows too—just in the most platonic way possible.

With a grand gesture and a little bow, Judge Morrow beamed. "I now pronounce you husband and wife."

Mrs. Zoey Fontenot. It certainly had a ring to it.

And now so did Zoey's finger. She held up her hand, admiring the simple gold band Linc had procured from a pawn shop on the mainland. She'd never been much of a diamond girl, so this simplicity suited her perfectly.

But would anyone suspect what they were up to without a big engagement ring to go along with it?

"Good news, Linc." Judge Morrow smiled at him. "You may now kiss your bride."

Um. Zoey's hand fell back to her side, and she cast a look at Linc, whose widened eyes revealed the same panic—they'd forgotten this part.

How had they forgotten this part?

Judge motioned to them with a chuckle as he leaned against the podium. "Come on, now. Don't be shy."

Amelia groaned. "I'll cover my eyes." She clapped her hands over her face.

"Okay." Linc raked his fingers through his hair with one hand, tugged Zoey closer with the other.

Okay? They were doing this?

Her breath caught, and she licked her suddenly dry lips. She'd forgotten lip gloss in her rush that morning, but maybe that was for the best, because Linc didn't seem like a Frosted Pink kind of guy.

She breathed in the familiar aroma of Linc and his balmy cologne as he drew nearer. He always managed to smell a little like saltwater and sun, even when he hadn't been on his boat.

His hand let go of hers and moved to her waist, warm against the thin fabric of her dress. They'd stood close before, but never like this. Never with the pressure, the expectation, the anticipation . . . Her chest heated, and she risked a glance into his eyes.

Linc, nervous? Now she'd seen everything.

Then, before she could begin to decipher why, he bent down and brushed a quick kiss against her lips. So light, he barely touched her. So quickly, she almost missed it.

Her stomach rolled.

He straightened immediately, looking back at Judge Morrow instead of at her.

Zoey schooled her features into a smile as her mind raced to process. She and Linc weren't the physically affectionate kind of friends. She knew that going into this arrangement—there was no reason to be sad. Nothing had changed, just like he promised.

Didn't he always keep his word?

Zoey squeezed Linc's hand, then chuckled at Amelia's still-hiding posture. "It's safe now."

The girl slowly lowered her hands, her scowl back in place. "Finally."

Well, at least Amelia assumed the kiss had been a good one.

After they settled up with Judge Morrow and retrieved their signed license, they made their escape outside, the sun a welcome relief as the courthouse doors closed behind them. Zoey inhaled a deep breath of air, ribs straining against her dress and that horrible underwire. Birds chirped from the nearby pines, and somewhere down Village Lane, a horn honked.

They'd done it.

They were married.

They filed down the courthouse steps, Linc's hand grazing Zoey's back as if protecting her from tripping in her low heels. Her heart skipped a little. See? He cared. Just because he didn't want to kiss her didn't mean he didn't *care*.

She had a feeling she was going to have to learn to be content with those kinds of gestures. After all, low expectations meant less room for disappointment. More room for sunshine.

And this family was going to need all that Zoey could possibly generate.

Linc jerked his head toward Amelia. "By the way, we're going to keep this just between us three for a bit. Keep the town busybodies out of it."

Amelia stopped walking. "That might be hard to do."

"Why do you say that?" Zoey frowned. "I mean, I know it's Magnolia Bay, but I figure we have a few days at least before word spreads."

Ugh. To that point, Elisa might kill her, but she'd deal with that later. Or maybe she could just tell Elisa, and make her promise not to—

"Because look." Amelia pointed.

Zoey followed her gaze to a limo parked in front of the courthouse, pink streamers and cans tied to the bumper. The back windshield read JUST MARRIED.

Uh-oh.

They all stopped short. Linc bumped into Zoey's hip. "Maybe

it's not for us?" Hope pricked his tone. "People get married at courthouses all the time."

"Guess again." Amelia pointed again—to the chauffeur climbing out the driver's side, holding a sign that clearly read LINC AND ZOEY FONTENOT.

"Was this you?" Zoey asked. Then realized there was no way Amelia could pay for something like that. But who—

Amelia scoffed. "As if. Probably one of your mushy friends."

Zoey met Linc's eyes, which had widened with a slight panic. Amelia was probably right. How would their friends have known?

"This way, please. There's a reception waiting for you." The smiling driver in a black hat grandly opened the back door of the limousine. "Ladies first."

Zoey slowly slid into the limo after Amelia, forcing a polite smile as the driver shut their door and Linc headed around the vehicle to the other side. She clenched her hands in her lap, staring at the glistening ring on her finger against the white fabric of her sundress.

She'd gotten everything she'd ever really wanted. Marriage to her best friend. A family. Even a surprise party.

So why did her natural sunshine feel so thoroughly blocked by clouds?

Eleven

THE MAGNOLIA BLOSSOM HAD BEEN TRANS-formed into a frothy, lacy, cupcake-laden reception hall. From her assigned booth by the window, evident by the white streamers draping the entire table and the BRIDE sign scribbled in marker, Zoey bit into a chocolate cupcake with hot pink icing. Frosting squished into her teeth. They'd probably be stained later, but the treat tasted so great, she didn't even care. She'd decided to chase away the clouds and have fun at her party—even if things weren't ideal.

As always, she'd look on the bright side.

"Okay, spill it. How did you guys know?" Zoey accepted a cup of creamy white punch from Elisa, who slid into the booth across from her. She took a sip, casting a quick look around the crowded room for Amelia. She'd lost her in the initial overwhelming fray of warm wishes and congratulations. Maybe she'd escaped to the bathroom.

"Mama D knows all." Elisa, wearing a sleeveless pink sundress that matched the decorations, toasted Zoey with her own clear punch cup. "Including someone who works at the courthouse, apparently."

Ah. They should have guessed that would happen.

Elisa set down her drink. "The question is, why didn't *I* know? I'm only your best friend."

Zoey couldn't quite tell if Elisa was upset or teasing. "Oh come on, you're the real bride around here. I didn't want to rain on your parade."

"I *love* parades." With a grin, Rosalyn slid into the bench seat next to Elisa, wearing a gauzy lavender dress with sheer short sleeves. Her long blonde hair was tied back, revealing the graceful long lines of her neck. "As long as Cade doesn't have to plan it, of course."

"They might throw us a parade next." Zoey cast a wary look at Mama D, who was busy stacking gifts on an empty table by the counter. "Someone sent a limo, after all. I felt like I was being kidnapped in the most polite way possible."

"We all pitched in for that one. I can't believe Linc got inside it, honestly." Elisa blew out her breath. "I half expected him to just run back home."

Rosalyn fluttered her long lashes. "The power of love."

Ha. More like the power of trying to keep up pretenses in front of his daughter.

"Zoey, for the record, you couldn't rain on anyone if you tried." Elisa's small smile assured Zoey she wasn't mad. "That's considerate, but there's plenty room in the Bay for more than one wedding this year." Then she elbowed Rosalyn. "Remember that."

"Hey, if I rushed down an aisle right now, I'd probably trip over my own feet." Rosalyn twisted a dainty gold bracelet on her wrist. "Cade and I are taking it slow."

"Yeah, that's the face of a man who looks like he wants to wait a long time to get married." Elisa leaned forward and discreetly pointed. Cade's eyes practically pulsed cartoon hearts from where he stood at the counter, holding a plate laden with bite-sized appetizers and cupcakes.

"Nah. He always looks like that when he's got food." Rosalyn smirked.

Linc, however—not so much. Zoey's gaze found him across the diner, standing in a circle with Noah, Owen, and Cade's father, Mayor Landry. Linc's stony expression looked like he'd rather be standing knee deep in the bay.

In a lightning storm.

Holding a metal rod.

Zoey caught Linc's eyes, raised her cupcake in a satire-laden toast. He glowered. She grinned. Teasing him was fun, even this far away. Then Pastor Dubois and Farmer Branson joined the men's huddle, which started another round of shoulder-slapping and cheers, forcing Linc to start over with niceties. Her grin morphed into a smirk.

"For the record, Zoey . . ." Rosalyn tapped her fingers on the tabletop between them, drawing Zoey's attention back to her friends. "Can't say we didn't all see this coming."

"You did?" Zoey blinked. Rosalyn had only been back in Magnolia Bay since that summer, didn't even *know* Linc before that. How did she—

"Yeah, you two were obviously a perfect fit during all the Cajun Circus fundraising." She elegantly peeled back the wrapper on a cupcake.

They were? Zoey glanced at Elisa, who held her gaze, eyes assessing.

Uh-oh.

"Definitely a perfect fit. And then all the close proximity of late, well, it was bound to happen. You guys moved fast, but that's what they say." Rosalyn pinched off a piece of cake. "When you know, you know!"

"Something like that." Zoey avoided Elisa's eyes that time, letting her gaze drift back to Linc. His strong shoulders, the broad span of his chest the confident way he carried himself.

What about when one person in the relationship knew but the other didn't?

She looked away. "We just figured it was good timing, with Amelia and all." She shrugged a little. "We were talking the other day, and Linc pitched the idea."

"Pitched? Don't you mean proposed?" Rosalyn asked with a little frown.

"Ha. You don't know Linc yet." Elisa laughed. But her eyes still held something, some spark of *knowing*, that made Zoey shift in her seat.

"I'll admit, the rush part is for Amelia." Maybe giving partial truth would keep the full truth from being exposed—that Linc didn't love her like that, that he was just a father trying to do the right thing for his kid.

"Everything happens for a reason, right?" Rosalyn toasted Zoey with her glass. "Cheers to God's creative timing!"

Hmm. That was one way to look at it. Zoey rolled the idea around in her mind, trying it on. Everything *had* happened so fast, and she *had* prayed. Seemed like the signs were pointing toward this being the right move. So, yeah—creative timing. She could drink to that.

And it was better than the alternative—that she had made a huge mistake.

They clicked their plastic cups together.

Amelia approached the Bride's table, clutching a white sack smeared with grease stains. Her name was Sharpied across the front of it. "This is for me?"

"Special order." Elisa gestured for Amelia to sit.

The teen eased onto the bench seat next to Zoey and opened the bag, brimming over with french fries. Her face lit like a Christmas tree, and she cleared her throat. Sobered. "Um, thanks."

Not deterred, Elisa raised an eyebrow. "Need ketchup?"

Amelia started to shake her head, then nodded. "Please."

Zoey paused. That was progress.

"I'll get it." Rosalyn slid out of the booth.

"I'll go with you and refill our glasses." Elisa took Zoey's cup. "Can't have a thirsty bride."

"There she is!" Mama D joined the booth just as the other two walked away. She beamed at Zoey with burgundy red lips. "I knew you two would finally see the light."

Apparently, everyone had seen it *but* them. Amelia jerked out of the way as Mama D leaned over the booth to hug Zoey, her floral perfume as strong as her grip. "Congratulations, hon."

Zoey tried to hold her breath. "Thanks, Mama D." New lipstick . . . new perfume. What was Mama D up to? There'd also been that whole panic over what to wear to Elisa's wedding . . .

Delia straightened and checked her gold watch. "I'm giving you exactly one minute to finish that cupcake, Mrs. Fontenot, then it's time for presents." She beamed before bustling off.

"Uh-oh." Zoey nudged Amelia again. "Pretty sure the only thing your dad will hate worse than a party in his honor is opening gifts while everyone stares at him."

"I would too." Amelia slugged a fry through a pile of ketchup. "So are you guys ditching me for the honeymoon? Where am I going?"

Zoey's stomach flipped. *Honeymoon.* There wouldn't be one of those, would there? Not that anyone else needed that information. And she couldn't let Amelia think they weren't interested in one.

"No way. We wouldn't leave you." She bumped Amelia's shoulder with her own, and to her surprise, the younger girl didn't jerk away. In fact, did her eyes light, just a little?

Amelia reached for another fry. "I'd be fine if you did. I'm used to being alone. Even like it, remember?"

Probably not as much as she pretended to. And this was also probably not the time to remind her it was illegal to leave a teenager home alone for several nights. "Your dad doesn't need to leave the tour business right now." Zoey waved one hand in the air, as if it were no big deal. "I'm sure we'll take a trip later."

Like when Amelia was eighteen. Or back with her mom. Or living in a college dorm . . . or maybe not at all. Dunkin' donuts, they really didn't know what was going to happen, did they? And now Linc was legally stuck with Zoey. Stuck taking care of her, providing for her.

What she always wanted. So why did it feel like such a burden?

Zoey reached for a fry from Amelia's basket, took a big chomp. She really needed to get this catering thing going, stop messing up the recipes and start making sales. She couldn't be dependent on Linc forever—even if he was technically her husband. Being a drain would eventually ruin their friendship . . . *marriage* . . . oh boy, this was weird. Despite Linc's misguided assurance, everything had changed. Yet later, they'd go home and sleep in their own rooms, wake up separately, have coffee on the porch.

Like nothing had changed at all.

She forced the rising storm cloud aside. *Nope.* It was her wedding day—only sunshine allowed.

Suddenly Linc was behind her, bracing against the back of the booth, his voice in her ear as he bent low. "Need anything?"

An involuntary tingle sprinted up Zoey's spine. She craned her head back to smile up at him—glad she didn't have to hold back her delight at the considerate question. They were supposed to be in love, after all.

Let people think she was a great actor.

"I'm okay. Elisa went to get me more punch. What about you? Do you need anything?"

"Besides my recliner and sweatpants?" He yanked at the collar of his shirt.

Amelia snorted.

Zoey grinned. "Just a little longer. Then we can bail." Felt like old times, leaving a birthday party together, making excuses for each other or using the other as the excuse. Canceling plans last minute to go out on his boat or taste test a new beignet recipe, instead.

The familiarity of him—of them—healed a bit of the ache that thrummed in Zoey's temples. Her shoulders relaxed. "The guys giving you a hard time over there?"

He shifted his weight. "Not too bad. I just kept changing the subject to Noah's mayoral campaign."

"Smart." Zoey gestured to the bench seat across from her and Amelia. "Want to sit—"

"Time for gifts!" Mama D clapped her hands so loudly, Amelia dropped a fry. "Zoey? Why don't you and your hunky new husband take a seat at the bar stools, here."

Her stomach flipped at the foreign word. *Husband.* Amelia scooted from the booth to let Zoey out, and the gathered crowd parted as she and Linc made their way to the counter. Did Linc feel any kind of reaction to hearing his new title too? Certainly didn't seem like it—though she knew from experience his somber poker face was strong enough to take down Doc Holliday.

"How in the world did anyone have time to buy presents?" Linc grumbled as he eased one hip on the high seat. Half in, half out.

Hopefully that wasn't some kind of symbolism.

Zoey took the stool next to him, in front of a stack of brightly wrapped packages and gift bags. The heat from his side warmed hers, and she fought the urge to lean into him. Once upon a time, she wouldn't have thought twice about bumping her hip against his, grabbing his arm, pulling him along.

Somehow now, a simple touch felt very, very different.

"I know, right?" She eased away a few inches, sitting fully on her own stool. "We only got the marriage license yesterday."

"It's Magnolia Bay." Mama D cackled as she rummaged through the pile of presents. "We keep some magic tucked away for rainy days, you know." She shoved a white box with a pink bow into Zoey's arms. "Now start unwrapping."

"You too, sugarplum." Madame Paulette nudged Linc's arm, which Zoey knew from experience was a bit like tapping concrete. "Help your bride, there."

He frowned a little but obliged, reaching for the ribbon on the box. The crowd gathered in, pressing on all sides, sipping punch and nibbling cupcakes. Sadie and Harper smiled at them while holding their own cups. Rosalyn and Elisa stood with Noah and Cade, while Owen and his older brother Sawyer stood clustered with their father, Pastor Dubois, and August Bowman, the local attorney. Miley's frown as she sipped a soda guaranteed good coffee later.

"Little lovebirds." Standing back from the counter, Mama D shook her head with a contented sigh.

Madame Paulette linked her arm through Delia's, stacked bangles clanging on her wrist, and released a matching sigh. "Have you ever seen a cuter couple?"

"Hey." Noah offered a mock frown.

Elisa reached up and patted his cheek. "I still think you're the cutest, sugar."

Linc had worked up to a full scowl now as he yanked at the tied ribbon. "I hate surprises."

Not sure if he meant the gift or the impromptu party in general, but in either case, Zoey had to disagree. If she couldn't have a real wedding, it *was* kind of nice to be doted on with a party.

Still—she shot him a warning look. "Be nice."

"This one is a together gift," Madame Paulette offered with a grin. "You should be able to figure out why."

Ah, it was from her. At least that explained why the wrapping smelled like essential oils.

Linc's expression lifted a little as he fumbled with the box flaps. "I guess a new coffeepot wouldn't be awful."

"Or baking sheets." Zoey winced. "I sort of burnt that one you had." She opened the lid to reveal several layers of tissue paper. "Here, you do the honors."

Linc reached into the box. Then he frowned, ducked his head to look inside, and froze. His eyes widened and he abruptly shoved the package away.

Madame Paulette cackled. "All clear on the together part now?"

Judging by the fact Linc's face had turned as burgundy as Mama D's lipstick, it must not have been a baking sheet or a coffee maker. Zoey rummaged under the tissue paper, and her hand brushed something silky.

Make that several silky somethings. And was that lace?

Oh, dear.

She tucked the flaps back into the box and cut her eyes at Linc, who had started chugging a glass of water. Leave it to Madame Paulette. "Um, thank you . . ."

"Here." Elisa shoved another present into her hands. "This one is from Mrs. Peters."

Ah, the librarian. That one should be safe to open in public. Zoey's shoulders eased from around her ears, and she cast her friend a grateful look. But just in case . . . She glanced at Linc. "Why don't I open this one?"

"Be my guest." Linc set his empty glass on the counter with a clank.

She carefully tore into the box, peeked inside. A toaster. Perfect.

A normal hue returned to Linc's face as they made their way through the remaining pile. Gift cards to Amazon from their friends. A basket of produce and canned salsa from Farmer Branson. A leather-bound set of books from Sadie. Stationery from Peggy at August Bowman's office. And a coffee maker from Mama D, much to Linc's delight.

Or, at least, as delighted as Linc ever got.

"This one is for you, sugar." Elisa gestured for Amelia, who had been hovering in the background with her bag of fries, to open the remaining package on the table. "We all went in together."

"For me?" Amelia's eyes widened, and she shot a half-panicked, half-hopeful look at Zoey.

Fighting the swell in her throat, Zoey gave her an encouraging nod. Maybe Linc and Zoey didn't have a lot of family in the Bay, but they had some *really* good friends.

Zoey glanced at Linc, the way his eyes softened as he watched Amelia cautiously tear off the gift wrap. He looked away long enough to meet her eyes, smile. He rested his hand lightly on her shoulder, and she leaned into him. Not for appearances, not for obligation. Just appreciating the nice moment together.

The moment that seemed to prove their hasty decision had been the right one.

Amelia unearthed a picture frame and another gift card, this time a generic one that could be used anywhere credit cards were accepted.

Elisa stepped forward, hands clasped in front of her. "We thought you could use some money of your own for shopping. Clothes, your room, whatever you want."

"Thank you." Amelia's whisper barely carried, but it was genuine, along with the small smile lifting her lips.

Linc squeezed Zoey's shoulder, mouthed a thank you to Noah, who nodded in return. Zoey smiled at Elisa, who offered a quick wink.

"And the frame is for a photo of your family." Rosalyn leaned across the counter and pointed with a smile. "The three of you."

Amelia's smile faltered. She stared down at the white ceramic square in her hands, back growing rigid. The room quieted. Zoey shot Linc a look of concern, but he was also frowning, clearly unsure what was happening.

She turned back to Amelia. "Hey, are you—"

The girl dropped the frame on the counter with a clatter. It cracked down the side, and without looking back, she bolted for the door.

It was Linc's turn to run after her.

His loafers pounded on the sidewalk, cramping his toe with every step. He was faster than Zoey had been the other day when she chased Amelia—not that in all his years of cross training he'd imagined needing endurance for this particular reason—and he caught up to her less than a block from the diner.

"For the record, you're not my family." Amelia spun in front of Chug a Mug, lobbing the words like a grenade.

Linc stopped. Cracked his neck to shake it off. "What are you talking about?" The descending sun cast long shadows across the sidewalk, swathing half of Amelia's face.

She crossed her arms, holding herself together. "You heard that blonde lady. I'm supposed to put a photo of my family in that frame." She swiped at her nose with her wrist. "What *family*? You're a stranger. And Zoey isn't my mom now just because you two got married on a whim."

"It wasn't a—" Well, it sort of was a whim. But not in the way she meant. He cleared his throat, unsure what to address first. "No one is trying to make Zoey your mother."

"Good. The last thing I need is *three* uninvolved parents."

Linc briefly closed his eyes. They were back to that. Why wouldn't she believe him? "I'm telling you, I never knew you existed until the other day. That's the truth."

Amelia's eyes shone with unshed tears. "*Mom* always said otherwise."

Of course she did. Because Kirsten lied. About love, about loyalty, about *life*. Linc wanted to punch a hanging bag, break a board. Bench press three hundred—*something* to let this frustration free.

He settled for a deep breath, squeezing his fist. "And you're going to believe her? She wasn't exactly mother of the year, you know."

"At least she was there."

"Until she wasn't."

They stared at each other.

More harsh truth . . . maybe too harsh. What had Zoey said—something about truth gently delivered?

He was ruining this again.

"Look." Linc tried to soften his tone, though the words felt like sandpaper on his tongue. "I didn't have a mom either, you know." He swallowed. "She died when I was really young."

"Well, did you have a dad?" Amelia glared. "Because I didn't."

Linc struggled not to physically step backward at the emotional sucker punch. Did teenagers come with a manual on how to best hit a parental target where it hurt? Amelia was two for two. "I had a father for a minute."

"And then what? You just chose to do life on your own?" She scoffed. "Guess I get that from you."

He frowned. "What do you mean?"

"You don't want me here."

"You don't want to be here."

She narrowed her eyes, dark like his. "Nice evasion."

"Back atcha."

Another stare-down. Linc refused to blink. If he let her win, she'd never respect him.

But maybe it didn't need to be about respect right now. Maybe it needed to be about trust.

They had to start somewhere.

"Amelia . . ." Linc looked away, giving her the win. He scrubbed his hands down his face. Good grief, this collar was too tight. "I never said I don't want you here. You were just a surprise."

Her nose scrunched. "A bad one, apparently."

"I didn't say that, either." He waited, letting that sink in—if she'd let it. A car drove down Village Lane. A few yards ahead, a couple walked hand-in-hand inside Chug a Mug, releasing the scent of freshly ground beans into the early evening air. "Are you finally willing to admit you *were* a surprise, at least?"

Amelia lifted her chin. "Maybe." Then she rolled in her lip. "You did seem pretty shocked."

"Trust me, I'm not a good actor."

She started to grin a little, then caught it.

He wanted more of those. Maybe she'd eventually relax enough to laugh with him.

She studied him. "Maybe I should drag you to the lamppost. Just to make sure."

He raised his eyebrows. "You know about that?"

"Zoey told me."

Of course she did. "I'll go if you want. If you'll believe me."

Amelia squinted, a smile still peeking just below the surface. "Too hot to walk that far."

He agreed. "Look, the truth is—I'm sorry the frame freaked you out, but there's no pressure or obligation with it." He held up both hands in surrender. "It's just a frame."

She sobered. "Felt like more."

"Put a photo of a rock in it, for all I care. Throw it away. Whatever you want."

"Really? I can do that?" She quirked an eyebrow, surprised.

"Better than running away every time something stresses you out." Linc shrugged. "We both gotta be able to say what we think. If you don't want the frame, say so. Let's be honest with each other."

She opened her mouth, and he quickly interjected. "Don't worry. I'm working on trying to be honest in a nicer way."

Her mouth snapped shut and she tilted her head. "I can do that. I think."

"We're not going to get all of this right—especially me. But just know there's a bunch of people in that diner who barely know you and already care about you." He hesitated. "Including me."

There. It was out there. She could believe him or not.

Amelia studied him, assessing. He stood still, fighting the urge to cross his arms. He tried to look open. Unintimidating. Unafraid—despite his heart about to pound out of his chest. How could Amelia *not* know how much she mattered? And yet he couldn't tell her the lengths he and Zoey had already gone to for her.

Guess they were just going to have to live it out until she did— together. That part brought comfort, at least. He wasn't in this alone, and neither was Amelia.

If she'd just believe it.

"So?" He couldn't bear the silence anymore. "What's it going to take for you to give me a real chance?"

Amelia tilted her head, hope rising in her expression. She took a tiny step forward, out of the shadows. Her brow arched. "There is maybe one thing you can do . . ."

Uh-oh. He shoved his hands in his pockets and rocked back on the heels of his loafers, working to keep his expression relaxed. Casual.

Not panicked. "Name it." He was going to regret this, wasn't he?

"Help me get my stuff out of the old apartment?"

Oh. He frowned, mind racing with the logistics. They had probably already cleared the space, maybe thrown everything away? There was no telling when the lease technically ended or where the belongings had gone. "Amelia, I don't know if that's poss—"

The disappointment immediately clouding the hope in her eyes snapped his mouth shut. He drew a deep breath, stared down at his shoes. Swallowed against the tight collar of his shirt. This was a problem dads would figure out, wasn't it? And he was a dad now.

So he'd do it. He'd figure it out.

He looked back at her. "Sure. Of course."

Relief flooded her young face, and a bit of the hope in her expression wormed its way into his heart. For her, he'd make a way.

He'd figure *all* of this out.

Twelve

T HE DINER LIGHTS WERE TURNED LOW, the chairs all flipped up on the tables. From the kitchen behind the counter, a cabinet door slammed as Elisa's head chef, Lucius, cleaned up in the back for the night.

The party was over. After Linc and Amelia had returned from Amelia's dramatic exit, everyone left for home, offering one last round of well wishes on their hustle out the door. The cracked frame had subtly been boxed up with everything else, and Zoey had yet to be alone with Linc to hear how the conversation between him and Amelia went.

Now, she contemplated snagging another cupcake from the bakery box Elisa was packing up, but her ceremony dress was decidedly tighter than it had been when she'd gotten ready earlier that afternoon. Probably shouldn't.

Then again, it wasn't like she needed to fit into any of the silky unmentionables she'd unwrapped an hour ago.

"I have a question, Mrs. Fontenot." Elisa nestled a leftover cupcake inside the bakery box, her tone overly casual—meaning the question would not be.

Uh-oh.

Zoey leaned against the countertop, craning her neck to look out the diner window—but no sign of rescue in sight. Linc and Amelia had gotten a ride back to the courthouse to get Linc's truck, and then they were supposed to come pick her up. She'd volunteered to stay and help clean, hoping to smooth over any lingering tension between her and Elisa over the elopement.

Had she known Elisa was getting suspicious of the truth, however . . . "Shoot."

Frosting smeared the side of Elisa's thumb, and she licked it off. "Why don't you marry Linc?"

Huh? Zoey waved her hand in front of her best friend's face. The flash of the gold band still looked foreign on her finger, and she lowered her hand, tucking her fingers into a fist. "Earth to Elisa. Didn't you just help host our *wedding* reception?"

Elisa tucked a strand of blond hair behind her ear, her eyes narrowed. "I hosted a party, but I'm not convinced it was for a wedding."

Uh-oh. What did that mean?

Zoey cleared her throat. "Do I need to pull out the marriage license for you?" It was in a folder in Linc's truck, in the nice little envelope the courthouse had provided. All neat and tidy, like their makeshift family was supposed to be now.

Though between her undeniable feelings for Linc, Madam Paulette's gift, and Amelia's second abrupt departure from Magnolia Blossom, it was starting to feel more like someone had started a second fire in her life.

"You need to pull out the *truth*." Elisa crossed her arms over her chest. Her eyes were kind, despite her firm tone. "Though I'm pretty sure God and I both already know what that is."

She should have known her best friend would see through the charade. "How did you figure it out?"

Elisa went back to packing cupcakes. Oh, and a small, only partially cut cheesecake. Where had that been all afternoon? "The comment you made earlier about my being a 'real bride' was a giveaway."

Oops. Zoey covered her face with her hands. "Do you think anyone else could tell?"

"Probably not. But why are you lying about marrying Linc? Is it for Amelia's sake?" Elisa frowned. "Because I don't think the girl needs any more lies in her life."

Zoey peeked through her fingers. "We *are* married."

"I know that. But only on a technicality." Elisa reached out, covered Zoey's hands with hers atop the counter. "Were things really that bad for you financially? Were you that desperate? Or was it because of Amelia?"

All of that, and none of it. Zoey released a sigh, grateful the truth was out there to someone. Her shoulders lightened, despite the knot forming in her stomach. One symptom for another. "Linc needed help. I needed help. Amelia needs help." Zoey offered a one-shouldered shrug. "I know it sounds crazy."

"It would." Elisa nodded. "Except I think you're both using this as an excuse."

"An excuse?"

"Sure. Think about it."

Zoey scoffed. "Right. Like Linc was so in love with me, he burned down my beignet shop and faked having a teen daughter to convince me to marry him."

"Not like that." Elisa chuckled. "Sorry, that was funny. I mean, I think deep down both of you wanted this with each other, and it just took all the sudden chaos of Amelia's arrival and the fire to make it happen."

Ha, again. "No way." Zoey shook her head, playing with the edge of a cupcake liner. "Linc made it very clear this was a business arrangement. Practicality, only."

Elisa's brow furrowed. "So what later? You just get divorced?"

"No." Zoey shook her head, paused. "Probably not."

Elisa sighed. "So you haven't thought any of this out long-term? You two just ran to the courthouse?"

Zoey lifted her chin. "We drove."

"*Zoey . . .*"

"I don't know, okay? We decided to handle what's happening right now, and deal with the future later." She was repeating Linc's almost exact words. As if she believed them.

As if he was right instead of Elisa.

"Sure." Her friend nodded slowly. "After all, it's just marriage. Family. A teenager's life. No biggie."

Ouch. "That's not fair." Zoey's chest heated beneath her dress. "We did what we had to do because it's such a biggie."

"Right. Because you *wanted* to do it."

She pursed her lips. "That's not helpful."

"Not helpful because it's true?"

Zoey started to argue, then hesitated, heart thudding. "Maybe it's true for me."

"Aha!" Elisa pointed, triumphant.

"A *little* true. But it doesn't matter, because it's not true for Linc, and no way am I going to mess all this up by being like 'oh by the way, I like-like you.'" Zoey rolled her eyes. "It'd ruin everything."

Elisa smirked. "Yes, falling for your husband would be tragic."

"You don't understand. You have a fairy tale going on with Noah."

Her friend's smile faded.

Oops. She wasn't being very sunny right now. "Which is great for you, and this is great for me." Zoey rushed ahead. "Everything is great exactly as it is."

She really needed to stop using the word *great*.

Zoey thought through her next words before speaking. "Linc and I have a plan that works for us and is good for Amelia." There. She smiled, channeling all things cheery. Silver linings.

Puppies and rainbows.

Elisa nodded. "I see. A plan that makes sure no one gets hurt."

Finally, Elisa was getting it. "*Exactly.*"

"Ha!" Elisa smacked the countertop with her hand. Zoey jumped. "That was a trap. Of course someone is going to get hurt."

Panic knocked. But Zoey refused to answer. Sunshine, puppies, rainbows . . . "Don't be silly. We're all adults here."

"Right. Adults with flesh-and-blood hearts."

"Actually, Linc's might be tin."

"You're playing with fire." Elisa winced. "Sorry. Poor word choice."

Zoey glared. "Why do people keep doing that?"

"You know what I mean. Someone is going to catch feelings— or from the sound of it, catch more of them than they already have." She widened her eyes pointedly at Zoey.

"I appreciate the concern." Zoey held up both hands. Dunkin' donuts, there was that ring again. She averted her eyes from it. "But Linc and I are best friends, we'll figure it out. This is ultimately about Amelia. Him and Amelia."

"Sure." Elisa's voice softened. "But you matter too."

"This feels like the moment in a movie right before the characters break into song."

"Funny."

"Just do me a favor. Don't tell anyone else in our group?" Zoey cringed. "This is complicated enough without having to keep up with who knows what."

"Fine. You win." Elisa held up one finger. "But I reserve the right to say a big fat *I told you so* if this blows up in your face later."

She was off the hook, finally. "Thank you." Zoey reached over and hugged her. It was nice to be loved, even if that meant interrogation. "Also, I know you'd never actually do that."

"You're right." Elisa hugged her back. "But I might think it."

"That's pretty hardcore for you."

"Or there's another option, like I suggested." Elisa gripped her shoulders. "*Marry* Linc."

Zoey pulled away, hoping the heat in her chest hadn't reached her cheeks. "Why don't you just focus on marrying Noah, huh?"

"Oh, I'm focused." Elisa squeezed Zoey's hand, eyes sobering. "I just want you to be happy too."

"*Happy*?" Zoey flashed a smile, the one she felt big enough for a teeth whitening ad. Big enough to convince people a lie was the truth.

Maybe even convince herself. "Way ahead of you. I'm pure sunshine, baby." Nary a cloud a sight.

But maybe only because she was scared to fully open her eyes.

She needed carbs.

Zoey padded silently down the hall. Past Amelia's room, toward the kitchen in smiley-face house shoes, her fuzzy purple bathrobe cinched tight. Linc and Amelia had finally picked her up at the diner, and by the time they'd put away all their gifts—the silky stuff going in the *far* back of Zoey's dresser drawer—and Amelia had gone to bed, Linc was sound asleep in his recliner.

Hardly a typical wedding night.

Zoey had gone to bed several hours ago herself, but couldn't sleep for tossing and turning, wondering what had transpired in the conversation between Amelia and Linc after the teen ran out of Magnolia Blossom. Wondering if anyone else was going to see through this marriage like Elisa had.

Wondering what her husband was thinking from across the house.

She rounded the corner of the hallway. The gravity of it all had hit her afresh, lying in bed alone, staring at the ceiling. No wonder

Cade stress-ate his way through the Magnolia Days fundraiser this summer. Apparently, Zoey had been missing out all these years by choosing to simply deny she was stressed.

Resignation and leftover cheesecake sounded way better.

She wouldn't even bother to turn on the light, she'd just grab a fork and—aw, man. A golden glow streamed from the open fridge door, blocking her view of whoever was on the other side. Was she too late? If it was Amelia, she'd let her have the leftovers without a fight.

If it was Linc, though . . .

She took a chance, leapt forward. "Step away from that cheese-cake!"

Silverware clattered to the ground. "What the—"

Linc.

She smirked as he emerged from the fridge, scowl firmly in place. But her smile faded as her eyes took in the fact that he, most definitely, was *not* in a robe. His dark hair was down, still damp from an earlier shower, and his tanned, muscular chest revealed several rows of abs that tapered into a pair of gray pajama pants. A muddled scar occupied his left rib cage, catching her stare much longer than it should have.

Linc raised his eyebrows at her.

She gulped. Bent to grab the dropped fork the same time he did. *Knock.* Their heads collided.

"Ow." Zoey pressed her hand to her forehead, backed into the island with a thump. "Oops." She straightened, nearly knocking into Linc again.

"You okay?" Linc steadied her with one hand, which immediately sent sparks shooting through her robe and up her arm.

She shook him off and banged her elbow into the island. "Ow!" Now she clutched her arm instead of her head. What was *wrong* with her? Dunkin' donuts, she'd seen Linc shirtless before—this was a beach town, full of pool parties and barbeques.

But never before in his home.

As her *husband.*

"You good?" Linc slowly held up both hands, eyeing her like she might be a wild animal in a trap. Which maybe wasn't too far from the truth, given the current state of her bed-head and spastic movements.

"I just really wanted cheesecake." Zoey slid down the length of the island to the floor, resting her back against the cabinet. Her head throbbed, and she had an incredibly uncanny urge to laugh. Cry.

Maybe scream, really, really loud.

Was that what happened when someone stuffed their emotions for too long? They all threatened to burst free at once?

Silently, Linc opened a drawer and grabbed a fresh fork. Then he sat down next to her, shoulder to shoulder, and handed it to her along with the cheesecake plate.

"Bless you." Zoey pressed the fork into the cake and took a bite. The cold, creamy texture mixed with strawberries soothed her nerves. Cade knew what he was doing with the stress eating, that was for sure.

"Bad night?" Linc plucked the fork from her hands, speared off a piece of cake, and popped it in his mouth before handing the fork back.

"Wasn't."

"Until you ran into me, you mean?" His lips curved upward.

More like until that tsunami of emotions tried to take her down. But it was before that, wasn't it? After all, she'd come to get carbs for a reason. Zoey stabbed her fork back into the slice, choosing to dissect the cake instead of her motivations. "Until you tried to steal my leftovers."

Linc smirked. "Thought marriage meant what's yours is mine."

"So I get a teenager, and you get my dessert. I see how it is."

He reclaimed the fork. "Guess we both get both."

"That works too."

They sat silently, the warmth of Linc's shoulder pressing into her robe-covered one comforting now instead of alarming. Funny how everything felt less chaotic in her head when she was near him.

Or maybe that was just because now she couldn't see his abs.

Speaking of—she couldn't help it any longer.

"What's this?" Zoey twisted toward him, touched the marred spot on his side. His skin was warm beneath her finger, despite the AC running in the kitchen, and his stomach shuddered at the contact.

She quickly pulled her hand away, clutching the cake plate again. Her fingers must have been cold. It's not like she had any effect on Linc—not like *that*. In fact, if he knew the way she'd checked him out in the fridge light, he'd tease her mercilessly. She schooled her features to casual, waited for his answer.

But he didn't answer, didn't even move—just remained silent and stoic next to her. She looked down at the crumbly remains of dessert, regret sneaking into her heart. Ugh, why had she asked? Just because they were married didn't mean Linc was obligated to explain every little—

"I had a tattoo removed years ago."

Oh. She looked back at it now with fresh eyes, resisting the urge to trace the mottled outline with her finger. Now she could see the faint remains of ink, not scar tissue like she'd always assumed. "I can't make out what it used to be."

"That's the point."

"Well, what was it?"

Once again, he didn't answer, so she turned her head to look at him, their faces inches apart. Her breath caught—so much for casual. Up close, the dark stubble staining his jaw begged to be touched, the furrow between his thick eyebrows smoothed. She gripped the plate tighter before she did something really dumb, like act on either of those impulses.

And risk breaking this fragile thing they'd created.

His eyes roamed her face. "Why do you want to know?"

She lifted her chin. Oops, bad idea, that just brought their faces closer. She inched away, tucked her hair behind her ear. "Why don't you want to tell me?"

"That's not an answer."

"Well maybe I want to know so bad *because* you won't tell me."

"Ah, there she is—the stubborn thorn in my paw." Linc tilted his head back against the island cabinet. "Figured you were in there somewhere."

"What do you mean?"

"You've been acting weird."

"I *am* weird, Linc."

"You know what I mean." Now it was his turn to swivel toward her, dark hair falling across his forehead. "Things have felt off again lately."

"Oh, you mean since I lost my business, became homeless, impulsively married my best friend, and helped take in the daughter he didn't know he had?" The words exploded from her lips, and she sucked in a tight breath. Wanted to take them back.

But he didn't seem offended. In fact, he only smiled, nodded slowly. "Yeah, since about then."

"What a puzzle." She rolled her eyes.

"Seriously. You doing okay with all this?" Linc asked. She studied his eyes, his expression deep, more serious than she'd ever seen without being accompanied by some kind of aggravation.

He was genuinely asking.

She nodded. "Talking like this—like we used to—helps."

"Agreed. We've always been a team . . . maybe against my better judgment." He bumped her shoulder. "And like I promised—nothing's changed."

She was starting to hate that phrase.

"I think we made the right decision." Zoey lowered her voice despite the fact they were alone in the kitchen. "But every now and then, the gravity of what we're doing hits, you know?"

"Tell me about it." He blew out a breath, looked up at the ceiling where Amelia slept upstairs. "I think Amelia and I reached some kind of understanding today after the party."

"Yeah?"

"Yeah. She seems to finally believe I didn't know she existed. That I didn't just bail on her all her life." He released a slow breath. The refrigerator hummed behind them. "I think she's going to give this a fighting chance."

"Good."

"Good, yes, but . . . also a lot of pressure." He sighed. "Like I don't even get three strikes."

"You're pretty decent at baseball." Zoey shrugged. "Maybe you only need one."

The corner of his mouth lifted. "Maybe." He reached for the fork again. "What about you? Why are you up?"

"Just thinking."

"About?" He speared a bite of cake.

"Why do you want to know?" she parroted, only half teasing.

He narrowed his eyes, and for the life of her, she couldn't keep her eyes off his lips sliding the bite of cheesecake off the fork. "Are you always going to be this difficult?"

"Don't think I'm letting the tattoo thing go indefinitely."

"What about just for tonight?"

"Deal." Zoey yanked the fork back, finished the last bite of cheesecake. "I guess I was up because . . . well, I didn't grow up thinking I'd elope at a courthouse, you know?"

"I get it." Linc shifted his weight, drew one sweat-pant-clad leg up. "As much grief as I give the guys for calling me a permanent bachelor, I kind of figured I wouldn't ever get married at all."

She pressed her lips together, thinking back over their ceremony. "No three-tiered cake. No professional photos."

"No bachelor party." He winked at her.

Zoey snorted, then sobered. "I didn't even dance at my own wedding."

"Well, *dear*, that's because you didn't have a traditional wedding."

"Exactly my point, *honey*."

The refrigerator hummed louder in the sudden silence.

"Do *you* think we made a mistake?" Her whisper carried across the dark kitchen.

With a sigh, Linc ambled to his feet. Her heart quickened. Was he going to bed? She'd gotten too negative. What was she thinking? She needed to be light for him. Sunshine. Joy.

Wasn't that why he'd invited her into this whole thing in the first place? To help?

She looked up at him towering overhead, sucked in a breath. "I'm sorry, I shouldn't have said anything. You're dealing with enough, *way* more than me, and here I am being super selfish and—"

"Come 'ere." Linc hauled her to her feet before she could even accept his offered hand.

She stood and started to let go, but he pulled her to him and clutched her hand between them. Her knuckles rested against his bare chest, and his other arm came around her back, hand lightly grazing her waist. What in the world—

He began to sway, slowly, side to side, the rhythm steady and beckoning like the waves on the bay.

Dancing.

Tears burned the back of her eyes. Oh no. She couldn't cry. Not in front of Linc.

She fought the lump in her throat. "But you don't—"

"Dance? Definitely not." He tugged her closer. "Now hush."

Gladly. She fell into the same pace, resting her upper body against his. His heart thumped under her ear, and hers matched his beat for beat. She closed her eyes, gripping his arm with her free hand, holding on for reasons she couldn't begin to let herself explore.

He began to hum, low and slightly off-key, the deep bass ricocheting in his chest.

Her throat burned with unshed emotion, and she squeezed her eyes shut. Water dripped in the sink. The scent of Linc's musky body wash wafted over her. His bicep under her fingers felt warm, strong. Familiar, somehow, though she rarely touched him.

Maybe they were making a huge mistake. Maybe this would all blow up in their faces. Maybe Elisa would get that chance to say *told you so* later after all.

But, for tonight, it was just them.

Zoey and Linc. Best friends. Sunshine and storm-clouds.

Dancing.

Thirteen

L INC SHOULD BE ON HIS BOAT RIGHT now, leading a tour. Or checking his equipment, or researching mainland festivals and markets for next season's haul, or talking to Anthony about ways to expand their business further until spring.

Instead, he was at the end of a three-hour drive north to Lafayette, Zoey riding shotgun with Amelia perched in the middle of the backseat of his truck, making good on the favor he'd promised her yesterday.

Marshland rolled past his window, rock music blaring from the speakers. That part prevented much conversation, which was exactly as he'd hoped. Hard enough keeping his mind on the winding ribbon of asphalt and not on the scent of Zoey's perfume next to him without adding further distraction.

"Turn here." Amelia tapped his shoulder, despite his GPS giving him the same direction, and pointed to the right as he approached a four-way stop.

He obliged, taking the opportunity to sneak a peek at Zoey's profile as he made the turn. Hadn't gotten much sleep, as last night's kitchen dance replayed every time he shut his eyes, but he was realizing today it replayed even when his eyes were open. He'd felt bad for her last night, for what she'd given up for him—for *them*—and figured he'd owed her a simple dance.

But the second her hand landed on his bare skin, her head tucked against his chest, any sense of obligation had cut and run. He'd become acutely aware of her scent, her softness, her warmth . . . and two very opposing facts.

She was his *wife*.

And she was *Zoey*.

Had that moment gotten to her too? He'd never know. Today, she was back to all sunshine, playing hangman and other note-passing car games with Amelia.

The only thing that had changed was the glint of gold on her ring finger.

He frowned. She deserved a diamond. Not that he could really afford it right now, but one day.

Assuming she had reason to stick around that long.

"Now left." Amelia tapped again.

"Got it." They meandered through a low-income neighborhood that had probably seen better days. Overgrown weeds poked through cracks in the street. Trash littered the sides of the road. An abandoned car, stripped of its tires, had become completely taken over by vines a block from the apartment complex the GPS directed him to.

He pulled into the parking lot, killed the engine.

Zoey edged forward on her seat, frowning as she peered up at the sagging gutter in front of the office door, the chipped paint. "You said you called ahead?"

"Yeah, the lease is up this weekend." Linc opened his door. "Manager said she'd let her in."

Amelia hopped eagerly from the backseat, practically jogging to the front door with the box of trash bags they'd brought tucked under her arm. "Come on!"

Linc grabbed a tub from the bed of his truck, braced it against his side. Zoey fell into step beside him. "Guess Kirsten didn't have a great job."

Or . . . "Guess she spent her money on what she wanted."

Zoey winced. "I wasn't going to say it."

"You're not going to offend me." He shot Zoey a look. "She is what she is."

Her voice softened. "This is a nice thing you're doing for Amelia, letting her get her stuff."

Linc shrugged. "She asked. And with school starting Monday, well—I figured it was the least I could do."

She slowed her pace. "Well yeah, I'm sure she'll feel more comfortable with some of her own belongings, but it's a lot more than the least, Linc." She looked up at him. "It's a good dad move."

The words washed over him, warming something deep inside, and he gripped the tub a little tighter. Zoey's approval had always carried a bit more weight than the average person—which wasn't hard, seeing how that amount was typically none—but this . . .

This was different.

Amelia hurried inside the office, where a potted plant fought to live, the air thick with the lingering aroma of cigarette smoke. A middle-aged woman with frizzy bleached hair sat behind the front desk. "Hey, Tara. Remember me?"

"Hey, doll." Tara's smoker's voice was as thick as the air. She set down the romance novel she'd been reading and fished in the desk drawer. "13B, right?"

"Right."

Tara handed over the key without a single word to Linc or Zoey, picked her novel back up, and waved them off.

Zoey and Linc exchanged a look.

Within minutes, Amelia had led them up rusty stairs to a nearby unit with cracked trim. The door across from Amelia's contained a flowered wreath and a worn welcome mat—clearly an effort to cheer up the place.

But Amelia's door was bare, save for the splattered stain of some kind of dark liquid. She burst inside, a rush of stale air mixed with rotting food drifting out the door in her wake. Zoey discreetly coughed.

Linc frowned, his bulk nearly filling the entryway of the small space. A nearly empty living room with a futon and a TV tray as a table sat next to a dirty window. Stains covered the threadbare carpet. The kitchen was to his left, clearly the source of the rancid smell. A short hallway led to the back, where he assumed the bedrooms and bathroom were. A bug skittered across the floor and vanished under the cabinet trim.

He was half afraid to set the tub down.

"Where's your room, Amelia?" Zoey ventured farther inside, then lowered her voice for Linc's ears only. "We should probably make this quick."

"Agreed." He risked setting the tub down, peeled off the lid.

Amelia set the box of trash bags on the counter separating the kitchen from the living area. "Down the hall, to the left. Mom let me have the bigger one." She cast a quick look at Linc, like he was supposed to be impressed. Like maybe that was proof Kirsten wasn't a horrible parent after all.

Zoey's hand on his arm kept his mouth shut. He cleared his throat. "Go on, then. Grab what you want."

Felt weird walking farther into Kirsten's personal space, so he let Zoey take the tub and go with Amelia around the corner. He shoved his hands into the pockets of his jeans, giving the room a slow once-over. No art on the wall, no framed photos sitting out. No motherly efforts toward making the space homey. Just an ancient television, a stack of magazines beside the futon, a yoga mat rolled up in the corner. How in the world had they lived here?

How had Amelia lived here *alone* as long as she had? Had she even remembered to lock the door at night?

Linc turned to study the weak deadbolt. He could kick that

in, easy, which meant someone else determined to could have as well. His stomach boiled with anger. Could Kirsten get any more foolish, any more selfish?

His chest clenched. How had he been so blind to who Kirsten really was all those years ago? He should have seen signs, had some indication. But he'd been duped. Blinded by love, or some hopeful teenage version of it.

Just a guy looking to find someone to stay.

They returned from down the hall, Zoey toting the tub half-full of what looked like some rolled-up posters, makeup, and a few boxes tucked inside. Amelia's arms were draped with clothes.

She stopped short, face washing pale as she stared into the kitchen.

"What is it?" Linc started toward her. "Another bug?"

She shook her head, stack of clothes going limp in her arms. Wire hangers clacked together. "It's just . . . those dishes weren't in the sink when I left."

Linc met Zoey's eyes, which looked as startled as he felt.

Amelia visibly swallowed. "Mom's been here."

Half an hour later, after drive-thru tacos, they were once again on the road. Zoey cast a look in her side mirror at Amelia, asleep in the backseat next to her meager belongings. She hugged a stuffed unicorn she told them was named Frederick on her lap. Linc had raised his eyebrows but wisely kept his mouth shut. No doubt he was remembering her angry dismissal of unicorn sheets when she first arrived.

From the driver's seat, Linc talked in quiet tones with Ms. Bridges, his expression drawn. Zoey alternated between trying to eavesdrop and trying to pray. Was Amelia right? Had Kirsten really been there that recently?

Linc finally disconnected the call, his face grim. The radio played low. "She hasn't heard from her."

Wow. Zoey fought to wrap her mind around that. "Well . . . I guess we don't know for *sure* it was Kirsten who made the mess."

Linc dropped his phone in the cup holder. "Amelia said she could tell. It was her mom's favorite coffee mug."

"Maybe someone broke in."

"And made sure to put their dishes in the sink after cooking?" He tilted his head, voice infused with doubt.

"Yeah, that was a dumb suggestion. I'm just trying to think who else it could be. The manager?"

"I doubt it. She'd have said something when she gave us the key. Besides, it's not like their apartment was a nice place to hang out."

All good points. Zoey's heart thudded, and she cast a glance over her shoulder to confirm Amelia wasn't listening. "So you're saying Kirsten went home at some point over the last few days, realized her daughter wasn't there, and just left again—without calling the police or social services or anything?"

"It's a different lifestyle, Zoey." His grip tightened on the steering wheel. A muscle jumped in his jaw. "It won't make sense to you."

Spoken like a man who knew. Zoey frowned. But that was impossible. "If it won't make sense, then how do *you* understand?"

"Because I've been in trouble before." He glanced in the rearview mirror. "Obviously."

"That's different. Accidentally getting your girlfriend pregnant isn't illegal."

"I've been arrested."

Zoey twisted her lips to the side. "Really?"

"And I've done drugs."

"*Oh.*"

"It was a long time ago, when I first started college."

"I never knew that." Apparently, she didn't know Linc as well as she thought. Maybe she knew him better than most people in the Bay, but what was that really saying at this point? What else had he kept from her?

"I straightened myself out before too long, got the scholarship. Made good grades." He stared straight again. "Mama D would say by the grace of God."

"She would say that." Amazing grace, even. The lyrics from their wedding rolled through her head.

"Broken people make mistakes." He huffed. "Again, obviously."

She glanced over her shoulder again. "Amelia isn't a mistake, Linc."

"No, I didn't mean her." He shook his head. "I meant my choosing Kirsten." The steering wheel creaked under his grip. "I pursued her, stayed with her when it was clear she was running around, getting into stuff. It's my fault Amelia is in this situation."

"Maybe partly, on a technicality." Zoey shifted sideways to look at him, the seatbelt pulling across her chest. "But to that same point, she wouldn't even exist without your so-called mistakes. God works all these things out for good."

He cut his eyes to her. "Everything?"

"That's what the book of Romans says." Zoey shrugged.

"Even fires?"

She swallowed, images from that fateful night flickering. The drifting ash, the smoke in her throat. The incessant strobe lights, the piercing sirens. "Even fires."

"You really believe that? Or are you spouting what your missionary parents would say?"

She drew a breath, thinking. "Both."

He shook his head. "How do you do it? Stay so positive."

"How do you stay so grumpy?" Zoey smirked.

"That comes easier."

They rode in silence, save for the soft rock playing from the radio. Yellow wildflowers and green mile markers flashed past the window. Zoey tapped her fingers on the middle console, restless. "Being positive all the time can be hard too."

"Then why are you?" He picked right back up, like the conversation hadn't stalled at all.

"People need me to be."

He frowned. "What about what you need?"

"You sound like Elisa."

"What?"

"Never mind." Zoey adjusted the air vent off her face. "It's just a habit, you know? Keeping people's spirits up, finding the bright side."

"Sometimes there's not one."

"We've had this conversation before. On your boat, remember?" She lowered her voice to imitate his. "*Some people see things that aren't there.*"

He turned down the radio even lower. "But don't you ever just feel like screaming? Letting out steam?"

Yes. "Sometimes."

"But you never do."

Only because last time he appeared with cheesecake and slow dances. She shrugged. "I didn't need to be another burden growing up. My parents were—*are*—missionaries, working with meager budgets and little appreciation. They'd come home from trips and be worn out." She shrugged. "I guess I felt like since I wasn't called to missions myself, I could still serve God by making their lives easier, you know?"

"Noble of you."

She shifted in her seat. "You think so?"

"*No.*" Linc shook his head at her. "You were just stuffing it all down—that's not helpful. Especially as a kid."

"Says the guy who bluntly expresses what he thinks about *everything*."

"Not everything." A muscle jumped in his jaw. "You can't appreciate the sun without a few rain clouds now and then."

"I guess you must *love* the sun, then, Mr. Grumpy."

Another side-eyed look. "I'm just saying it's okay to have a storm come through."

"Storms are scary."

"Rain is necessary."

She leaned back in her seat, shifted her gaze out the window. He was right. She knew that on a logical level, but emotionally . . . it felt dangerous to let go. To actually scream, yell, throw something. Say what you thought.

Release the pressure inside.

Storms came with side effects, as the whole town of Magnolia Bay had seen after Hurricane Anastasia. She glanced at Linc, then at Amelia, before focusing back on the road.

It wasn't worth the risk of widespread damage. They'd made it this far. She couldn't stop shining now.

Or everyone she cared about would suffer.

Fourteen

WHAT KIND OF SCHOOL INSISTS PARents attend a field trip the *first* week?" Linc grumbled. The bus was sticky—so sticky. He crossed his arms over his chest, his shoulder bumping Zoey's in the constricting, peeling leather seats. Overly applied adolescent perfume and body odor competed in the small space, as the bus bounced over a pothole still yet to be fixed on Marsh Street.

"Well, it's the only middle school in Magnolia Bay, for starters." Zoey gripped the seat in front of her, grinning as a row of kids in the back broke into a rousing chorus of *This is the Song That Never Ends*. In her graphic T-shirt and ripped jeans, she didn't look much older than a teenager herself. "And this is what parents do—I'm assuming."

"Then why are we the only ones here besides the teacher?" He gestured with his chin to the front of the long vehicle, where an already-tired-looking woman rode behind the bus driver.

"I don't know. Amelia said Principal Vaughn needed chaperones or the field trip to New Orleans would get canceled." Zoey shrugged. "So here we are."

Yep. Trapped. When he needed to be fixing that loose board at the concession shack and prepping the boat before the next tour tomorrow. "There's so many . . . kids."

"On a school event? Shocking." She rolled her eyes with a little grin. "We couldn't tell Amelia no. I think it's a good sign she asked."

Good point. It'd been five days since their return from her apartment, four days since she started school, and the week had been . . . interesting. Not that he expected their post-run-from-the-diner-talk and impromptu road trip to get her stuff to be a massive breakthrough, but she still kept her distance more than not. Slept with that ratty unicorn. Argued.

Slammed her door a lot.

Ms. Bridges had checked in Wednesday on the phone, and he tried to tell her only the good stuff. Like Amelia had eaten a vegetable on Wednesday without protest and had stopped being rude to their friends. Not that he was too worried about Ms. Bridges taking Amelia back—where was she going to go?

But in the middle of the night, as he lay in bed staring at the ceiling, he wondered if Amelia could ever choose to leave.

Choose the state home over him.

He swallowed. "You're right. Her wanting us to come along seems like a good sign." Either that or Amelia just really wanted to leave school for the day.

"Is that your dad?" A boy's voice whispered from two rows back, near where Amelia sat.

Linc fought the urge to turn, scowl at him. Nosy little scamp.

Amelia's voice was low in return. "Yeah."

"He's so . . . big."

Okay, maybe the kid wasn't all bad. Linc grinned.

Zoey nudged his arm. "If your head gets much bigger, I'm going to have to open the emergency exit window."

He grunted. "Like you even could. You're so behind on your pushups."

The eighth-grade teacher, wearing turquoise wire-rimmed glasses and looking like school had been in session for a whole semester instead of just a week, made her way toward them. A paper airplane bounced off her hair as she sank into the empty chair beside them. She smiled. "So you're Amelia's parents?"

"Stepmother, yes." Zoey shook her hand. "Zoey Lake—Zoey Fontenot."

Hmm. He liked that. Even if theirs wasn't a typical marriage, it sounded . . . nice.

"Penny Thompson." The middle-aged woman shook Linc's hand next. "I'm glad you were able to come. Amelia said you insisted." She smiled. "That's so nice, really. And rare for this age group."

Insisted? Linc frowned. That was hardly the way it went.

Another airplane bounced off the teacher's head and this time stuck in her curls. Zoey snatched it free, tossed it on the floor. "Amelia said that?"

Penny patted her hair. "We didn't need chaperones for this trip, since it's only a few hours and a small group. Principal Vaughn meets us there too, and the museum provides an escort. But it's so refreshing to see parents who want to get involved!"

Uh-huh. Linc turned, caught Amelia's eye. She grinned, wiggled her fingers.

He spun back around. "We've been set up."

Penny frowned. "Pardon?"

"Nothing." Zoey elbowed him in the ribs. "We're happy to be here."

A boy in the back kept singing loudly, off-key. Someone behind him started burping the alphabet. The window ledge stuck to Linc's arm. He nodded, feeling strangled. "Thrilled."

With a confused smile, Penny went back to her seat. Two girls in front of them began taking a string of selfies on their phones, while two boys across the bus started an aggressive game of thumb war.

He nudged Zoey's bag on the floor between their feet. "Got a time machine in that purse of yours?"

"It's possible." Zoey bent to retrieve it. "Which part of time would you like to go back and change?"

Good question. Maybe the part where he said yes to this field trip. There had to be a different way to connect with his daughter than in a bus of screaming kids, especially when he needed to be doing a dozen other things for work. He had been worried enough about getting the tour business off the ground even before he suddenly became responsible for two other people's welfare.

Was this what parenting was like? Constantly choosing between the hard and the harder? The right decision and the best decision? What was more important—time spent bonding with Amelia, or time spent providing for her financially?

His head swam.

Zoey hauled her purse to her lap and began to paw through it, moving a screwdriver and a jump rope out of the way. "You might have to settle for some gum."

A black-and-white photo slipped out the front pocket, and he went to grab it before it could fall to the sticky floor. And paused.

It was a picture of him, from the other week, when he was driving the boat. When he'd been thinking of her.

Why was she carrying around a picture of him?

He glanced at her, but she hadn't seemed to notice what happened as she ducked her head, reaching into the depths of an interior pocket. He quickly tucked the picture back into the oversized bag as she emerged triumphant with a package of peppermint gum.

"Here." She pulled out a stick, handed it to him. "You never answered my question about which part of time you'd change, by the way."

He took the piece, unwrapped it. Popped it in his mouth as he eyed the bag where the photo lived. A rush of warmth spread through his chest. "Maybe I wouldn't change anything after all."

Oh, man. Hadn't meant to say *that* out loud.

Zoey shot him a quick look, brow furrowed, and he quickly chomped into the gum. "I mean, like you said . . . it's a good sign Amelia wanted us here."

Disappointment—was it disappointment?—briefly flooded her expression, then was gone. A passing cloud. She smiled, loosely, the shine not quite meeting her eyes. "Exactly."

Aye. What had he done? Did she know what he had really meant? Had he freaked her out? He'd promised nothing would change, and yet here he was, reading into something as simple as a photo in her purse. It could have been anyone. She probably just was proud of the shot.

He was such an idiot.

Linc scrambled to keep the conversation going, away from the truth. "I mean, even if Amelia just meant this whole thing as a trick to punish us, she's obviously not embarrassed by us enough to hide us from her new friends."

"We could fix that, you know." Zoey wiggled her eyebrows. "Throw some slang her way." She twisted to look over her shoulder, her body angling toward Linc's.

He caught his breath, held it, as she shifted back forward, her gaze locking with his. "What? Too far?"

She meant the slang idea. But the scent of her perfume, the warmth of her side, the memory of her body next to his in the dimly lit kitchen as they danced . . . He swallowed. Nodded. "Yeah. That would be going too far."

Maybe time for him to pull back a little. Before he ruined this very fragile thing he'd created.

Everything with Linc lately felt like two steps forward, two steps back. Not regressing, exactly, but definitely not progressing. At least not in the way she kept daring to imagine.

Zoey stood in front of a portrait in the New Orleans Cabildo museum, the polished wood floors gleaming under the sneakered feet of two dozen eighth graders. The kids had poured off the bus like a pack of hungry wolves earlier, but to their credit, most of them had been properly awed by the ornate historical building on their way in.

Linc had reluctantly taken a group down the other end of the museum hall at the teacher's request, much to Zoey's surprise. But maybe he was trying to avoid her after that—*whatever* that was on the bus. For a minute, she'd thought he'd meant he wouldn't change anything about them. But that was silly. After their kitchen dance and that random comment about time, she was obviously reading into things that simply weren't there. Getting her hopes up.

She knew better.

She turned her attention to Amelia, who had hung back from the group near Zoey, taking in all the paintings with twice as much interest as the rest of her class. Her thin arms wrapped around her T-shirt-clad waist as she gazed at a landscape, so intently Zoey half wondered if she might try to run straight into it, like Harry Potter boarding the train at 9 ¾.

Zoey couldn't help it anymore. She leaned in close. "What do you see?"

Amelia jerked, as if she forgot Zoey was there. She frowned a little. "I was just thinking that some of these are not very good."

Zoey blinked and straightened. "Oh." Not what she'd expected her to say—though Amelia had yet to be real or vulnerable about anything yet.

Took after her father that way.

She started to move to the next portrait, give her space, when Amelia spoke again, her voice smaller. "Kinda makes me feel like maybe I could draw something that was important one day too."

Zoey paused, turned. "I bet you could. You seem to have a natural gift."

A flush tinted her pale cheeks. "You're just saying that because you're my stepmom."

Stepmom, wow. That felt like a promotion from their earlier conversation. "I mean it. I've seen your backpack, all your doodles." Zoey nodded toward the framed hillside speckled with flowers. "Personally, I'd much rather come to a museum with drawings of turtles and cupcakes."

"That would be *so* much more fun." Amelia glanced over her shoulder, to the museum guide and the rest of their class farther down the hallway. "Why are the paintings in museums sometimes so . . . boring?"

"Art is subjective." Zoey shrugged. "A lot of people like this style. The good news is there's plenty of room for all kinds of art."

Amelia squinted at the hillside, tilted her head. "Even mine?"

Oh, but she wanted to give this kid the moon. Make her believe in herself. Zoey nodded, her throat tight. "Especially yours."

And if she felt that way about Amelia, how much more must Linc feel it?

Guilt nudged. She was expecting too much from Linc during a time in his life when he was least capable of giving it. She knew what she was getting herself into from the beginning—an arrangement of convenience, not love. She had no right to want more.

"Maybe you could take art lessons one day." Zoey wished she had the money right now to sign her up. But surely Linc could figure that out eventually. He'd had several more tours book in the last few days. Now if Zoey could just get the claims department to come through, or have the time to figure out some decent recipes, she could help too. Pull her weight. Earn her spot.

"I don't like starting stuff." Amelia twirled a lock of hair around her finger, casting a glance at her classmates laughing in front of a sculpture. "It never works out."

Zoey frowned. "What do you mean?"

"Anytime I've joined a club at school or whatever, we've moved." Amelia shrugged. "It's pointless to try."

For a woman she'd never met, Zoey was really starting to hate Kirsten. She fought the urge to scoop Amelia into a hug. "I think this is different now."

She didn't look convinced. "But I've done this so many times. I can't even imagine feeling like this place is my home. Odds are it won't be for long."

No wonder the kid held back. Zoey frowned. "Well, getting involved is a good way to make friends, meet people. You should take the chance."

"Maybe." She studied the painting again, a frown creasing her young face.

Poor girl. Zoey couldn't promise her that she would be in Magnolia Bay indefinitely, not with things with Kirsten so up in the air—though she did know that Linc would never give her up without a fight.

But how could she convince Amelia she was wanted . . . that she had something to offer right now, exactly as she was?

Zoey took a chance. "You know . . . I'm not the only one who thinks you have talent. Your dad commented on your backpack the other day too." Granted, he'd been complaining she'd left it in the middle of the kitchen, but technically, it was still a true statement.

"Yeah?" Amelia frowned, but her chin lifted a little with interest.

See? The girl cared what her father thought, despite pretending not to. "We both believe in you." That part Zoey *knew* was true.

"Linc doesn't seem to." Amelia looked back at the landscape.

"Your dad"—maybe if Zoey said the word *dad* enough, Amelia would start thinking of him that way—"isn't always great at saying what he feels."

"He sure says what he thinks." Amelia huffed.

"That's different." Zoey shot her a sideways glance. "Pretty sure you get that from him, by the way."

Amelia rolled in her lip. "He doesn't include me in a lot. I think I'm just like a pet at this point. Someone he has to feed and water because it'll make him a bad person if he doesn't."

Zoey's heart ached. "Amelia . . . that's not true."

"Maybe not, but we never do anything."

"It's not been long."

"He hasn't invited me on the boat, or to the gym or fishing."

"He doesn't think you'd want to go." Zoey raised an eyebrow. "Is that why you tricked him into coming today? Because you assumed he wouldn't come otherwise?"

"Yeah."

Oh, Linc. Zoey drew a deep breath. "Keep giving him a chance, okay? You guys actually have more in common than you think."

She smirked. "I doubt that."

Linc approached from the other end of the hallway, then, as if they'd somehow summoned him. Their eyes met, and Zoey's stomach flipped, and suddenly she was back on the bus in close proximity. Noting the way his shirt sleeve cut into his bicep as he braced one arm on the back of the seat. Feeling the weight of his stare at he suggested maybe he wouldn't change things after all.

He stopped in front of the landscape portrait, gave it a once-over, and then scowled. "Why are museum paintings so boring?"

Amelia snorted. Zoey covered her mouth with her hand. Nudged her. "See?"

"See what?" Linc frowned.

Amelia pursed her lips, and then they both burst out laughing.

"Women." Linc shook his head. "I better get back to the boys."

Zoey watched him walk away, then shared another secret smile with Amelia. Her heart warmed, and she even risked slinging her arm around Amelia's shoulder as they headed to join the rest of the class.

If she could break through and connect with Amelia, surely Linc would be next. Zoey swallowed, heart thumping. And then maybe . . . *maybe* . . . he would be in a place to want the same things Zoey wanted.

Fifteen

AH, FINALLY. LINC CLOSED HIS EYES and drew a deep breath of metal, sweat, and chalk. *Home.* His workout routine had been off, to say the least, since the sudden arrival of two women in his house.

He had a lot of reps to catch up on.

Thunder rumbled overhead. While today's storm was frustrating in that it canceled one of the tours he desperately needed, it also provided a chance to kill a few birds with one stone—or rather, kettlebell.

He shot a glance at Amelia, whose tangled mane was pulled up in a ponytail. She planted her hands on her skinny, shorts-clad hips as she cast a dubious look around the gym, surprisingly vacant for a Saturday afternoon. At least there wouldn't be a lot of witnesses for this potential train wreck. Of course, that all depended on how Amelia and Zoey worked out.

"Why are we here, again?" Amelia asked.

Because his mental health was tanking under all this recent stress? Because if he didn't lift something heavy, he might actually lose his mind? Because Zoey had told him about her and Amelia's museum talk yesterday, and challenged Linc to initiate doing things with Amelia? Pick a reason.

Not that he could say most of those without throwing Zoey under the bus.

"Because I'm going to show both of you a healthy way of taking out frustration." Linc pointed at Amelia. "And it's not by running away or slamming your door every time you don't get your way." He then swiveled to point at Zoey. "And it's not by pretending that you're not frustrated in the first place."

"The door thing works fine for me," Amelia whispered to Zoey, who grinned as she dropped a backpack on the bench by the door. The two of them had been all giggly since yesterday's field trip, a fact that made him happy and also incredibly jealous. Why did she trust Zoey so much more?

"Don't mind him. He just wants to show off." Zoey, wearing a tank top and running shorts, stage-whispered back, making sure Linc heard.

He tried to scowl again as he headed onto the matted floor, but she wasn't far off from the truth. Okay, maybe she was completely on target. Still, what he said was true too. It'd been five days since Amelia had started school, and she still grumbled that she didn't have any real friends. That the homework was harder than in Lafayette. That she didn't know her way around town.

None of which seemed true, as she yammered on about some kid named Sarah regularly, could easily get to Chug a Mug and Magnolia Blossom, and had A's so far in her classes.

He was starting to think teenagers just enjoyed complaining.

"What do those do?" Amelia poked at the J-cups mounted on the tall steel rig.

"They let you adjust the height of your bar on the rack." He pointed across the gym, to the barbells resting in their stands. "You won't be doing any of that today. Not on day one."

Though the idea did sound fun. Get his kid interested in fitness, share the hobby. Teach her how to power clean, squat snatch. There was something so empowering about throwing around a few hundred pounds when life felt out of control.

He figured they could all use a bit of that power lately. "Remember when we talked about endorphins?" he asked.

Amelia scrunched her face. "Is this about to be a science lesson? Because it's Saturday."

He ignored that. "Endorphins are proteins in your brain. They make you happy."

"And exercising gives you those?" Amelia looked doubtful.

"They really do." Zoey began bunching her hair into a ponytail. "I promise."

Amelia shrugged. "Okay. If you say so."

"Let's do it then." Amelia cracked her knuckles. "Hand me a bar."

"In this family, pushups always come first." Zoey dropped to the mats on her hands and knees. "Come on, might as well get this over with."

She'd said *family*. A knot pressed against his throat, and he coughed. Man, he'd been living with women too long if he was getting this sappy over a single word.

But it took a bit of the sting off Amelia's lack of trust in him, compared to her obvious trust in Zoey. They *were* a family—and the reason they'd even started this unlikely unit in the first place was paying off. Further confirmation that he needed Zoey in his life.

In their lives.

Though after that whole bus slip-up, he still needed to keep his guard up with Zoey, keep as much distance as the same household would allow.

Kind of hard when they were supposed to be in love in front of Amelia.

Amelia reluctantly knelt beside Zoey and mirrored her position.

Both of their forms were terrible, but it made them think they were actually doing a pushup, so he let it go. Never mind the fact their chests were a mile away from the mat.

"He has . . . to do them . . . too." Amelia gasped as her thin arms wobbled.

Zoey shifted into a knee pushup. "Try these."

They actually had the right form that time. Linc moved into position next to Zoey, set himself into a plank, and then casually stuck his left arm behind his back. Pushed up on just his right. It took three reps before they noticed.

"A one-arm pushup?" Zoey shoved back on her heels, out of breath. "Oh my gosh."

"What *are* you?" Amelia scowled. "Alien?"

He sat up, chest on fire, refusing to show it. He shrugged. "Do more pushups, you'll get there."

Zoey tilted her head. "Not sure that's a personal goal of mine."

"Bet he can't do a handstand pushup." Amelia's dark brows shot up in challenge. "I saw that on YouTube."

He winced. "You're probably right."

She wasn't.

He walked to the nearest clear piece of wall, making a show of looking confused. "So I just, like, what? Flip into a handstand?"

"Yeah, and then do a pushup while you're upside down." Amelia stood to join him, folded her arms. "If you can, anyway."

"Like this?" He easily launched into a handstand, feet smacking the wall. He pulled his legs straight up, no longer using the wall for balance, and, bracing his wrists, dipped into a pushup. Two. Three.

His pecs were on fire, his shoulders lit up, but the upside-down, shocked expression on his daughter's face made his inevitable ice bath later worth it.

"Maybe I'll do a few more pushups after all," Amelia mumbled under her breath as she walked back to her mat, but not before he caught the awe in her eyes.

"Well done, Super-Dad." Zoey joined him as he stood upright, lowering her voice, her own gaze lit with admiration. Over his actual pushup, or the way he'd impressed his daughter, he wasn't sure.

Hopefully both.

"My cape's at the cleaners." The blood rushed out of his head, and he steadied himself on the wall. Or maybe that was a rush from the look Zoey gave him.

"Wow, you're actually cracking jokes. The gym *does* make you happy."

So did she.

Zoey looked over her shoulder at Amelia, who was cranking out a few knee pushups with surprising speed. "Any more phone calls from Ms. Bridges?"

He rested one shoulder against the wall. "Not since the last one you knew about."

Ms. Bridges checked in semi-weekly, but hadn't had any further updates on Kirsten. But this past call, she'd started throwing around court terminology. He'd hidden in the pantry on the phone, facing a row of canned vegetables and lowering his voice to a whisper. "Amelia's not ready for permanent. There's no reason to rush this."

Ms. Bridges had hummed under her breath. "Amelia's not ready, or you're not?"

"*She's* not." He'd hissed. "Making this official in court with her mom still MIA would spook her. Poke the bear."

The bear being, of course, the hormonal teenager who alternated between sitting between him and Zoey on the couch at night, laughing at sitcom reruns, and slamming her door hard enough to shake the house when she got upset.

"I understand. But sometimes what's best for Amelia isn't what's easiest."

Linc sighed. "Am I legally at risk of losing her if I don't take this step soon?"

"Possibly." Ms. Bridges' voice pitched with concern. "It just depends on when—or if—Ms. West returns, and what she is willing to do when she does."

So, once again, everything was up to Kirsten. Linc pinched the bridge of his nose. "I don't want to mess this up—we're finally on the same page, the three of us."

"Getting married was a smart move," Ms. Bridges said. "It'll look good to the judge if this ends up in a trial of some kind."

His heart lurched. "You think that will happen?"

"Unlikely. Though, unfortunately, I've been in this industry long enough to know to expect anything. Especially the worst."

Hadn't they all had enough of that? So now he had a decision to make about a court hearing. Should he move forward now and risk losing the progress they'd made with Amelia? Or risk losing her in a different way if Kirsten showed back up again?

"Can I try next?" Zoey's voice jerked him back to the gym, to the hope in her eyes as she eyed the wall behind him.

He scoffed. "Are you crazy? You can't even do a regular pushup."

"Spot me."

Before he could agree—or, more likely, protest—she kicked up into a handstand. Or rather, a handstand attempt. Her bottom end slammed into the wall with more force than she intended, and her legs crumpled instead of shooting up. One sneaker clocked Linc in the jaw, and he stumbled back, reaching at the last minute to steady her.

But she took them both down.

They landed with a heap on the mats, his fall slightly more controlled than hers. She flipped onto her side, face flushed red and laughing. "Did that count?"

He lay on his back next to her, rubbing his jaw. It clicked. "Definitely did not."

She inched closer to him, propping up on her elbow, still giggling. Her ponytail flopped over her shoulder, and her eyes lit with laughter as she looked down at him. "I should at least get points for bravery."

Linc started to respond with sarcasm, but something about the way she hovered over him, that light in her gaze, the genuine joy—the real stuff, not that manufactured, forced rainbow crap—stopped him.

Still lying flat, he reached up and tucked a strand of hair behind her ear instead. "I think you're one of the bravest people I know." *Aye*. So much for distance.

Zoey's eyes widened, and her bubbling smile dialed to a simmer. Her gaze studied his, more seriously this time, and he forced himself not to look away, not to hide. She deserved the compliment, plain and simple.

Deserved a lot more, actually.

"Thank you." The words were a whisper on her lips, and he wanted to catch them with his own. He'd kissed her at the courthouse, yeah, but that hadn't counted. He'd made sure. Because he'd promised nothing would change. Nothing could change.

Yet right now, he suddenly wanted *everything* to change.

They held eye contact. His breath hitched. Her eyes darted to his mouth. Then—

"Look!" Amelia shouted from across the floor. "I'm doing it."

They craned their heads in time to see her perform a perfectly executed pushup.

"Nice job!" Zoey hopped to her feet, clapping. "You'll be ready for that handstand way before I am."

Linc ambled to his feet, a little more slowly. His jaw throbbed, but it was a mild inconvenience compared to the sudden ache in his chest. What had just happened? What had he almost *let* happen?

The excitement lingering on Amelia's face as Zoey congratulated her reminded him what they were really there for—her. The last thing Amelia, or Zoey for that matter, needed was for Linc to take stupid risks with their family. If Zoey had expected more in their marriage, she'd have made that clear. It was up to him to hold to what he promised. They'd stay best friends and raise his daughter together, without pressure or expectation for anything more.

Because in Linc's experience, *more* always led to *less*.

"Did you see that?" Zoey called to him, ponytail swishing as she pointed to Amelia. Her eyes lit with pride, and his heart twisted. Losing Zoey wasn't an option. He'd rather keep her forever as just a friend than risk not having her at all. A brief moment of chemistry wasn't worth everything else.

Linc nodded, crossing his arms over his chest. "Sure did." He watched his daughter attempt a one-arm pushup and chuckled as she nearly face-planted on the black mat. Looked like he lived with two brave women.

He drew a breath. Maybe it was time to call Ms. Bridges back. Because at this point, he couldn't bear to lose either of them.

Sixteen

INC LEANED BACK IN THE CAPTAIN'S chair of his pontoon as he killed the engine, stretched out his legs. "You know, you guys could just outright invite us somewhere sometime, quit tricking us."

Especially on his own boat.

Not that he really minded. The evening breeze was the perfect temperature, the sky clear, the salt water warm as the wake sprayed his face. Zoey had just handed him a cold drink from the cooler, which paired perfectly with the spicy crawfish meat pies Elisa had baked.

He'd blame the endorphins from the gym for his good mood, but—his eyes darted to Zoey—he wasn't sure science could fully back that up.

"We didn't think you'd come properly celebrate your elopement if we didn't make up some story to get you to the dock." Noah sat next to Elisa, portside, his arm draped around her shoulders. She leaned against him, a contented smile on her face as she sipped from a thermos.

"Yeah, you two have been sort of MIA lately." Cade, sitting

opposite them starboard with Rosalyn, air-toasted Linc with his soda. "Not that I blame you, newlyweds."

Yikes. Awkward territory. He forced his gaze not to drift to Zoey, though it felt a bit like fighting a magnetic pull. "Don't forget that small, time-consuming matter of suddenly raising a teenager."

"Speaking of, nice call, having Mama D take Amelia shopping with her new gift cards." Zoey pointed at Elisa. "I'm guessing that was your idea."

The blonde grinned. "Guilty as charged. Seemed like a win-win."

"Owen, drop that anchor for me, will you?" Linc pointed to the bench seat nearest his friend. "We can hang here a bit."

Owen stood to open the compartment, stumbling as a wave bumped the boat. He lurched forward. "Oops."

"Not again." Zoey shot Linc a knowing smirk as she rummaged through the cooler near Cade. "At least that one wasn't possibly my fault."

"Good thing. I don't think dolphins are going to save me a second time." Linc snorted.

"Just look at them." Cade shook his head with a *tsk*. "Already obnoxious with the inside jokes."

"Oh hush. It's cute." Rosalyn nudged him in the ribs.

Elisa shot Zoey a look, one Linc couldn't quite interpret.

Owen dropped anchor, took his seat again. The wind mussed his usually kempt hair, making him look more pirate than banker. "Any apple tarts left?"

"Pass the meat pies too—unless Cade's finished them all." Linc held out his hand.

Cade dug in the picnic basket and passed Owen a tart, then leaned forward, swung the woven container toward Linc. "Have at it. I have no reason to stress-eat now."

"I'll take some credit for that." Rosalyn tilted her head back and kissed his cheek.

The boat erupted into a mix of *awws* and *ewws*, depending.

Zoey maneuvered her way toward Linc, sparkling water in hand. The wind blew her hair, which was loose and tucked behind her ears, causing her wide eyes to appear even bigger. "I should probably sit with you." She lowered her voice, back to the group. "You know. Keep up appearances."

Oh, right. They were supposed to be mushy newlyweds.

So much for his determination to keep his distance.

"Sure." Linc set down his pie and looked around to see which seat she meant. But before he realized there wasn't one, she plopped on his lap and cracked open her canned drink, as casually as if she were sitting on a lawn chair.

His throat ran dry, his back stiff. Her body warmed his leg, the scent of her shampoo competing with the salty air and the fried apple tarts. Linc swallowed. Where the heck did he put his hands? He picked up his neglected pie with one, and the other, he attempted to rest on the steering wheel. But that just braced his arm against Zoey's side, his forearm grazing her shoulder, bare in a thin-strapped tank.

If he moved again, it'd be obvious. He'd have to deal.

Again—not that he really minded. He should, though. He really, really should.

"So, how's family life now that it's been a week?" Rosalyn shifted positions near Cade, pulling her long legs up on the bench seat beside them.

"Yeah, is everyone bonding?" Elisa tucked her arm through Noah's flannel-clad one, resting her head on his shoulder.

"It's a work in progress. Good days and bad." Zoey shrugged. "Today was good, I think."

It was, wasn't it? Getting better by the second, at this rate. And now that he'd finished his tart, Linc's left hand had nowhere to go except to reach around and rest on Zoey's knee.

She glanced back at him, a measure of surprise in her eyes, and then understanding dawned. She assumed he was doing that for show, because the other couples were snuggled up.

He tried to convince himself that was why too, but his erratic heart rate wasn't buying it. Neither was the way he wanted to lean in, inhale her hair, soak in her warmth.

Oh, brother. He should throw himself into the bay, shock this out of his senses. He knew better. Zoey was obviously nothing like Kirsten, but heartbreak was heartbreak.

And he and Zoey had too much to lose.

Owen wiped his hands on a napkin. "Any updates on Amelia's mother?"

Linc's hand tightened on Zoey's knee, and she reached over, covered his knuckles with her own. Supporting him. "Sort of."

He double-tapped Zoey's knee, which she accurately took as a cue to explain what happened last week at the apartment. "We're still in limbo." Zoey shrugged. "But Amelia seems to be taking it in stride. We haven't had any issues lately, and we're all getting along better."

"I still feel bad about that picture frame." Rosalyn winced, covering her face with one hand. "I had no idea it would trigger her that way."

Zoey shook her head. "You couldn't have known."

"Yeah, it was a nice gesture." Linc cleared his throat. "We appreciate it. All of it."

The boat grew quiet, everyone processing the shock that he'd said that out loud. Well, if anything was going to make him eat a little humble pie, it'd be his daughter.

Though he much preferred the crawfish ones.

"So here's a question." Cade leaned forward, bracing his elbows on his knees. The wind tugged at his shirt collar, but his gelled hair didn't move. "Some of us were debating this at your surprise reception last week—how did you guys meet?"

Uh-oh. Linc stiffened.

"Yeah, I asked because I had no idea." Rosalyn raised her hand. "Everyone has a different theory."

"And we're all wrong." Noah laughed.

"Yeah, I told them you two just always knew each other." Elisa grinned. "But that's probably not right, either."

Zoey hesitated, twisting sideways to catch his eye. He automatically steadied her with both hands on her arms, her skin soft under his calloused hands. His palms tingled with the contact.

"You want to tell them?" she asked.

"I don't tell stories."

Then he quickly realized she wasn't asking if he wanted to be the one to tell the story—she was asking if it was *okay* to tell the story. The one no one knew.

On second thought, yeah, he better tell this one. "I mean, yeah, why not?" He didn't have to tell *all* the details—like the ones Zoey herself had only learned last week.

She twisted back around, and he took advantage of the excuse to loop his arms around her. Her proximity somehow simultaneously grounded and unsettled him. "So one summer, back when I was around fourteen, my fos—my, uh, aunt decided to host this cooking class for local kids." Geez. One sentence in and he'd almost slipped.

"I remember that." Cade grunted. "My mom tried to get me to sign up. Thankfully, my dad didn't make me."

"Too bad." Rosalyn rolled her eyes. "Maybe then you wouldn't burn water."

"I don't have to know how to cook. One of our best friends is a chef." He grinned over her head at Elisa, who shook her head back.

"Anyway." Linc shook his head. "Zoey came to the class."

"So *that's* where it all began." Owen nodded, eyes shining with approval. "Did you make beignets that first day?"

"We didn't bake cookies, I can tell you that." Zoey squeezed Linc's hand.

The inside joke warmed his chest. He leaned around Zoey's hair fluttering in the wind, proud of himself for not pausing to take a big whiff. "They were making gumbo. So, Zoey shows up—"

She chuckled. "My scrawny, ten-year-old self."

"I thought she was eight, tops."

Zoey slapped his wrist.

"What? It's important to the story." He chuckled. "They were putting all the ingredients in the pot when I came through the kitchen—"

"Too cool for school," Zoey interjected.

"I was *not*."

"You were so moody." She turned around to look at him again, a smile playing on her lips. "Wore a leather jacket in the summer."

Linc shrugged, unbothered. "That proves nothing."

"Come on. You were like a cross between a teenage Mr. Darcy and Danny Zuko."

He grimaced. "I know you're not comparing me to a musical from the seventies."

"But you don't mind being compared to a brooding foot-in-his-mouth fictional hero?"

He held her gaze. "He got the girl, didn't he?"

Linc only then realized the entire boatful of his friends were staring directly at them as if watching a movie, starry-eyed with giant grins. Except for Elisa, whose brow furrowed.

Aye. He'd gotten carried away.

Zoey's questioning gaze held his, then once again, it seemed to register that he was flirting for pretenses. "I guess he did."

"Technically, Danny got Sandy too," Cade pointed out. "He just wore tighter pants."

Linc looked away, shifted his weight under Zoey. "So anyway, they were cooking, and Zoey dropped half her ingredients and didn't notice. I pointed out the shrimp, but she thought I was *calling* her a shrimp, so she came after me."

Rosalyn nearly sprayed her water. She wiped her mouth with the back of her hand, eyes wide. "Are you serious?"

"Jumped right on my back like a spider monkey." Linc could still feel the weight of her, if he thought back hard enough. Her tiny fists pummeling his shoulders. "Started yelling for me to take it back."

"Oh, my gosh." Elisa's eyes sparkled with laughter. "Zoey!"

"What? He tried to scrape me off on a door frame." She chuckled, shoulders bobbing.

"You were *choking* me."

She winced. "I finally realized what he'd meant and apologized."

"Did your aunt kick Zoey out of the class?" Owen asked.

"Actually, no. She thought it was funny." It was what happened next that changed things. Linc hesitated. Maybe that was enough of the story . . .

But Zoey wasn't done. "A few classes later, Linc's aunt had to take a phone call. She'd always told us not to use her professional-grade knife set without her permission, but I knew she'd be right back."

"Uh-oh." Elisa scrunched her face.

"I tried to hurry and chop the pecans for my brownies and just . . . missed." Zoey rubbed her hand, as if remembering the cut. "Blood was *everywhere*. Linc came through the kitchen and didn't even blink an eye, just grabbed the first aid kit and started fixing me up."

"Oh, man. Did you get busted?" Noah asked.

"No. She still doesn't know to this day." He'd been so scared that if his foster mom knew what had happened, that there had been an accident, they'd lose their license. That he'd get sent elsewhere.

That he'd be alone again.

He shook off the memories, that gut-deep sensation of pending loss that never fully left. "Anyway, joke's on me. Apparently whatever Band-Aid I used on Zoey's finger stuck her to me permanently."

She leaned into him, smirked. "Hasn't been able to get rid of me since."

"But you moved up north, right? After high school?" Cade frowned. "Did you two keep in touch then?"

"A little." They didn't know—or need to know—that Zoey was part of why he came back. "I moved with my aunt and uncle after I graduated, but got a scholarship to a different college and eventually came back to start Boiling Bayou."

And to be near Zoey, near her light. Her warmth.

Somehow, her annoying, friendship-stalking behavior all through his high school years remained one of the only familiar things he had left, after his foster parents decided their job in raising him was done at eighteen.

After Kirsten and he had started a snowball in motion that turned into an avalanche fourteen years later.

"That's really cute." Elisa brushed tart crumbs off her lap. "I can't believe I never heard that story."

Good. The more times it got told, the more likely it'd be someone would find out his aunt and uncle weren't related to him. That he was a foster kid.

Granted, it wasn't as big a deal as it had been when he'd moved back to Magnolia Bay. The description wasn't a label he stuck on himself anymore as a grown man with a growing business. It was part of his past—and now, a large part of his motivation in doing whatever it took to keep Amelia out of the system.

He watched the wind toss Zoey's hair, the way she held it back with one hand while trying to catch the piece of tart Elisa aimed at her mouth. The way she laughed as it bounced off her nose, hit his shoe.

He just didn't want to get into the *why* of his being a foster kid. Not even with Zoey.

Seventeen

F UN PARTY." ELISA STOOD ON THE DOCK holding her woven picnic basket, a slight smirk on her face. The aroma of crawfish pies and salt water drifted over them.

Zoey followed her gaze to the end of the pier, where Linc and Noah secured the boat. Dusk settled over the bay, and she shivered a little in her tank and jeans. Owen, Cade, and Rosalyn had already cleaned up the party trash and left, and now she and Elisa waited under the glow of the security light for the guys. "It *was* fun . . . but somehow I get the feeling that's not really what you mean?"

"I'm talking about you and Linc. The PDA, the adorable meet-cute story . . ."

Oh, that. Zoey winced.

Elisa pursed her lips. "Don't worry, you two have everyone fooled—to the point you're fooling yourselves."

"What do you mean?" But Zoey knew. She knew exactly.

Elisa shifted the basket to her other hip. "Come on now, sugar. Don't try to convince me that while you're actually married, you're just *pretending* to be in love."

"Some of us more than others." Zoey groaned.

"You love Linc." A soft statement, not a question.

And it wasn't a question. Hadn't been for a long time. Zoey nodded, watching to make sure the guys stayed out of earshot. "I've always loved Linc." She huffed a breath. "Maybe since that moment he put a Band-Aid on my finger."

Elisa shot her a knowing look. "And now he's put a ring on your finger."

Zoey looked down at it, twisted her hand so it caught the glow of the overhead light. "You know it's not that simple."

Elisa hugged the basket. "It could be."

"Not if he doesn't feel the same." Zoey clenched her left hand into a fist, hiding the evidence. "I agreed to our terms."

"Terms? Marriage isn't a contract." Elisa winced. "Well, okay, technically it is. But you know what I mean. It's so much *more* than that."

"But I committed to this, the way it is. So I have to see it through." Zoey unfisted her hand, stared again at the gold band. "At least for now."

"Giving yourself an out isn't going to solve your problem."

"I'm not giving myself an out." Stars began to prick through the gray sky above. From the dock, Noah laughed at something Linc said. "It's more the fear that Linc's going to give me one."

"Then you should talk to him. Tell your husband how you feel." Elisa's tone, gentle but firm, pierced Zoey's convictions. But easy for her friend to say—she had the fairy tale. Zoey had . . . well, she had Papa Bear and cold porridge.

"You don't understand. If I tell Linc I want the real thing with him, and he doesn't feel the same way . . . it'll ruin everything. We wouldn't be able to stay together. Then all that we've done for Amelia, all her progress and security, would be gone." Zoey's heart cramped at the mere thought.

"Back up a minute." Elisa finally set the basket down at her feet, planted her hands on her hips. "You said *we wouldn't be able to stay together.*"

"Right."

Her eyes took on a knowing sheen. "*That's* what you're afraid of. You think the only way to stay with Linc is to keep denying your feelings for him. To hold him at arm's length."

"So?" Zoey huffed. "I don't exactly see him coming any closer."

"You two sure looked cozy on the boat tonight."

"He was just putting on a show for you guys. Keeping suspicions at bay." Zoey waved one hand in the air. "I have zero proof that tonight—or the dance in the kitchen—was anything more than him doing what we agreed to do."

"Dance in the kitchen?" Elisa's brows shot higher. "You skipped that part."

"It's nothing. He was just being sweet, letting me have a wedding dance."

"Linc." Elisa squinted. "Being *sweet*. And you say you have no proof?"

Zoey cast another look at the two shadowed figures leaving the boat. "I know he cares for me. I've always known that."

The fact that he'd let her—and basically no one else—stick around all these years was proof enough of that.

She lowered her voice. "But that's not romantic love or passion. That's not the grow-old-together kind of stuff that lasts. It's just friendship. Loyalty."

Elisa sighed. "I think you're overthinking this because you're scared."

"And I think you're under-thinking this because you're happy and want me to be too." Zoey reached over and took Elisa's hand, drew it up to her own throat in a begging posture. "Please, I'm begging you. My wedding is over. Let's focus on yours, okay? Don't I have a bridesmaids fitting this week?" Not that she had any idea how she was going to pay the balance.

Elisa rolled her eyes, but squeezed Zoey's hand in return, allow-ing the subject change. "You do, and you better not be late or I'll put shoulder pads in yours."

Zoey released her and clapped. "I'll be there with bells on."

"Coming from you, that's a threat." Elisa grinned. "Honestly . . . I am getting excited."

"As you should be. It's going to be a great night." Whew, just in time. They were striding up the dock now, Linc's shadow significantly more hulk-sized than Noah's.

"Ready to go?" Linc called toward her.

Oh, this part could go to her head too. Being a couple, a team. Belonging.

"Ready when you are." She thought about throwing a 'babe' at the end of it, but her heart had been through enough confusion for one night.

"They're probably talking wedding stuff." Noah grinned at his bride-to-be. "That's usually what I catch her doing these days."

"Speaking of, don't worry." Elisa winked as she picked up the picnic basket, handed it to Noah. "I changed your name in the program to Zoey Fontenot."

Her stomach swirled. "Great, thanks."

"And your title to matron of honor, instead of maid of honor."

Zoey knew what she was doing—exposure therapy. Tossing around words to make Zoey remember she was married. Trying to make it feel normal.

She cast Linc a look as they waved goodbye to Noah and headed for his truck. Normal was one thing. Anyone could eventually get used to something, to consider it normal.

But would it ever feel real?

Fifteen minutes later, she and Linc were on their way home, just the two of them, windows down, radio turned low. He hadn't touched her since their impromptu story time in the boat, when she'd sat in his lap. But she could still feel his fingerprints on her arms, her knee, her waist. Like tiny tattoos, permanent claims. She'd always be his, for better or for worse.

And not just because she spoke those words at a courthouse.

"Mama D is bringing Amelia home?"

Linc's deep voice broke the silence, making Zoey jump.

"That's right." She cleared her throat, hating how stiff her voice sounded. Could he sense her tension? Would he guess why? Obviously he had no issue being close to her like that on the boat, probably didn't think anything more of it than the hugs and high fives she'd bestowed over the years. She might just give up her beignet business all over again if she could remain as naive to the chemistry as he seemed to be.

Or worse yet—maybe he wasn't naive. Maybe it simply wasn't there for him.

And that's why he could easily marry his best friend.

Mama D's car was waiting in the long drive as they pulled up—thank goodness. Zoey didn't want to be alone with Linc a moment longer. Not until she got her head on straight.

Amelia got out of the car, arms loaded with shopping bags. Mama D slid out the driver's side, shielding her eyes from Linc's headlights as he swung the truck into reverse and parked. She wore a floral blouse over hot pink pants—the exact shade of her lipstick. Zoey could tell from here. Another new color experiment?

"Have a nice date, lovebirds?" Mama D grinned as they climbed out.

Linc grunted. "All you liars. Can't just invite a guy to hang out."

"Not when the guy always says no." Mama D grinned bigger. "You're welcome."

Amelia said nothing, stared down at her bags.

Hmm.

"We had a good time." Zoey shot Linc a pointed look. "Why don't you help Amelia with her haul?"

Linc glanced between her and Amelia before taking the hint,

fisting most of the bags out of her hands. "What'd you get?" He led the way up the stairs to the porch, good-naturedly nudging her with an elbow. "These better not be a bunch of crop tops."

The screen door slapped shut behind them. Zoey turned to Mama D. "Is everything okay?"

"Oh, we had a lovely time." Mama D reached up, fiddled with the cross necklace dangling from a silver chain around her neck. "Went shopping and to the Burger Barn for dinner."

"Not Magnolia Blossom? Wow." Zoey grinned. Maybe she'd misread the tension earlier. She was full of her own right now, it wouldn't be unlikely for her to—

"There was just the one incident." Mama D's hot pink lips curled downward.

So she hadn't misread. "What happened?"

Mama D cast a quick look over her shoulder at the lights glowing inside the house. "She ran out of money pretty quick, as you can see from all the bags. She bought mostly clothes, though I think she found some cheap jewelry too. A ring, was it? Or earrings . . ."

"You're stalling."

"I am." Mama D wrung her hands. "I hate to get her in trouble, because she put it back. But I thought you should know."

"Put what back?" Then the implication registered. Her stomach clenched. "Wait. Did she steal something?"

Mama D nodded, so slight her head barely moved. Her gray brow furrowed. "A floor model cell phone."

"*A cell phone?*" Oh, Amelia. Zoey briefly closed her eyes, sighed. Linc was going to hate this. After all the progress they'd been making . . .

"She put it back, like I said." Mama zipped the cross faster along the chain. "I saw it immediately in her purse, thank heavens. She grumbled a little about no one using it, and it going to waste—but put it back without further issue."

Was that supposed to be comforting? That she didn't fight Mama D in the middle of a store?

Zoey pressed her fingers against her temples. "How do we handle this? We completely skipped potty training and the 'don't touch the hot stove' lessons most parents get to teach first." She ran her hands down her cheeks, her chest heating. "Now we have to go straight to the 'stealing is wrong' lessons?"

Mama D murmured in sympathy. "I know it's a lot, hon. Parenting isn't for the faint of heart. But you'll get it." She hesitated. "That's actually why I told you first—because you'll know the right way to tell Linc. Maybe you can even talk to Amelia before he has to know."

There it was—Linc's bad-boy reputation, biting him. Everyone assumed he'd have a temper, go off on Amelia just because he was a grumpy kind of guy. Zoey knew better.

But while she didn't think he'd yell at Amelia, it *was* entirely possible he'd say the wrong thing right out of the gate. He needed time to process this information before he addressed it.

Zoey sighed. "I'll talk to her. Break the ice."

"Good." Mama D nodded briskly. "We had a wonderful time outside of that. She warmed up to me after a little while." She chuckled. "I think my springing for ice cream helped."

"Thanks for taking her out." Zoey hugged her, and for a moment, she couldn't help but wonder if her own mom would have been this involved. She couldn't even tell her she was married yet because of the lack of cell service where they were serving.

But this wasn't about Zoey. It was about Amelia.

She pulled back. "Guess I better go figure this out."

Mama D slid back inside her car, lifted one hand in a wave. "I have no doubt you will, dear."

Zoey stared toward the lit house and blew out a breath. That made one of them.

Linc had gone to bed roughly half an hour ago, but once again, couldn't sleep. Too many thoughts jumping through his mind, like errant sheep. Or what had Zoey said—rabid squirrels?

Would the tours be enough to keep Boiling Bayou in the black before next crawfish season? What else could he do until spring to keep things going?

Why wouldn't Amelia tell him about her night? Was that a normal teenager thing or a she-didn't-want-to-talk-to-him-specifically thing?

Would Kirsten come back? Should he give Ms. Bridges the green light for court?

And the one thought that kept circling, the most rabid of them all. The only one not in question form.

He wanted to kiss Zoey.

No denying it. He'd thought about it in the kitchen that night, at the gym earlier. But this . . . this was different. This was need.

This was bad.

Linc flopped on his side, tucked the pillow under his neck. The ceiling fan whirred overhead. He'd finally confessed the truth to Noah while they were docking the boat and the women stood on the pier, chatting about wedding plans. He sort of figured there was a good chance Zoey had already told Elisa the conditions of their marriage, anyway, so Noah was the safest bet. And Linc had to say something.

Noah hadn't seemed surprised, which meant he had probably been right about Zoey spilling the beans to Elisa. "Sometimes relationships take time to develop."

Linc had wrapped the anchor, set it back in the bench compartment. "We've been friends forever—you heard the story."

"Talking about more than friends, bro." Noah clapped his shoulder. "You remember how long it took me and Elisa to figure it out. We went from one romantic summer as teenagers, to essentially worst enemies—until my grandfather's will forced us to work together. Ended the family feud."

"Unfortunately, I don't have a grandfather giving me instructions from beyond the grave." Linc snorted.

"No, but you've got a daughter from the past giving you motivation. I'd say that's pretty close." Noah grinned, then sobered. "Look, you made the decisions that put you here. So why not fully commit? Give it a chance."

"I don't think Zoey wants that." Linc brushed it off as thinking of her, trying to look noble. But deep down, it wasn't so much fear that Zoey didn't want to take a chance with him. It was fear that she *did*.

And that he'd still eventually end up alone. Not be someone worth staying for.

Judging by the look Noah shot him, he probably could tell Linc's altruism was misplaced. But he didn't push it. "You're married now, man, so you got time. Pray about it."

He'd shut the compartment lid. "I'm sure Zoey's got that covered." God would rather hear from her, anyway. Not that he'd tell Noah that.

Noah stepped onto the dock, turned to look down at Linc as if he'd somehow heard it anyway. "You can pray too, you know. There's no quota on topics per household."

"I know." Linc hesitated. "I'm just out of practice."

He believed in God as a kid, thanks to his mother's early efforts—he still did. But his foster parents hadn't instilled much of a lifeline in that department over the years, and getting tangled up with misdemeanors, recreational drugs, and then Kirsten hadn't helped. After all that, he'd kept his head down, went to church as often as he could get up on Sundays. Figured he owed it to God to straighten up. But that's where he kept his distance.

Zoey believed God worked teenage mistakes and commercial fires for good, and he could see her logic there.

It was much harder to see the good in his own father turning him over to the courts.

Linc abruptly threw back the covers, stood up. Enough sheep counting. He pulled on a T-shirt and house shoes, the boring gray slippers only reminding him of Zoey's smiley-faced ones, and there went the rabid squirrels again.

Probably wasn't anything good in the fridge, but even a glass of water might help at this point.

He shuffled into the hallway, pausing at the light shining down the hall from Amelia's room. What was she still doing up? Last he'd glimpsed the clock—quite a few squirrels ago—it'd been nearing eleven p.m.

He headed to knock on the door, which stood just a little ajar, but stopped again at the muffled voices inside. Amelia's—and Zoey's. He shook his head. Leave it to Zoey to initiate girl talk at nearly midnight. He started to head for the kitchen.

"... don't tell Dad."

He stopped short. Craned his head.

"Amelia, I can't do that."

He released a little sigh at Zoey's logical response. Of course they wouldn't gang up on him like that.

"Please?" Amelia's voice shifted into tearful begging. "He'll be so mad if he finds out I tried to steal a phone."

She *what*? His chest tightened.

Her young voice pitched. "What if he kicks me out?"

"He's not going to do that."

Of course he wouldn't do that. But what was she thinking? Shoplifting while out with Mama D? He bit back a groan.

"But he'll be mad."

Silence.

That part Zoey couldn't refute, because he was mad. A lot mad.

Mad enough to knock down the door but not mad enough to realize he shouldn't.

Linc drew a shaky breath. At least Zoey was on his side, had his back. He'd cool off, talk to Amelia in a little while. Sucked she didn't trust him enough to tell him before she told Zoey, or even tell them at the same time—but at least she trusted one of them.

That was something. He'd hold on to that.

"...when Mama D told me, I was mad too."

Oh. So Zoey had known first? He frowned, inched closer to the door. Why hadn't anyone told him?

"You were?" Amelia's voice shrank.

"Of course I was. That's a pretty shady thing to try, especially when someone is doing something nice for you, like taking you shopping."

"I know." Her voice was tinged with regret. "I said I was sorry."

"And I believe you." A beat. "Parents can get mad. That doesn't mean they don't care—or that they don't want you around."

"You're not my parent."

Zoey's sigh was long. "I know."

"But I'm glad you're here."

Oh. That sentiment should have been nice, but it hit Linc like a sucker punch in the gut. Zoey, Amelia trusted. Zoey, she confided in. Zoey, she was glad was there. Not him.

Would it ever be him?

Then again, how much could he really blame Amelia? Zoey was his comfort too. The one person he wanted around when things were bad. The one person he wanted on his team.

Then Zoey's voice sounded again, quieter this time. "I guess I don't have to tell him right now."

Aye. So much for a team. His stomach flipped. He'd heard plenty for one night.

Before he did something dumb, he stalked to the kitchen, yanking open the fridge door and staring blindly at the meager contents. Half-eaten bag of grapes. Square of cheese. End of a gallon of milk. He didn't know what he wanted.

Well, yes he did. But he couldn't have it.

He didn't know how long he stood there, staring, cold air rushing over his face, but at some point, footsteps sounded. He turned from the fridge.

"Oh, hey. We've got to stop meeting like this." Zoey, her hair gathered up in a messy bun, grinned at him as she tightened the belt on her fuzzy robe. Her face fell as he didn't smile back. "What's wrong?"

"Oh, nothing." He bumped the fridge door shut with his hip, casting the kitchen into shadows save for the dim light over the sink. "Just processing the fact my daughter shoplifted and my wife was going to keep it from me." Almost tripped over the W-word, but managed not to stutter.

The anger helped.

Zoey crossed her arms over her chest, eyes flashing. "You were listening at the door?"

Incredible. He crossed his arms, mirroring her position. "*That's* what bothers you? Not the fact you two were ganging up on me?"

A bit of her fire dimmed. She uncrossed her arms. "That's not what happened."

"Keeping secrets. My kid is already convinced I'm the bad guy—you're just confirming it with antics like that." He jabbed his hand toward Amelia's room. "You're making her think I'm not safe. That I can't be trusted."

"Look, I've never been a parent before either, okay?" Zoey stepped forward, finger pointing toward his chest. "I'm doing the best I can. Mama D implied I might need to talk to Amelia first, because you might do something rash." She narrowed her eyes. "Ironically, like get mad before you have all the facts."

"I have the facts." He ticked them off on his fingers. "She tried to steal a phone, got busted, 'apologized,' and now she's working one over on you with all the compliments. To stay out of trouble."

"That's not how it happened."

"She's manipulating you."

Zoey blew out her breath. "Will you just listen for a second?"

Anger was easier to manage than rejection. He braced his hands on the countertop. "I did listen, remember? Heard plenty, trust me."

"Well, maybe if you listened a little longer, you'd have heard *why* she wanted the phone in the first place."

"To be cool? To see if she could get away with it?" Linc gestured with a wild wave toward Amelia's room. "I'm sure I can figure that out. Not that it matters."

"You missed one." Zoey glared.

"What? To pawn for cash?"

"To be able to talk to her mom."

Oh.

Oh.

The faucet dripped. They stared at each other, chests heaving. The back of Linc's eyes burned. His temples throbbed.

Then Zoey wilted, her entire body slumping toward the counter. "Are you mad at me?"

"No." The word barely escaped his throat. He opened his arms. Even he could tell this was the time for a hug.

Maybe needed one himself.

She flew into him, tucking herself against his side. "You're probably right."

"No. You're right."

"Maybe we both are."

He leaned down, spoke against her hair. "This parenting stuff is hard."

She pulled away, just enough to look up at him. "Will be a lot easier if we stay on the same team."

"How? She trusts you more." He didn't try to hide the defeat in his voice.

Zoey's tone softened. "Only because she has less to lose with me."

Huh. Maybe so.

Her eyes flickered. "Give her time, Linc. And some patience. She'll come around."

He pulled her back against him, ignoring squirrels and needs and what-ifs. Just grateful for the fact Zoey was there, and cared enough to do this gigantic task with him. "When did you become an expert in this stuff?"

"I'm not." She snuggled a little closer, nearly undoing him. He tightened his grip, her voice muffled against his chest. "I just . . . I know you."

That she did.

And somehow, despite that fact, she was still there.

But for how long?

He held her, barely daring to breathe, as if she might dissipate in his arms. As if this whole thing they'd made might go up in smoke. And then what would he do?

But at this point, even if she really did stay long-term, would their carrying on as they were now—friends, roommates, team-mates—ever going to be enough?

Was he still destined to be alone, even in a house full of family?

Eventually, Linc let go of her, and Zoey smiled at him, a truce in her eyes. They went to their separate rooms, every fiber of Linc's heart and body fully aware that she was only a hallway away. And somehow, at the same time, a light year away.

In the midst of all the questions circling his mind, one thing was certain—he wouldn't be getting a wink of sleep tonight.

Eighteen

ALMOST READY!" ELISA STOOD BEHIND a dressing screen in the converted bride's room in the Sunday school building of the church, changing into her bridal gown. Zoey sat in a tiny blue child's chair at an equally short table, adjusting the peach roses in her bouquet. "Can't wait to see!" She inhaled the fresh aroma wafting up her nose. Her friend's big day had finally come—maybe slightly more bittersweet than Zoey anticipated.

She shoved that part aside. This was her friend's day. She grinned toward the screen, despite Elisa not being able to see her. "I still don't believe you about my bridesmaid dress. I know you paid for it."

"And I keep telling you I didn't." Elisa singsonged back from the other side.

"Don't look at me either." Rosalyn, who was standing in front of a full-length mirror, twisted around to smooth the back of her sage-green one-shouldered dress. Her long blonde hair hung in cascading ringlets down her back. "Sounds like a Mama D thing to do."

Hmm. Maybe so. Zoey's bank account had rejoiced at the surprise payoff, but it also felt odd, being taken care of. Then again, it *was* a total Mama D move. Especially considering how Zoey had never worked up the nerve to ask Linc for help. It was one thing to live in his house, use his utilities and baking ingredients . . . but asking for money outright felt way too strange. Especially considering how her latest attempt at snickerdoodles had flopped, being nearly as inedible as her attempt at cinnamon rolls. Maybe she needed to forget cinnamon.

Maybe she needed to forget baking. She *needed* the darn insurance payment to come through, and then she could stop being a burden.

"How have things been lately, Zoey?" Rosalyn continued primping. "I feel like I've barely seen you since your surprise party on the boat."

Zoey pinched off a dried leaf, schooling her features to hide her churning thoughts. "Good, mostly. Just busy." The last two weeks had flown by in a flurry of disciplinary efforts toward Amelia—whose punishment for the shoplift attempt was helping out with Linc's tours after school—dress fittings and wedding errands with Elisa, and researching new recipes online.

Somehow, though, her Google searches kept drifting away from baking and into food photography, casting her down several rabbit trails of lighting tips and lens comparisons.

"I understand busy." Rosalyn bent closer to the mirror, ran a finger under her eye to clear a smudge of mascara. "I've been helping Cade study for the bar and added a second aerial class at Madam Paulette's."

"Which the kids *love*," Elisa called from behind the screen. "By the way, I'm almost ready for the zipper—please."

"Of course! Just let us know," Rosalyn called back. She lowered her voice and shot Zoey a wink. "I think Mama D was more of a Bridezilla when I did her makeup earlier than our actual bride is being."

Zoey snorted. "I believe you."

Rosalyn uncapped a lipstick. "Any more updates from Amelia's social worker?"

"No, she's checked in once, but that's it."

"I guess no news is good news, then."

Linc sure hoped so. Zoey held the bouquet in front of her, adjusting the height of the baby's breath. "It's weird—there was so much happening when Amelia first arrived, and then with our eloping, but I think things have finally reached a bit of a lull."

A nice lull, like when Zoey bobbed on Linc's boat after a tour (since she still wasn't allowed on the boat *during* a tour), stretched out in the sun, discussing fresh marketing ideas. Some of her ideas he scoffed at (dressing up in a crawfish costume and spinning a sign at the end of the pier), others he didn't dignify with a response at all (sky-writing in the clouds).

But a few of her suggestions made it into his black notebook. Subtly, of course, when he thought she wasn't looking. Like partnering with Elisa to sell crawfish pies on the tours, and asking Amelia to design an official logo for Boiling Bayou.

It was fun, partnering with him. Like maybe she actually benefited other areas of his life too, not just this new parenting role. Made her feel like *slightly* less of a burden.

Just not enough to ask for cash.

"I saw Amelia in the church a while ago, picking a seat in the back." Rosalyn smiled. "I complimented her dress, and she was quick to tell me it was yours."

Zoey rested the bouquet on her knees. "Probably because she still thinks it's too long on her, though it's barely to her knees. I'm starting to understand that old nursery rhyme, about girls being sugar *and* spice." She snorted. "It's definitely both."

"Sounds like a teenager, all right." Rosalyn laughed as she took the other tiny chair across from Zoey.

"Some days I almost forget she's been through so much. It's like she's always been around." Zoey winced. "Then other days . . ."

Rosalyn twisted her lips to the side. "How are she and Linc doing?"

"They have their moments. But most of the time? Like oil and water."

"It's only been, what, about a month?" Rosalyn frowned. "It'll get better."

"That's what I keep telling him." Zoey and Linc seemed to have found a good rhythm between the two of them, at least. Fewer awkward moments, more banter. Though sometimes, she caught Linc looking at her, his eyes serious, and she'd give just about anything to know what he was thinking. Was he regretting their decision? Worried about Amelia? Still jealous of how she and Amelia had bonded faster than he had?

She had no idea, and didn't want to risk stirring the pot to ask.

"Ready!" Elisa stepped from behind the screen, her professionally made-up face glowing.

Zoey and Rosalyn jumped to their feet and gasped simultaneously.

"Elisa!" Zoey pressed one hand against her cheek. "Dunkin' donuts, you look stunning." The white, form-fitting strapless bodice, covered in a delicate lace pattern, flared at the hips and drifted into a princess gown of multiple soft layers.

"Absolutely perfect. Noah is going to want to skip his own reception and whisk you away." Rosalyn grinned.

A flush of pink tinted Elisa's contoured cheeks. "He better not, after what we paid for that cake. I should have made it myself, but—"

"Don't be silly. It's your day to enjoy, not work." Zoey stepped back as Rosalyn rushed behind Elisa to finish pulling the zipper.

"Speaking of, Zoey, I almost forgot to ask." Elisa winced. "Our photographer has to leave after the ceremony—apparently her babysitter had an emergency, and she can't stay all evening. Would you be able to take photos during the reception?"

A tiny thrill leapt in Zoey's stomach. "Of course."

"Even if it's just with your phone." Elisa waved one manicured hand through the air. "We have that photo booth we rented, but I really wanted some candids of people dancing too."

"I actually have my camera in the car—I learned about this lighting hack, thought I'd try it during your big exit." One of those rabbit trails she'd fallen down the other day.

"Oh, perfect." Elisa turned as Rosalyn finished zipping. "Thank you."

A heavy knock sounded on the door—clearly a man's. Zoey raised her eyebrows at Elisa.

She shrugged. "Whoever it is can come in. Noah knows not to even try."

Ha. Smart man. Zoey set down her bouquet and headed for the door as Elisa and Rosalyn moved to the mirror. She swung it open.

Linc stood in the carpeted hallway, buttoning the sleeve of the white dress shirt he wore under a fitted gray suit. His hair was down long, combed back with a bit of gel.

Just like Zoey had imagined while daydreaming with Rosalyn at Chug a Mug last month.

She swallowed, tried to speak. He seemed to be having the same problem, his gaze sweeping over her floor-length, sage-green matron-of-honor dress.

He cleared his throat, hands falling to his side. "You look . . ."

"Matronly?" She tried to remember how to breathe, but his gaze, lasered in on hers like that, made it hard to remember any basic survival skills.

He snorted. "Hardly." Then he took her hand, raised it above her head. Inviting her to spin.

Zoey obliged, the chiffon skirt with a slight slit on one side flaring, then settling once more about her legs. The sweetheart neckline dipped below her collarbone, while thin straps created cold-shouldered, sheer sleeves that fluttered around her upper arms. She'd felt pretty when she put it on a half hour ago, but now . . . now she felt like the only woman in the church.

Which was pretty dangerous, all things considered.

She cleared her throat. "Need me to get that for you?"

Linc was still staring. "Get what?"

She pointed to the unbuttoned cuff of his sleeve.

"Oh. Right." He held out his burly wrist, his musky cologne subtle but powerful.

"Is that why you came?" She fumbled with the button, her fingers shaky.

"Partly." His voice was low, his skin warm against her fingers. Why couldn't she operate her hands? "And partly because Cade sent me to check on you ladies."

"Cade?" Seriously, it was like she'd never buttoned a button before. Zoey squinted, tugging the fabric tighter.

"Yeah, Noah's nervous as all get out. I think Cade figured if Noah got a report on Elisa, he'd calm down a little."

"That's sweet."

"Sweet?" Linc scoffed. "Nothing to be nervous about. He needs to just man up and get down the aisle."

"Is that what you did?" Zoey raised her eyebrow at him, fingers pausing over his wrist. "Manned up and got down the aisle?"

"That was different."

"Right." Their wedding had been *very* different—a fact she kept trying to distract herself from, to no avail. Here, there were candles, and flower arrangements, and formal gowns. A decorated arch to stand under. Friends to stand with.

No robed judge or courthouse in sight.

But Zoey found her smile before it got away, squared her shoulders. She was happy for her friends—they deserved a dream day. Noah and Elisa were marrying for love. Zoey and Linc had married for friendship, for need.

No reason to compare their situations when they were beyond comparison. So what if Linc thought she looked pretty in her dress? Nothing had changed.

Just like he wanted.

There, finally. She patted his buttoned cuff. "Report to Cade—and Noah—that all is well. We'll see you guys in there." She took a step back.

"Great." Linc started back down the hall, toward the men's Sunday school room, then stopped. Turned. "Oh, and Zoey?"

She waited, one hand on the door frame. "Yeah?"

"I realize we didn't have an aisle at the courthouse, but for the record…" The corner of his mouth lifted. "There was no 'manning up' required."

Then he turned and disappeared around the corner.

Leaving her with her expectations decidedly more wrinkled.

This wedding was getting to his head.

Or maybe Zoey was.

Linc tapped his fork in rhythm to the live band playing from the stage. The reception hall, a venue on the outskirts of Magnolia Bay, was bursting with people, all dancing, laughing, eating cake. Sadie, Harper, and Mrs. Peters sat at a circular table laden with floral centerpieces, while Trish, wearing a form-fitting halter dress, stood nearby, batting her eyelashes at Sawyer Dubois, who was attempting to ignore her while talking to Owen.

Elisa's dad, Isaac, helped himself to the buffet with August Bowman and Miley. Sheriff Rubart had shed his typical uniform tonight and stood off to the side of the stage, mouthing along the words to the trendy pop song. It was as if the whole town had turned out to see the age-old family feud of the Bergerons and the Heberts officially come to an end.

And in the center of the tiled dance floor, Noah and Elisa swayed, her head resting contentedly on his chest.

Had to admit, they were a great couple—brought out the best in each other.

The fork stilled in his hands. Sort of like Zoey did for him. She coaxed all the best things out of Linc—what little bit of good there might be. Not that he'd been great lately about returning that favor. He frowned. What was Zoey even getting out of this arrangement with him besides a roof over her head? She was doing so much for him and Amelia . . . and with zero complaining. Sure, he was taking care of Zoey financially for now, but it didn't seem fair. Didn't seem like enough.

Across the table from him, Amelia sat, chin propped in one hand. She swiped her finger through a glob of leftover icing and licked it off. He raised an eyebrow at her. "Having fun?"

She raised one back. "Would you, if you were thirteen?"

Fair enough. He tossed her a table mint, wrapped in green and peach wrapping—the wedding colors. Which Zoey wore the best, if he were honest. Sure, Rosalyn was movie-star beautiful in whatever she wore, but Zoey . . . that green brought out her dark hair. Her eyes. That faint smattering of freckles across her nose, the ones that had only recently developed after so much time on his boat the past few weeks.

He cast a glance toward the photo booth—he only allowed himself one every five minutes or so—which Zoey had manned for the past half hour, helping arrange the guests as they chose props on sticks and posed for the flash.

Made him sort of want to snag her picture too, though she wouldn't need the flash. She lit from the inside out, her joy contagious with everyone around her. She'd seemed a little . . . off . . . when he came to the bridal room before the ceremony, but whatever that was had clearly worn away. Funny how Zoey used to bug him a little, with her endless talking and energy and ideas.

And now he just wanted to be around her as much as possible. She charged him, like a solar battery. The sun.

He glanced back at Amelia. "Want to hit up the photo booth?" The words escaped his mouth before he could realize it might be a bad idea. He didn't do pictures. Or anything in the spotlight or intentionally cringe, for that matter. And wearing fake glasses or holding a cardboard hat up to his head was definitely that.

But Amelia's eyes lit and she sat up straight, dropping the unwrapped mint back on the table. "Yeah!"

Well, that was the first exclamation point he'd gotten out of her in a week. Make that two weeks, if he was going for *positive* exclamation. He shoved back his chair. Looked like they were doing this.

"Come on, then." He gestured for Amelia to lead the way, her borrowed black dress swishing around her knees and making her look way older than almost fourteen.

Another stab in the gut of how much of her life he'd missed already.

Madame Paulette stood next to Zoey, wafting essential oils as she gestured to the photo booth. "So you hook your camera up to this machine here, and it prints them immediately?"

Zoey nodded. "That way, the guests have souvenirs."

"Hey, these are good." Madame's jewelry clanged and she cackled. "You should come take some class pics of my young students. Their parents would pay good money for these."

"That'd be fun." Zoey hadn't noticed his and Amelia's approach yet, which provided Linc the perfect opportunity to study the way her eyes sparkled as she looked at the preview screen. The way her slim shoulders curved against the sleeves of her dress, the way her neck arched gracefully toward the camera . . .

Then she turned, and he was busted. He swallowed, elbowed Amelia. "Amelia wanted a picture."

Amelia shot him a strange look, but thankfully didn't correct him. He made a mental note to start her an allowance later.

Surprise lit Zoey's face, but she concealed it quickly. "Sure, come on. Pick your prop."

Amelia began pawing through the basket of costumes, pulled free a red boa.

"You should all get in there." Madame Paulette took the camera from Zoey's hand before anyone could protest. "Go on. You too, Muscles."

"I'm assuming she's talking to you," Zoey whispered.

"Obviously, since you're skipping pushups."

Zoey stuck out her tongue at him before plucking a cardboard prop from the pile—a red bowtie. She handed it to him with a grin.

Why not? It was probably the lesser evil in the stack. He took it with only a mild groan, got into position beside her. Amelia stood in front of them, squatting slightly, boa draped around her neck.

"Okay, everyone. Smile now." Madame Paulette held up the camera.

He moved the bow tie on a stick under his chin, refusing to smile despite Madame Paulette's repeated instructions. Thankfully, no one seemed to be watching, as the band had picked up another fast song, the floor filling quickly. What prop had Zoey picked?

He glanced sideways at her, taking in the cardboard mustache she held over her lips, and couldn't stop his grin.

Flash.

"Perfect!" Madame Paulette handed the camera back to Zoey.

Amelia tapped Linc's arm, mischief dancing in her expression. "You should ask Zoey to dance."

"He doesn't dance."

"I don't dance."

He and Zoey spoke at the same time, connecting eyes. Both of them lying, because it'd happened before, and they both knew it. But the kitchen was one thing. A *one-time* thing. A dance floor in a public setting was by far another.

But something about the hope in Zoey's eyes, and her past comments about not having had a cake or photos at their wedding, stopped him short. His own thoughts taunted him. *What was Zoey getting out of this?*

He held out his hand.

Madame Paulette gasped. "Oh, honey, go. I'll man the booth." She shoved Zoey forward, and he caught her, led her toward the floor while Amelia grinned and Madame Paulette swooned.

Aye. He led the way to the dance floor, heart pounding, couples giving him double takes as they quickly cleared his path. Zoey trotted to keep up with him, and he parked them in a spot off to the right, farthest from the stage. The song was slow, had just started. He held out his arms.

And just like that night in the kitchen, Zoey stepped into them, fingers curling into his bicep. His hand curved around her hip, and she moved in close, smelling like leftover roses and shampoo.

Heaven.

Torture.

"Good call." Zoey cleared her throat, smiling at him. "People would expect us to dance."

Right. Appearances. He spun her in a quick circle, pulled her back in. Nodded vaguely, not wanting to confirm the lie.

Not wanting to tell the truth.

Which was getting more obvious to him by the minute.

The music crested, and he spun her again, missing her warmth every time she left the circle of his arms and forgetting how to breathe every time she landed back in close. He had to say something.

Had to stop himself from falling.

But that wasn't going to happen, was it? And maybe that was what he could do for Zoey in return for all she was helping him with—hide the truth. That he was dangerously close to loving her more than he'd ever imagined loving anyone.

Maybe the best way he could serve her in return was to keep his promise that nothing would change.

Even if it slowly killed him inside.

He cleared his throat, fighting the moisture building behind his eyes. "People seem to really like your photos." And said people were no longer watching them, thankfully. In fact, looked like all eyes were on Mama D and Farmer Branson, slow-dancing together by the band. He did a double-take. "Did you know about that?"

"About what?" Zoey turned to look over her shoulder, and her eyes widened. Then she grinned. "I did not. But it explains a lot."

"I've never seen Farmer B in anything outside of overalls." Granted, he'd traded them for jeans, but that was dressed up for him.

"Looks like he trimmed his mustache too." Zoey's grin widened. "Hope he appreciates the lipstick efforts Delia's been making."

"I can guarantee you he doesn't." He nodded toward Zoey's photo booth. "Also just realized the real reason Madame Paulette wanted to get rid of you."

Zoey followed his gesture, where Madame Paulette was apparently trying to gather all of the single men in the room, and shook her head. "I should get back there or Elisa will end up with nothing but footage of Sawyer Dubois."

"Ah, she'll be okay a little longer." He turned her again, but not so fast he didn't catch the surprise lighting her eyes.

She relaxed back with him, humming a little under her breath. "This is going okay, isn't it?"

What, them? The dance? The wedding?

He thought back to their conversation on the porch the first night Amelia arrived. *Define okay.* He definitely wasn't.

But he would be, for her. For everyone.

Linc shrugged, opting for the latter—the safest topic. "Sure. I mean, they're married—that's the end goal of a wedding, right?"

Zoey's smile slipped. "Right."

He waited a beat of the music, two. "I didn't mean it like that."

"I know." Her stiff shoulders suggested otherwise, and he wanted to fix it. Fix them. Maybe he couldn't admit his feelings, but he could keep their normal dynamic going. He had to have that like he had to have oxygen. So much that just a little bit of truth wouldn't hurt.

He took a breath. "I'm not a romantic guy, Zoey."

Her gaze flickered. "I know that too."

"I think tonight was great. The wedding…Noah and Elisa…" He swallowed. "You."

"You think I'm great?" Her lips curled.

He coughed. "Pretty."

"Pretty great?"

"No." *Aye.* "I meant, I think you *look* pretty."

She knew, she was teasing him. It was evident in her eyes. She tilted her head back, grinning.

He groaned, spun her again. "You're enjoying this, aren't you?"

"You're cute when you're awkward."

"Only then?" Good grief. How was he even managing to dance if he had both feet in his mouth? Though he couldn't complain, really. Their banter was back, and he'd gladly suffer a little embarrassment if it meant they kept their footing.

"Not just then." She ran her hand down the arm of his jacket, and the entire left side of his body lit on fire. "But you did clean up extra nice tonight."

The compliment, even if half-coerced, sank in deep. Too deep for his own good. "Better than Farmer B?" He tried to keep his tone light, despite every instinct wanting to pull her off the floor. Scoop her up. Go home and be fully married.

Aye, he was in trouble.

"Way better." She grinned.

"So we've established we both look nice. Guess you and I are still a good team, then." Good grief, a new song had started, and he hadn't even noticed.

"Good thing." Her grip tightened on his arms, and he decided not to spin her. Wanted to keep her close. "Because you're stuck with me now, remember?"

Man, he hoped so.

With all his heart, he hoped so.

nineteen

HAT A NIGHT.

Zoey stood by the dock near Linc's pond in her bridesmaid dress, the cool night air grazing her bare arms. Fall had officially arrived, as evidenced by the burgundy and coral leaves crunching under her low-heeled shoes. Despite the chill, she went ahead and toed them off, let the damp wood ground her. She drew a deep breath.

Dancing with Linc had unnerved every cell in her body. Grumpy Linc, she could handle. Sullen Linc, busy Linc, selfish Linc—no problem. She knew how to cheer him, make him grudgingly smile, call him out on his attitude or harsh words.

Sweet Linc, romantic Linc, slow-dancing Linc—that Linc she had no idea what to do with.

She tossed a rock into the pond, watching the ripples dance across the dark surface, breaking the reflection of the half-orb moon overhead. Amelia was in bed, and Linc had started rummaging through the pantry for a snack, so she'd taken the opportunity to slip outside, gather her thoughts. Her emotions.

But they kept slipping through her grasp.

Why was he making this effort toward her lately? Did he suddenly feel what she felt, want what she wanted? Or did he just feel guilty for roping her into his mess and was trying to be nice? There'd been that hug in the kitchen after the argument over Amelia . . . the way he looked at her while dancing at the wedding . . . she'd wanted to rise up and kiss him, test the waters, hope he felt the same way she was feeling.

If she guessed wrong . . . it could ruin everything.

But was missing out on something potentially amazing any better? What was worth the risk?

The tired dock creaked behind her, and she stiffened. Linc. She closed her eyes.

"You okay?"

She slowly turned to face him, her sunshine generator feeling decidedly cracked. She didn't want to shine. She wanted answers. "Why do you keep doing things you don't typically do?"

He tilted his head, shoved his hands in his pockets. "Like what?"

"Dancing, for one."

He looked down at the wood beneath their feet. At the inky water visible through the cracks. "I don't know. I guess I feel like I owe you."

Right—she should have guessed. Obligation, duty. She was still the burden, someone else for him to take care of. A second dependent. "You don't owe me."

"Good to know."

She narrowed her eyes. "I went into this whole thing willingly, in case you don't remember."

"I remember." He wasn't getting annoyed back, which only annoyed her worse. "I was there."

"So, I don't need any favors. Don't do things you don't want to do." She crossed her arms over her chest, shivered.

He pulled off his jacket, draped it around her shoulders. "Who said I didn't want to?"

Oh. She stared up at him, her fire extinguishing. He wasn't joking.

"I wanted to pay for your dress too. So I did."

She drew a breath. "That was *you*?"

"Well, yeah. What are husbands for?"

Husband. Not friend. Her stomach turned to mush.

His eyes searched hers. "Why didn't you ask me?"

She shrugged. "You've done enough already."

"Look." He sighed. "You got the short end of this stick, Zoey. We both know it—paying for a dress is hardly equal to what you're doing for us. For me *and* Amelia." He stepped away from her, raked one hand through his hair. "You got a grumpy, clueless father and a moody teenager in this deal. If I can do something to help you be happy, then I'll do it. Even dance."

"I don't see it that way." She took a step toward him.

"Then you're blind."

She licked her lips. "I just see my best friend and his brilliant daughter, both of who are going through a really hard time."

He nodded. "That's why I need you."

Need.

Not want.

She inhaled. Once again, that was as good as it was going to get with them. And she had to be okay with that—because she'd known all along exactly what she was getting. And painful as it was, she still didn't consider it a short stick.

Maybe that's what love did.

Painful as it was.

But maybe she could get a little something from it. She tucked deeper into his jacket, fisting the collar in both hands. "If you feel like you owe me, how about telling me about that tattoo you got removed?" She teasingly arched a brow.

He groaned. "Seriously?"

"Hey, I didn't even know you grew up in the system until a

few weeks ago." She tilted her head. "Or that you'd been arrested before."

"Or had a kid. I know, the surprises keep coming." He scuffed one shoe across the dock. "Though to be fair, one of those I didn't know either."

She stepped toward him, tugged at the white dress shirt he'd untucked at some point after they got home. "Tell me."

He didn't stop her from lifting the hem, running her finger over the healed, slightly scarred skin on his lower ribcage. His corded side shuddered. Must be ticklish—she never knew that either. And all of that was what hurt the most—that she didn't know him as well as she assumed.

That maybe she wasn't as special to him as she'd hoped.

Zoey looked up at him just as he looked down. Their gazes tangled. "It was something to do with Kirsten, wasn't it?"

He blew out his breath. "I was young and dumb. Got her initials. She was supposed to get mine too, but chickened out."

Ah. Zoey touched the mottled spot with renewed interest. He'd cared enough about Kirsten to do something like that. Surprisingly, the fact didn't make her jealous. It just confirmed what she knew deep down—despite his reputation and shell, Linc loved hard.

And when he committed, he went all in.

His voice deepened. "Should have taken the hint that day, but didn't."

"Did it hurt?"

"Hurt worse removing the tat than getting it." He made no move to lower his shirt, and for the life of her, she couldn't stop touching him. This link to his past, this chain that had brought Amelia to them. Brought their new family together in the most unlikely way imaginable.

She swallowed. "I think it's beautiful."

Linc frowned, tugged the hem down. "Funny."

"No, I'm serious." Zoey stepped back, clutched his jacket around her shoulders. "Scars are stories. They show where we've been."

"To hell and back." His expression tightened.

"And look where you are now." She couldn't stand it any longer, had to touch him again. She took his hand, and he didn't pull away. "You're a *dad*."

"More like half a dad." Linc swallowed. "I missed so much."

"You're doing all you can now, and that's what matters. Amelia sees that, whether she'll admit it yet or not." She squeezed his hand. "You're showing up. You're taking care of her."

He glanced toward the house, mostly dark save for an upstairs light. "You really think she understands?"

"If she doesn't, she will." Zoey squeezed his hand. "It just might take a little more time."

"I'm afraid that's what I don't have. Kirsten could dump this latest loser and show back up, want to go back to normal with her kid." His Adam's apple bobbed. "Is it weird that Amelia is still distant with me, but the very thought of her going back to Lafayette rips me apart?"

"See? You *are* a good father." The jacket slipped from one shoulder. "Not weird at all. Those are your protective dad instincts coming out."

He grew quiet, lips pressed together. His hand shook a little, and he used his free one to pull the jacket back up around her. One corner of his mouth curved up, his eyes surprisingly gentle. "What would I do without you?"

Zoey looked down at their joined hands. "Eat less fast food?"

"Probably." He snorted.

"Do more pushups?"

"That too." He ducked his head, catching and holding her gaze. "I don't know why you put up with me. But I'm glad you do."

Oh, she didn't know what to do with serious Linc. She needed jerk Linc to come back, make an off-handed comment to annoy her. Stabilize her. Because if he didn't feel what she felt, if he was just being nice . . .

"What are friends for?" *Friend*. Not husband. She diffused casual into her voice, despite her heart threatening to thump right out of her dress and into the pond.

"You've been a much better friend to me than I have been to you."

"That's not true. You were there when Bayou Beignets burned . . ." She distinctly remembered the way he held her, protected her, tucked her face into his broad chest so she couldn't watch.

He shook his head. "I mean lately." He was so close, moving closer. Drawing their joined hands up to his chest. His facial hair, clearly as stubborn as he was, had long made an appearance post-wedding.

Unable to help herself, she used her free hand to run her thumb over his jaw, exploring the square line of his face, the scruff over his chin. His eyes hooded, darkened, and a jolt of regret sliced through her midsection.

What was she doing?

"I'm sorry." She pulled her hand free, heat flaming her cheeks. "I don't know what—"

But he took her hand back, returning it flat against his cheek. Oh.

Then he turned his face to press a kiss into her palm.

Oh. Definitely not a friend move. Her legs tingled, wobbled. Tentatively, she continued her journey, tracing his lips with one finger, then two. The top one dipped in the middle, and he had a small scar where most people might have a dimple. How had he gotten that one? Had she never asked?

She wanted to know it all.

Wanted to know him.

"Linc . . ." Her finger then trailed down his corded neck, running horizontally across his collarbone, until both hands slid to land on his chest. Even through his shirt, his muscled pecs flexed under her fingers. On instinct, maybe. Because Linc would never *try* to impress her—he

didn't have to.

Didn't he know she stayed that way?

With a growl in the back of his throat, he picked her up, pulled her against him, face-to-face. Her heart threatened to burst. Joy . . . trepidation . . . adrenaline. She easily wrapped her legs around his waist, held on tight. His hands exploded fire on her hips, his lips inches from hers. Her stomach trembled. What had he called her the other day—brave? Oh, she felt anything but.

Felt like she was throwing gasoline into a pile of fireworks.

Yet somehow—rather bravely—her arms snaked around his neck and held on. A question lit his eyes, and she forgot how to speak.

But she knew how to say yes. And this *was* her husband, after all.

Risking everything, she pulled him toward her, closing the short distance until their lips met.

Zoey's lips were softer than he'd imagined, so surprising Linc inhaled a quick breath. This was how he should have kissed her at her wedding—the way she deserved. Full stop. Because nothing about Zoey was halfway or halfhearted. She gave her best to everyone around her, to her own detriment, and rarely asked for anything in return.

He was more than happy to volunteer it.

Linc supported her with one arm, his other burying deep into her hair at the nape of her neck, deepening the kiss. His senses lit on fire. Zoey. *His* Zoey.

She kissed him back as if she'd wanted to for as long as he had.

Maybe that was true, or maybe it'd never crossed her mind. It didn't matter. Nothing mattered except her. This.

Them.

She turned her head, gasping for breath. Apparently oxygen still mattered. But he couldn't stop, couldn't let her go. He pressed a kiss against her cheek, her jaw, the dip in her neck. She smelled like lingering perfume and cake. Coconut deodorant. His jacket had long since slipped to the dock, but he didn't care, stepped on it, even, as he fought to keep his balance, keep Zoey lifted within his reach.

Then her lips were back on his, and his head buzzed. He stumbled forward a step, swept away with the need rising in his chest. Not because she was homeless and he was obligated. Not because he couldn't parent on his own. Not because of money or convenience or tax breaks.

Just because it was her.

His best friend.

He'd officially fallen for his wife.

Linc shifted Zoey, trying to get a better grip without breaking their kiss. She moved at the same time, knocking him off balance. He sidestepped, but the jacket bunched beneath his shoe.

And then they were both falling.

Linc sat in the living room, wrapped in a fleece blanket, bare feet propped on the ottoman as he waited his turn for the shower. He ran his hands over his cheeks, bristle scrubbing his fingers.

Guess that was one way to end a kiss.

Zoey had come up from the murky water shrieking, laughing, shocked, her dark hair plastered to her head. Linc hauled her back onto the pier, and they'd laughed together, squishing up toward the house, her soggy dress probably weighing a million pounds. He'd stripped off his wet shirt and tossed it in the laundry room, thrown on a dry tee and sweatpants while she dripped her way upstairs to the bathroom.

The impromptu cold dousing was exactly what he needed, to the point he'd wondered if an angel had tripped him instead of his own suit jacket.

What would have happened if Linc hadn't knocked them both in? Would it have gone farther? They were married, but . . . He groaned. He hadn't been thinking clearly—obviously. Maybe they'd rushed down the proverbial aisle, but rushing *this* would be the end of them.

If it wasn't already.

His stomach clenched. What was Zoey thinking? Did she assume he'd taken advantage of the conversation, of the vulnerability between them? Did she want to keep moving forward as a real couple—a real marriage? Or was that kiss a one-time fluke?

What did they do from here?

"You stink."

He looked up at Amelia's voice, her wrinkled nose as she stood by the fireplace in a sweatshirt and pajama pants. Took him a moment to realize she meant literally. "Fell in the pond."

"I wondered what all the yelling was." She perched on the end of the recliner, rocking forward. "How'd that happen? And why are the stairs all wet?"

He opened his mouth, closed it. Narrowed his eyes. Uh . . .

"Never mind." Amelia rolled her eyes. "I can figure it out."

Linc held up one hand. "We tripped, fell off the pier. It was an accident."

She seemed to accept that, thankfully. "Hope you don't ever run with scissors."

Ha. "Good advice. I take it you've heard that one before?"

"Well, yeah." She pulled a strand of hair over her shoulder, started plucking at a split end. "Mom wasn't *that* bad of a mom, you know."

"I'm sure she wasn't." He shifted positions on the couch, angling to face her.

Amelia paused. "Why do you say that? I thought you were mad at her."

He drew a breath. Couldn't be honest with one woman in the house tonight and not the other—though the vulnerability felt strange on his lips. "I say that because, well. You've turned out kind of great." He coughed. "I know she must have had some role in that, at least."

Amelia plucked faster. To her credit *and* Linc's surprise, she didn't make a move to leave. "Mom did teach me how to make really good grilled cheese sandwiches."

Linc nodded slowly, imagining the scene. Amelia and Kirsten in that nearly vacant, dirty apartment, cooking in a skillet. Maybe laughing together. Maybe it wasn't all as bad as he'd thought. It couldn't have been, or Amelia would have been more eager to leave that life.

He lowered his voice. "Tell me what else was good."

Amelia's hands drifted from her hair to her lap. "She liked driving with the windows down. I mean, the AC didn't work a lot, so she had to, but she'd turn up the radio, make me sing with her."

A smile tugged at Linc's mouth. "Sounds fun."

"And she said we'd get a dog one day, maybe when I was in high school." Amelia's smile faded, her eyes glossed over. "I guess that's not happening now."

Ouch. He hadn't meant for this conversation to take a sad turn. But maybe it was long overdue.

"That's why you wanted the phone, wasn't it?" Linc dipped his head toward her. "You miss her. Wanted to be ready to talk again, if you got the chance."

She sniffed, avoiding his gaze. Shrugged one shoulder.

"You *can* talk to her again, you know. As soon as we know where she is." He frowned. "No one here is trying to keep you away from her. We just need to keep you safe, and teenagers can't live alone."

"I know." Amelia's voice cracked. "It was . . . hard . . . to think of good things just now."

"I'm sure that's normal to get choked up over it."

"No." She shook her head. "I meant hard because there weren't a lot of things to pick from. We did some goofy stuff, but that's because she never felt like a mom. Felt more like a babysitter, or an older friend." She snorted. "Clearly she's selfish."

They sat in silence a moment. What did he say? This moment felt . . . important. But he couldn't rail on Kirsten to their kid, even if she did deserve it.

He drew a breath. "Sometimes parents make bad decisions that affect their kids. Some are just bigger than others, have bigger consequences."

She nodded. "Like this."

"Yeah, like this." Linc winced. "And I'm sure I'll make mistakes too. Parents aren't perfect—and I've only been one for about a month."

Amelia side-eyed him, pursed her lips. "You're not doing horrible."

A compliment? This night kept getting more and more unreal.

"Even if you did ground me."

There it was. He grunted. "For stealing? Right, how off balance that was of me."

"I really am sorry about that." She pulled at a thread in her pants. "I just knew you wouldn't let me have a phone."

Linc shrugged. "To be fair, you also never asked."

She quirked a brow, interest lighting her face. "So can I have a phone?"

"Of course not."

She huffed, but a smile slipped through.

He grinned. "Nice try, though."

Overhead, the shower shut off.

"Guess I better go to bed." Amelia stood from the chair, fiddling with her hair again as she headed across the room.

"Okay." He wanted to tell her how glad he was she came downstairs, how glad he was that she was *there*. But it felt like too much, too soon, and he didn't want to scare her off. It'd been a good conversation—he'd leave it at that. He leaned back against the couch, readjusting his legs on the ottoman. "Good night."

"Good night." Amelia half turned, her eyes darting to meet his before flicking away. She paused. "Dad."

Twenty

"THANKS FOR CALLING BACK SO FAST."
Zoey paced the concrete in the church parking lot the next afternoon, keeping her voice low and a steady eye on the front doors for Linc's emergence. She'd hurried outside after the service when Elisa had called, hoping to snag the brief opportunity to update her best friend on the big news. "Linc kissed me."

"He *did*?" Elisa's pitched with excitement over the phone. "Finally!"

A car pulled away from the church—Sadie. She waved. Zoey waved back. "Or maybe I kissed him. I don't know. It happened really fast." Ended rather abruptly too, with their swan dive off the pier.

"What did he say? What did you say?" Elisa's voice muffled, as if she turned away from the phone. "Linc and Zoey *kissed*."

In the background, Noah let out an exclamation Zoey couldn't quite decipher.

"By the way, your friendship is really over and above for responding to my SOS text message on your honeymoon." Zoey winced. "Tell Noah I'm sorry."

"Are you kidding me? We're both totally invested in this." She could hear the smile in her friend's voice. "Besides, we're just sitting at Louis Armstrong International right now, waiting for our flight."

As if on cue, an intercom buzzed. "Hang on." Elisa listened as the voice announced the next flight number. "Okay, not us. Continue."

"It was after the wedding, outside by his pond. We started talking and then he got really serious and said he was grateful I was around and then it just . . . happened." Zoey pressed her fingers against her flaming cheeks, despite the cool fall breeze swooping through her hair.

"And then what?" Elisa's voice dipped.

"Then we sort of tripped and fell in the pond."

Elisa burst out laughing. "That sounds about right."

Her chest warmed. She could stand there, if she wanted, and easily recall the way his arms had hauled her up, his soaked shirt clinging to his chest, the barely extinguished fire in his eyes as he held her steady.

Probably shouldn't remember all that in the church parking lot, even if Linc *was* her husband.

She cleared her throat. "We cleaned up after that and I thought we'd talk about it, but, get this—Amelia called Linc *dad* last night."

"What?" Elisa gasped again. "That's huge. Good gravy, what a night."

"Yeah, we started talking about that first, and then both fell asleep on the couch." Her legs stretched across his lap, his hands resting on her ankles. Had been nice, despite the lack of closure with the elephant in the room.

Zoey looked over her shoulder—coast was still clear. She ducked her head low. "Then we all three overslept for church and rushed around trying to get here on time. So I don't really know what he's thinking."

"Well, is he acting normal?" Elisa grunted. "Never mind. Noah just said you can't go by that with Linc."

"Good point."

"I'm sure you'll talk soon. Don't worry. Things are happening, which is great." The intercom buzzed again, and Elisa sucked in her breath. "That's us. Gotta go."

"Have fun in the mountains!"

"We will. Text me when you have more news." Elisa's voice muffled again, then she laughed. "Noah says I might not answer right away."

"Fair enough." Zoey snorted. "See you guys later." She hung up, pocketed her cell, grinning at her friend's happiness—daring to think it might become her own.

Could that finally be her and Linc one day? For the first time since the courthouse, she dared to think it was possible. That maybe their friendship could turn into a real relationship, a real marriage in every way.

Maybe even a real honeymoon.

She started for the church, then paused at a familiar figure walking under the awning, wearing a skirt and carrying a briefcase. She frowned. Then her heart dropped.

What in the world was Ms. Bridges doing here?

A rogue petal from yesterday's flower girl basket still resided under the pew in the front row of the church.

From the sixth row back, Linc jiggled his leg, nerves flooding his system. Zoey had headed somewhere after the service—the restroom, maybe. And Amelia had left right away with Mama D for lunch at the Burger Barn again—which he figured was Amelia's way of apologizing to her for their last disastrous outing. Never mind the fact Linc was paying for it, having slipped Mama D a twenty-dollar bill during the closing song of the service. The congregation had also cleared out, leaving Pastor Todd alone at the front of the church, humming to himself as he flipped through his sermon notes.

Linc jiggled his leg faster. He should go up there, ask for prayer. Zoey was praying about them, sure, and he'd tried a few times, but this—his *family*—seemed too important to not have backup.

But he felt glued to the seat. Pastor's words from the sermon, some verse he read from in John, rang in his mind. *You did not choose me but I chose you . . .*

He wanted to know what that meant. Because it sounded a little too good to be true.

Zoey would probably know, but they hadn't had a chance to talk about anything yet, including that kiss. Amelia calling him Dad had temporarily distracted them from the obvious Thing between them. Or maybe he and Zoey had let it distract them on purpose. This new element to their relationship seemed so fragile, dissecting it might completely break it.

If so, Linc was okay with *not* talking about it for now. Noah's words from the boat lingered. *Relationships take time to develop.* And he and Zoey had time, didn't they? Their entire marriage to figure it out. Because, like Zoey kept saying—she wasn't going anywhere.

So why the fear . . . the sudden urge to get extra prayer . . . to make sure God agreed with Linc on this one?

Before he could change his mind, he stood, hauled himself to the front row. Pastor Todd looked up from his Bible with a jolt. "Oh, Linc. Good to see you." He held out his hand, which Linc shook. "How you doing?"

"I need prayer." He blurted the words out before he could keep them.

"I'd be happy to pray with you." Pastor smiled, his dark goatee sprinkled with gray. "Any particular topic?"

He swallowed. "Family. Marriage."

"That's right, I heard the good news. Congratulations." He rested his hands on his podium, angling toward Linc. "Everything going well on the home front?"

Couldn't fully get into that, and definitely couldn't lie to a pastor. Linc hesitated. "We're all adjusting." There, that was the truth.

"Ah. It can be tough, blending families so suddenly." He tilted his head, studied Linc so hard he shifted his weight. "What else is on your mind, before we pray?"

Man, the guy was good. Linc pushed up the sleeves of his shirt. "You read a verse today."

He dipped his head. "John 15:16."

"Yeah, that one. I guess I'm struggling to believe it."

"That God chose you?"

No one ever chose him. Linc nodded, throat tight. He glanced over his shoulder for Zoey, hoping she didn't catch this. The last thing he wanted right now was to look weak in front of her.

"The good news about the Bible, Linc, is that it's truth. And that truth remains true whether we believe it or not." Pastor Todd crossed his arms over his chest, his smile open and welcoming. "So I suggest we start by praying for God to help you believe it."

That sounded . . . nice. "Okay."

Pastor winked. "And while we're at it, we'll pray for your marriage and your daughter too."

Throat burning, Linc nodded again, afraid to speak.

Pastor clapped Linc on the shoulder and began to pray, his voice low. As he spoke, peace washed over Linc. The fear he always carried wasn't completely gone, but it was significantly lighter. Something he could only assume was hope pierced through the shadows in his heart, letting him believe there could be a future for his family after all.

He should have prayed like this weeks ago. If he could fully believe that God chose him . . . that God wasn't going to leave . . . then maybe he could believe God also cared about his family as much as he did. That God, like Zoey kept saying, would work things for good.

Even all of Linc's mistakes.

The sanctuary doors burst open. He looked up as Zoey rushed inside, eyes wide. Pastor's voice broke off mid-amen.

"Are you okay?" Linc's heart stopped, jump-started again at Zoey's quick nod. Then he drew a sharp intake of breath. "Is it Amelia?"

"No, she's fine too." Zoey rounded the last row of pews to join them up front. The red dress she'd paired with a denim jacket flared around her knees. "I just saw Ms. Bridges outside."

"What? Here?" Linc frowned, checked his phone and grimaced. "Two missed calls. It was set to silent during the service." He jabbed the screen, calling her back.

"Do you need a private place to talk?" Pastor Todd shifted his Bible to his other arm, dark brows pinched in concern. "You're welcome to one of the Sunday school rooms."

"Thank you." Zoey pushed on Linc's arm, nudging him toward the back hallway. "You can call her from there—"

Ms. Bridges appeared in the sanctuary before the phone could ring twice. Linc hung up as she walked toward them, briefcase in hand. Creases marred her forehead, and she sighed as she approached.

Bad news.

Linc gulped. "It's Kirsten, isn't it?" He should have known. She was back, wanted Amelia. But *now*, when things were going so well? When she was calling him Dad?

When he'd finally started to believe in good things?

"Actually, no. It's not Kirsten." Ms. Bridges hesitated, shifting her weight from one high-heeled foot to the other as she stopped in front of them. Her gaze flicked to Zoey, then Pastor Todd, and finally back to Linc. "It's you."

"This can't be happening." Linc paced the room, his shoes leaving creased tracks in the carpet.

Zoey had given up pacing after him—couldn't catch him, so once again, she sat in a child's chair in the small Sunday school room, knees nearly reaching her chest. Ms. Bridges leaned her hip against the chalkboard liner on the far wall, her face drawn.

Zoey's heart ached, could only imagine what was going on in Linc's.

"Are you sure?" He stopped pacing to stare at Ms. Bridges, despite the question being one he'd repeated twice already with no different answer.

"We're *not* sure, which is why I'm here." Ms. Bridges crossed her arms over her blouse, sympathy turning her lips. "Like I said, you were due a surprise visit, and on our last call, you mentioned you were attending church regularly, so when you didn't answer this morning, I thought I'd try to find you here. Figured it better to break the news in person."

"We appreciate it." Zoey spoke softly, since Linc didn't seem to be in a position to.

His face was hard, drawn. Fierce. Nothing like the Linc she'd kissed last night on the pier. "Who is he?"

Ms. Bridges hesitated. "That information would need to come from Ms. West."

"But I don't have that option, do I?" Anger sparked in Linc's eyes, and he shook his head. "I'm sorry. It's not your fault there's another guy."

Zoey swallowed. Surely Linc wasn't jealous. Not after everything they'd learned about Kirsten. Still, Zoey had only kissed Linc, and felt like she could turn a truck over with her bare hands if another woman so much as smiled at him. And Linc and Kirsten had obviously been much closer than that.

Now, something feral lit Linc's eyes, dark and protective, like a wild animal determined to keep its territory safe.

This wasn't about Kirsten. This was about how much he'd come to love Amelia.

Zoey cleared her throat, focused on Ms. Bridges—and not on her accelerating heart rate. They had to figure this out. All of them. Calmly. "What do you recommend we do?"

"A paternity test would be the obvious solution, if you want a guaranteed answer as to who Amelia's father is." Ms. Bridges cast a cautious look at Linc. "But I don't think you need to panic yet."

A little late. Everyone in the room knew that, including Linc.

Ms. Bridges continued. "There's more to this story."

"Now what. A *third* potential father?" Linc scrubbed his hands down his face.

"No. But the other potential father passed away two years ago."

Zoey stilled. Linc's hands froze on his cheeks, then slowly lowered. "Really?"

"Our agency contacted Ms. West yesterday, after she'd been picked up by the local police." Ms. Bridges cut her eyes to Linc, lips pursed. "And no, I can't tell you what she was arrested for."

He wearily motioned for her to continue.

"She asked about Amelia, and we told her that she was safe with her dad. That was when Ms. West informed us that you might not be Amelia's biological father after all. That it was either you or this other man."

A muscle in Linc's jaw jumped, and he resumed pacing. "Why did she only tell Amelia about me, then?"

Zoey had the same question. She wanted to go to him, take his hand. Support him. But the fire in his eyes—and her uncertainty over exactly what it was motivated by—kept her rear end glued to the blue chair.

"Who knows? Maybe she didn't want to give Amelia a bad impression. Maybe she never thought it would matter." Ms. Bridges sighed. "I know these situations are messy. But the good news is, you're not in immediate danger of losing custody of Amelia. Kirsten will be detained for some time, and with this arrest added to her existing record, I don't see a full custody plea going in her favor—if she were to even request it."

Linc nodded, pacing, clearly processing.

Zoey tilted her head. "So why the paternity test?"

"To have proof of parental rights, if you were to go to court in the future. But also because this could mean you're not obligated to care for Amelia."

Linc's head snapped to stare at her. "Obligated?"

Ms. Bridges lifted both hands. "I'm only saying, a paternity test could give you more options should you want them."

"Of course I don't want them," Linc grunted. "Amelia stays with us. Final."

As attractive as Linc had been last night, all dressed up for the wedding, it was nothing compared to how appealing he was fighting for his daughter.

Who might not even be his. Her stomach churned. How would they address this?

"At least now we know where Ms. West is, and she knows Amelia is safe." Ms. Bridges nodded at them. "I can relay a message to her, from you or Amelia, if you'd like."

"Can Amelia talk to her?" Linc asked, shooting Zoey a look. She knew what that question cost him, and her respect for him swelled further. "We think she's been wanting to."

"I don't know that seeing her mom in jail would be in her best interest, but that's a decision for you two to make." Ms. Bridges picked up her briefcase. "The paternity test is also available if you want it."

He lifted his chin. "Don't need it."

"That's fine." Ms. Bridges shrugged, her eyes studying Linc, then Zoey, and back again. "I suppose Ms. West being detained right now worked out for good in this particular case."

Like her favorite verse in Romans promised.

Zoey took a deep breath. Maybe Linc would believe her now. All of this *was* working toward good—for Linc, for Zoey, for Amelia. For their family. Even for Kirsten. Maybe she'd be forced to clean her life up from here, start making better decisions.

Become a mother that Amelia could get to know again one day.

Ms. Bridges checked her watch, began walking toward the door. "Something official will have to be done in the future to maintain permanent custody, but for now, if you feel it best not to upset Amelia with the news, I understand."

"Oh, no, we'll still tell her." Zoey looked at Linc, at the firm press of his lips, the little shake of his head. She frowned. "Wait. We won't?"

His face was granite. "No reason to. Nothing is changing."

"But Linc . . . I think we need to be honest. She deserves the full story."

His jaw set. "Nothing. Is. Changing."

She opened her mouth, then shut it. Nodded slowly. "Okay." Denial it was. Because everything about that particular promise of his hadn't been kept so far.

Linc cracked his neck to the side as he walked through his house, toward the light glowing from the kitchen. First he was a dad, now maybe he wasn't. The ultimate roller coaster he hadn't wanted to ride.

But the question at hand ultimately meant nothing. Amelia was *his*.

She had to be.

Because if she wasn't, then all of this had been for nothing. His and Zoey's marriage, his bonding with Amelia, their developing family.

He'd lose it all.

He walked into the kitchen, the overhead light bright against the darkness outside. Zoey sat at the table, unclaimed photo prints from the wedding covering the wooden surface. Had that only been yesterday? Felt like a week's worth of events had happened in the past twenty-four hours.

He studied the way she bent over the pictures, one arm braced on the table, the other propping up her chin as she studied each one before adding it to the growing stack. His heart twisted. They still hadn't talked. The kiss was still hanging over them, like an anvil on an old Looney Tunes cartoon, waiting to drop.

And now this. How was he supposed to focus on that—on *them*—now?

His life had become a giant question mark. Too many important things pulling at him at once. He wanted to sink onto the couch, throw a blanket over his head.

Or better yet, kiss Zoey again until all of this went away.

"Hey." Zoey looked up. Her smile immediately calmed a bit of his stress, and she scooted the chair beside her out from the table with her foot, an invitation. The wedding band on her finger glinted under the kitchen lights, and he wanted to take her hand. Kiss her palm, the move that had started everything between them the night before.

But he fisted his hands, kept them to himself as he sank onto the chair. It'd been a wild, unsettling day—if he opened that door now, no one would be able to shut it. "These all from the wedding?" Obviously, but he didn't know what else to say.

"Yep." She moved a pic of Mama D and Farmer Branson from

one pile to the next. "I'll surprise her with this one. Maybe frame it first."

"She'll like that."

Zoey pointed to the next print of Noah and Elisa shoving cake in each other's mouths. "Funny what you can see in a photo that you miss in real life, isn't it?" In the background, behind Noah's shoulder, was Trish—glaring at Sawyer Dubois engaged in conversation with Harper.

Linc snorted. "That'll be interesting later."

"Like I said." She tapped another stack of photos together and grinned. "Funny what you can see sometimes."

They sat in silence, looking down at the photos. He stared until his vision blurred and the images swam.

Zoey's voice was soft. "She has your eyes, Linc."

He grunted, unable to meet her eyes. "Lots of people have dark eyes."

"She has your attitude too."

He cut her a look, then.

Zoey tapped his arm. "I think you're worried for nothing." A beat. "But I do think you should tell Amelia."

He stiffened. "I don't know that I want to talk about it right now." Every decision he'd made lately felt like a ticking time bomb to destruction—to the loss of everything he'd just gained. Discussing it put him at risk of having to admit maybe some of those decisions were wrong.

"But think about it." Zoey pointed upstairs, toward Amelia's room, where she'd disappeared after having spent the afternoon with Mama D. "Honesty is a big deal to her. If she hears about it another way, she'll be hurt you didn't tell. Might break trust."

His frustration ebbed. Zoey was right. But—"I don't want to give her a reason to leave."

Zoey frowned. "She won't leave. She doesn't have anywhere else to go."

"Maybe she won't physically leave, but she won't think of me as her dad anymore." Linc swallowed. "We just got there . . . It's too risky."

"Love takes risks." Zoey clamped her hand over his. "Personally, I think she can handle it. She's pretty mature for her age, after everything she's been through."

"I agree. But not right now." He shook his head. "Later."

Maybe.

His breath tightened. He'd just wanted to come downstairs, forget about that horrible conversation with Ms. Bridges today that changed *nothing*, and reset. Veg with Zoey on the couch or even help make another inedible cookie recipe, if she wanted.

He didn't have anything beyond that to give right now.

"Well, Ms. Bridges said she can pass messages to Kirsten in jail." Zoey leaned forward, her eyes earnest. "What if you asked her about giving up her legal rights? Making this official now."

"What? *No.*" Why was Zoey being so pushy about this? Linc pulled his arm free, edged away from the table. "That's a horrible idea." He was being overly blunt again, but he hated feeling pressured.

Zoey didn't understand.

"Why not?" She blinked at him.

He could explain—*should* explain—but the words stuck in his throat. The memories, raw, unfiltered in his head. Hot tears on his young face. Muffled screams—his own. The social worker tugging him through the doors, his dad's stone-cold face.

Linc bolted from his chair. "I said *no.*"

She looked up at him, confusion and hurt in her gaze. "I just thought that way you wouldn't have to worry so much about—"

"You don't get it." His voice shook. He was always going to worry.

"Then help me understand."

Maybe he was ready to pray with Pastor Todd at church—lot

of good that had done so far—but he wasn't ready to be this vulnerable with anyone. Not even Zoey.

Maybe especially not Zoey.

He was *Linc*. He had the reputation to maintain, the shell that had kept him safe this far. Alone, maybe, but safe. Look what had happened the minute he let his guard down.

Everything went up in smoke.

He shoved his chair back under the table. "Just because she likes you better doesn't mean you know what's best."

Her eyes flashed with hurt. "Fine."

They stared at each other, and he hated himself more with every blink of her eyes.

He made a conscious effort to control his tone. "I'm going out on the boat. I'll be back in a bit."

"Sure." Her voice stiff, Zoey went back to her photos, flipping through the pile she'd just stacked.

Regret gnawed. He hesitated in the doorway, not wanting to leave it like that. Wanting to kiss her forehead, assure her it wasn't her. It was *him*.

But he couldn't do that without telling the whole story, and he'd never done that before. And couldn't start today—not with everything else happening, everything else that was still unsaid between them. A month ago, he was a bachelor with a crawfish business, content to spend his evenings in the gym or in front of the TV. He'd never even considered getting a dog, for crying out loud.

Now he had the weight of two women he cared about resting permanently on his shoulders. Their lives. Their futures.

He wasn't equipped for this—how could he be?

It was all too much.

He turned and walked out.

Twenty-One

UNKIN' DONUTS, BUT THAT MAN DROVE her nuts.

Roughly an hour after Linc stormed away, Zoey packed up the pictures and put them in her room on her dresser to hand out later. She couldn't focus on the photos anymore tonight, even though she wanted to. Even though they'd been a surprisingly pleasant distraction from the fact her real career was permanently on hold.

Everything in her heart seemed on pause too, until she and Linc could talk. Maybe, when he got back from the boat and cooled off, they could work through *all* of it.

Including what happened between them last night.

Her lips tingling from the memory, she shut the dresser drawer with a snap, waffling between annoyance and fear. Annoyance, because if Linc wanted to be a team like he kept saying, then he couldn't keep pushing her away when things got complicated. She'd never let him get away with that before as a friend, and she couldn't let him now that they were married.

Even if part of her wanted to push him right off the dock in return.

She ran her finger over the dresser handle, her anger wilting a little. There was plenty of annoyance, yes—but also fear that she would fail. She *had* to keep it together, stay strong, stay positive.

Because who was going to hold all this together if she fell apart too?

Zoey headed back down the hall, pausing in the doorway of Linc's bedroom. His familiar, musky cologne lingered in the air, along with the spice of his aftershave. She closed her eyes and breathed a lungful of it all, briefly considering flopping on his bed and inhaling his pillow.

There was clearly another part of her that still very much wanted to kiss him again, wanted to see where this relationship could really go.

If he'd ever let it.

Music played from Amelia's room, per usual. Zoey hadn't heard much from her since she'd gotten back from lunch with Mama D—also not unusual. Had she been that much of a hermit when she was a teenager? Or was she just hurting?

Zoey shut her bedroom door behind her, then knocked softly on Amelia's. "It's Zoey."

No response. She tapped again, louder.

Nothing.

Zoey edged the door open, slowly. "Amelia?"

Silence, save for Evanescence blaring.

She pushed the door all the way open. The room was empty. Amelia's bed was rumpled, though, like she'd been in it earlier. A book lay open on the floor, the spine bent. Pages of doodles and a pencil were abandoned on the desk, under lamplight.

Maybe she'd gone to the bathroom while Zoey was in her room—to which point, Zoey better get *out* of her room or risk the wrath if she got caught.

A frame sitting on the desk caught her eye—the cracked one from the surprise reception party. Zoey walked toward it, squinting. Was that—*oh*. She pressed a hand against her chest. The family photo from the wedding that weekend. Amelia in her red boa, Zoey with her cardboard mustache. Linc, with his bow tie.

Except Linc wasn't smiling at the camera, which would have been shocking to her. He was smiling at *her*.

Funny what you can see in a photo that you miss in real life.

The way Linc looked at her . . . Zoey swallowed. Maybe the kiss last night hadn't been a fluke. Maybe the slow dances . . . the gentleness he'd shown . . . maybe it meant something, and she just needed to wait this out.

Give him time.

Zoey's eyes burned, and she picked up the frame, running her finger over the long crack. Amelia had kept it anyway, saved it— and done exactly what Rosalyn had said to do. *For your family . . .*

Linc needed to see this, bad. Maybe it'd mend a few of his own cracks.

She carefully replaced the frame where it was on the desk, next to the open notebook of doodles. Turned, being careful not to trip over the backpack that was always set at the foot of the bed.

Zoey blinked. The backpack was gone.

Something heavy pressed on her chest. Had she even seen Amelia in the last few hours? Zoey thought back. She'd heard her music . . . but definitely hadn't heard the front door open or shut. Amelia hadn't gone on the boat with Linc, had she?

He hadn't exactly seemed in the mood for company.

Zoey spun a slow circle, taking in more details of the room. The open closet door, the pajama pants sticking out of the dresser drawer. The curtains pulled back . . . the window cracked.

She rushed to the window, the frame barely lifted as if someone—Amelia?—had left it in a hurry.

Zoey peered out the window into the darkness, toward the ground. It'd be an easy enough descent with a backpack, down the split-level roof, to the dormer window, then just a hop to the patio cover and a four-foot drop to the ground, if she dangled over the side.

Her heart hammered, and she tried to control the erratic pace with a deep breath. Just because the window was open a smidge didn't mean Amelia had run away. And the backpack could easily just be downstairs, or even left in Linc's truck after church. No need to panic. After all, why would Amelia frame that photo of them all, just to up and run away?

Unless . . .

Zoey closed her eyes, remembering the conversation with Linc. What if Amelia had overheard them, gotten upset?

No. She was being paranoid.

She strode back toward the bed, pausing to pick up the creased book from the floor. Shut it, dropped it on the messy covers.

And stared at the empty spot on the rumpled pillow case.

Frederick, the ratty unicorn Amelia had brought back from her apartment, was missing.

Stars twinkled overhead as Linc let his boat drift across the bay. He hadn't dropped the anchor, just allowed the pontoon to go where it wanted.

Free.

Aimless.

Alone.

He propped his foot and leaned back in the captain's chair, looking at the sky. He shouldn't have come out here. Shouldn't have left Zoey like that. Linc closed his eyes, groaned. If Noah or Cade had acted like he had, he'd have told them in no uncertain terms what idiots they were. Hadn't he done exactly that when Cade almost screwed everything up with Rosalyn a few months ago?

Problem was, Linc didn't have anyone to tell him this kind of stuff, because he didn't let anyone close enough to find out.

He opened his eyes, picked out a constellation. He'd started opening up to Noah a little, but the man was on his honeymoon now—hardly the right time to confess Linc's idiocy. It'd have to wait until he got back. But he needed to change *something*, or he was going to mess it all up.

Those two women in his life deserved more.

He shifted in the chair. There had to be a way to make things right with Zoey without having to dive into the gritty parts of his past, the parts that no one knew—save for a social worker he'd heard passed away a few years ago.

Linc's cell chimed from his pocket, and he briefly thought about letting it ring. If it was Zoey, they really needed to talk in person, and he hadn't yet figured out what to say. But he couldn't ignore her, either.

He answered the call.

Zoey's voice immediately filled his ear, panicked. "Amelia's gone."

"What?" He rocked upright, feet landing on the boat floor with a thump. "What do you mean?"

"I went to her room, and she's gone."

"Maybe she's in the shower." Dumb. He knew it the second the words left his mouth. Of course Zoey would have checked other rooms before calling him in a panic.

"She's not in the house. I've looked everywhere, even out by the pond. And your boat is still pulled up on shore."

"Did she leave a note?" He grabbed the wheel, started aiming the pontoon back toward the dock. Where would she have gone? And why? She had no idea about Ms. Bridges' visit. No one else in the church knew, either, except Pastor Todd, and he wouldn't have said anything to her.

Unless . . .

Zoey's voice pitched. "There's nothing. And Linc . . ." She inhaled. "Her backpack and her unicorn are gone too."

A word he hadn't used since getting back in church filled his mind. He pressed his lips together.

"I think she overheard us."

"Impossible. We would have heard her in the hallway too." His heart hammered. Water sprayed as he gunned it for the slip.

"She's a *teenager*. They're practically born with ninja skills."

"Say she did, then." He thought back over the conversation. "What did we say that she could have—"

What if you asked her about giving up her legal rights? Making this official . . .

That's a horrible idea.

He gripped the wheel, dread pinching his gut. "I screwed up."

"*We* screwed up."

"No, you had this one right." Zoey always had it right. Why did she always have it right? "If I had told her like you suggested, she wouldn't have misheard."

"We don't know for sure that's what happened."

"Why else would she leave?"

"There's something else." Zoey's voice was muffled. "Hang on, I'm sending you a photo."

The dock rapidly approached, and he expertly swung the boat into place. His cell dinged. He looked at the display, opened the text.

A photo in Amelia's room, of the three of them from the wedding.

Displayed in the broken frame.

His chest tightened. "She must have done that earlier today."

"And then heard us tonight?"

Of all the timing . . .

"It'll be okay." Zoey's voice rallied, though weaker than usual. "We'll find her. It's Magnolia Bay. She couldn't have gone far."

Unless she hitch-hiked to the interstate, up to New Orleans or beyond. But no need to put that fear in Zoey's mind. "I'll call Sheriff Rubart." He grabbed his keys, climbed out of the boat. "How long do you think she's been gone?"

"An hour, maybe two? But Linc, he won't do anything until she's been gone twenty-four hours."

"Oh, he will. Trust me." Determination—fueled by raw fear—shot through his veins. Not even Sheriff Rubart would cross him on this. "Meet me at the jail. We can start from there." Thunder rumbled overhead as he hung up.

Great.

They could really use some sun right about now.

Twenty-Two

WHAT DO YOU MEAN, STANDARD PROcedure?" Linc leaned so far over the counter at the Magnolia Bay Parish Jail, Zoey thought he might bump noses with Sheriff Rubart. The fluorescent light above buzzed. "My kid is *missing*."

Unperturbed, Sheriff crossed his arms over his protruding belly. A half-full coffee mug sat next to a pad of sticky notes and an overflowing in-box of papers. Obviously, the front desk admin had gone home for the night, and Sheriff Rubart didn't seem very eager to take her place. "For all you know, the girl went shopping."

Exactly as Zoey predicted—and feared. She winced.

"That's ridiculous. She's thirteen, and it's Sunday night. Nothing is open to shop at." Linc stabbed his hands through his hair. Thunder boomed, rattling the glass in the front windows. He pointed to the sky. "Plus there's that."

"Exactly my point—she's a teenager. A troubled teenager. And teenagers get wild whims all the time, including running around in the rain." Sheriff narrowed his eyes. "Did she happen to get mad at you recently?"

Linc glared. "Yeah."

"Again, my point."

"And when she does, she slams her door! Not packs a bag and vanishes into thin air."

Sheriff raised a bushy gray brow. "I seem to remember her running out of the diner when she got upset at that reception." He tilted his head toward Zoey. "Congratulations on the nuptials, by the way."

Zoey opened her mouth, shut it. Unable to tell if the comment was satire.

"I know how this looks, but Amelia promised she wouldn't do that anymore." Linc pushed away from the counter, paced a tight circle before landing back.

Sheriff reached for his coffee mug. "Teenagers break prom—"

"I know!" Linc slammed his hands on the counter. The entire structure shuddered. "But something could still be wrong—and you're doing nothing."

Sheriff frowned, set his mug down. Reached toward his belt, which held a weapon and a pair of handcuffs.

Okay, so they weren't getting anywhere with vinegar. Time for sugar.

Zoey placed a steadying hand on Linc's arm, despite her own nerves threatening to send her over the counter next, and stepped in front of him. "Look, Sheriff." She smiled, tried to gentle her tone enough for the both of them. "Could you maybe just make a call? Have some of your deputies watch out for Amelia while they're on patrol?"

"That I can do." Sheriff reached for the walkie-talkie on his belt while Linc glowered. "If she actually stays out all night, check back with me in the morning."

Zoey's stomach flipped. All night, alone . . . in this storm? She glanced at the rain knocking against the front window, the darkness stretching beyond it. A gust of wind howled.

The sheriff must have seen her look, because he rushed on. "Don't worry. Chances are she'll come home tonight, especially if she gets wet. That's usually the case." He shook his head. "Teenagers think running away is real cool until they miss their free food and electronics."

Linc back-stepped toward the door, face stony. "You better be right."

Zoey tugged his arm. "Let's go." Another gust slammed against the window panes. She flipped up the hood on her jacket, then followed Linc out into the night, knowing what he had to be thinking—because she was thinking it, too. That Amelia wasn't just any typical teenager.

She was theirs.

Linc pulled his truck back into his own gravel drive an hour later, a desperate prayer on his lips. Rain beat his windshield, the wipers doing little to sluice it off. He shifted the truck into park. *Please let her be here.*

Amelia hadn't been anywhere else around town—not Magnolia Blossom, or Second Story, or Chug a Mug, which was the only place in town open this late on Sundays, and even they'd been in the process of closing. They hadn't seen her huddled under any store awnings as they drove by the Burger Barn, or hanging out in the courtyard by the library.

His hitchhiking fears were becoming stronger, and at some point, he was going to have to tell Zoey what he suspected. But saying it out loud made it feel more likely, and he wasn't ready for that.

"Are you praying?" He glanced at Zoey, who sat still in the passenger seat, her eyes closed. Droplets of water coated her cheeks.

She nodded. "Have been all evening."

"Why hasn't God answered yet?"

She opened her eyes, lips curved downward. "I don't know."

"I prayed with Pastor Todd this morning." The words felt like a confession, like an experiment gone wrong.

"Yeah?"

"Think it made things worse."

Zoey took his hand, her skin damp and chilled. "I'm sure it didn't."

He'd had all that peace, for a minute. But then—"Ms. Bridges showed up right afterward, and everything went downhill after that." With Amelia. With him and Zoey.

Granted, he was the common denominator in all of those.

He looked at their joined hands, then back at her. "Why do you pray so much? If there's no guarantee."

"My parents always said *faith and prayer—that's what moves mountains. You do your part and God does His.*" Zoey shoved her wet hair out of her face. "So I guess prayer helps me feel like I have a say in what's going on."

Linc frowned. "I thought Pastor Todd said before that the point of prayer is to remember God is in control—*not* us."

"Oh, He is, but we get to participate." Zoey nodded. "Another verse I love is in Colossians . . . chapter one, I think. It talks about how in Christ, all things are held together."

There was that *all* word, again. Working good, even through fires and denied claims. Missing kids. His frown deepened. "So is that what you're doing when you pray? Trusting God to hold it together?"

She opened her mouth, then slowly closed it. Her brow furrowed. "I—"

Lightning split the sky, followed by a crack of thunder. *BOOM.* They jumped. Linc cast a glance toward the house, wishing to see their answered prayer via movement behind the curtains, lights turning on—*something* to indicate Amelia was there. Safe.

Home.

Because if she wasn't inside, wrapped up in a blanket or drying her hair after a shower or rummaging for a snack . . . He swallowed. What if Ms. Bridges found out about this? Would they take Amelia away, prove him an incompetent father?

His gut tightened. Maybe he was.

"Let's go." He got out, slammed the door. Knowing deep down, with every pounding footstep through the rain, that Amelia wasn't inside. He continued to plead with God to let him be wrong.

A pile of mail sat at the front door, tucked close against the wall, next to a giant box of protein powder he'd forgotten he'd ordered. He didn't care. He brushed past it, burst through the front door, dripping water all across the entryway. Didn't care about that, either. "Amelia!"

Nothing.

He hollered again, louder. Judging by Zoey's wince and the way she clamped her hands over her ears, he figured Amelia would have heard him, even if she was out in the woods.

More silence.

He started to shake. "This is all my fault."

"Don't do that." Zoey shook her head. "We can go back out. We'll find her."

"And look where?"

Her silence confirmed his fears. There was nowhere else to look. This *was* his fault—he should have just talked to Amelia earlier, like Zoey suggested. Who knew what would happen next when they found her?

If they found her.

His stomach flipped. Prayer hadn't helped—God wasn't working this for their good. Linc was, once again, alone. Amelia had literally run away from him. And he had Zoey, but for how long? When all of this fell apart, when they took Amelia away, Zoey might not stick around either.

Because people left.

Linc pressed his lips together, went to the porch, and scooped up the soggy mail, dumping it on the table in a heap. Zoey's name was listed on several envelopes, with a big red FORWARDING ADDRESS stamped in the corners.

The one on top caught his eye—must have caught hers too.

Zoey frowned. "This is my insurance company." She slowly picked up the envelope, tore it open.

A check fluttered to the table.

"Linc." She gasped. "It's the full amount."

He set his jaw, huffed a breath. Of course. Now, of all times. "That's . . . great." Perfect, really. He could get rid of everything he wanted, everyone he cared about, in one awful night. Rip the Band-Aid.

"Wow." Her eyes lit, the check shaking slightly in her hands. "I can't believe it. So much earlier than we thought." She looked up. "I didn't know if it was coming at all."

Obviously, which was the only reason she'd agreed to marry him in the first place.

The only reason why she'd stayed.

Well, now she could be like everyone else.

"Congratulations." He stalked to the pantry, grabbed a few bottles of water and almond-free granola bars. Two bananas. Amelia might be hungry in this storm, and he wanted to be prepared when he found her.

If he did.

"You seem mad."

He slammed the pantry door. "Just worried about my kid still out there."

"Of course." Zoey shoved the check away. "I'm sorry, I was just so surprised. Let me grab a dry hoodie and we can—"

"Don't bother." He shoved the water and the protein snacks into a duffel, zipped it shut. "I've got it. No reason in making anyone pretend any longer."

"Pretend?" She took a step toward him. "What are you talking about?"

"You don't need me anymore." He gestured toward the check. "And with all this happening with Amelia, well. Looks like I won't need you either." The words stung leaving his lips.

Zoey flinched. "*Linc.*"

He couldn't stop now, or the pain would consume him. Destroy him. He tossed the strap on his shoulder and headed for the door.

She followed. "Why are you doing this? We never even talked about us." She drew a shaky breath. "Or about last night."

"No point." He shot the words over his shoulder, like he didn't care. Like he hadn't relived that kiss in his mind from every angle, every breath, a hundred times. "Was just a fluke between friends, obviously. We felt sappy after that wedding." He shrugged. "It happens."

"No, it doesn't. Not with us." Zoey stepped closer, wrapping her soaked arms around herself. Her hair hung in damp waves down her back. "You said nothing would change, but everything changed, Linc."

So add that to his list of failures. He couldn't keep his word.

"Change it back, then." He turned and pointed to the pile of mail. "You have your money—you're free. We can annul, if you want. It's all the same to me."

His chest hurt—almost as much as the hurt filling Zoey's eyes. He looked away, started to crumble under the regret, then stopped. This whole scene had always been inevitable. Why put it off? He'd known all along he would lose them both. Probably why he kept fighting so hard to keep them.

The little fight he had left had to go toward getting Amelia home safe. Then—well, Zoey could live her life, and Amelia could go wherever she wanted. He could be alone again.

"Annul." Her voice grew cold, still. "Is that what you want?"

No. He closed his eyes, summoned everything in him, and opened them. Met her gaze. "It's the way it was meant to be."

Then without looking back, he wrenched open the door and walked out into the rain.

Her money had come.

Just when Zoey thought she wouldn't have to be a burden anymore, just when she thought she could contribute, get back to having a purpose and a career . . . finally feel like she had a whole life again . . . she'd lost the only parts of her life she'd come to enjoy living.

She wanted to rip that check into shreds.

Rain sluiced off her windshield as Zoey drove, faster, down Village Green. As hurtful as Linc had been, she couldn't let him search for Amelia on his own. She'd given him a head start, then got in her SUV and headed back toward town. Surely they'd missed something, somewhere.

Amelia couldn't have just vanished.

She watched out the window for any sign of the teen. Streetlights glowed in puddles on the flooded road. Thunder rumbled, farther in the distance this time, the lightning less bright and frequent as she drove past Magnolia Blossom, then Chug a Mug.

She hadn't driven this far past the coffee house in a while—almost to her old shop. She hesitated, foot over the gas, ready to floor it past. Not look, per her usual.

Then she braked. Hard. Her tires skidded on the wet pavement as she pulled over and parked. Got out.

Zoey stood in the rain, staring up at the remains of her building, water soaking her skin and the dry hoodie she'd thrown on before she left. There it was. Her precious, crispy building, stuck in limbo just like Zoey had been.

She closed her eyes, still able to easily picture the cute black iron tables that once sat inside, the clusters of fairy lights and fleurs-de-lis wall sconces. Could remember painting those green walls, ironically the same color as her bridesmaid dress, painstakingly one weekend before opening, kneeling for hours, cutting in the baseboard and trim all by herself. She'd spent more time in that shop than in her apartment, baking, creating, dreaming up new marketing ideas. It'd paid off too. She'd become a local favorite, had even won Best Dessert on the island last year. She couldn't bake cookies to save her life, apparently, but her beignets and kolaches were award-winning.

And just like that, it was all gone.

Funny how one decision—the purchase of a new fryer—had changed the entire course of her life. She opened her eyes, studied what remained of the framework with a fresh realization. It'd never be the same again. Even if she rebuilt it.

Forever changed.

Tears pricked. What if she had never ordered that stupid fryer? Her building wouldn't have burned. Zoey would have never been broke, or homeless . . .

Never would have married Linc. She swallowed. Bonded with Amelia.

Fallen in love with her husband.

Okay, so maybe God really did work good in all things. Or at least, they *could* have been good, had Linc not turned on her tonight. Made her the enemy somehow, rejected her.

Not sure how God was going to pull this one off.

She wiped water off her face, chest burning. It didn't make sense. She'd prayed about their marriage, prayed before going to the courthouse. Prayed after they drove away in the limo. Every day since.

Maybe she still hadn't prayed enough. Or maybe she'd been too negative—didn't have enough faith. *Faith and prayer—that's what moves mountains. You do your part and God does His.*

Somewhere along the way, she'd gotten something wrong.

He is before all things, and in him all things hold together.

The thought came through, louder than the others. Solid. More secure. She drew a breath, staring at the exposed beams of Bayou Beignets. The blackened shell of a dream.

And then it clicked.

She had gotten something wrong, but it wasn't in not praying enough or having enough faith. It was in trying to hold everything together herself. Her parents, her career, her relationships. Her heart. She'd never allowed herself to fall apart because she never knew if she'd find the strength to put it back together.

Never allowed herself to tell her parents what she really felt about their absence, in case she created conflict that couldn't be repaired.

Never allowed herself to admit to Linc her changing feelings for him for fear of losing him completely.

And all she'd accomplished with all of that "holding" was a whole lot of grief. A whole lot of loss. Fake smiles that led to empty hands.

Her tears mixed with the rain, slowly, then steadily, until she wasn't sure which was which. She grieved—for her shop, her sudden loss. Her uncertain future. For her inevitably changing friendship with Elisa, for the pain Amelia had endured in her short life. For her own parental absence over the years. For her marriage. For the end of her friendship with Linc.

Because just like her shop, even if she rebuilt it, it'd never be the same again.

Forever changed.

But maybe that was okay? She sniffed, wiped her eyes. Wasn't that what she tried to tell Linc? That God worked it all out, for good. Even when it hurt.

Maybe especially when it hurt.

She squinted through the rain. Tried to see the vision. Tried to hope. Who knew? Maybe her next shop would be even *better* than her old one. Maybe her relationship with Linc *could* eventually thrive. The possibilities were limitless when God was involved. She just had no idea.

But one thing she did know for sure.

She'd burn it all down again if she could just find Amelia.

Twenty-Three

THE STORM CONTINUED—THOUGH THE one in Linc's head thundered much louder than the one outside his truck. He turned the radio down, the wipers on high. His chest heaved for each breath, like he was running instead of driving.

He couldn't do this anymore.

"God, you have to show me where she is."

His hands tightened on the steering wheel until his knuckles ached. Guilt nudged. He wasn't really in a position to boss God around, was he? He stopped at the stop sign on Bayou Boulevard and tossed the truck into park. Rested his head on the steering wheel. "Please."

Silence, save for the rain pelting the roof. Oh, what was the use? He was on his own. If God cared, He had a funny way of showing it. Maybe Linc had pushed Him away too. Like he'd done with Amelia. With Zoey.

Pastor Todd's words echoed in his mind. *Truth remains true whether we believe it or not.*

Linc swallowed. He'd been in church enough times to know God never changed, and God couldn't lie. If those facts were true—then, well, God *had* to care. The Bible said so.

Which meant there was still good being worked in all this, despite the evidence to the contrary. There was still something to hope for, fight toward.

Maybe even for his family.

Pray for God to help you believe it.

He squeezed his eyes shut. "Help me." It was all he could utter. And yet somehow, in the deepest parts of his heart, a measure of that same peace washed over him. Cleansing. Like the rain streaking the windshield.

You did not choose me but I chose you . . .

Oh, how he wanted to believe that. Wanted to believe that not everyone walked away.

That someone picked him.

You did not choose me but I chose you . . .

The words seeped in, slow, deep. Taking root. His neck muscles slowly relaxed. Maybe he could believe it. After all, had *not* believing done anything besides shove away everyone he loved the most?

Okay, God. I believe. He swallowed. *I believe what Your word says, even when I don't feel it.*

And then . . . he was feeling it. The peace spread. Along with it, a seed of hope, planted deep. He drew a clear breath, first one in a while. It was time for some changes, and that had to include being willing to believe all of these hard things. And being willing to tell the truth.

Then he tensed again. Wait. *The truth.*

He knew where Amelia was.

Linc shoved the truck into gear, peeled out. Nearly took out the bush on the corner, correcting just in time as his tires searched for purchase. He turned left and made the curve, back toward Village Green, but this time, the other end.

He parked in the lot, barely remembering to turn off his truck as he jumped back out into the rain. The trail was covered in wet leaves, downed branches as he jogged the path past the playground equipment and the gazebo.

To the lamppost.

Sure enough, a tiny figure sat hunched on the ground under the light, next to a backpack, arms wrapped around drawn-up legs. Linc's chest nearly burst as he picked up the pace. "Amelia!"

She looked up but otherwise didn't move.

He came to a stop next to her, lungs heaving.

She stared at him. "You sure are breathing hard for someone who works out so much."

"I—oh." All the things he planned to say when he found her fled. "Guess you'll have to come with me to the gym, again. Motivate me."

She looked away. "I doubt that."

"Doubt you'll come or doubt you'll motivate me?"

She shrugged. "Both."

He waited a beat, then dropped down beside her. Wanted to say something encouraging. Something hopeful.

Wanting desperately to *not* put his foot in his mouth.

"I think God told me where you were." Well, that was one way to start.

"Not really sure why anyone cares I was gone." Her eyes were red-rimmed, her cheeks pale. She shivered, and he wished he'd thrown a blanket in the duffel.

"I brought you snacks." That he left in his truck. In said duffel.

She shot him a bewildered look, looking around at the obvious lack of snacks.

"They're in the truck, sorry." He ran a hand through his soggy hair. Messing this up, once again. But that was okay. They had time.

He had to believe that.

"It's okay. I'm not hungry." She rested her chin back on her jean-clad knees.

"Not just about that. I'm sorry about a lot." He pulled his legs up, mirroring her position. "I haven't been honest with you."

"I know."

"I should have told you what I'm pretty sure you overheard."

She narrowed her eyes. "How'd you know I was eavesdropping?"

So they'd assumed right. "I didn't at the time, but Zoey and I pieced it together." He waited a beat. "Saw the window cracked in your room. The missing unicorn . . ."

"Frederick."

"Right, Frederick."

Her hair dripped water off her face, and she swiped it away with the back of her arm. "You can stop pretending now."

"Pretending what?"

"That you want me around. You don't want to ask Mom to give up her rights, so obviously you don't want me."

"I was afraid you thought that." Linc brushed water off his eyes. "You broke a promise, you know."

"Not to run away?"

"Yeah."

"Felt like the deal was off when it was clear you didn't want to keep me." She scowled.

"See, that's where you're wrong. We do want to." The inclusion of Zoey came naturally, but for a moment, he wondered if it was applicable. Would she forgive him? He had to find her next.

Had to step out in faith.

He cleared his throat, repeating the sentiment. "Zoey and I both want you."

"Then why did you—"

"I just didn't want to go to court, put you through all that." Linc shook his head. "That's a totally different conversation."

Hope hovered in Amelia's eyes. "So you mean—"

"We do want you? Yep." He tapped her zipped backpack, where he knew the unicorn was tucked safe and dry. "Frederick too."

Amelia winced. "So I—"

"Ran away, broke your promise, and sat outside in a thunderstorm for nothing?" Linc nodded. "Yep."

"Oops."

He could stop now—maybe should stop now—on this high note. But it wasn't the full truth, and if he'd learned anything tonight, it was that the truth mattered. "There is one more thing that you probably didn't hear."

"I know Mom is in jail."

Ah. That took one item off the list. Still a doozy to go. "There's something else."

She hugged her knees. "What?"

He twisted his lips to the side, thinking through the best way to censor this news for a thirteen-year-old—one who didn't need an even worse image of her mother than she already had. "There's some confusion over who your father is."

She stiffened. "What do you mean?"

"Meaning it was either me or another man." He paused. "A man who died several years ago."

Amelia grew quiet, tugged at a loose thread on the ripped knee of her pants. "Okay."

That definitely hadn't been Linc's reaction, but hey. He wasn't thirteen. He waited.

"But we don't know for sure?" She frowned, tugged harder. The rip spread.

He nodded. "We don't know for sure."

"Can we find out?"

"If you want to, yes. There's this thing called a paternity test that can match DNA, prove it one way or the other." Man, that prospect hurt. But it needed to be Amelia's choice. Linc knew in his heart who she was—his daughter.

Amelia needed to know it for herself.

She let go of the thread, looked over at him. Studied him. Then . . . "Nah."

He nearly swallowed his tongue. "*Nah*?"

"Nah. I don't need the test." She shrugged a little. "I want you to be my dad either way."

He was suddenly grateful for the rain, hiding the tears falling free. "Yeah?"

"Yeah. I guess if you're willing to come search for me in a thunderstorm, you must care more than I thought."

She wasn't the only one found in the storm tonight. Tears held his throat in a vise. He croaked out the only words he wanted to hear. "You promise?"

She looked up at the lamppost over their heads and grinned. Reached up and slapped her hand against it. "Promise."

Oh, this kid. He struggled to his feet, maybe using the pole for support more than he should have as relief and adrenaline coursed through his veins. He reached around, grasped the other side of the post. "Looks like I want you to be my daughter either way too."

"Guess we're stuck with each other, then."

"Yep." Best news ever. "There might be some legal stuff to deal with down the road, but we'll handle it as it comes."

"Okay." She nodded. "I'm in."

Linc hesitated. "You know . . . we haven't ever hugged before. Is this—"

"Seems like a hugging moment to me."

His heart lifted. "Was hoping you'd say that."

Amelia's skinny arms launched around him.

Linc held on tight, tears of gratitude burning his eyes. "Looks like you were meant for me, kid."

They stood, hugging, under the light of the lamppost, until Linc thought his heart couldn't grow any larger. *Thank you.* The prayer came naturally, and with it, the faith to believe for more.

For their entire family.

He stiffened. Now, if only he could find Zoey. Convince her he was a jerk, convince her he didn't just need her, he wanted her. First part wouldn't be hard, but the second. He swallowed, hugged Amelia tighter as the rain continued to pour.

Time to hope the sun would come out, just one more time. For them all.

Twenty-Four

MELIA!"

She pulled away from Linc's hug, squinting across the park. "Did you just hear my name?"

"I think so." Linc turned, searching the shadows around the lot. Another shout echoed across the field, and a light flashed over the hill behind the gazebo. What in the world?

Then a flashlight beam shot across his face. He shielded his eyes with his hand, scowled. "Who is that?"

Amelia's mouth opened. "That's . . . everyone."

She was right. Sure enough, the whole town crested the hill, converging on the park, holding lanterns, toting flashlights, wearing headlamps. Sheriff Rubart led the charge with an umbrella, flanked by Sadie and Harper and Mrs. Peters, wearing a clear plastic rain slicker. Even Peggy, the eighth-grade teacher, wasn't far behind them, marching alongside a handful of other teachers Linc recognized from town. There was Pastor Todd and Isaac Bergeron and Mayor Landry, Madame Paulette in an oversized poncho. Several deputies, Captain Sanders from the fire department. Sawyer Dubois, in a graphic tee featuring a guitar, his long hair dripping.

Cade and Owen yelled as they jogged toward them. "There she is!"

Miley, with a dark hoodie over her head, tagged close behind with Trish and Rosalyn. Bringing up the rear was Mama D and Farmer Branson, who gallantly held an umbrella over her head.

"She's here!"

"She's all right!"

"We found her!"

The shouts mingled—the inaccurate last one making Linc smirk—as ten people tried to group-hug Amelia at once. Her eyes widened and her back stiffened before Linc lost sight of her completely in the mob of ponchos and ball caps.

There was only one person missing.

But that was his fault. Linc waited a moment, then whistled between two fingers. "Let her breathe."

Everyone backed off, except Mama D, who kept one arm around Amelia. And okay, that was fair, because she'd dealt with enough over the last few weeks. She'd earned it.

Amelia's eyes flicked from one person to another. "What is everyone doing?"

"Looking for you." Mama D squeezed her tight, and to Linc's surprise, Amelia didn't edge away.

Rosalyn stepped forward, nestled in next to Cade. "You had us worried sick!"

Linc looked toward the crowd, then back at Mama D. "But how did anyone even know that she was missing?"

Cade snorted, wrapping his arm around Rosalyn. "Madame Paulette heard Sheriff Rubart dispatch the deputies to start searching for Amelia."

Finally, the man had come to his senses. Linc nodded at him, eyes narrowed. "Glad to hear you shoved protocol where it belonged."

"Yeah, you big softie." Trish winked at him.

Sheriff Rubart frowned, flustered. "Well, the storm was getting worse, and . . ." He paused. "The bigger question is what was Madame Paulette doing on the police scanner?"

All heads turned toward the dance teacher.

Madame Paulette shrugged sheepishly. "I keep an eye on things." She regally lifted her head. "Never know when one might meet a fireman." She winked.

Captain Sanders coughed. "Uh, we'll work on that, Sheriff."

"You really all came to look for me?" Amelia pulled in her lip, eyes big and cautious as she took in the crowd smiling at her.

"Of course." Rosalyn couldn't help herself. She sidled in for a hug on Amelia's free side. "You're one of us."

Amelia coughed, and Linc could tell the moisture on her cheeks wasn't from the downpour. She smiled, cautiously, then wider. She looked up at Mama D, then Rosalyn, and then Linc. "Thanks." Her soft voice carried through the group, as everyone murmured how glad they were that she was okay.

The rain started again, lighter this time, colder. Miley clapped her hands. "Okay, I love a good mush fest, but let's take this party back to Chug a Mug."

"But it's closed." Trish frowned.

"I know the owner." Miley rolled her eyes. "Hot chocolate on the house."

Everyone cheered.

"Can we go?" Amelia asked Linc, her eyes wide, smile hopeful.

At this point, he'd give her a pony if she asked. But he also had to find Zoey. Had to try to try to fix his mistakes while they—God willing—were still fixable. He opened his mouth to explain when another figure appeared in the shadows by the gazebo.

Zoey.

His heart stammered. Would God grant him one more answered prayer tonight? He touched Amelia's arm. "Go on ahead with Mama D. I'll meet you there soon, okay?"

Amelia followed his glance to Zoey, and understanding lit her eyes. "Okay."

Linc met Mama D's gaze, and she winked. "Don't worry. I won't let her out of my sight."

Then, before Linc could move, Zoey was running, scooping Amelia into a hug. Linc's heart jumped, fresh emotion burning his eyes. Mama D stepped back as Amelia hugged Zoey in return, their heads buried next to each other, two wet curtains of dark hair. They rocked back and forth until finally Zoey pulled away, smoothed Amelia's hair back from her face, and said something Linc couldn't catch but that made Amelia laugh.

Then Amelia's voice, clear as day. "Give him a chance, okay? I did."

Well, he was just going to puddle right onto the ground, wasn't he? The question remained, would Zoey take Amelia's advice?

Zoey looked up after that, right at him, her smile fading a little as their gazes locked. His breath hitched.

"Let's go, now." Mama D's voice was soft as she led Amelia to the rest of the group whisking up the path toward the coffee shop.

Zoey wiped her eyes and made her way toward Linc, the voices fading as half the town crested the hill and rounded out of sight.

He met her halfway, wet grass squishing beneath his shoes. Zoey's hair and clothes were soaked, mascara smudged under her eyes. Still, she hung back, cautious. "I see you found Amelia on your own. You were right." She shrugged, offering a sad smile. "You don't need me after all."

Oh, man. That was so far from true. His chest burned, and he wished he could take back every awful thing he'd said. He coughed, words tumbling together for escape, sticking in his throat. "No, you were right. I told her *everything*. The truth behind what she overheard, her mom in jail, the chance that I'm not her real father."

"Wow." Zoey's shoulders relaxed. "Seemed like it went well."

"We agreed neither of us wanted to take the paternity test." He swallowed. "She said she wants me to be her real dad no matter what."

"Linc, that's amazing. I'm glad to hear it." Zoey's eyes glistened. She was too far away for a hug, and he hated what that maybe meant. Hated how that tightened his chest and made his stomach drop. "Happy for you both."

The pronoun choice jabbed. You. Not *us*.

Didn't she know there was none of that without *her*?

He fought the urge to snatch her up. Kiss her. Make things right between them without having to use words. But he'd gotten them into this mess with his hurtful comments, and he'd make it right the same way. By talking.

Even if it cost him.

He drew a breath. "I need to tell you a story."

She tilted her head, surprise lighting her weary eyes. "You don't tell stories."

"I also don't dance, and we've been down that road a few times."

She crossed her arms. "You don't have to do this, Linc. You made your thoughts really clear earlier. I just came to check the lamppost for Amelia, thought she might have come here."

"Your hunch was right." Linc nodded. "She did."

"Then I saw the crowd, and wanted to make sure she was okay."

Of course she did—because that was Zoey. Unselfish to the same fault that he was selfish. He reached toward her, but she stepped back.

He started anyway. "Once upon a time . . ."

Zoey narrowed her eyes, but Linc kept on, crossing the wet grass as she continued inching back. "There was a young boy whose mom got really sick. He didn't have any grandparents or other family, and his father was uninvolved, more interested in his career and side relationships than his family."

"One day, the mother went to the hospital and never came home, while the dad decided that was the perfect time to turn his hobbies into addictions."

Oh. Her heart stammered.

Linc inched forward, close enough to touch her now, but he didn't. Did she want him to? *Yes.* Her heart ached for him, her arms ached to touch him. But his earlier words still rang in her head, rejecting her . . .

He stood still, hands shoved in his pockets. "The boy tried to make him happy, but nothing worked. The dad was gone more and more, until finally the courts got involved."

Zoey froze. She knew he was a foster kid, but—

"The boy's father signed away his parental rights, right there in the courtroom that day. Surrounded by business suits and security guards and hard wooden benches, the boy became an orphan. Just like that."

Oh my gosh. The ache spread. "Linc . . ."

"His last memory of his father was through a curtain of tears, as he was physically dragged off. Sliding on his belly across the courtroom floor, screaming, while his father looked the other way."

No wonder. Hot tears crested her cheeks. "I'm so sorry. I had no idea."

"I never told anyone that." Linc looked down, then up. "And I don't tell you now for pity. I just wanted you to know why it was so important to me that Amelia never have that memory for herself. That's why I didn't take your advice—even when you were right."

Ha. She'd hardly gotten it right. And yet . . . "Everything turned out the way it was supposed to." Working for good . . . mostly, anyway.

"Not everything. Not yet." He reached out, pulled her hand free from her pocket, threaded their fingers. Her skin lit on fire.

"I've always been alone, Zoey. I had foster parents who took care of me, but it was never a family. It was a job for them. It's why I never tried to make us more than friends before."

Her weary heart soared. "You mean . . . you thought about it before?"

"Of course I did." Linc took her other hand, rubbed the ring on her finger with his thumb. She stared at it, vision blurring. "But you were always more important than my wants. I couldn't risk messing it up. Messing *us* up. Was afraid I'd lose you."

"Until Amelia came along."

He nodded. "I thought marrying you would guarantee your staying. Then everything started falling apart."

That was one way to put it.

"When we kissed, I thought for sure I'd messed it up. But you seemed to want the same thing, and—"

Boy, did she.

"—for a minute, I had this . . . hope." Linc shook his head. "It's dumb. But the stuff with Kirsten threw me back to the past, and then when Amelia left, I panicked."

"Understandably." She loosened her grip on his hands. "I panicked too. Felt like I couldn't show it. Felt like I had to hold us together."

"You can't hold broken pieces, Zoey. They'll cut you."

"That's awfully poetic of you."

"Don't you know by now?" He let go of one hand to swipe a tear off her cheek. "I'd write a sonnet, for crying out loud, if it made you smile. Or what's the one with the syllables?"

"Haiku." She choked on her laugh.

"That too." His fingers trailed her jaw, then cupped her cheek. "I realized, after our fight, that I was so afraid of you leaving, I pushed you away."

She nodded.

"I said awful things."

She nodded again.

"I was such a jerk."

Nod.

He hesitated. "Feel free to jump in here."

"You're doing great on your own." She pressed her hand against his, the one still on her cheek. "I'm sorry too. I wasn't real with you—if I had been honest about how I felt all along, none of this would have been so bad."

"Are you really forgiving me?"

"What are friends for?" She smirked.

He winced. "I deserve that."

"Before I came here, I stopped at my old shop." Zoey drew a shaky breath and let go of his hand. "I finally released it—all of it. I'd held too much in for way too long."

She might have let go, but he didn't. He wrapped his arms, his ridiculously strong arms, right around her waist. Held on tight. "Good."

"Earlier, in the truck, I told you something my parents always said to me, about faith and prayers." Zoey winced. "And I think I got it wrong."

"How so?" His brow furrowed.

"Well, I mean, yes, God invites us to participate in His plans, and our prayers do matter. But it's never up to us. It's never God *plus* our efforts. It's God, working it all for good." She blew out her breath. "Usually despite us."

"I think that makes me Exhibit A." Linc snorted.

She grinned. "And B."

"I said I didn't need you, and that was a lie." He pulled her in tight against his damp chest, whispered against her wet hair. "But the even bigger lie would be to say I don't want you."

Tingles rushed down her back. She snuggled closer into his arms. "Then you definitely shouldn't say that."

"I'd much rather say something else."

"Mmm?"

He abruptly pushed her away, stepped back. "Zoey Lakewood Fontenot." He dropped to one knee. "Will you marry me?"

"Again?" Dunkin' donuts, this was happening. Her heart leapt. Joy burst.

He held her gaze, the depth of his feelings shining through his eyes. "Still."

She didn't even try to hold back this second round of tears. Because as she was learning, sometimes the sun could shine even through the rain. Like grace.

Amazing grace.

"I love you." Still on one knee, he grasped both her hands. "Always have." He let out a little huff. "I should have known I'd somehow end up with a woman who jumped on my back during a cooking class."

She let out a half laugh, half sob.

"Zoey, you need to know I still mean every word I said during our elopement. Every vow, every promise." His voice sobered. "But I'll do it all again for you. Big wedding. Whatever you want."

She already had everything she wanted.

"Well . . . *will* you marry me?" He lumbered to his feet, as if suddenly concerned she hadn't actually said yes.

"Yes." She tapped her chin, pretending to think about it. "On one condition."

"Condition?" He frowned.

She fought to hold her straight face. "Twenty pushups."

He tilted his head. "You're kidding." But he really couldn't tell if she was or not, and she loved it.

Loved him.

"I never joke about fitness, Linc." Zoey pointed at the ground, shot him a saucy wink. "Count 'em off, Muscles."

"Better than a haiku." He hit the ground, his lats bunching under his wet shirt. "One. Two. Three."

She waited until he got to ten, then dropped down to the ground in front of him. He paused at the top of his next rep, a question in his eyes. She flipped over on her back and scooted across the wet grass until her face lined up perfectly under his. "Ten more."

He grinned, pushing down into his next rep, lips grazing hers. "Eleven."

Kiss.

"Twelve."

Kiss.

She giggled. "I would have worked out much sooner if I knew this was an option."

He growled, then came to his knees, grabbed her. Hauled them both to their feet. She shrieked with laughter, and he held her up against him, like he had on the dock. Tucked in his arms. Safe.

Secure. He pressed his lips to hers, a kiss full of promise and anticipation.

Zoey's heart soared. "I love you too, by the way. You big jerk."

"Glad to hear it." He pressed his damp forehead against hers. "Ready to go get our kid? I'm sure she's all sugared up by now, if Mama D had anything to do with it."

Zoey snorted. "Yep." Linc kissed her one more time, stealing her breath. She closed her eyes, relishing his scent. His strength. This moment. "And then let's go *home*."

Where they were meant to be.

Epilogue

L INC HADN'T BEEN TO JAIL IN A REALLY, really long time.

Couldn't say he missed it.

Noah, perched next to Linc and Cade on the hard wooden bench inside the Magnolia Parish Jail, narrowed his eyes as he looked around the cramped holding cell. "This feels familiar."

Down the hall, Sheriff Rubart paced, keys dangling from his belt. The lobby of the facility buzzed with eager voices.

Linc elbowed his friend. "Yeah, not sure a jail cell is a good look for a new mayor."

"Guess I was sitting right here with my dad, what—a year ago?" Noah winced. "Gotta say, the company is infinitely better this time."

"Happy to help." Linc stood, grabbed for one of the overhead bars. Knocked out a strict pull-up.

"Oh, come on. Show off. Just because you can . . ." Cade leaned back against the wall, then seemed to think better of it as his pastel, dress-shirt-clad shoulders brushed the dirty surface. He winced. "Hey, when do you think they last cleaned in here?"

"Don't ask," Sheriff called from down the hall.

"Guess your favorite designers don't make an appropriate 'rot in jail all day' line, huh?" Noah smirked.

"Don't hate." Cade brushed his hands on his creased slacks. "I'm a lawyer now, man. I have to dress the part."

Linc grunted as he leaned one shoulder against the wall. "You looked the part way before you passed the bar and started practicing."

"Hey, you gotta dress for the job you want, not the one you have." Cade spread his hands wide. "At least I'm aware other materials exist besides flannel."

Noah shot him a sideways look. "Guess your wardrobe explains why August Bowman was so eager to add you to his practice when you passed the bar, then."

"Right. Had nothing to do with my test scores, reputation, hard work ethic . . ." Cade droned.

"Ethics, huh? How are those treating you while in jail?" Rosalyn approached from the other side of the bars and leaned in close, eyes light with humor. The giant engagement ring on her finger sparkled under the fluorescent lights.

Cade groaned. "Why do I get the feeling you're the one paying the most money to keep me in here?"

"At least we're not married yet. Otherwise it'd be your money too." She winked. "Boys, is he complaining much? Or just worried about his clothes?"

"Both." Noah and Linc answered at the same time.

Zoey and Amelia came up behind Rosalyn, wearing matching grins. Linc's heart stammered a little at the sight of his wife, dark-haired and blue-eyed—and all his. Suddenly made him wish he'd gone for a few pushups after the pull-up.

Zoey gripped the bars with both hands, blinked up at him. Her purple top brought out her eyes, which she'd probably done on purpose to torture him. "This whole jail thing probably won't help your bad-boy reputation, you know?"

"Very funny." He joined her at the bars, wrapping his fingers around hers. "Did you pay to bail me out?" Been several hours. At this point, he just wanted to go home.

With her.

Zoey tossed back her hair, feigning nonchalance. "Actually, Amelia talked me into paying to keep you in. Just until after the Spring Fling this weekend."

"*What?*"

She chuckled. "Kidding, kidding."

"Come on, Dad. I really don't want to fight you over my dress." Amelia crossed her arms, cocked her hip—attitude as usual. Except now, there was a smile accompanying it, not to mention that title he'd never get sick of hearing. *Dad.* "I know you're going to think it's too short."

"Because it probably is." He narrowed his eyes. "You're not going with a boy, are you?"

She rolled her eyes. "It's just Michael."

"Sounds like a boy."

"It's not like that. He's my best friend."

He glanced at Zoey. "Heard that one before."

"Don't worry. I won't let them keep you in here too long, even if it is for a good cause. I miss you." Zoey rested her forehead against the barred door, a slow smile curving her lips. "Though I have the feeling you could probably bend these bars enough to get out, if you wanted."

He pressed his forehead against hers. Inhaled the scent of powdered sugar and sunshine. Growled a little. "Don't tempt me."

Cade and Noah groaned. "Come on, guys, you're not even newlyweds anymore."

"If they're not, then we're not." Elisa walked up next, hands planted on her hips. "Does that mean you don't miss *me*, Noah Hebert?"

Noah hopped up like the bench was on fire, brushing off his

flannel shirt. "Of course not, *Mrs*. Hebert." They tried to kiss through the bars.

"Oh man. This is nauseating. I'm going to Chug a Mug." Amelia held up both hands in surrender. Then she brightened. "Oh, wait. Almost forgot! The new cards came in." She reached into the back pocket of her jeans and pulled out a Boiling Bayou business card.

Geez, a lot had happened in the two hours he'd been stuck in here. He took the card through the bars while she grabbed another one to show Elisa and Rosalyn.

"Amelia—you drew that?" Elisa's eyebrows shot up. "That's amazing."

Rosalyn hugged her, her long blonde hair almost completely hiding Amelia's face. "I'm so proud of you!"

"So are we." Zoey beamed. "She's going to start art classes this summer at the community college."

Something a lot like pride welled in Linc's throat as he studied the hand-drawn Boiling Bayou card. He'd seen the design before they printed them, of course, but hadn't viewed the final product yet. Amelia had created a new logo of a crawfish reclining on a raft as it floated in the waves, sunglasses dangling in one claw. It provided the perfect addition to the previously plain cards—along with Zoey's name as co-owner and official photographer.

Maybe that was his favorite part.

"Turned out even better than I thought." He tucked the card in his pocket, fought to swallow. Good grief, no one warned him that everything about having a daughter would make him emotional. "Good job, kid."

Amelia twirled one strand of hair around her finger, smiled self-consciously. "You mean it?"

"Can't reach the lamppost from here." He narrowed his eyes again as an idea struck. "Bail me out and we'll go see."

"Nah. I really like this dress for the dance." She snickered. "Want me to bring you back a latte, though?"

He sighed. "You know I only drink coffee."

"That's *sooo* boring."

"What, my coffee isn't hip enough for you?"

She wrinkled her nose. "No one says hip, Dad."

"Fine. My coffee not bussin' enough for you?"

Cade snorted from the bench.

Amelia blanched. "That's it, I'm out." Face twisted in horror, she started down the hall.

"Just remember who pays your cell phone bill," Linc called after her, and she turned, laughing. He watched her practically sprint down the hall, mixed emotions churning his stomach. She was blossoming—which was good. So good.

But also growing up fast—which was good *and* painful.

Elisa followed his gaze, offered him a soft smile as she stepped closer to the cell door. "How's her mom?"

He cleared his throat. "Been in rehab the past month."

"Yeah, and if she sticks it out for the duration, the court will allow supervised visitation with Amelia," Zoey added. "Then we go from there."

"That's a good thing, right?" Noah asked.

Linc shoved his hands in his pockets, blew out his breath. "Hope so." Regardless, Amelia wouldn't be leaving the Bay anytime soon. That much he knew for sure.

"Yoohoo!" Delia ambled up next, waving a fistful of bills. Clad in overalls, Farmer Branson ambled behind—as usual, these days. Rumor had it Delia even got him into the movie theater last week. "I paid for someone to stay longer and for someone to go free. Guess who is who?"

No telling. "This is the wackiest town fundraiser idea you've had yet," Linc grumbled at Cade. But maybe he didn't mind that much. It'd been kinda fun—not that he'd ever admit it to the guys.

Cade grimaced. "Yeah, I didn't think I'd be the one in here

when I dreamt up this one. I somehow ended up in the dunking tank last summer too."

"Hey, I liked that one." Rosalyn winked at him. "Think you'll be out of here in time for our date tonight?"

"I better." Cade stood, waved at Delia. "Mama D, I beg you."

Delia stopped at the cell door and smiled at Cade. Her lipstick today was back to normal—apparently, she'd snagged her man and had no more use for burgundy or fuchsia. "You can go, honey. I'm sure your fiancée needs you."

"What about me?" Noah asked, clutching the bars.

"Actually, your wife is busy." Elisa tucked her hair behind her ears. "Me and Zoey are about to go whip up the weekly batch of beignets at the Magnolia Blossom."

"I thought you only baked from the diner on Fridays?" Linc looked at his wife. Man, he'd never get sick of that phrase. *His wife.*

"Right. But we missed last week because of the engagement party, remember?" Zoey asked.

Rosalyn wiggled her glistening ring finger in reminder.

Ah, that's right. That was the same night he and Zoey had stayed up late at the pond, night-swimming. He grinned. Probably why he didn't remember the prior part of the evening.

"Then I had all those photos to edit." Zoey continued. "Been busy since Anthony went back to school full time and I went from having no job to three."

"I love that you've got a photography hustle now and are just baking on the side at Elisa's." Rosalyn touched Zoey's arm. "Your photos are so great, I can't decide if I want you to do my wedding pics or be a bridesmaid this summer."

"Definitely both." Zoey flexed one arm, which made Linc do a double-take. She'd been working on her pushups.

"Yeah, I'm catering it too, so we can figure it out." Elisa laughed. "Double-duty bridesmaids it is."

Madame Paulette swooped down the hall in a wave of patchouli, followed by a reluctant Captain Sanders, who wore his fire department uniform. "Linc, you're being traded for Captain."

"Finally." He stepped back as Sheriff ambled over to open the door.

"This is really unfair." Noah sighed. "I'm your fearless leader, for crying out loud.'"

Ha. "Probably why you're raising the most money."

Noah tilted his head. "Not sure if I'm flattered or offended that my loyal subjects are *paying* to keep me locked up."

The barred door opened with a clank. Cade rushed out first. Linc stepped into the hall and only had to wait approximately two seconds before Zoey's arms were locked around his waist, hugging him as hard as if he'd actually been arrested.

Fine with him—he'd take the excuse. He wrapped her up, breathing her in.

Zoey looked up at him as Sheriff locked Captain in the cell with a protesting Noah. "Did I tell you my mom called today?"

"No. Been in the slammer."

"Right." She grinned. "Well, my parents are finally back in the US, and they're coming to town next week. They can't wait to meet Amelia . . . and bring us our delayed wedding gift."

"Sounds good." He raised his eyebrow. "They weren't upset they missed our elopement?"

"Nope. Actually, Mom already is hinting about grandkids."

"She's already got one." Linc nodded his head in the direction Amelia had just left.

"She's super thrilled about that, for sure." Zoey wrinkled her nose. "But I think they're also hoping for the baby variety."

"Tell her teenagers are less sticky." He thought back to the New Orleans field trip and winced. "Usually."

"Or . . ." Zoey's grin stretched, and she hugged him a little tighter. ". . . we could just give her what she wants."

"Oh man, lock those two back up." Cade rolled his eyes. "Do the town a favor."

Elisa and Rosalyn grinned. Madame Paulette clapped her hands together, bracelets jingling. Sheriff looked like he halfway wanted to oblige. Mama D shook her head, released a happy sigh. "From lovebirds to jailbirds."

Linc ignored them all, focused on his wife and the heat of her arms around him. Her smile. Her light. "Suppose it's not a horrible idea."

Zoey tilted her head. "Could be as good as your last one."

"Which one was that?" Hard to remember anything when she stood this close.

"Marrying your best friend, of course."

"Ehh." He schooled his expression, but almost couldn't hold it. "Guess it worked out okay."

"Almost like we were meant for each other?" Zoey quirked her brow.

"Now you're just getting sappy." He lowered his voice the way she liked. "Mrs. Fontenot."

"Okay, that's it. Back in the cell, all of you." Sheriff drew a circle in the air with his finger.

No way. "Time to go." Linc scooped Zoey up with both arms.

She let out a little shriek, clutched the sleeve of his T-shirt. "Is this to make up for not carrying me over the threshold last year?"

He bounced her a little in his arms, just because he could. "Hope I never make it up to you."

She gripped him tighter, eyes sparkling. "Why's that?"

He swallowed. "Because I don't ever plan to stop trying."

"*Aww.*" Madame Paulette, Elisa, Rosalyn, Mama D, and even Noah joined in on that one.

Linc was seriously going to lose his reputation, but maybe he didn't care anymore. He adjusted his grip on Zoey. "Ready to go home?"

She reached up, pecked his cheek. "Already there."

Where she'd stay.

Thank You!

Thank you so much for reading *Meant For Me*. We hope you enjoyed the story. If you did, would you be willing to do us a favor and leave a review? It doesn't have to be long—just a few words to help other readers know what they're getting. (But no spoilers! We don't want to wreck the fun!) Thank you again for reading!

We'd love to hear from you—not only about this story, but about any characters or stories you'd like to read in the future. Contact us at www.sunrisepublishing.com/contact.

Read on for more from the

Magnolia Bay

series

Return to Magnolia Bay and see where it all began in *Where I Found You.*

From beloved author Betsy St. Amant comes an enemies to more, Hatfields and McCoys swoon-worthy contemporary romance set in a small beach town that reminds us that true love is worth fighting for.

Noah Hebert recently inherited the Blue Pirogue Inn—along with all its problems. He needs money to keep his beloved childhood home from being shut down by his family's longtime nemesis, Isaac Bergeron. So when Noah's lawyer approaches him about an additional segment of his late grandfather's will, it's just in the nick of time. But even from beyond the grave, his grandfather is up to his usual games. In order to receive the last portion of inheritance, Noah must follow the clues. But there's one condition...

Magnolia Blossom Cafe manager Elisa Bergeron is shocked to discover an acquaintance from the local Puzzlers Club left her something in his will—and even more surprised to discover they are clues to a portion of his estate. When she learns she must work with introverted inn-owner Noah Hebert to solve the puzzle, she's torn. Growing up in the middle of a multi-generational feud between their families, she's been taught by her father Isaac that Heberts can't be trusted.

When these two exes must work together to save their future, will love get a second chance or will the longstanding family feud claim another generation?

One

NOAH HEBERT NEEDED TO GET BACK home—he didn't have time to watch paint dry.

"You got the wrong blue." Peter, Noah's apprentice at the Blue Pirogue Inn, clearly felt confident enough to point out the obvious as he stood beside Noah, his scrawny arms crossed.

"I can see that." Noah pushed one hand through his hair as he stared at his mistake—one of many over the past several months he'd been fixing up the inn since his grandfather's funeral—and sent a scattering of sawdust onto the taped off floor. The humidity of his coastal Louisiana hometown wet Noah's flannel shirt and stuck it to his back, despite the spring breeze rustling through the pine trees outside. Not that the humidity was much better in north Louisiana.

Figured. They were finally at the finish line of these endless renovations, meaning his return to Shreveport and his real job as a land man in the oil and gas industry was in sight . . . but now he was being mocked by slate blue and—

"Sky blue. How did you even do that?" Peter squinted up at him beneath his side-swept dark hair. The kid had chosen to work a trade instead of going to college, and had proven to be a hard worker and fast learner. Noah could trust him to notice details.

Especially this one glaring at them in matte finish.

"Lot on my plate, kid." Noah checked his watch with a grimace. "And now I'm late for an appointment with the one man in Magnolia Bay who probably hates me the most."

Peter's eyes widened. "Must be a Bergeron."

"Isaac Bergeron, and if you're a praying kind of person, you might start working on that now."

"That bad, huh?" Peter made a *tsk* with his tongue.

Worse than the kid knew. But some parts were public. "As county inspector, Isaac's the one holding the keys to this kingdom." Noah gestured around them, at the multitude of mostly-finished projects, at abandoned tools lying on heaps of folded tarp that hadn't been put away yet. And now even more projects would be delayed, all because of the stupid paint. "I'm hoping I get the inspection certificate from this meeting so we can reopen and call this a wrap." And never have to see the wretched man—or his daughter—again.

Not that Elisa Bergeron would be at the Magnolia Blossom Café today. Just the ghost of her memory.

Peter clasped his hands in front of him in a posture of prayer. "On it."

Noah headed for the front door, stepping over a discarded roll of painter's tape. "I'll grab the right blue on my way home."

"Slate blue!" Peter called after him.

Noah shot him a thumbs-up over his shoulder as he hurried outside. He steered around a crew member perched halfway up a ladder on the porch, measuring for the decorative trim left to hang. Better him than Noah—he'd never been a fan of heights.

He breathed a gulp of air not thick with sawdust as he hurried down the porch stairs, careful to avoid the rotten spot on the second step. No, wait. That had been fixed, along with the shingles that begged for attention the past year. Everything was finally coming together, just in time for tourist season.

Assuming Isaac Bergeron didn't hold a grudge and did his job fairly.

There's more where this one came from. Noah might not ever get Isaac's last words to him—or the sight of the bitter man cleaning a shotgun on his porch, out of his mind. And now he had to sit down with him for coffee.

He started toward his grandfather's Chevy truck that had become his along with the inn during the reading of his will. For the first time in a long time, Noah's chest didn't tighten at the sight of the tired but sturdy three-story structure he'd inherited—the lingering symbol of a family feud multi-generations thick. That'd be one way to market for the upcoming tourist season. *Come see where the infamous Bergeron/Hebert battle first began . . .*

His cell vibrated in his pocket, and he pulled it free before hauling himself into the truck cab. Hopefully his backorder of tile hadn't been delayed again. He snorted at the display indicating a string of missed messages. Thankfully, none from the tile guy.

Noah opened the group text labeled "GONE FISHING."

CADE
Fishing tonight at 7, right? 🐟

Linc
Aye. I'll bring the cold ones.

Owen
You always bring the beer, Linc. 🍺

Linc
Only because we never know if Noah is gonna
bother to show.

Noah winced. Yet lately, the accusation wasn't inaccurate. He typed back.

Noah

I'll be there this time, I promise.

Owen

Hey guys, I might need to borrow some bait again.
😌

Noah dropped his phone into the console cup holder. The familiar scent of Armor All mixed with the evergreen air fresheners he kept dangling from the rearview mirror wafted over him. Partly his scent now, partly his grandfather's. Grandpa Gilbert used to keep candy orange slices in the glove box. There were probably still melted traces of them clinging to the interior.

Noah gripped the steering wheel and took a breath. Time to get this over with. He started the engine just as his phone rang.

Noah grunted as he reluctantly hit the speaker feature. "Yeah?"

Cade's voice filled the cab. "Just making sure you're really coming tonight and not blowing smoke."

"I'll be there. I could use the break . . . after I get this certificate and slate blue paint, anyway."

"Sure you don't want to stick around Magnolia Bay a little longer? Enjoy the hard-earned fruits of your labor at the inn?" Cade's grin was evident in his voice.

Noah looked both ways at the end of the drive. "I'm sure. This town is too small for Bergerons and Heberts to coexist again."

"Especially with a certain blond one?"

"I didn't say that."

"Didn't have to." Noah turned off the private road, the bay in his rearview. "Three months of working on the inn has been plenty. I need to get back to Shreveport ASAP."

For several reasons, and fine, maybe one of those reasons was blond. Not that Elisa Bergeron lived in the Bay anymore—she was probably a famous chef somewhere on the mainland by now.

But he'd seen her memory more around town in the time he'd been back than he had in the twelve years prior combined.

Cade sighed. "That's too bad, man."

Noah cleared his throat. "You know I was just here long enough to get the Blue Pirogue fixed up for tourist season." He ignored the pinch of guilt that always followed that fact. He *should* keep the inn—it was his favorite childhood landmark, his safe space growing up during his parents' tumultuous marriage. It was his grandfather's legacy.

But he couldn't live in a town that judged him. Judged his family.

He pressed the gas. "I have a real job in Shreveport." One he'd been on hiatus from. He didn't have a boss to go back to, since technically, he was self-employed as a landman, but the project manager might not trust him with future projects if he stayed gone too long.

"Running an inn is a real job. Regardless, you're good at construction—I've seen what you've been doing at the inn."

The compliment might have sunk in if there hadn't been so many mistakes made the past few weeks. "Don't worry. I'll hire someone to keep the Blue Pirogue running for me. I definitely don't want to sell."

Cade's voice dropped in understanding. "To Isaac?"

"To any Bergeron, but definitely not to him." The thought of Noah's beloved childhood inn going to that man was inconceivable. Grandpa Gilbert would flip over in the grave.

"Don't worry about meeting Isaac today, by the way. I think he's mellowed a little over the years."

"Maybe to you. You're not a Bergeron . . . and you didn't break his daughter's heart."

Cade snorted. "I think that breaking part was a bit mutual, if I recall."

Noah's grip tightened on the wheel. "Water under the bridge."

And if that statement didn't remind him of the time he and Elisa would walk the beach to the coastal bridge onto the island, picking up seashells, throwing back the broken ones and collecting Elisa's favorite in a little mesh pouch he'd bought her just for that purpose . . .

"I guess you'll see." Cade chuckled. "She might be there, you know."

"What?" Noah hit the brake harder than he meant to at the stop sign. "She's back?"

"Been back, bro. She manages the café."

Impossible. "I thought she went off to culinary school." Not that he kept up. But small towns talked, and some gossip threads strung all the way up the state to North Louisiana.

"She came back."

Noah's foot slipped off the brake pedal and he quickly stomped it again. "You could have warned me."

Cade laughed. "What do you think this is?"

"I meant sooner."

"If it's water under the bridge, what's it matter?"

If Noah could reach through the phone and wipe the smirk off his friend's face, he would. With his fist. "Thanks a lot." He eased off the brake and turned onto Village Lane, Magnolia Bay's main drag, flipping his visor down against the mid-morning sun.

"You haven't seen her around town at all the past few months?"

"Been keeping to the inn and the hardware store." And eating enough Chinese take-out to merit his jeans fitting tighter, all to avoid public restaurants and the chance of running into . . . well, anyone.

"She didn't come to the funeral, did she?" Cade asked.

"No. But I wouldn't have expected her to. She owes me nothing." And he probably owed her even less.

He coasted into a parking spot in front of the Magnolia Blossom

Café, then killed the engine. The truck idled into silence. "I'm here, man. I'll see you on the pier."

"You got this," Cade coached. "Get in, get the certificate, and get out."

"From your lips to God's ears." Maybe the Lord would hear one of them.

Noah sat for a moment, slowly withdrawing the keys from the old ignition and stalling as he took in the café's front. Not much had changed in the past decade plus. The turquoise curtains tied back in the front windows had faded and the welcome sign on the porch now hung slightly crooked. The potted flowers celebrating spring were new, though, as was the cheery yellow paint on the door.

His erratic heartbeat was also new. How many times that fateful summer had he coasted up to this very parking lot, waiting for Elisa to get off work so she could hop in his truck? Hit up the drive-in movie the park hosted every June, toss popcorn in each other's mouth and miss. Share a large soda and fight over the last of the Milk Duds.

Noah reluctantly released his seat belt. Of course Isaac would choose this spot to meet—probably got free coffee from his daughter, if she ran things now—and Noah wasn't in a position to argue the specifics.

He pushed through the front doors, the turquoise walls immediately closing in on him in a rush of memory. He avoided looking at the patrons seated at the spinning barstools at the serving counter—more so, at anyone potentially *behind* said counter—and scanned the crowded room for Isaac. The unmistakable aroma of waffles and syrup wafted over him like an air freshener someone needed to invent. He inhaled deeply, then moved through the maze of various-sized yellow tables toward the back, where Isaac was most likely to be seated. He definitely didn't want to draw attention to himself lingering in the doorway.

The breakfast crowd was in full swing. Forks clanked against dishes, the abrupt holler of "order up" sounded through the swinging doors behind the bar, and the chatter from townsfolk eager to start their day filled the diner with a low hum.

Despite Noah's determined attempt to keep his gaze away from the counter, it traitorously darted there anyway, ping-ponging back and forth until he was certain Elisa wasn't one of the two aproned people pouring coffee.

Relaxing, he walked past Sadie Whitlock, owner of the local used book shop, who sat at a table reading a hardback and nursing a glass of chocolate milk. She'd always been kind, a little older than him, and usually had her face in a novel. "Hey, Sadie."

"Noah! Good to see you out and about." She looked up from her book with a smile, her green eyes bright. "How's progress on the inn?"

"It's getting there. You'll be seeing less of me around here soon." Noah's grandfather had been a regular at *Second Story*, devouring American history texts as far back as Noah could remember. He'd accompanied Grandpa Gilbert into that used bookstore more times than he wanted to that last summer spent on the island when he was eighteen.

"That's too bad, but I understand. Not everyone can take over a business suddenly, like I did from my great-aunt." Sadie gestured with her book—what looked to be a romance novel, judging by the cover. "Surely I'll see you before you leave."

Old Farmer Branson—who looked exactly the same as he had a decade ago—raised his head from a plate of bacon as Noah passed, but didn't nod. The grizzled man had always been close with the Bergerons, taking their side in the ongoing feud over who rightfully owned the inn's grounds. Most people in Noah's generation seemed mature enough to realize the majority of that beef had occurred in the past, but some old-timers still liked to play favorites.

Especially if they'd only ever been told one side of the story.

"Noah! Fancy meeting you here." August Bowman, his grandfather's probate attorney, stepped in front of Noah and held out his hand. "Come for the pancakes?"

So much for avoiding conversation. He liked August, though, as far as lawyers went. "No, sir." He returned the handshake, noting the older man's signature tweed blazer. The man had been born in the wrong century. "I have an appointment—Blue Pirogue business."

"Speaking of the inn, I was going to call you later this morning, so this is rather fortuitous." August set his briefcase on the empty table beside them, then pushed his glasses up his nose. The man's untamed salt-and-pepper hair was the only thing about him that wasn't always perfectly in order. "Could you come by my office this afternoon?"

Noah hesitated as the dozens of unfinished tasks on his calendar filled his mind, including finding slate blue paint. "I'm afraid I've got a full—"

"Here, take my card, in case you need a refresher of the address." August handed over the rectangular business card. "It won't take long, but it's important."

"I'll try, but—"

"Great! Two o'clock?" August clapped Noah on the shoulder before he could protest. "See you then, son."

Noah was more likely to be August's grandson than son, but he didn't get to protest that or the fact he couldn't come by before the older man scooted toward the exit.

Great. Noah needed to find Isaac, before he got swept into any more obligations.

He scanned the café a final time, his gaze bouncing off the various magnolia blossom centerpieces, the kitschy teal and yellow wall art, and the hardened stare of Sheriff Rubart—another Bergeron fan—until . . . *there.*

Isaac Bergeron sat with his back to the restroom wall, his iPad on the table before him next to a mug. The Magnolia Blossom Café had never used a designated set of coffee cups. Delia Boudreaux, the long-time owner and town "mama," had told Noah when he was a kid that she was clumsy and would end up breaking them, so if they never matched, no one would know.

The thought brought a smile. Maybe he'd missed this quirky town just a little.

Isaac looked up from his iPad, squaring his shoulders under his dark polo shirt. His face was clean shaven save for a tidy goatee peppered with gray. "Noah. Glad you could make it."

Noah's burst of generosity dissipated. He dipped his chin as he slid onto the bench seat across from Mr. Bergeron, then remembered a childhood's worth of Delia's reminders to take off his hat during greetings. He tugged his favorite ball cap free from his head and nodded again. "Sir."

Isaac wasn't a gambling man, but his poker face could have won him a bundle. He revealed zero hint of how sharing a table with a Hebert affected him, if it did at all. Especially this particular Hebert.

Noah, however, worked hard to keep his thoughts off his expression. He replaced his hat and searched for polite conversation. "Have you ordered?"

"I had a bagel. Would you like some coffee?" Isaac cocked one brow, the intentional movement creating the exact intimidation factor Noah was sure he intended.

"I think I'm set, thanks." He wanted a stack of pancakes, but not at the expense of making this meeting longer than necessary.

Under the table, Noah flexed his hands against the worn denim of his jeans. During the inspection last week, they'd kept their distance. Isaac had done his official thing, while Noah hovered just close enough to be reached if the inspector had any questions. Thankfully—for both of them—there had been few, and their forced interaction hadn't taken long.

Isaac took a leisurely sip from his mug, and Noah dug his fingers harder into his knees. Surely Isaac wanted to get this over with as much as Noah did. But the older man didn't seem in a hurry to hand over the coveted contents of the closed manila folder sitting on the table.

"As you might expect, I have some news for you." Isaac set down his mug, then draped one arm across the length of the booth seat.

There was the poker face again. He braced himself for a request to tweak a few things. But Noah knew the inn, knew the work that had been done with his own sweat and blood, not to mention the crew he'd hand-picked that had come highly recommended. He'd had a tight budget to work with from his construction loan, but he'd gotten the best and even bartered a handful of favors when finances got tight.

That reminded him—he owed Peter a few bass.

Noah cleared his throat. "I'm ready."

"I have to warn you, it might not be good news." Isaac drummed his fingers on the bench as if it were a regular day, not as if he was holding Noah's golden ticket just out of reach. "But it's how these things go sometimes."

So it was as he'd feared. Noah gritted his teeth, keeping his gaze on the syrup-sticky menu between them rather than on Isaac's smug expression. "I assume there are some changes you'd like to see?"

"Only one big one." Isaac finally reached for the folder and slid it across the table to Noah, then flipped open the cover. The bold stamp boasting the words FAILED INSPECTION met him like a red-inked slap in the face.

Noah's mouth went dry. He stared at the unexpected words until they swirled against the other type. "I don't understand. How?" His renovations couldn't have failed. Noah had personally attested that everything had been done up to code.

But he did understand, didn't he? He should have known a Bergeron wouldn't play fair.

Noah wished he could rip the paper into tiny shreds and throw it in Isaac's face. Wasn't that what his grandfather had preached all those years of Noah's childhood, as he grew up in the inn? That the land under the Blue Pirogue was rightfully Hebert property, despite their petulant claims otherwise, and that the Bergerons were simply "too lazy to make their own good business deals"?

Isaac's face was less than sympathetic—in fact, that appeared to be a smirk hovering around the corners of his mouth. Then the man schooled his features and picked up the condemning paper before Noah could give into temptation. "I'm sorry it wasn't what you hoped."

"I bet." The words slipped out before Noah could censor, but as a flush of heat crawled up his chest, he realized he didn't want to. This was injustice. "There is nothing wrong with those renovations, and we both know it. I followed all the rules."

"What are you implying?" Isaac tilted his chin a degree, his gray eyes narrowing.

"More like assuming. I'm assuming the fact the Blue Pirogue happens to be on the exact acreage our families have been feuding over for generations has nothing to do with this." Noah jabbed his finger at the folder.

"Of course it doesn't," Isaac snapped. "Are you questioning my professionalism?"

"Yes, along with about a dozen other things right now." Namely, what in the world had he taken on with this inheritance? Hadn't his dad, who'd been successfully managing a luxury hotel chain in California for the past fifteen years, warned Noah when Grandpa got sick the first time? *He's going to pawn that old dump off on you in his will, you know. It'll be a money pit. You don't have to accept it.*

But Noah had. And until this moment, he hadn't regretted it.

Isaac's eyes flashed.

Noah took a deep breath, trying to regain control. He laid both palms flat on the table, releasing his breath. "Let's just say I'm questioning the timing. You've had your eye on that inn since before Grandpa started chemo."

"That has nothing to do with this and you know it." Isaac's voice turned to steel. "In fact, if you'd bothered to read the report before making accusations, you'd see there's a good reason the inspection failed." He nudged the paper closer to Noah. "Black mold."

Noah's fire tempered a bit. "That's impossible." He'd have seen it.

"Afraid not." Isaac pulled a few photos free from the folder pocket and turned them around for Noah.

His heart dipped in his chest as he stared at the evidence in the walls. Not so impossible after all. He picked up another glossy image. "How did I miss this?"

"It probably happened after the storm. You know Hurricane Anastasia didn't play favorites last summer." Isaac's haughty expression sobered. "Left more damage in its wake than a Kardashian."

"I know. It even hit us in Shreveport. Mom and I have lived there for fifteen years, and we'd never seen anything like that reach so far up north."

Was it his imagination, or did Isaac's eyes narrow at the mention of his mother?

"Regardless of where it came from . . ." Isaac began stacking the photos. "The mold exists. It'd be *unprofessional* to approve this inspection before the problem is fixed."

Noah stared at the way Isaac calmly slid the photos that were ruining Noah's life back into the folder pocket. He'd thought the Blue Pirogue hadn't taken much damage during the storm, and what little there had been had easily been swept into the round of renovations.

He'd thought wrong.

"Black mold is a massive liability." Isaac leaned back in the booth, his expression tight. "You clearly can't operate with guests until the mold is taken care of."

"But I can't afford this." He'd barely made budget on the renovations needed to get the inn up to date—and up to code—for the pending tourist season. The inn's books had been in the black—barely—when Noah took over, but having to close temporarily for the repairs had given the dwindling business account a hit. So far, he'd managed to keep his own meager savings out of it, hoping to get the inn back up running before he decided whether or not to keep it.

Isaac shrugged a little, downing the last of his coffee. "Maybe if you hadn't expanded the third-story suite, you'd have some money left over for emergencies."

Noah stiffened. The last thing he needed was yet another person telling him how to manage and market the Blue Pirogue. "Not that it's your business, but that expansion was necessary to draw honeymooners and guests who want more space." He folded his arms over his hammering heart. "Statistics prove it'll pay for itself in a few years."

"That's great—except you can't start the clock until this is handled." Isaac tapped the folder.

He was aware. Noah cleared his throat. These next words were going to taste like sawdust. "Then what do you suggest I do? I don't have that kind of money left." Or energy. Or time. The inn was supposed to be finished in the next few weeks so he could figure out his next steps in life.

Not take several backward.

"Do like everyone else does—get a loan." Isaac raised his eyebrows in challenge as a slow grin curved the corners of his mouth. "Or you could always sell."

Noah's gut tightened. "Nice try."

Isaac leaned forward and lowered his voice, all pretenses gone as he braced both hands on the table. "If you don't handle this one way or another, I'll call Judge Morrow. You'll have a cease and desist slapped on you faster than you can say—"

"Afternoon, gentlemen." A slender, tan arm stretched past Noah and started pouring coffee from a carafe into Isaac's mug. The familiar scent of vanilla and honey hit Noah like a two-by-four from the past and he didn't need to look up to know.

Elisa Bergeron.

But he did look up, because there wasn't a man on the planet who was unable to spare Elisa a second glance. He swallowed hard, watching her pour her father's coffee, his gaze skimming over her high cheekbones and pink lips. Her blond hair, shorter than he'd ever seen it, was tucked back into a tiny ponytail, revealing her slender neck.

"And can I get you anything, hon?" Elisa's voice, twangy with a southern drawl just as he remembered, trailed off as her eyes met his. Just as blue as he remembered, too, though they darkened as recognition paled her cheeks. She jerked the carafe upright. "Noah Hebert."

He spread his arms in a slightly exaggerated, resigned gesture. "That's me." And that had always been the problem between them, hadn't it? His name. What he represented.

She lifted her chin, her smile wobbly around the edges. "Well, I'll be. It only took you four months of being back in town to stop in here, didn't it?"

"I've been pretty busy with the inn." He waited. Elisa had always been a master at keeping her emotions in check. Hard to tell if her words carried a genuinely pleasant undertone . . . or if she was contemplating stabbing him with the fork resting near Isaac's mug.

She resumed pouring, her back rigid but her tone fluid as if he hadn't spoken at all. "I didn't think men who wore flannel every day were afraid of anything."

He scooted the fork out of reach. "Never said I was."

"You're right. You didn't say much of nothing, did you? Some things never change, I suppose." Her voice flowed like molasses, but the look in her eyes as she met his gaze full on packed a punch he hadn't expected.

And just like that, he was eighteen again, sitting on the pier out by the bay and memorizing the curve of her sun-kissed shoulder beneath his arm. The smell of sunscreen and vanilla wafting off her hair, lapping over him like the waves beneath their feet.

Naively believing that summer would last forever.

He held her challenging stare. "And some things do." Unfortunately, and fortunately, all at once. He watched a hurricane of emotions flicker through her eyes, but he couldn't have named a single one.

And he refused to look away first.

"Elisa!" Isaac yelped.

She finally broke eye contact, looking down with a gasp. Coffee spilled over the brim of Isaac's mug and formed a river on the table, cascading toward Noah. He jerked back, but not before a stream of scalding brown liquid struck the leg of his jeans.

Forget Hurricane Anastasia—Elisa would always be the biggest storm he'd ever encountered.

And it looked like his brief respite from the rain was over.

Acknowledgments

This is the first book I've ever had to write without a critique partner reading along the way. (Side-eyes Megan and Georgiana.) Like so many things this past year, that threw me into scary waters, BUT like with everything else this past year, I wasn't actually alone in the waves. Thank you, Holy Spirit, for Your sustaining grace and endurance...in this novel and in everything else. You didn't (and will never) let me sink. This I know.

Tamela Hancock Murray—I'm very blessed to have you as an agent...not just for your expertise, encouragement, and industry connections, but also for your caring heart and prayers. Hugs!

Susie May Warren—So glad we did this. Thanks for taking a chance on Magnolia Bay! Your belief in me and my little southern town was so healing. And to the entire talented team at Sunrise, thank you for all your hard work in making my books the best they can be. What a crew!

Megan—Thanks for always being on the other side of my "OH! WHAT IF THE LAMPPOST MEANT THIS" type random text messages. And to you, Josh, Julia, AND Caleb—thank you for cheering me to the finish line for this deadline. That family photo was epic.

Sara Rose—Special thanks for letting me randomly call you and ask a zillion panicked insurance claim questions! You were a lifesaver. Any mistakes in the process are mine, not yours!

To my family at No Ceilings CrossFit—you all knew I was going to have to put a character in CrossFit eventually. LOL. I can't do a handstand pushup like Linc yet, but I'll get there. Good thing I have the fiercest female inspirations ever in Coach Megan, Coach Morgan, Coach Keri, Coach Miki, and Coach Amy.

Maddie—You know what this means! My deadline is over. Time for more Ramen! Love you, friend.

Hubby & Kids—I'm sorry for what I said while I was on deadline. (hahaha) Let's go to Andy's Frozen Custard. Seriously, though, I love you guys and appreciate your support and patience so much! (Also seriously—let's go to Andy's.)

About the Author

Betsy St. Amant Haddox is the author of over twenty romance novels and novellas. She resides in north Louisiana with her hubby, two daughters, an impressive stash of coffee mugs, and one furry Schnauzer-toddler. Betsy has a B.A. in Communications and a deep-rooted passion for seeing women restored to truth. When she's not composing her next book or trying to prove unicorns are real, Betsy can be found somewhere in the vicinity of an iced coffee. She writes frequently for www.ibelieve.com, a devotional site for women.

Learn more about Betsy at www.betsystamant.com.

MAGNOLIA BAY

Where southern charm and romance intertwine...

"Heartwarming, genuine, and utterly captivating."

–SUSAN MAY WARREN
USA Today bestselling author

We solve the problem of what we read next.

Available on Amazon

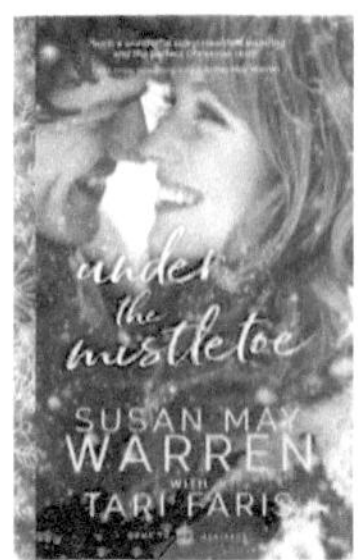

SUSAN MAY WARREN and **TARI FARIS**

with **Mandy Boerma** and **Andrea Michelle Wood**

We solve the problem of what we read next.

Available on Amazon

YOU MAY ALSO LIKE...

When a blizzard strikes Deep Haven and Megan is overrun with catastrophes, it takes a former Ranger to step in and help. But the more he comes to her rescue, the sooner she'll move out... Come home to Deep Haven in this magical tale about the one who got away... and came back.

Still the One by Susan May Warren and **Rachel D. Russell**

Working together to keep Fox Bakery from going under, Robin and Sammy find that something more than friendship is simmering between them. But will Robin follow her old dreams back to the glamor of Paris, or will she discover how sweet it is to be loved in Deep Haven?

How Sweet It Is by Andrea Christenson

Back in Hearts Bend for the first time in ten years and thrown together at Haven's Bakery, Chloe and Sam have a second chance at first love. The more time Sam spends selling pastries, the more he sees a new future. But where does Chloe's heart belong? Can they find the recipe for leaving regrets behind and start something new?

One Fine Day by Rachel Hauck and **Carrie Padgett**

We solve the problem of what we read next.   Available on Amazon

**WHERE EVERY STORY IS A FRIEND,
AND EVERY CHAPTER IS A NEW JOURNEY...**

Subscribe to our newsletter for the latest news, weekly giveaways, exclusive author interviews, and more!

follow us on social media!

Shop paperbacks, ebooks, audiobooks, and more at
SUNRISEPUBLISHING.MYSHOPIFY.COM